Visions of the Heart

Visions of the Heart

Book Two of The School of Dreams Series

Julia Sutton

Acknowledgements

Thank you to all at Creativia Publishing, for believing in me.

Many thanks to my family and friends for all your support and encouragement.

Finally, thanks to you the reader, I hope that you enjoy this book.

I dedicate this novel to my children: Jack and Isabel
Love you to the moon and back

Chapter One

Will Bentley was stuck in *the* most delicious dream. He was lying on a powder white, deserted beach, with one other person: Hema.

Above them was an azure blue, cloudless sky, where the sun beat down a ferocious heat. Close by drifted the sound of water lapping, the gentle swell of waves breaking over shimmering sand. The smell of salt and the fresh, heady aroma of the natural, unpolluted world, permeated the air. Overhead a bird swooped and dived, its body arched into a graceful crescent that cast a long shadow on the ground. A contented sigh escaped from Will's lips, he turned to his right, reaching for her hand, but she was gone, up and away, running erratically down to the majestic ocean, laughing and jumping high in the spray and the bubbling surf. And Will smiled, his eyes crinkling with pleasure at the sight of the girl he loved. She turned and beckoned him with the hook of a seductive finger, a radiant smile that pulled him to his feet and propelled him forward, towards her lithe, playful figure. Then as he was almost there, ready to dive into the crystal blue coolness beside her, he was suddenly awake, alone in a cold, small bedroom, deposited back into reality with a thud, where a clock ticked rhythmically and the chill of the morning air nipped at his bare feet.

Will tugged at the duvet with an irritated sigh, wishing himself back into dreamland, but sleep eluded him, he struggled into a slouched position, peered at the wall clock then gazed distractedly at a peeling piece of royal blue wallpaper. The February wind rattled at the window pane. It was a dreary month, where the cold and ice settled across the city of Chattlesbury like a cloak. The desk in the corner overflowed with books and paper, reminding him of university commitments; essays, deadlines and texts waiting to be read. He shook away the last remnants of sleep, rubbed at his tired eyes, then swung himself up out of the warm bed to cross the landing, pausing to listen to the soft sounds of his mother's warbling drifting up from downstairs. The bathroom door was closed firmly, the sounds of the power shower rumbling rhythmically through the woodwork. Will swung on his dressing gown then wandered downstairs. Flora was busy in the ground floor toilet, head bent and marigolds snapped firmly in place, as she scrubbed at an already gleaming, marble sink.

"Morning," Will mumbled, as he staggered through the open door.

"Will," she turned in surprise, "you're up early for a weekend love." Her smile was radiant, her face brightly lit, as she surveyed her only child.

"Places to go, people to see, essays to write," he winked playfully, "can I use the bathroom Mom?"

"Of course," she stepped aside, then chattered away until he reappeared.

"Have a nice time son, whatever you plan on doing."

Will nodded, averting his eyes, there was no way he could tell her he was meeting Hema. As far as his parents were concerned, that relationship was well and truly over, he didn't want them finding out that they were back together and closer than ever. Still, he felt guilty for deceiving them, especially his sweet, kind hearted Mom.

"So, what are *you* up to today?"

"Oh I'm busy Will, housework, shopping and uncle Evan is coming over for tea, won't that be nice?" Flora cocked her head to one side and peered up at Will, who was grimacing at the thought of his Mom's older brother. Uncle Evan was a retired army corporal and aspiring local M.P. He was short, stocky, with a penchant for shouting, intimidation and hearty back slapping. Nothing like his younger sister with her gentleness and endearing naivety. Will quickly swilled his hands, glancing in the mirror at a youthful face, lined by faint stubble and framed by a halo of wild, upright hair.

"Would you like breakfast love?" Flora enquired, "I've got some lovely Applewood smoked sausages. You can have an egg with it too."

"Great Mom, I'm starving," his stomach rumbled in agreement.

Flora bustled into the kitchen, chattering about the weather, how she could never get the washing dry and the expensive cost of using the tumble drier. Will perched on a stool and scrolled through Facebook. The news feed reminded him of stranger's birthdays, another celebrity death, explicit animal cruelty shots which made him shudder and pleas for donations to cancer research. Ah, but there was a cheeky status from his mate Jimmy, who was feeling fed up of having to work on a cold, Saturday morning. A girl from his old secondary school, and an aspiring model, had also posted a portfolio of half-naked selfies which had accumulated 200 likes. Not from me he thought, as he resolutely scrolled past.

"Mom, why don't you join Facebook?" Will grinned across at her, as she turned the spitting sausages.

"Now can you imagine what your Father would have to say about *that*."

"None of his business I reckon," Will retorted.

"He's a prominent head teacher Will, of a very successful Catholic primary school. How would it look if his wife began cavorting on social media?"

Will snorted with laughter, "you *are* allowed a life of your own. Maybe you could befriend a couple of hunky men."

Flora chuckled along in good humour, "and maybe I could also get a tattoo."

"On your buttocks?"

"Yes, a love heart with your Dad's initials."

"And the Chattlesbury Football club logo on the other cheek?"

Will collapsed over the table, shoulders shaking with mirth. While Flora wiped away tears of merriment.

"What's the joke?" Max Bentley enquired, as he strode into the kitchen.

"We were just discussing the pros and cons of Facebook."

"Worst thing ever invented," Max replied in a firm tone, "every head teacher's nightmare. Causes problems with staff, pupils, parents, a school's reputation. I say ban it."

Will rolled his eyes, "I am so glad I'm not going to be working in education."

Max spun towards his son, "well, what *are* your employment plans then? Your Mother and I are longing to know."

"Er, I'm still working on it." Will ran a hand through his tousled hair, maybe winding up his Dad this early on a weekend wasn't such a good idea. He noticed Flora looking across at him, a small smile playing on her lips. She then proceeded to distract Max with subsequent chatter on household finances. Will's phone buzzed to signify a message from Hema, reminding him of their lunchtime rendezvous.

"So yes, we've managed to save a fair bit on the electricity this quarter," Flora cracked an egg into the pan with a happy glance at her husband.

"Good," Max grumbled, "have you seen my striped tie? It had a tea stain on, I put it in the washing basket last week."

Flora pointed to the clothes horse wedged against the radiator. Ruby, the family Border Collie was pacing agitatedly, she paused in front of Will for a fuss, her nose was turned upwards as she frantically sniffed out the succulent smell of cooking meat.

"So, how is uni going dear?" Will frowned at his mother's question. The first year was almost over, lectures, seminars, debates and discussions, culminating in headache inducing essays, to show that it had all been understood and your own opinions of the texts formulated into a cohesive argument.

"It's flown by," he confirmed, "I'm looking forward to the summer."

The end of term was just a few months away. Light nights beckoned, bringing the possibility of warm sunshine and time off to relax and unwind. Although he had planned on increasing his shifts at the Student Union bar, he wanted to purchase Hema a ring, a token of his love and commitment. He'd spotted the perfect one, last week in the jeweller's window, emerald and diamonds curled into an exquisite pattern. Now he had to find out her ring size, which could be a bit tricky, but Jimmy's girlfriend Sadie had declared that she would find out for him, which was cool with Will.

"You really need to study more," Max Bentley voiced, with a shake of his head. Droplets of water dripped from his still damp hair. "Prolific reading is the key to a successful English degree."

"Er, wasn't your degree in Maths?" Will questioned.

"It was," Max confirmed with a proud smile, "and let me tell you, I worked bloody hard to attain my first. Maths is straightforward, you either get it or you don't, but English, it's a tricky subject. Some people think it's easy - it's not. A lot of reading and that's just the primary texts. Then you must be proficient at writing, spelling, grammar, coherence and fluency. It's hard work."

"You don't need to convince me; I'm living it remember."

"So then set more time aside for study," Max suggested, "it's three years of your life. Your mates will still be there at the end of it."

Will knew he was right, his sensible Dad, perfection personified.

Max was pulling on his tie, adjusting it in the steamed-up mirror, "a few of my teachers are English grads, I could introduce you if you need extra help."

"No thanks," Will replied firmly, "I can manage."

"Will is doing really well love," Flora interjected, jumping to her son's defence, "he's trying his best and that's all he can do."

"It's a competitive world out there and grades count. I wouldn't consider employing a teacher with a degree below a 2.1"

"I don't *want* to go into teaching," Will snapped in anger.

"Let's discuss holidays," Flora said brightly, "I stopped at the Travel Agents the other day, there's some super deals at the moment, with really cheap flights and you really do need a holiday love." She peered at her husband with sympathy.

Max nodded, looking thoroughly fed up, "I *am* looking forward to the end of this year. It's been a tough one. Pupils behaviour is worsening and parents seem devoid of any respect and support for the teachers now-a-days."

"Well at least it's the weekend," Flora stood on tiptoe to plant a kiss on her husband's lips, "where are you off to anyway, all spruced up?"

"St Mary's," Max sighed.

"On a weekend? Surely it can wait until Monday?" Will raised an eyebrow at the tetchiness in his mother's tone.

"Just half a day," Max replied curtly, "it's parents evening next week, I need to make sure that everything's organised and the PTA are holding a meeting this morning, so I want to keep an eye on things, otherwise they'll be running me down like the rest of the staff do." He bit into a cold piece of toast, which had been intended for the dog.

"What's the PTA?" Will asked with a yawn.

Flora answered for him, "it's the Parent Teacher Association dear. There are some very outspoken ladies in it, that seem to enjoy making your Dad's life even more difficult."

"Oh. Why do you stick it there?" Will grumbled, "no job is worth this constant hassle, surely."

"My job pays for this house and your education," Max snapped irritably, "besides I'm not about to let a gang of bitter, stressed out teachers and a bunch of menopausal PTA members run *me* out of a career."

"Whatever!" Will's eyes lit up at the sight of the oozing sandwich heading his way.

"Can't your deputy take some of the burden dear?" Flora piped up, ever helpful.

Max's top lip curled in disdain, "Marcia Bent is a nutcase, admittedly a very educated one at that. I've had so many staff threaten to file a grievance against her, it's a miracle she's still in employment. Parents are terrified of her. Even the priest hides behind the font when she's around."

Flora clutched at her bosom, "Father McGregor? But he's such a lovely man."

"I know!" Max agreed, "but one surly look from that woman could turn water to ice."

"Sack her then," Will commented, as he wiped a blob of runny egg from his chin.

Max laughed, "it really is a good job you're not going into teaching my lad. I really wish it were that simple. She's a governor Will and has a lot of influence within the school. Her husband is a solicitor, specialising in employment law. Then there's the Unions – don't get me started on them. I've tried to get rid of her before, but she managed to wheedle out of it and all the other staff are too busy watching their own backs to lend me a hand, or to support a bullied colleague. No, I've got to wait until she does something *really* malicious."

"Sounds like a bitch to me," Will concluded.

"What a thoroughly nasty person," Flora was shocked by the revelations, "and in a religious school too."

"You'll find her at church every Sunday," Max revealed with a shake of his head.

"Yeah, she must think that if she prays for forgiveness, then her behaviours okay." Will was reminded yet again why he no longer attended church. He thought of Hema and her religion. Karma seemed a pretty cool ideology to him.

Flora rubbed at her reddening throat, "well Will, there are a lot of truly good people attend church too you know."

Will looked across at his mother, noting her fingers hovering over her gold cross pendant.

"Yes I know Mom," he sighed, "you're an absolute angel."

"Exactly," Max snapped, "don't tar us all with the same brush. Anyway, what I personally think of the staff is irrespective. As long as they do their job, then I'm happy."

"Don't work too hard dear," Flora admonished gently, "I'll have a nice lunch waiting for you when you get home."

"Oh?" Max brightened at the prospect of food.

"Crusty cobs, your favourite," she beamed, "do you want two saving Will? I've bought some of that crumbly, extra mature cheddar you love."

"Maybe tomorrow Mom, I'm off out for lunch with mates," Will hated lying to Flora, but Hema had insisted there was no other way for them to be together. Their relationship *had* to remain a secret. He noticed Max lingering by the door, with a suspicious look on his face.

"Don't forget your briefcase," he mumbled to his Dad.

"Have a good day," Max nodded, then strode from the room.

Will lobbed the last remaining piece of sausage into Ruby's metallic bowl and bounded up the stairs for a revitalising shower, a couple of hours' study and then a lie on the bed, with his iPod blasting Arctic Monkeys. Soon enough it was mid-day, he stood in the kitchen staring despondently out at the lashing rain.

"Do you want a lift son?" Flora enquired.

She dropped him on the outskirts of the city centre, waving and tooting cheerfully as she chugged off up the street. Will jogged towards the bank, swerving around lines of shoppers clutching umbrellas. The bad weather could not dull his spirits, he felt happy and excited to see her. To hold her in his arms and hear her chattering about her day. He could see her now, leaning against a high wall, shielding her head with a large, shiny bag, as she looked for him, searching the crowds of people. As he neared her, he slowed his pace, appreciating her striking beauty, thoughts of kissing her full lips and staring into her honey golden eyes distracted him, so he was clumsily tripping over his own feet. He could see a range of emotions flickering across her visage; anxiety, trepidation and genuine fear. A lump rose into his throat, as thoughts of her strict parents niggled at him. Then she spotted him and a small, sweet smile wiped away the other emotions and quelled his own sense of anxiety.

"Hema," he panted breathlessly as he strode to meet her, "are you okay?"

"We need to talk," her reply was soft, but direct.

"What's wrong?" He grasped her hand, pulling her towards him.

Gently she shrugged him off, "not here."

Will followed her through the crowds, down a deserted alleyway and into a quaint tea shop.

They sank down at a table covered in pretty red and white gingham. A smiling waitress jotted down their order, then retreated to leave them alone, silently facing each other. Will moved the vase of flowers to one side and reached across to take her hand.

"Would you like a muffin to go with your tea?" Hema asked in a high pitch, that was different from her usual subdued tones.

Will nodded, feeling a little bemused at the strained atmosphere that surrounded them.

She called across to the busy waitress, "two blueberry muffins please."

Will leant forward in his seat, attempting to catch her eye, but Hema was looking anywhere but at him.

What on earth had got into her? He thought with agitation, as her beautiful eyes flickered around the café. At the table next to them a baby wailed and a harassed looking mother lifted it onto her lap, making cooing noises as she did. Hema's gaze fixated on the child, then she pulled her hand away sharply.

"Is it your family?" Will enquired, "have they found out about us again?"

Hema shook her head firmly.

"Thank God," Will breathed a sigh of relief, running a terse hand through his floppy hair.

"Do you love me Will?" The question rattled him and he gaped at her with surprise.

"Here you go," the waitress chirped cheerfully, as she set two china cups and a plate of cakes down in front of them.

Will waited until she had moved away before replying, "of course I do, you know I do.

Hema spooned sugar into her drink, not looking convinced.

"Are you ill?" He quizzed, "Talk to me!"

There was silence. Will sighed and relaxed back in his seat. The door pinged open, a lady with a metal zimmer frame plodded inside. She looked wet through and thoroughly fed up.

"Looks like it's still raining," Will commented, wondering why he was talking about the weather. Hema chewed her bottom lip, staring at the rivulets of water trickling down the misted window pane.

"Fancy a movie night tonight? There's a new Brad Pitt film out and I've heard he wears nothing more than a loin cloth in it," he winked salaciously at her and was rewarded by a curve of her mouth. "Then we could grab a pizza after, maybe drop in and watch Jimmy play pool, Sadie should be there, you could have a good girly ch…"

"I'm pregnant."

Two whispered words and Will felt his world crumbling apart.

For a split second he felt he was freefalling, the air rushed from his lungs, the colour drained from his cheeks. He thought he must have misheard her, a slip of the tongue maybe, a cruel joke. Anytime now she would burst into laughter, point across at him and giggle, "gotcha." But she did none of those things. Hema sat perfectly still, like an impassive statue, a beautiful work of art.

"What?" He scratched his head in bewildered denial.

"I'm having your baby Will."

Now there were more words. A confirmation. Bloody hell, was this a dream?

Heat coursed through his body as he stared at her, open mouthed, dazed and shocked.

"Are you okay?" Hema asked, with a frown.

"But wh-what…how?" The words stuttered from his mouth, louder then he intended.

A few of the other diners paused to stare his way, interest piqued.

Hema's lips pursed into a thin line. She folded her arms across her chest in a defensive gesture, turning her face away from him.

Silence stretched between them. Then suddenly a soft, furry rattle landed on their table, jolting them both from their reverie. Will looked down at a chubby, red face, flailing fists, the sounds of an angry child in mid rant. Oh.My.God!

He took a slug of lukewarm tea and let out a long shaky breath. Hema meanwhile was picking apart her muffin, arranging the pieces in an intricate pattern on the plate.

"Are you *sure?*"

Her head snapped back to face him. For the first time ever, her usually molten eyes were stone cold.

"Two positive tests, 99% accurate, I'm sure."

Will rubbed his forehead, closing his eyes momentarily.

"We were so careful."

"Then there's the morning sickness, the constant fatigue, the strange metallic taste I have in my mouth right now actually."

"But you haven't mentioned feeling unwell, why didn't you say something?"

"Technically speaking I'm not unwell," Hema snapped, "I just presumed it was too much indulgence at Christmas, the time of year. Everyone feels shitty in February right?"

"This must be a mistake," Will decided, "we used contraception, we were so careful." He was genuinely puzzled by the anger emanating from her. "We'll go to the doctors and he will confirm that the test was wrong. Everything will be okay."

"It's not a mistake Will, I can feel it, my body is changing."

Will gaped, "you look the same."

Hema rolled her eyes, "no contraception is totally safe, you know that Will. How many times did they drum that into us at school? Remember old battle-axe Brookes preaching that to abstain from all sexual activity was the most effective form of contraception." She tittered, then her eyes filled with tears, "we obviously weren't careful enough.

Maybe we were carried away in the heat of the moment. I don't know," she shrugged with resignation, "it's too late now to ponder on the whys and how's, it's here, this is real and it's happening right now!"

She jumped to her feet, burst into a flood of tears and loud sobbing, then fled away, out of the café, leaving Will alone shouting her name in desperation, panic and utter fear.

Chapter Two

As the rain petered away and the sun broke through the hazy clouds, Evelyn traipsed out into the garden, relieved to be out of the stuffy house. All morning she had been cooped inside, cleaning, tidying, sorting old clothes into charity bags for the less fortunate. She stood on the wet lawn, trying to decide which area to tackle first.

"Nice day for ducks," commented her neighbour.

Evelyn smiled at the sight of his bald head peeking above the fence panel.

"It sure is Ted."

"How's Nora? I haven't seen her about much this winter."

Evelyn frowned at the mention of her mam, "She's not been too good Ted. Can't seem to shift this nasty cold."

"That would be the jet stream I reckon. This country is getting milder and milder. Bugs are festering like crazy. It's just not cold like it used to be. The winters of my youth, well they were bad, but they sure killed the germs. Now it's all tropical like and the central heating and disinfectants don't help do they lass?"

"I suppose not," Evelyn agreed, "although Mam is ninety-seven, so it is to be expected that her health is going to deteriorate one day."

"Well give her my love lass. I best get back to work. Her indoors has a chore list for me as long as her arm."

Evelyn waved him off, then pulled open the dilapidated shed door, searching for garden tools.

She set about pruning the heads off a patch of wilting winter border flowers and was humming softly, when she heard an almighty crash emanate from the house. She sprang to her feet, dropping the secateurs, rushing back up the sloping garden to tug on the sliding doors.

"Mam," she called, frantic with worry.

Nora was still in the lounge where she had left her, slumped in a velour flecked chair, staring despondently down at a shattered tumbler and a pool of spreading water.

"Are you okay Mam?" Evelyn squat down next to her.

"I don't seem to have much energy this morning. Sorry dear."

"You don't need to apologise Mam, it's fine, don't worry," Evelyn pulled strips of tissue from a nearby balancing box and began mopping at the sodden floor.

Nora was wracked by a sudden coughing fit that had her whole body heaving and her hands clutching at the arm rests.

"I think a call to Doctor Dunn is in order Mam," Evelyn placed a hand across her forehead, shocked to feel the hot clamminess. Her countenance was grey and pallid, the usual florid hue from her cheeks was missing.

"I really don't want to make a fuss," Nora protested weakly.

"Shush," Evelyn soothed, as she wiped gently at her mam's wet mouth, "you're not well."

"I just need a good sleep," Nora replied, as her eyes fluttered closed.

"I'll get some more water, then make a quick call," Evelyn straightened, knees cracking as she did, then rushed off down the hall, reciting the number for the surgery.

Doctor Dunn was swathed in a long, grey rain mac, with expensive looking spectacles hanging from a chain around his neck and a fancy looking pen wedged firmly behind his ear. Evelyn almost pulled him through the entrance, she was so relieved to see him.

"Come in," she mumbled, ushering him inside.

Mam's eyes flickered open as he strode towards her.

"Well now Nora, what have you been up to?"

"Can't get rid of this blasted cough," she spluttered, "I hope I haven't taken you away from your family."

"I'm always available for my favourite patient," he assured her smoothly, as he delved inside a sturdy doctor's bag.

"How long has she been like this?" He asked Evelyn, who was hovering nearby, a worried frown on her face.

"Since early morning, but she has got progressively worse."

The doctor nodded, "I'm just going to listen to your chest Nora."

She slumped back as he explored with his stethoscope.

"Can you help me lift her forward?" He motioned to Evelyn, then together they bent her slightly in the chair so he could check her back.

"Any pains in your chest?"

Nora nodded, clutching her bosom with a wince.

"Okay lovely lady," he patted her hand gently, "you need a little bit of help to get you better. I'm going to call for an ambulance to take you to the hospital."

Nora's eyes widened in consternation.

"I'll be with you Mam," Evelyn reassured her, choking back the lump of emotion.

Doctor Dunn left the room to make the emergency call and Evelyn sprang into action, rushing around to pack a small holdall with toiletries, a warm woollen dressing gown and a Mills and Boon novel. The ambulance was soon tearing down the street, sirens wailing. Evelyn stood to one side, fighting back the tears, as two young paramedics jogged into the room and secured Nora to a stretcher.

"She's never been in hospital," Evelyn whispered to Doctor Dunn, "not even to have me, she'll be frightened."

"They will take good care of her," the doctor replied, "they're good people, try not to worry."

Evelyn clutched Mam's hand as they headed up the path. Neighbours congregated at the edge of their picket fence, murmuring in hushed tones and watching with sympathy as they loaded her into the vehicle. The kind paramedic pulled Evelyn up into the ambulance, pushing her onto an antiseptic smeared seat.

After an energetic whizz across the city, Nora was wheeled into an assessment room, where a doctor and a nurse were waiting.

Evelyn paced outside, fumbling in her bag for some change to purchase a cup of lukewarm, watery tea. She stared down a long corridor which tapered off into numerous cubicles. The sounds of a child sobbing could be heard, the bellowing of an inebriated youth as two porters grappled with him. The minutes seemed to tick by interminably slow. As a distraction, she read a wall poster which listed the benefits of hand washing, underneath it was a sink and disinfectant soap. Evelyn crossed to clean her hands, while around her bustled numerous hospital workers. Their rubber shoes squeaked annoyingly loud as they rushed to and fro. The smell of cleaning fluid hung in the air, an invisible cloud, heavy and cloy. Magazines protruded from a wall rack, she pulled one out and speed read through it, the words swam in front of her, blurry and indistinct. It was futile trying to concentrate on Sabrina and Tom's magnificent competition wedding win in the Seychelles. She snapped it shut, just as an exhausted looking nurse appeared from Mam's cubicle.

"The doctor will be with you shortly," her name tag informed Evelyn she was called Sonia.

Evelyn nodded a thank you, then drained the remains of her drink. She straightened her shoulders, preparing herself for bad news.

"Ms Cooke?"

"Yes." Evelyn turned to stare expectantly at a small, jolly looking lady, with ruddy cheeks and flaxen hair.

"I'm Doctor Flavell," she held out a hand in a friendly greeting, "I've assessed your mother."

Evelyn's spirits sank as she noted the doctors sympathetic frown.

"I'm sorry to inform you that Nora has pneumonia, she does need to be admitted straight away."

Evelyn felt a tremble begin in her hands and raised them to her mouth in shock. "She will be okay though?" Evelyn searched the other ladies countenance for signs of hope.

"We are doing all we can, but I must tell you that your mother is very poorly. We have started her on a course of strong antibiotics and I've arranged for a chest x-ray. Would you like to see her briefly before we take her up to the ward?"

"Oh Mam," Evelyn sighed with emotion at the sight of Nora, looking weak and frail in the hospital bed. "I love you," she murmured, as she bent to plant a tender kiss on her cheek.

Beneath the oxygen mask, Mam's lips lifted to form a small smile. "Don't forget to pay the milkman and the paperboy and let Jacob know where I am dear." Nora rasped, her chest shaking with the effort of speaking.

"Shush, just concentrate on getting better," Evelyn took her hand and squeezed it gently.

The nurse led her out of the cubicle, "we'll take good care of her," she said with a kind smile.

As Mam was wheeled away, up the dimly lit corridor, Evelyn was overcome with a feeling of dread, the hairs on the back of her neck pricked up, goose bumps covered her arms and she felt an irrational urge to run after the retreating figures and to fling her arms around Nora and never let go.

Chapter Three

"Happy birthday to you, happy birthday to you, happy birthday to Josh and Jake, happy birthday to you!" Sophie stood in the kitchen, arms wide and face beaming, as she greeted her twin boys. "Nine years ago you were tiny, tiny babies. Now look at you, all growing up."

Josh rubbed at sleepy eyes, while Jake hitched up the trousers of his too large pyjamas.

The kitchen floor was covered with presents, cards, brightly coloured streamers and shiny balloons which floated about and drove the dogs into a complete tizz.

"Stop that!" Sophie tapped the Labrador's shiny snout as he skittered around with excitement.

"This is awesome," Josh decided, as he fell to his knees and began inspecting tags, "even better than Christmas. Here," he handed a large rectangle to his younger brother by ten minutes.

Jake, the quieter twin shook the gift, before tearing the paper off and adding it to the growing heap in the centre of the room.

"Wowee," he exclaimed, as he gazed in delight at the limited edition Star Wars Lego set.

There was a creak from the door that had the dogs bounding over to investigate. Ryan O'Neill staggered into the kitchen, stretching a muscular torso, hips and legs covered by a snugly fit pair of pyjamas bottoms.

"Happy birthday lads," he boomed.

"Dad, dad. Look, a skateboard," Josh skidded towards him, grinning with delight.

"Cool," Ryan ruffled his hair then glanced at Sophie, "any coffee on the go?"

"Just made some Mr O'Neill," Heidi their housekeeper interjected, as she stumbled out of the utility, carrying an armful of laundry.

"Cheers love," he winked playfully, causing a red flush to stain the older lady's cheeks.

"Here, let me," Heidi dumped the freshly washed clothes into the ironing basket, before hurrying across to pour Ryan's coffee, just as he liked it.

"The club has been on the phone," Sophie whispered, drawing Ryan away from the boys, "something about a commitment that you made to open a charity fun day?"

"Oh man," Ryan clamped his hand across his mouth, "I totally forgot. Yeah, I promised them babes."

"It's your sons' birthday," hissed Sophie, "how could you forget?"

"It's for charity," Ryan protested, taking a loud slurp of coffee, "it won't take long babe. Just a quick speech and maybe a few autographs, I'll be back in a flash and Del can come with me, keep the crowds in order."

Sophie grimaced at the mention of 'Del', aka Derek, their multi-talented gardener. He was a decent enough bloke, but whose loyalty to Ryan could be rather overbearing at times. Sophie felt she was constantly vying for Ryan's attention, whenever Del was around.

"He's our gardener, not your bodyguard," Sophie shook her head and sighed with resignation. "Make sure you're not long then, I need you back home to help supervise things."

"I'll be super speedy. I'm doing it for the disadvantaged kids honey," Ryan's voice took on a whining tone, his eyes wide, looking for sympathy. Sophie softened, he knew how much she loved children.

"Fair enough," she mumbled, as he held her in a bear like vice and began nibbling her ear.

Inwardly she was fretting over all the organising that today's magnificent party had entailed. Her stomach was flipping with worry and she had been up half the night planning what to do if the weather turned bad. Maybe a trip to the *Wacky Warehouse* or *McDonalds* would have been more sensible, Sophie surmised. Then a glance out of the window showed the promise of a sunny day, which lifted her spirits and allayed the pangs of creeping doubt. Hopefully it would be just perfect for all the outdoor activities which she had planned. And Jules was coming; funny, sweet, kind Juliette, her university buddy and confidante. That alone was enough to instil happiness and excitement.

"Wowzers Mom, Dad, look, a candyfloss machine from uncle Del."

Sophie mustered a grin, while silently cursing the sugar overloaded, rotten teeth inducing present. Maybe she could place it into strategic hiding, somewhere dark and cobwebby that the twins would be too frightened to search. No such luck, they were slitting open the box in excitement and ferreting around for instructions.

"Can we have candyfloss for breakfast…please?"

"Urm, er," Sophie tried not to be swayed by two cherubic, upturned faces.

"There's a candyfloss machine!" She erupted with glee, "coming later, when the party starts."

"Awesome," both boys shouted in sync.

"I'll make some homemade pancakes for you," Heidi said with a fond look their way, "you can have syrup and lemon juice with them, your favourite." Sophie threw her housekeeper a smile of gratitude.

"I *love* candyfloss," Ryan high fived them and Sophie wondered who really was the biggest kid.

"Mr O'Neill, what about your figure?" Heidi tutted good naturedly.

"What this?" He lifted his t-shirt to reveal a set of impressive pectorals, "all paid for by Chattlesbury FC. They're mega firm, would you like a feel?"

Heidi had the grace to blush, while looking anxiously at Sophie.

"Take no notice of him," Sophie laughed, with a roll of her eyes, "it takes him hours in the gym to look that way."

"Hey, hey, I'm a natural beauty!" With a cheeky wink, Ryan disappeared up the stairs to get ready, with the dogs chasing and yelping after him.

"Well, I suppose we had better tidy up," Sophie surveyed the wrapping paper debris and began stuffing it into black refuse sacks.

"How many gifts have you had?" Heidi asked, as Josh and Jake finally opened the remaining parcels.

"Twenty-seven! Each!" Josh cried triumphantly.

"Oh my, you are lucky, lucky boys," Heidi commented.

Sophie knew that their housekeeper adored the boys and had not intended to chastise them, but still, Sophie felt irked. Once again she had gone completely over the top, it was the same for every birthday and Christmas. There were way too many and there was still more to come.

"I forgot how many I had bought," Sophie muttered with embarrassment.

Heidi shrugged, "If you can afford it why not. They are lovely boys Mrs O'Neill, so polite and kind, you don't need to how you say, expose?"

"Explain," Sophie corrected, "thank you."

While the boys grappled with new skateboards and Heidi started on the washing up, Sophie consulted her to-do lists. She pondered on how many children would be coming today. Truthfully she had lost count. There was the whole of Josh and Jake's class for a start, then a large group of the younger village kids were expected, as well as a few moody teenagers. She also suspected that Ryan had been inviting some of his footballer buddies, along with their families. Oh well, she sighed, better just get on with it. The doorbell chimed and Sophie hurried through to the hallway. Sophie's mom, Yvonne, stood on the doorstep, posing in a long, fur, winter coat, her eyes shielded by oval sunglasses.

"Morning babes," she air kissed her daughter's cheeks, "are you sure it's a good idea to have an outdoor party? It's blooming cold."

Sophie tutted at her mother's air of negativity, "of course I'm sure. Look, it's going to be a beautiful day." She pointed at a bright, rising sun, "besides, I have fifty rain macs on loan from the Disney store, just in case."

"What about the grown-ups?" Yvonne persisted, "I've just had my hair styled."

"There's an adult tent for us all to shelter in," bit back Sophie, "come in and see your grandchildren."

They traipsed back into the kitchen, where the twins paused their game of fling the frisbee, to catapult themselves instead at their Nan.

"Woah!" Yvonne laughed, hugging them tight, "darlings, I have an extra special surprise for you." She clapped her hands in delight, "come with me. You too." She winked at a puzzled Sophie, then took the boys hands, leading them outside to the huge driveway. There was nothing there, except for a small selection of gleaming sports cars.

"We're ready," Yvonne yelled.

The rumbling sound of an engine could be heard emanating from behind the large hedge, then two long haired youths appeared, driving what looked like quad bikes.

"Wh-what?" Sophie stared open mouthed, as they performed circles on the drive, before coming to rest in front of Josh and Jake.

"Happy birthday darlings," Yvonne drawled, with a proud smile, "go on, have a go, they're yours now." Yvonne looked as if she were going to explode with excitement.

Josh and Jake whooped with delight, flinging themselves at the throbbing machines.

"Helmets," screeched Sophie, as she clutched her throat with worry. The two youths duly plonked safety headgear on the twins, strapping them securely and giving them a pep talk on the basic mechanics of the bikes. Then they were off, careering around the drive, skidding and twisting, spluttering mud and gravel everywhere.

"I feel faint," Sophie mumbled.

"What's wrong with *you*. It's an excellent present, you should be pleased," Yvonne sniffed, "don't be such a killjoy."

Sophie turned on her mother, eyes blazing, "you should have told me. Aren't they a little young for quad bikes? Besides the safety implications, they must have cost a fortune. It's too much Mom."

"Bah!" Yvonne turned her nose up, "the man in the shop said they're all the rage now and it's my inheritance money, so I can do whatever I like with it." Sophie had almost forgotten that her mom was loaded and had never worked a day in her life. Money was like a turned on tap for the Fletchers, ever flowing and taken a lot for granted.

"Make sure you're careful," Sophie yelled, as Josh and Jake disappeared out the drive, to begin spinning around the cul-de-sac.

"Don't worry Mrs O'Neill, we'll watch them," the gangly youth and his friend lumbered after them, shouting 'brakes' and 'slow down'.

Sophie spent the next half hour peering after them, gasping each time they bounced off the kerb or narrowly missed a tree trunk. There were no cars parked in the street, of that Sophie was thankful, but still, her nails dug into her palm each time they manoeuvred a tricky bend.

"Best present ever," chirruped Jake, as he pulled to a shuddering stop, almost flattening his nan's toes.

Sophie breathed a shaky sigh of relief, as she snatched the keys from the ignition, "that's enough for today boys."

Josh jumped from the vehicle, high kicking with excitement, "wow, thanks Nan. Totally awesome!"

Ryan had surfaced from his male beauty administrations, looking gorgeous and smelling like a male perfume counter. His verdict on the quad bikes was predictably positive.

"Me and you later Del eh?" He slapped the gardeners back.

"You're on!" Del replied, as he climbed into Ryan's new Audi R8.

"See you later baby," Ryan hugged Sophie tightly, his hands lingering over her buttocks.

"Don't be long," warned Sophie, "or I'll send Mom after you."

Ryan chucked her under the chin, "it's a promise."

Then with a salacious wink he was gone, zooming away, sunglasses snapped firmly in place, leaving a trail of billowing dust.

Sophie glanced at her Mom and let out a resigned sigh, "it is a fantastic present, thank you. Now come on, you can help me prepare for the kid's party of the century and boy have we got a lot to do."

* * *

By early afternoon the garden had been transformed into every child's fantasy; a world of wonder and delight. Sophie and Yvonne had struggled to open the double gates which led into the back garden, allowing a fleet of brightly painted vans to set up position near the patio. There were vehicles selling all sorts of delicious, child friendly foods: ice-cream in an assortment of flavours, candyfloss and sweets, hot dogs and burgers, chips and pizza.

"The kids are going to love this," Yvonne commented, as they watched them preparing their counters.

"It's not very healthy," conceded a worried Sophie, "but look, there *is* a jacket potato van."

"I think that's more for the adults," laughed Yvonne, "don't stress honey, it's just for one day, they can have salad for the rest of the week."

Then came the bouncy castle, the crazy golf, the face painters and the balloon artists. The last people to arrive were the circus folk – clowns, acrobats, jugglers and extremely tall men walking on stilts. Josh and Jake tore around the huge garden, not sure what to do first.

"Bouncy castles ready love," a burly man shouted over the noise of the disco music.

The twins dived on and began performing a competitive series of high kicks, forward rolls and belly splats.

"Nan, nan, come on, have a go."

Yvonne's face erupted into a huge grin, then she was pulling Sophie across the lawn, flinging her shoes off in the process. The attendant hoisted them unceremoniously onto the inflatable. They were tumbling and falling and rolling and swaying in the most unladylike manner, but it was amazing fun and all four of them were giggling uncontrollably as they bumped and jostled each other for space. Above the din of the exuberant shouting, Sophie could just make out the sound of her name being called. She looked sideways towards the house, to see Juliette advancing on her, flame haired and grinning. On either side of her clung two children. They all looked completely mesmerised by the extravagance of their surroundings.

Sophie hopped off the castle, "Jules," she squealed, running to embrace her tightly.

"Hello," Juliette replied, "oh my, it looks like the party has already started."

"Oh we were just testing it out," Sophie laughed boisterously, "hello," she said, squatting down in front of a mini replica of Juliette, "you must be Molly. Your hair is beautiful." She ruffled the copper curls affectionately.

"Hello," Molly said shyly, hiding behind Juliette's thighs.

"You must be Harry?" She held out her hand to be taken by a tall, slim, dark haired boy.

"Yes," he replied, his face crinkled into the loveliest, widest smile.

"Would you like a go on the bouncy castle before everyone else gets here?"

Two young heads nodded with excitement.

Juliette ushered them away from her. Harry dived straight onto the inflatable, causing Yvonne who was attempting to clamber off, to fall onto her backside. Molly was very sensibly removing pretty, sparkling shoes, placing them in a neat line, before executing a perfect jump onto the bouncy castle.

"She does gymnastics," Juliette explained to an impressed Sophie.

"Wow, you can tell. Come on Mom stop fooling around."

Yvonne slid to her feet, patted her hair and adjusted her clothing, which had ridden up and was revealing a large section of thigh.

"I think I'll just stay on for a bit longer and watch the children," Yvonne said happily.

Sophie rolled her eyes and tugged at Juliette's sleeve, "want a quick game of crazy golf?"

"This is amazing," Juliette said, as she followed her across the grass, "I do love crazy golf. Have your children had a nice birthday so far?"

Sophie explained about the quad bike saga, then thoughts turned to university.

"I'm totally loving Introduction to Poetry," Sophie admitted, "I've almost finished the essay, go me huh?"

"Wow, that's brilliant," Juliette smiled her way, "it's not due back for a week or so is it?"

"No, but after my last low marks, I wanted to make an extra effort."

"You'll be fine," Juliette assured her, "it makes such a difference if you enjoy the subject."

"Yes, the teachers not bad either," she winked Juliette's way, noticing how she coloured slightly. There was a pause, "so how did your date go?"

Juliette thought back to her night out with Ben Rivers. Castleford had been *the* most perfect setting; in fact, the whole night had been exhilarating from start to finish. It had been the most romantic date she had ever been on. Her mind felt like it was stuck in reminiscent heaven, thoughts filtering back, replaying conversations and lingering kisses.

"It was good," Juliette revealed, trying to sound calm and casual.

Sophie was no fool, "oh come on," she pestered, passing her a golf stick, "I want more information than that."

"Okay, it was amazing. He's just wonderful Soph, a really lovely guy, fun to be with and a gentleman too."

"Gorgeous as well, huh?"

"Yes, totally," Juliette nodded, her face had taken on a dreamy glaze.

"Sexy as hell?" Sophie peered at her face, "did you?…"

"No!" Juliette let out a shocked laugh, "what kind of girl do you think I am? On the first date, really?"

"Second then," Sophie chuckled, "so what happens now? Are you officially an item?"

"I don't know," Juliette said truthfully, "We're trying to keep it quiet, but I am er, cooking him a meal the weekend."

Sophie clutched her arm, "oh heavens, this is so exciting. Maybe he'll stay over."

Juliette laughed, "no, no I'm cooking at his place and I *won't* be staying over."

"Maybe you should take your toothbrush just in case, huh?"

"No," Juliette shook her head firmly, "it's too soon Soph, we need to take things slow, get to know each other." She didn't let on that she had been fantasising of a naked Ben, lying on silk sheets, beckoning her. Her mouth felt suddenly dry and she let out a series of coughs.

"You alright there Jules?" Sophie whacked the ball high. They watched as it looped through the air and crashed through the conservatory window.

"Shit," Sophie gasped, "was that a hole in one?"

Juliette stifled a giggle, "who is that woman shouting? I think you nearly hit her Soph."

"Oh it's just Heidi the housekeeper, I'd better go sort it out, will you be okay here for a bit?"

Juliette waved her away, "of course, I'll say hello to your Mom."

* * *

Juliette waved at Yvonne who was sprawled on the grass, buckling up her shoes.

"What are you girls up to?" Yvonne queried, as Juliette jogged across to her.

"Just having a chat," Juliette smiled, "do you remember me?"

Yvonne gazed at her face, "of course, yes, you were at the New Year's party. Are you one of Soph's university friends?"

"I am," Juliette nodded, "it's lovely to see you again."

"Likewise," replied Yvonne, "I see Ryan's missing again."

"Is he? I hadn't noticed," Juliette was secretly pleased he was not here. She didn't like him one bit. She hadn't forgotten the way he had mocked Sophie, his own wife, for going to university. She also remembered with distaste, how he had encouraged an already intoxicated and maudlin Yvonne, to drink even more alcohol at the New Year's Eve party. Shots and cocktails had left her stumbling around the kitchen and into the arms of the gardener, if Sophie recalled correctly.

"I know he's my son-in-law, but sometimes I wonder why Sophie stays married to him. He's such a big kid, but then aren't all men!"

Sophie thought of Ben and a warm feeling circled her stomach, "I don't think so," she replied.

Yvonne glanced at her with disbelief, then sniffed, "yes, well, I think it's better the devil you know with those two. Although I must admit, he does take care of her financially. Totally spoilt she is."

Juliette was distracted by the sounds of Molly and Harry whooping as they ran circles around the stilt men. Sophie felt encompassed by a feeling of strong motherly love, the fierce need to protect. Their dad Marty was still pestering for access. To be fair, as yet he hadn't let them down. He had turned up at the agreed allocated dates to take them out. However, from past experience, Juliette had braced herself for the tears and upset when he did not show. This was why she was cooking at Ben's house. There was no way she was going to complicate her children's lives by introducing another man into the equation. As far as her and Ben's relationship, it was very early days. Juliette knew she had to get to know him a lot more before she introduced him to her precious children. Their date in Castleford had been beautiful. At the end of the most perfect night, he had been a true gentleman, walking her to her door, making no comment on the shabby maisonette, where she lived. He had taken her in his arms, kissing her so tenderly that her head had spun with desire and longing. So no, not every man was cut from the same cloth as Ryan O'Neill or Marty, Juliette thought with resolution, but still she felt she ought to be a little cautious and take things slowly.

* * *

Sophie was bent over sweeping shards of glass up, when the first guests began to arrive.

"Here," she thrust the dustpan at Heidi, "I'll get the door."

A line of children stood waiting outside, hopping up and down with excitement, even the parents looked thrilled to be invited to a real-life footballer's kids' party.

"Come in, come in," Sophie said with a cheery smile. For the following half hour, she was occupied with welcoming guests. In the end she managed to grab hold of a harassed looking Heidi and delegated the door duty to her.

"I need to mingle," she said, as she checked her reflection in the large, ornate mirror. The garden was full of children swarming everywhere and luckily the weather had remained nice, with just a few clouds in the sky. Although she did notice the wind had picked up, tossing leaves and garden debris around and dimpling Sophie's arms with goose bumps.

"You should have worn a cardigan," Yvonne berated, looking warm and snug in her tightly fitting coat, "get some whisky down you, that'll warm you up."

"Where on earth did you get whisky from?" Sophie was genuinely puzzled, "Mom, surely you haven't brought alcohol to a children's party?"

"It's on sale in the adult tent!" Yvonne shrieked, "although I doubt they'll be much left, the vicar was at it the last time I looked."

Sophie let out an exasperated sigh and made her way towards the white, flapping marquee. Just inside the entrance sat an elderly man wearing a boater hat and a dazzling white suit. He was strumming on a banjo and warbling in low tones. He looked like he should be at a wedding. Sophie had no idea who he was or what he was doing here. She definitely had *not* booked him as entertainment. Maybe he has wondered in by mistake she fretted. She was just going to interrogate the man behind the refreshment stall, when she was accosted by the vicar.

"Bless you and your family Mrs O'Neill, this is a grand party."

"Thank you Mr … er," she trailed off with embarrassment.

"Mr Pobble, but please call me David."

"Er yes, thank you," Sophie stared wide eyed at the decanter of whisky in his hand.

"Just for medicinal purposes my dear," he winked her way, "I've had a nasty cough this winter, can't beat a tipple to clear your chest. I wasn't going to come, but as a lot of my parishioners are here, I felt it my duty and also dear I wanted to thank you and your husband for the kind donation to the church repairs."

"It's a pleasure," Sophie beamed, "my friend Amber, I mean Mrs Lavelle had told me that you were short on funds."

"We are that," he said, with a sombre shake of his head, "money is an evil necessity in this climate I'm afraid," he burst into a rendition of a biblical proverb, "whoever loves money never has enough; whoever loves wealth is never satisfied with their income."

Sophie feeling suitably chastised looked down at the floor

Mr Pobble seemed not to notice her discomfiture, "but can you and your lovely family find it in your schedule to celebrate one day a week visiting the house of the Lord? Our Sunday congregation is growing, I'm sure the villagers would make you very welcome."

Sophie was touched, "thank you, that would be lovely, we will try David."

Mr Pobble nodded with agreement, "ah, but Sophie, you must understand that there is to be no press there. We don't want a repeat of your New Year's Eve party shenanigans. Mrs Pobble was so distressed it bought on her asthma and David junior was so angry, that he threatened to sue the newspaper for that libellous picture and caption."

"Can I say again how sorry myself and Ryan are," once again Sophie felt mortified by remembrance of it all, "we have no idea how the press got hold of those pictures."

"It's all in the past," the vicar soothed, taking a furtive sip of the light brown liquid, "but obviously if it happens again, we *will* have to take action Sophie."

* * *

"Probably one of his own parishioners," drawled Yvonne, after a worried Sophie had confided in her, "maybe if he behaved with more decorum, he wouldn't have to worry about sneaky photographers."

"Hush Mom," Sophie warned, "he has a right to a life like everyone."

"Not when he spends it preaching missy,"

Sophie paused at her mother's words. Tarquin Haverstock, the English course leader, had addressed her as missy. A smile curled her lips as she thought of him and his quirky persona; the untucked hippie shirts, the big, blond spikes for hair and his animal, conservationist friendly office. She found herself looking forward to next week and being back at uni. After a shaky start, she really had started to enjoy herself there and she had made some lovely friends. Not that Ryan had noticed she thought with dismay, he had shown little interest in her status as a student and was more interested in the gossip surrounding Chattlesbury FC. The club was up for sale and coach Jones had been sacked. It was all rather turbulent there at the moment, Ryan seemed distracted and was working more hours than usual. The football season was in full swing; the players were under pressure to get the club promoted. Sophie had been making more of an effort just lately; cooking nice meals for her and Ryan to enjoy alone, asking about his day, she had even popped to Ann Summers and purchased a flimsy, satin negligee. No matter how hard she tried, things just didn't seem right in their marriage. When she had tried to broach the subject, Ryan had accused her of being paranoid. So Sophie had flounced off on a shopping spree with Amber, determined to lift her mood, by spending her darling husband's money.

As she was pondering on whether to ask her mom for marital advice, Ryan and Derek burst into the marquee, followed by a group of star struck women. He began signing his name on scraps of paper, items of clothing, he even covered an arm encased in plaster with dozens of kisses. Sophie watched him, arms folded.

"Your husband sure is good looking," commented Yvonne, as he dipped his head to kiss a proffered cheek.

"Too good looking," Sophie agreed, "so how are things with you and Roger?"

"Not good at the moment," Yvonne admitted, "he really isn't coping with his sciatica, it's making him terribly grumpy and I shouldn't have to be a nurse-maid for him. I am after all in the prime of my life, I should be enjoying myself."

Sophie rolled her eyes, another man bites the dust, she thought with ill humour. Although she held no love for Roger, she did feel sympathy for him. Her mother was certainly hard work; she could be terribly selfish and shallow. Where men were concerned, she had little patience, it was either her way or nothing. But still, Sophie was keen to show a sense of loyalty, so she found herself agreeing and sympathising with Yvonne.

"Maybe you need to move on," Sophie suggested.

Yvonne nodded, "so how is your gardener? Has Derek mentioned me?"

"I don't know," Sophie replied, with a shake of her head, "he's not going to confide in me is he? I'm his employer remember. Anyway," she sniffed, "he *is* married. You really shouldn't have anything to do with him. If he cheats on his wife, he'll cheat on you!"

"Hmm," Yvonne considered the argument, "he is terribly butch and virile though. Maybe I'll see how it goes, it's just a bit of fun after all."

"Just be careful," Sophie warned, "now, let me go and speak to the assistant and ask why there is a wedding singer and a booze tent at *my* kids' party."

* * *

The afternoon passed in a whirl. The children had great fun, even the adults commented on what a great party it was. At five o'clock the rain decided to make an appearance. Macs were flung casually on and the festivities commenced. Adults crammed into the marquee / beer tent, waving at their children as they raced around the wet garden. Soon the weather had turned torrential, the hovering clouds turned a filthy grey colour that opened a tumultuous torrent on the people below.

"Inside! Inside!" Sophie yelled, ushering all the children into the conservatory. They were so noisy and fidgety, she had to blow the dogs whistle to gain their attention. When fifty eyes were all looking at her, she had no idea what they should do. Party games, nursery rhymes? In the end the circus people came to her rescue, staging a fantastically exaggerated show and causing a complete brouhaha in the process. It was with relief that the party came to an end an hour later. Parents came swaying out of the marquee to collect their cherubs, kissing Sophie warmly and proclaiming it had been the best kids party EVER!

"Just look at this mess," Sophie stood with Yvonne and Juliette, surveying the debris strewn all across the lawn. Already the trucks had started to move off, leaving trails of imbedded mud in the garden. Derek was holding his head in his hands, emitting low groans of anguish.

"My beautiful garden," he cried.

"Don't worry, you'll soon get it back to normal," Yvonne sidled up to him, "are you exclusive to my daughter, or available for contract? My bushes are in a desperate need of a good trim." She tittered girlishly, causing Derek to look her way with what can only be described as wanton lust.

Sophie turned away, "come on Jules. Want to give me a hand?"

Juliette took the refuse sack with a rueful smile and together they set about tidying up the magnificent garden.

Chapter Four

Ann had been hunched over the kitchen table for two hours now. Her back was aching and her fingers were sore.

"Have a break," her husband Jon suggested, as he finished off ironing his sports t-shirt.

Ann nodded, closed her books with a resounding bang and pushed away her writing pad. She watched as her pen rolled across the table, coming to stop at the edge of a crystal vase full of beautiful, multi coloured flowers. They were a present from Jon, not for anything in particular, just a plain *you are my wife and I love you* type of token. The romantic that he was, had picked them up while doing the weekly shop, while Ann had been tucked up in bed, snoozing under a warm, winter duvet.

"You're so good," Ann said quietly.

Jon grinned, "I'm getting better at ironing, I'm down to ten shirts in an hour now."

Ann chuckled, "no, I mean you're so good in general, at everything. You never complain, you just get on with it. I don't know what I would do without you mister."

Jon hung the shirt on the dresser then came to squat down beside her.

"And without you lady, I would be completely heartbroken and lost. Besides, no one else could cope with the smell of my dirty socks."

Ann tutted, "you would be a catch for any woman."

"I only want you... always," he kissed her nose, her forehead, cheeks and then her waiting mouth, "now stop distracting me with your womanly wiles and let me get on with my chores." He went to tip more water into the iron and a cloud of steam puffed out around him.

"How is your essay going?" Jon enquired.

"Not too bad," Ann replied, "I am finding it more challenging to analyse poetry then prose but it's very interesting. Ben Rivers is an excellent lecturer."

Jon lifted a pair of Ann's jeans from the bottom of the basket, "He seems a nice guy, but I'm really surprised that Juliette has started a relationship with him."

"Why? He's lovely, I can certainly see the attraction."

"I mean, won't it make things a little awkward, you've already said a few of the other students have been gossiping about them."

"They are adults Jon. Frankly it's no one else's business, as for the gossips, I think that's more jealousy and wishful thinking that it was them, to be honest. Anyway, they've only had one date. It might be their last for all we know."

"True, I wonder how they got on though?"

Ann exhaled, "I haven't seen Juliette to ask her, but she *was* extremely excited."

"You've got to admit, it is romantic," Jon quipped.

"Yes," Ann conceded, "even cynical, bitter me, feels a bit warm thinking about the pair of them together."

"Anyway," Jon changed the subject, "are you looking forward to seeing Glenda this afternoon? It was nice of her to invite us over hmm?"

"It was, but a little surprising. I thought she might have forgotten about us."

"No chance. I think we made an impression Ann and hopefully a good one."

Ann thought back to the adoption meeting that they had attended before Christmas. Glenda was one of the parents who had shared her experiences. Herself and her husband had adopted a brother and sister. Apparently they had been mere babies when they had been taken into care. Whisked away from a drug addict mother who neglected them and her temperamental partner. Ann had immediately hit it off with the amiable, older lady, with the kind eyes and the welcoming aura. Telephone numbers had been exchanged, which had resulted in a recent invitation to lunch, an opportunity to see a snapshot of life within the adoption system. So, after the adoption meeting and lots of time ruminating over it, Ann and Jon had sent their applications off and were now just waiting to hear back from them. Ann was excited and a little bit nervous of the prospect of having a child living with them permanently. Yet Jon was all positivity, happiness beamed from him whenever he spoke of the children who needed a good, stable home.

"We're doing a fantastic thing you know," he reiterated for the tenth or so time, "this is going to bring us so much joy and satisfaction. I wonder if we'll have a boy or a girl? Do you have a preference?"

"Of course not," Ann chided, "but just slow down okay? We haven't had the all clear yet."

"Just paper," he replied with a wink.

* * *

To find Glenda and Jim's house, they had to make a short journey on the motorway. The sat-nav then proceeded to send them the wrong way off a round-a-bout. By the time they reached the large detached residence, they were half an hour late.

"I'm so sorry," Ann explained as Glenda answered the front door.

"Not to worry at all," Glenda replied, "it's just lovely to see you both again."

Glenda then began chattering about the food she had prepared; a cold buffet which was awaiting their attention. Ann was staring with dismay at the narrow door opening, she glanced at Jon, *my wheels are not getting through this door*, her eyes told him.

He looked completely unperturbed, "can Jim give me a hand with Ann's wheelchair?"

"Oh, of course," Glenda called for her husband, who appeared munching on a piece of pork pie.

Jon lifted Ann into his arms with ease and instructed Jim in the art of wheelchair folding.

He carried her through the house, waiting while Glenda plumped the cushions of a high backed chair.

"Comfy?" He asked, setting her down gently.

"Perfect," she replied, smiling at her hosts, "so where are your cherubs?"

"In the garden with their auntie at the moment, I'll call them in." She slid back the door of a French window and hollered their names. They careered into the room, calling for their mom and dad.

Glenda swung a dark haired toddler up into her arms, "this is Maisie, she's two next week."

Jim was trying to grapple a mouldy watering can from the little boy, "this is Archie, tell them how old you are."

"I'M FOUR and I start school soon." He stared defiantly at Ann with huge, blue eyes.

Ann liked him immediately, "that will be exciting! What would you like to be when you grow up?

Archie thought for a moment, "a stunt man!"

Ann gave him a big thumbs up.

"Why have you got a wheelchair, can't you walk?"

"Archie!" Glenda berated, "sorry."

Ann shook her head, "it's okay, I really don't mind talking about it. Well Archie, a few years ago I was in a car accident and now I can't move my legs like you can. But everything else is okay, look," she waved her arms about in wide circles. Archie watched wide eyed, then burst into giggles, "spaghetti arms," he shouted, as he whizzed around the room, pretending to be an aeroplane. He stopped in front of Ann, "would you like to see my transformer? It's a robot *and* a dinosaur."

"That sounds awesome Archie, show me, show me."

So the following hour passed by quickly. Jon stretched out on the floor with Maisie, helping her pour imaginary tea into pretty, pink cups.

"Teddy want one," she urged Jon, who duly lifted Mr Shanks, the golden bear, onto his lap.

Archie pulled his toy tub next to Ann's feet then climbed onto her lap, so he could show her the intricacies of his transformer toys.

"Are you okay Ann? He's not too heavy?" Glenda enquired, hovering next to them, ready to snatch him up.

"He's just fine," Ann replied, in return Archie wound his arms around her neck, giving her the biggest hug.

Glenda smiled widely, "he's always been affectionate, such a lovely, kind boy."

"Kind boy," repeated Maisie, who was sitting astride Jon, blowing raspberries on his uncovered belly.

"That's Jim who taught her to do that," Glenda laughed, "you'll be there all day."

Just after midday they enjoyed a lovely lunch, washed down with cups of English Breakfast tea and fruity, homemade scones that crumbled as you bit into them.

"This is delicious," Jon commented, as he smothered jam onto his second scone of the day.

"Can't beat our Glen's home baking," Jim boomed, "let's put the television on for the kids, then we can have a proper chat."

The Teletubbies appeared on the screen, frolicking and singing. Toys were flung aside as the two young children plonked down in front of the glass screen.

"I do try to limit their T.V watching time," Glenda began, "but I must admit, it does give us a rest, they can be very tiring when they are both together."

"It must be hard at times, although they are both lovely and extremely sweet." Ann glanced at their faces, transfixed by the action in front of them.

"Oh yes don't get me wrong, we love them both dearly, but they can be exhausting." Glenda yawned, as if to reinforce the fact.

"We wouldn't be without them though," Jim said gruffly.

"Oh no!" Glenda returned, "they have certainly changed our life, but it's definitely for the better. I can't imagine a day without them, I love them so very much."

Ann smiled, "we can see that." She picked at a thread of cotton on her trousers, "but tell me, how has it changed your lives?"

Glenda cocked her head to one side and thought for a moment, "well, before Maisie and Archie came to stay with us, we had been on our own for twenty-five years. I had pretty much given up on having children. We'd been trying for years, had lots of tests, but they couldn't find a problem with either of us."

"Did you consider IVF?" Jon asked, "or surrogacy?"

"Gosh not surrogacy, but we did think about IVF. We even went for a consultation."

"Wasn't it the nurse there who told us about adoption?" Jim asked, patting his wife's hand.

"Yes, yes it was. Martha, that was her name. She had two adopted sons, couldn't praise them enough. So we paused the IVF idea, went to a few adoption meetings, did a lot of research and then decided to go for it. Eight months later we had Maisie and Archie."

"That's wonderful," Ann said, "and how was it when they first came to stay?"

"Oh it was hard; I do have to be honest with you Ann. The first month was difficult, they were unsettled you see. Missing their mother, awful as she was. It took us weeks to get them into a bedroom routine. Archie wouldn't speak to either of us and Maisie cried and cried. But we had lots of support off social services and we persevered. Suddenly one day something clicked between us and them. They started communicating, talking – well jabbering in Maisie's case. They were sleeping for longer and oh, I don't know how to explain. It was like the wall around them started to crumble."

Jon was nodding, "that sounds excellent and how are they with you now?"

"Cuddle monsters!" Jim said with a hearty laugh.

"Very tactile," agreed Glenda, "and Archie is so talkative and en-quiring, he questions everything. His teacher said he is forward for his age," she beamed with pride, "and Maisie, bless her, she's a real sweetheart, loving and affectionate. The apple of Jim's eye."

"Definitely a Daddy's girl," Jim's face was suffused with love for the tiny toddler, "but enough about us, have you decided to go ahead with adoption?"

"We have," answered Jon, with the biggest, widest smile ever. He began a spiel of their life story; how they had met, his career as a physiotherapist and Ann's dreams of becoming a university lecturer. His longing to be a Dad and to give a child a good home. Ann let him ramble on, happy to see the light in his eyes and his passion for the subject of adoption shining through. She thought about everything he did for her, the selfless way he loved and cared for her. Maybe a part of her was worried adoption would change their relationship, would a child take him away from her, monopolise his affections? Maybe she was just too selfish to be a parent. But when she looked at Jon Stokes, she knew that she would do anything for the man she loved. He was her hero. He was her everything.

Chapter Five

The library was busier than normal on Monday morning, especially the line to the self-service machines. Students queued to return books which had been borrowed over the weekend. Some people were grumbling about the fines they accumulated if their books were overdue. Others chatted about their weekend; the parties they had attended, family time away from study, books and essays. Juliette was standing near the front, trying to converse with an extremely distracted Will.

"Are you okay?" She asked, wondering why he looked as if he had no sleep.

"What?" He ran a hand through his already perfectly tousled hair.

"Have you had a good weekend Will?"

"It's been okay," he lied, gritting his teeth, "what about you?"

"Oh yes, I went to Sophie's, remember I told you ten minutes ago."

"Hmm," he gazed down at his mobile, willing it to life. Frustratingly for him, it remained blank, his message box was well and truly empty.

"Well anyway, it was a good party, nothing like the New Year disaster," Juliette laughed, "she's meeting us in the canteen in about... well now actually."

Will heaved his heavy rucksack onto the table and waited while Juliette scanned her books back in and collected her receipt.

"Is Hema okay?" She asked, with a sideways glance at him.

"Urm, yes she's fine thanks."

Juliette noticed his worried frown and decided to drop the subject. I hope they haven't broken up again, she thought with a sigh, he had been so happy when they had reunited at the Christmas party.

They made their way out of the library and across a pristine clean courtyard. The cleaners were out in force today, sweeping the pavements free from last week's detritus. A couple of gardeners had mowed the grass and were now hoeing the borders free from weeds. Even the canteen workers seemed to be working extra hard, scrubbing at tables and mopping the floors until they shone.

"Morning," Juliette greeted, "is there something going on here today?"

Sophie looked up from her muesli, "morning guys, I think the mayor is coming."

Juliette bent over to give Sophie a welcome hug, then perched on the seat next to her.

"Oh Will before I forget, here," Sophie searched in her bag and pulled out two glossy photographs; signed team shots of Chattlesbury Football Club. "There's one for you and one for your friend." She smiled warmly up at him.

"Thanks Soph, that's cool," Will glanced at the pictures, then started messing with his phone.

"Er, I'll just put them here then," Sophie decided as Will disappeared, mumbling something about needing the toilet, "what's got into him?"

Juliette shook her head, a face a picture of bemusement, "I think it might have something to do with Hema. He's certainly not his usual, talkative, outgoing self."

"Not again!" Sophie pushed her bowl away with a grimace and eyed the cooked breakfast station longingly.

"Are you dieting?" Asked Juliette, "you do know you have the most beautiful figure Sophie."

Sophie sniffed, "not according to Amber and Mom. You can never be too thin they reckon."

"You shouldn't listen to other people," advised Juliette, "it's inside what really matters."

"I'm not so sure, I just feel under constant pressure to look perfect Soph. Some of the women of the footballing world can be vicious, believe me. Then there's the press. Did you know a camera shot taken at the wrong angle can put pounds on you?"

"It must be difficult to be under the spotlight," conceded Juliette, "just be careful okay, if you get any thinner, you'll start wasting away."

Sophie laughed, "I don't think there's any chance of that, even Ryan teases me about my wobbly, protruding belly."

"Well he shouldn't," Juliette patted her hand, "you are lovely just the way you are."

Sophie felt touched by her friend's kind words, "I'm so lucky I've met you guys. Coming to university is the best thing I've done. After my kids of course."

"Yes," agreed Juliette with a huge grin as Ben Rivers strolled into the canteen, "it is pretty awesome here."

Sophie following her line of vision and elbowed her in the side suggestively, "are you going to say hello?"

Ben was talking to another lecturer Brian Hodges, but she noticed him glancing in her direction a few times. Her stomach began a slow series of flips.

"No I'm not. When we're at university it's purely professional. We're trying to keep it quiet Soph remember?"

Sophie winked and placed one finger over her lips, "of course, your secret is safe with me and I know the rest of the gang can be discreet."

* * *

Down the stairs, another student was worrying about secrets. But this secret was huge, life changing and absolutely terrifying. Will was staring at his reflection in the toilet mirror, running through the speech he had prepared last night. I'm here for you, I love you, I'll support you one hundred percent, whatever you decide to do. After firing off about thirty texts, Hema had finally responded. She wasn't willing to speak to him over the phone, but she had agreed to meet him at university, so that they could discuss their predicament. He glanced at his watch, fifteen minutes to go. For once Will was determined to be punctual, this was too important. Hema was too important. What if she was early? He wrenched open the door and paced outside the student union bar. Nobody came down here this early, that's why Will had suggested it. They needed complete privacy, away from prying eyes. He was longing to see her, to reassure her that he would stand by her. They were both so young, they had their whole life ahead of them, but a child, it would ruin everything; their future together no longer looked so rosy. What was going to happen to his dreams of travelling? And what of Hema's dreams of completing her degree and becoming a social worker? A baby, oh blimey, even the word bought him out in a cold shiver. Maybe I'm still in shock, Will thought, as he stared at a poster affixed to the door. Apparently, 'Five Shades of Purple' were playing here next weekend. He liked them and he knew Hema did too. Yes, we'll go, that's what we need, an uncomplicated night out. Act our age, rebel and have fun. Live a little before it's too late. He thought of his stressed out Dad, weary with responsibility. His closeted mother, suppressed by family life. This is bad. This is serious.

He heard a noise and looked upwards. It was the scrape of her heels as she slowly descended. He longed to rush forward and take her in his arms, but wariness stopped him. Would she yell? Would she lash out? His words in the café had been pretty insensitive, but he had been so shocked, even now he couldn't quite believe it.

"Hello, I..." Will began.

"I've got class Will, this really isn't the time to talk." Hema's eyes flashed, hot and molten. The passion was back, that was something at least. He had dreamt of the cold emptiness that her eyes had portrayed, a nightmare that had woken him, dripping with sweat.

"I've booked us a study booth, for lunchtime. Can you meet me in the library?"

"Let me check," Hema fished inside her bag for a crumpled timetable, "yes I'm free at midday."

"Great, that's great," Will stepped closer, "can I walk you to class?"

"No, no, I'm fine Will. I'll see you later," she backed away from him, then turned on her heel and was gone, back up the stairs, while Will was left alone, feeling a little more positive. At least she was willing to talk and boy did they have a lot to discuss.

* * *

Ann was already settled in the huge lecture theatre. She had an enviable, birds eye view of the projector screen and podium, with hundreds of tiered seats behind her. The room was decorated in the university's colours of red and gold and on the far left wall there was a plaque with a crest entitled 'Learning enables us to be Free'. On one side of her, sat Melanie the note-taker and on the other was a jolly looking man, who was also in a wheelchair.

He had introduced himself as Fabian, a nice name, thought Ann. He was studying a combined English degree with History and aspired to be a secondary school teacher. At the moment they were studying The Great Depression apparently, it sounded hard and Ann was relieved that she had decided to study just English. Melanie was chattering away about her weekend, when Evelyn rushed towards them, a grave look on her face.

"Evelyn, whatever's the matter?" Asked Ann, shocked by her pale pallor and the dark circles underneath her eyes.

"Mam's in hospital," she gabbled, "pneumonia."

"Oh heavens," Melanie interjected, "can we do anything to help?"

"Well I have to leave at lunch to visit her, but I wonder if you could photocopy any notes from the afternoon lectures?"

"Of course," Melanie replied smoothly, "I'll see to it, no problems."

"Sit down Evelyn," Ann instructed, pointing at a seat behind her.

Evelyn sank downwards, "I'm so worried, I've been up half the night." There were tears glistening in the corners of her eyes

"Are you sure you should be here?" Ann asked with concern, "I'm sure the lecturers will understand if you explain to them."

"I can't visit until this afternoon," Evelyn explained, "I thought it would be a good idea to try to take my mind off things. Besides, Mam was adamant I should carry on as normal." She blew into a tissue.

Ann was overcome by a swell of sympathy, Evelyn was such a lovely lady, she hated seeing her distressed.

"Well let me know if Jon and I can give you a lift to the hospital, or if we can do anything else to help."

"Thank you dear," Evelyn reached forward to pat her hand, "you're very kind."

The lecture theatre soon began to fill up, with students scrambling for the best seats. Sophie and Juliette managed to grab two next to Evelyn and plonked their bags on another seat for Will. They listened in shock, as Evelyn explained about Mam and offered their sympathies. The English lecturers were all there at the front of the room, conversing quietly. Juliette tried not to stare, but her eyes were constantly drawn to Ben Rivers, who looked extremely smart in a suit and tie. He looked her way, smiled and bubbles of happiness fizzed inside her. Stay professional, she reminded herself, but still she was overcome by her wandering thoughts. In her mind she daydreamed about kissing his neck, running a trail with the tip of her tongue down to his chest, her hands splayed over his soft hair, her hair trailing provocatively, as she moved lower and lower…

"Juliette," Evelyn whispered, passing her a handout.

"Oh, th-thanks," Juliette cleared her throat and looked down at the itinerary for the next few hours. Apparently, there was a guest speaker, a distinguished lecturer from another top Midlands university here today. Where was I? She thought, Ben River's erogenous zone of course, or was that called a G-spot in men? Whatever, she was sure she could find it. Her tongue darted out to moisten her dry lips, when he stared directly at her, his countenance dark, brooding and totally mesmerising.

Then Sophie nudged her and spoilt it. "Will you two stop it," she whispered with a giggle, "I can feel the heatwave from here."

Juliette blushed and looked away.

Sophie herself was staring at Tarquin Haverstock the course leader. He looked tiny in stature compared to Ben Rivers, but he had the loveliest, cheeky smile and a real aura of warmth about him. He waved at Sophie then hopped up behind the podium.

"One, two, one two," he tapped the microphone, "anybody out there?"

The room resonated with laughter.

"Right, I think we're ready to start," Tarquin gripped the podium and gazed around at the hundred or so pairs of eyes fixated on him, "you don't need your pens and papers yet. This is just an introduction, a pep talk. Welcome everyone..."

He was interrupted by the door at the back slamming loudly. Then Will came bouncing down the steps, all gangly long limbs and tousled hair.

"Woo-hoo," Sophie stood up and pointed at the reserved seat. Will looked suitably embarrassed and slunk down the row, eliciting a few tuts along the way.

"Where was I?" Tarquin scratched his head, "yes, welcome, welcome everybody. So from myself and the rest of the English staff, we want to say a big well done to you all. You are working hard and we're impressed. This year's batch of students are showing great promise." He glanced at Sophie, "we're almost at the end of this school year, just a few months left, so keep up the good work and if you need any help or advice, please come to us. In fact, I do recommend that you all have chats with your personal tutors, they can help guide you and assist with your progress. That's what we're paid for, so please, come say hello, we don't bite."

A few titters spread around the lecture theatre.

"But anyway, we hope you're having a great time at Chattlesbury University. Let's face it though, when this is all over, you'll forget ninety-five percent of what you learn here. What it does do is get you thinking outside the box, questioning and exploring. We ignite those brain synapses and you'll never be the same again. So ask those awkward question, don't just settle, don't just accept things. You people are the future, the leaders that this country needs. Be brave, be honest, be rebellious. Most of all be you!"

A few claps ricocheted around the room. It soon grew into deafening applause. People got to their feet, cheering Tarquin Haverstock, the enigmatic English course leader.

"Thank you," he raised his hands signalling for quiet, "and now we are extremely lucky to have a guest speaker who is going to give a talk on the abuse of power in the literature of Charles Dickens." A few students could be heard groaning, but the majority were happy to pick up their pens, ready for scribbling.

* * *

After the lecture finished, student satisfaction questionnaires were circulated.

"I'll do mine at home," Evelyn decided, as she snatched the sheets up and folded them into her handbag, "I'm leaving now, do you think I should notify the lecturer?"

"It might be a good idea to give them a heads up," Melanie advised with a smile.

"I hope Mam's okay," Sophie and Juliette chorused together. Ann reiterated her offer of assistance if required. Evelyn stooped down to hug her gently, "thank you...everyone, I'll be in touch." She hurried off towards the group of lecturers, while the others slowly made their way to the exit doors.

"So," Ann drawled, "who wants to come with me to see the Mayor open the new computer suite?" Juliette and Sophie nodded.

"Why not," decided Melanie.

"I've got to, urm meet someone," Will said with an apologetic smile, "see you later in European Literature?"

"You sure will," Ann replied waving as they drifted away in opposite directions.

The new computer suite was housed in a high, red brick building, tucked behind the imposing church of St Pauls, with its intricate, archaic stonework and pretty public gardens.

"It's so peaceful here," Juliette commented, as they wandered up a winding path, which was bordered by colourful winter violas, forget-me-nots and evergreen bushes, "shall we eat our lunch here afterwards? It's such a beautiful day." They all agreed that would be a lovely idea.

"We can come here in the spring, with Evelyn and Will too," Sophie suggested, "hopefully Mam will be okay and everything will work out with Hema."

"Will certainly isn't himself," Juliette divulged, "he hardly made any notes today and seemed to be constantly checking his phone."

"The angst of teenage love," Ann replied, "I'm sure he'll be alright, as for Mam, let's hope she makes a speedy recovery."

The double doors of the computer suite slid open and a security guard gave them the once over.

"Straight up to the second floor," he instructed, when they had told him why they were here.

There was already a large group of people congregating in the corridor. Sophie groaned as she spotted a few press badges affixed to coats, and tucked her head down as they sailed past them to the lift.

"Phew!" She exclaimed, as the doors closed, "hopefully they didn't see me."

No such luck, when they arrived at their destination, there was a couple of burly looking men waiting.

"Hi Mrs O'Neill, can we have a photograph with you and your friends?"

Sophie laughed nervously, "aren't you here to photograph the Mayor?"

"Come now, one won't hurt will it?" the other man took charge, positioning them all in a semi-circle, "smile ladies." The camera clicked a dozen or so times.

"Have they finished?" Ann asked through gritted teeth, "I'm not used to smiling so much."

There was a commotion from the other end of the corridor. The mayor had arrived in all his finery. The reporters rushed off, cameras clicking frantically.

"How do you put up with them?" Ann asked, "it's so intrusive, doesn't it annoy you?"

"I've got used to it I suppose, they're more interested in Ryan to be honest and any gossip about Chattlesbury FC." Sophie paused to survey her surroundings, "anyway, this new computer suite, so we'll be able to come use these computers then? There is never enough spare in the main building."

"Yes," Melanie nodded, "it's all very ultra cool modern technology, but with thousands of other students, you will have to book to use them."

The crowd watched with bated breath as the Mayor cut the ribbon and said in a loud, booming voice, "I declare this computer suite officially open." There was a small round of applause, then people surged forward to look around the fresh smelling, open plan floor.

* * *

Will was pacing outside the reserved study booth. He glanced at his wrist watch, another ten minutes had elapsed since he had last checked. That meant that Hema was now twenty minutes late. The row of glass rooms stretched the length of the library, full of people reading, writing, or just listening to music on their i-pods.

"That one's taken," he said to a man and woman who were walking towards it, with their arms wrapped around each other and canoodling on their minds.

Then he saw her, half hidden behind a shelf of hard back books, peeping at him. What was she doing? he wondered with an exasperated sigh.

"Hema," he mouthed her name, beckoning her with his hands. She pulled at her fleece, unzipping it in the warmth of the library. Will's eyes were drawn to her stomach. She looked exactly the same for goodness sake. She saw him look and her hands fluttered downwards, in a protective gesture. He still couldn't quite believe that there was a baby in there.

"Hello," he began, taking hold of her dainty hands, "were you held up in class?"

Quickly she nodded. He noticed she looked tired and drawn, her cheekbones were more pronounced and she looked as if she had lost weight off her frame, if that was possible. Shouldn't you put weight on when you were pregnant, Will surmised, ah the dreaded 'p' word crops up again. He closed the door firmly and pulled out a chair for her to sit on.

"So, Evelyn's Mam is in hospital," he began, as he perched on the desk and swung his legs up, "pneumonia, really poorly apparently."

"Oh no," Hema's hand flew to her mouth, "please give her my well wishes."

Will nodded, "and how are you feeling?"

"Not too good," she replied, "I constantly feel sick, gone off tea, coffee and even prawn cocktail crisps."

"No way," Will looked flabbergasted, "already?"

"Yes."

Will stood awkwardly, "have you any idea how far gone you are?"

Hema shook her head, "no, I'm booked in to see the midwife at the end of the month."

"So you're going to keep it then?"

"Of course I'm keeping the baby," Hema said, eyes flashing, "I'm keeping *our* baby Will."

Bloody hell thought Will, as he raked his fingers through his hair, "o-okay, if that's what you definitely want. Are you sure Hema?"

"I am," she snapped, "I've thought it through carefully and I'm going to have and keep the baby."

"But what about your parents?"

"I don't care, they will have to accept it," her chin jutted out with defiance.

"Well good but what about uni? This is a huge decision you've made here."

"Uni?" Hema looked shocked by Will's words, "I can defer my course, I can finish it anytime! I know how difficult this is going to be! I'm still having our baby."

Will looked down at his feet, *what about me*, he wanted to shout. But instead he painted on a bright smile, "I'll stand by you then, I'm here for you. I love you, you know that."

Hema rose, her hands trembling slightly, "you have no idea how relieved I am to hear you say that. I'd prepared myself to being alone, to going through this without you. I'm so happy that you're supporting me." She skipped into his arms, flinging her hands up to cradle his face, then smothering his cheeks with kisses. Will kissed her back, sank into the warmth of her. As they hugged and caressed he leant his head on her shoulder and for the first time in years he prayed, God help us.

* * *

After a lovely lunch seated on benches in the gardens of St. Paul's, the ladies made their way back to the university. They grabbed hot drinks from the canteen before making their way up to the second floor. Rather uncharacteristically, Will was already seated at a front table.

"Are you okay?" Juliette asked, as she plonked her bag next to him.

"Think so," he looked shell shocked, as if he had been the recipient of life changing news and Juliette was unable to detect if the vibes were good or bad. She slid onto the seat next to him, smiling at him warily.

Dr Smythe was ten minutes late for class. Rumour was, that she liked to keep her students waiting and therefore her lectures always ran over. The room was quiet when she entered, carrying a big box of handouts and a bohemian looking handbag.

"Goodness, what a civilized class, are you all okay?" Her accent was posh, quintessential standard English. She removed a floppy, multi coloured hat and placed it down on her desk as a few murmurs of assent could be heard, "well I hope you are all ready to speak up. We have a lot to discuss today."

Juliette regretted sitting so near the front now, Dr Smythe had a reputation for picking on the quieter members of the class.

"Can I have a volunteer to assist me in distributing the handouts." There was total silence.

"You," she pointed at Juliette, then passed her a wad of stapled paper sheets.

Juliette scraped back her chair and meandered to the back of the class.

As she passed the sheets around, Wilomena Smythe was writing on the board, her letters were fancifully scribed, looping into attractive swirls.

"European mythology," she read to the class, "is what we are going to be studying for the next few weeks. Today we are going to be looking at French mythology, legends passed down over the centuries. In particular we shall be focussing on tales of French legendary creatures, the Beast of Gevadan, the Cheval Mallet, the Gargouille, you will find many more on the literature you have been given, so sit back class and prepare to be amazed."

So the next three hours flew by. Towards the end, Wilomena declared that next week they would be looking at extracts from films which explored myths, such as *Jason and the Argonauts*.

"I shall give your wrists and hands a break," she said with a smile, "although you may take notes for the seminar discussion if you wish to." Dr Smythe then went onto discuss the presentations which were due at the end of the semester, "I want you all to get into small groups of two or three and work on your presentation. You can choose any subject from any European myth to discuss. Please feel free to use projector slides or other forms of accompanying media such as music, film clips to enhance your presentation, but the focus *must* remain on discussion and you must all take it in turns to speak. The exact criteria is in the module handout." With that, she waved the class away, bit into a juicy, red apple and began flicking the pages of her current read: *Lady Chatterley's Lover.*

"That was really interesting," Sophie exclaimed, as she stuffed her pens back into her handbag, "I'm not sure about the presentations though, I don't really feel confident enough to speak to a whole class."

"You won't be on your own," Ann replied gruffly, "I'll work with you, if you'd like me to."

"Oh wow," Sophie gushed, "will you Ann, that would be awesome, thank you."

"Looks like you've got me," Juliette threw a lopsided grin Will's way.

"Cool," Will nodded, digging in his pocket for his phone.

"And Evelyn can join our group too," Juliette continued, "this should be really interesting. It will certainly be different to writing an essay." They made their way towards the lifts, chatting about what category myth they could choose, when suddenly Juliette heard her name being called. She spun around to see Ben Rivers, his head poking out the side of a classroom door.

"Erm, I'll catch you up guys," Juliette said breezily. She hurried back down the corridor, where he was waiting inside the empty classroom.

"Hello," she whispered as she closed the door and leant against it.

"Just wanted to check you are okay," he pulled her away from the transparent glass panel and into his arms. Juliette smiled up at him, winding her fingers around the nape of his neck.

"I'm very well thank you Dr Rivers," she teased, pursing her lips, "why are you sneaking about?"

He laughed, deep chuckles, "you are such a tease. For your information, I am preparing for a very important afternoon lecture with my third year students."

"How very conscientious of you," she replied, lifting her nose high into the air.

"Are you still available Saturday evening Miss Harris?" He pecked her cheekbones, the upturned curve of her dainty nose. Juliette felt her stomach flipping with anticipation.

"I suppose so," she replied, ducking her head down towards the floor. He lifted her chin and slowly kissed the corner of her mouth. Her breath caught as she slipped her fingers upwards to twine into his hair, pulling him down so she could plant her lips firmly onto his.

"I'm looking forward to it," he admitted casually, "I've installed a fire extinguisher in my kitchen though, just as a safety precaution."

Juliette pulled away, her mouth gaping open in mock outrage, "I can assure *you* Dr Rivers, you will enjoy it."

"I can believe it," he murmured, pulling her back towards him to kiss her again and again.

Minutes ticked by and Juliette's head was spinning. Then the worry of being caught intruded her thoughts, reluctantly she pulled away, "I should go," she gasped, placing her hands against his firm chest, "your students will be here soon."

Ben nodded, "I'll wait to hear from you," he called, as she walked away, outside into the February sunshine.

* * *

The journey to the hospital took longer than anticipated, making an already anxious Evelyn feel completely stressed out. There had been a major hold up on the main road due to roadworks, creating a line of tooting traffic and irate commuters. The bus had therefore taken a detour around the less busy streets. Evelyn watched the scenery flying by, thoughts of Mam occupying her mind. When it was time to disembark, she never noticed that she had left her handbag on the seat until the driver had called her back. When she finally arrived, the hospital ward was quiet and extremely hot. Evelyn pulled off her coat as she made her way towards Mam's bay. A jolly janitor was mopping the floors, humming along to the sounds of the hospital radio, playing from speakers overhead.

"Afternoon love," he called as she neared, "watch your step now, this bit 'ere is wet through."

Evelyn skirted around it, passing a nurse dispensing drugs from a trolley.

The bay that Mam was in was small, with two other beds occupying the room. Mam was nearest the window. To get to her she had to pass two other ladies. One was sitting up knitting, while the other was lying flat, the sheets pulled tightly up to her chin.

Just across from Mam's bed a slightly ajar window allowed a cool breeze to enter the room. The blinds fluttered to and fro and the sound of workmen shouting and bird song permeated the air.

Evelyn stared down at Mam, who lay fast asleep, chest rising and eyelids flickering.

"She's been asleep for a while," whispered the lady in the next bed, click, click went the sound of her knitting needles, "none of us slept well last night, it's so noisy in here and the heat is unbearable." Evelyn nodded politely and perched on the chair next to Mam's bed. There was only an hour left of visiting time, but then she could come back this evening. She relaxed back in the squashy chair, feeling some of the tension draining away, now that she was here and could see Mam looked comfortable.

"Would you like a cuppa?" The other lady asked, "there's a relative's room just down the hall with tea and coffee making facilities."

"Oh no it's okay, I've got water, but thank you," Evelyn smiled her way.

A nurse bustled into the room dispensing painkillers and checking patient charts.

"How has she been?" Evelyn asked the fresh faced looking young lady.

"She's stable at the moment, the Doctor has been this morning and prescribed more antibiotics."

Evelyn stared at the IV drip attached to Nora's arm and the oxygen mask covering her nose and mouth. There was a sudden clatter from just outside the room and Mam shifted slightly in the bed. Her eyes fluttered open.

"Where am I?" Nora said drowsily.

"You're in hospital Mam," Evelyn gently took her hand and leant towards her.

"The confusion is to be expected," the nurse said with a touch of sympathy, "she needs complete rest at the moment." She inserted a thermometer into Mam's ear then scribbled the results down on the chart at the bottom of the bed.

"Would you like a sip of water Mam?"

Nora nodded weakly and watched as Evelyn tipped some fresh liquid into a plastic cup.

"Here," she raised Nora slightly so she could drink. "How are you feeling?"

"Sore and old," rasped Nora. She fell back against the pillows, coughing slightly.

Evelyn patted her hand, "it's a lovely room they've put you in," she stared around at the brightly painted walls and the spotlessly clean floor, "thank heavens for the NHS."

"Evelyn," Nora was tugging at the oxygen mask.

"Shush Mam, you should be resting. Let me tell you about my day." So Evelyn launched into a spiel of what had transpired at the university. Nora listened keenly as she chatted about Juliette and Dr Rivers.

"So it seems that they had a marvellous time in Castleford, I'm so happy for them. I was thinking when you come out and the weather is warmer, maybe we could go for a day trip there. I've heard it has beautiful restaurants and plenty to see and do. Would you like that Mam?"

Nora was silent, staring wide eyed at something over Evelyn's shoulder.

"Mam, what is it?" Evelyn glanced around at the blank wall.

"Your Dad Evelyn, he's here."

"No Mam, there's no one there, you're poorly that's all. Hush now, you need to rest."

Again Mam pulled at the mask, "he's been here all night. He's waiting for me," tears glistened in her eyes, "it's time Evelyn."

Evelyn clutched at her throat, she could feel her colour rising, "don't talk so Mam, I'm going to fetch the nurse," she jumped to her feet but Nora grabbed her wrist, she was surprisingly strong for someone so poorly.

"Promise me Evelyn that you'll be okay, you'll carry on, you'll succeed," cough, cough, "finish your studies and publish your book. Find love Evelyn, find love…"

Evelyn watched aghast as the frail, familiar hand slipped away to flop down on the bed.

"Mam, Mam," she shouted, "wake up, wake up." But her eyes were closed and Evelyn noticed the colour fading away from her cheeks. She knew then it was her life ebbing away, it was her spirit leaving. As the nurses ran towards them and the alarm began ringing, tears cascaded down her cheeks, "I promise Mam, I promise," she whispered, "I love you, sleep tight."

Chapter Six

Juliette was checking off her shopping list at the supermarket, putting a big tick next to all the goodies she already had in her trolley. Now where was the white chocolate? She wondered as she swerved around the aisle, almost careering into a buy one get one free display. Saturday mornings were always horrendously busy in the shops, but today seemed even worse. Aha, there it was, Juliette picked up a slab of heavenly creamy chocolate and balanced it on top of the raspberries. Then it was off to the meat counter for four of the butchers finest chicken breasts. On the way, she passed Harry and Molly in the magazine aisle, their heads were bent, as they chuckled together over animated jokes.

"Pop them in if you really want them," Juliette was feeling a bit flush, a spare pound she had found at the bottom of her bag yesterday had been spent on a scratch card (not something she usually bought) and to her delight, she had then won fifty pounds. So in went *Animal Monthly* and *Shoot* without her having to check she had enough in her purse. Juliette paused at the greetings cards shelf, her eyes skimmed over the condolences section. Sophie had rung to inform her that Evelyn's Mam had passed away. Ninety-seven was a great age to reach, but still Juliette was shocked and concerned for Evelyn. She thought of her own dear parents and a shudder of fear ran down her spine. Old age came to everyone, that was a surety, but still Juliette worried over how she would cope without them.

"Mom, can we have marshmallows to go with our drinking chocolate tonight?" Molly pleaded, eyes big and wide.

"I should think so," Juliette replied with a warm grin, "do you fancy some squirty cream too?" Molly whooped with delight and rushed off towards the refrigerator section, with her brother in tow.

Juliette browsed the shelf, flinging in paella rice and hunting the spice section for smoked paprika. She was making a chicken paella this evening, followed by white chocolate and raspberry trifle. All from scratch of course. The recipes had been torn from a weekly magazine. The pictures looked lovely and very appetising. She had toyed with the idea of making a starter, but thought it may be too filling, so instead she headed towards the wine section and chose a lovely sounding French white, that was on special offer.

Harry and Molly were back, clutching two cans of squirty cream and a bumper pack of fluffy marshmallows.

"Can we go now?" Harry asked, scuffing his trainers on the linoleum floor with impatience.

"One last thing to get," Juliette assured him, "peppers." Off they marched to the vegetable aisle, then joined a queue to pay.

They were walking across the car park with their bags of shopping, when her phone buzzed an incoming text. She paused to glance at the screen and grimaced as she recognised Marty's number. He wanted to know if her and the kids were free this evening for a family quiz night at the local pub. Juliette suppressed a sigh and typed out a quick succinct reply, sorry – busy. He had been pestering *again* for them to spend time together as a family. No way, she thought with resolution. She knew he was eager for them to get back together, but Juliette felt only anger and pity towards him. There was certainly no love there for him anymore, in fact she wasn't sure that she even liked him. A minute later the phone was ringing loudly and vibrating in her pocket.

"Who's that Mom?" Molly asked, as she skipped in front of them.

Harry was dawdling behind, "do you want me to answer Mom?"

"No!" Juliette replied sharply, "it's probably just sales people pestering, don't worry love, I'll pick it up when we get home."

When they arrived back at their maisonette, Harry and Molly disappeared into their bedrooms.

"I'll make you a sandwich, Juliette hollered, "will cheese and cucumber do?"

There were muffled affirmations. She unloaded the bags then grabbed the margarine from the fridge. Just as she was slicing the cucumber, her phone rang again.

"Hello," she said breathlessly.

Her spirits sank as she recognised Marty's cheeky greeting.

"Hi Jules, it's me, hope you're not avoiding me."

"Marty…of course not, what can I do for you?"

"What can I do for *you*, is the question," he guffawed and Juliette waited silently. "Why don't you come tonight Jules? It's a great night out, there's a beer garden for the kids to play, it's got slides and climbing frames, they'll love it and I guarantee that *you'll* have fun."

"No Marty," Juliette said firmly, "it's nice of you to think of us, but no, sorry."

"You need to get out, live a little, let your hair down. Come on, I'll pay for everything if that's what you're worried about."

The hairs on the back of Juliette's neck stood upright as she clenched the phone.

"I've already made plans, sorry, but if you want to spend time with the children, we can arrange another weekend for you to take them out."

"I want to spend time as a family," the whine in his voice reminded Juliette of a petulant child, "Harry and Molls would love it."

"That's enough," Juliette snapped, "we're not together anymore, haven't been for years, so why don't you drop the idea that we're going to reunite; we're not."

"Okay, okay," Marty rasped, "there's no need to be nasty. I get the picture. Where are you going anyway? Miss high and mighty, never goes out."

"I really don't have to answer that, it's not your concern," Juliette was close to yelling, it was none of his damn business, instead she bit down on her lip and tasted a sliver of blood.

"So you're going out with a man then?" Marty yelled.

"So what if I am," the retort escaped from Juliette's lips.

"What about our kids?" he ranted, "who's looking after them, oh let me guess, Marie the perfect sister from the perfect fam…" Buzz went the line as Juliette hit the red button with fury. She switched the phone completely off, then flung it away from her.

Ten minutes later, with the help of a cup of chamomile tea and a garibaldi biscuit, Juliette was feeling much calmer and determined that Marty would not be spoiling her evening. She set about making the trifle, simmering the custard and prepping the raspberries. As she was placing the completed glass bowl, full of delicious creamy trifle into the fridge to chill, Molly wandered into the kitchen, wrapped in her fluffy Disney blanket.

"Where are you going tonight Mommy?" She asked, climbing onto a stool.

"I'm going to have a meal with a very lovely friend," well he was more than that, thought Juliette, but she didn't want to confuse her seven-year-old daughter with complicated matters of the heart.

"What's your friends name?"

Juliette thought for a moment, how much should she reveal and then decided that honesty would be the best policy.

"His name is Ben sweetie"

"Are you coming home after your meal?" Molly looked anxious, her forehead crinkled.

"Yes of course Molly," Juliette frowned, "why don't I tell Auntie Maz to let you stay up late. Then when I come back I can tuck you in."

"Okay," Molly seemed happy with that and climbed down off the stool, "can I watch Harry Potter?"

"*Again*?? Of course you can, as long as your brother doesn't mind."

Molly skipped off, calling her brother's name and Juliette was left alone ruminating over what she should wear this evening. Marie of course found fault with her attire, when she arrived.

"Jeans Jules, really?"

"I want to be comfortable, I'm cooking remember," Juliette bristled, "and we are going to be eating at his house. It's not like we're going to a swanky restaurant."

"Okay, okay, your top is pretty though."

Juliette looked down at the floaty, butterfly covered blouse and smiled.

"Hope you've got matching undies on, nothing worse than a black bra teamed with white knickers." Marie chortled and Juliette blushed at her sister's forthright manner of speaking.

"He won't be seeing my underwear, so I don't need to worry."

"Okay sister, whatever you say," Marie winked, a salacious gleam in her eyes.

Juliette laughed along, just as Dave, Marie's husband sauntered into the kitchen.

"You look smashing Jules, and the grub looks good too," he was almost salivating over the trifle, which was all ready to go, wrapped in cellophane.

"Ere, give Jules a hand carrying the stuff to the car," Marie deposited the bulging bag of ingredients in his arms. Juliette hugged the dessert to her and let out a shaky breath.

"Do I look okay?" She asked, with a nervous glance in the mirror.

"Beautiful as always," Marie pecked her on the cheek, "let me know you're alright and text when you want picking up, okay?"

Juliette nodded, "I'll leave my phone on, so call me if you need me for…anything."

Marie rolled her eyes, "have fun," she shooed her out of the flat, watching as they clattered down the concrete stairs.

Dave programmed Ben's address into his sat-nav, then joined the steady flow of traffic heading towards the outskirts of the city.

"So this geezer, he's okay is he?" Dave asked, as he changed gear and sped up.

"His name's Ben," Juliette replied a little tetchily, "and he's lovely."

"Hmmmm," came the unconvinced reply.

Juliette tutted, "why have you and Maz got such a problem with me seeing him?"

"What d'you mean?" Dave glanced sideways at her.

"Well it's obvious Marie doesn't approve and you don't seem too happy about it either."

Dave sighed, "we don't want to see you getting hurt, he is your teacher Jules."

"He's not my teacher, he's a university lecturer. I'm not a dizzy sixteen-year-old. I know exactly what I'm doing, so please don't worry."

"Okay, okay sorry, it's up to you, as long as you're happy."

Juliette settled back in the leather seat with a happy smile, which froze at Dave's next words.

"You know I've got a lovely mate. Clive, remember him from school? He's got his own business, doing really well for himself. A top bloke, nothing like that scum bag Marty," he paused to check his mirrors and manoeuvred his car into the left hand lane.

"Why are you telling me this?" Juliette's pretty eyes were narrowed, as she stared out of the steamed up window.

"We could go for a meal, me, Clive, you and Maz. There's a new Indian restaurant opened on the high street, I've heard the food is cracking."

"Dave," Juliette began firmly, "you know I love you, but there is no way I am going on a blind date with one of your friends."

"But…"

"No," Juliette held up her hand, "that's enough, let's just listen to some music." She reached forward to snap on the radio and music flooded the car. They whizzed away from the built up grey, city buildings and onto narrow country lanes. Juliette sat forward with excitement and stared out at the setting sun, the golden red skies kissing the tops of swaying trees. She wound down the window and took big gulps of the bracing, country air.

"According to Mr computer, we're almost here," Dave said as he tapped the side of the sat-nav, "I hope this signal doesn't give up on me."

"It's here," Juliette squealed with delight, "Thornberry Road."

Dave took a sharp left, kicking up dried dirt and stones as he followed a long, winding lane. They passed a small, country pub where children played outside and a quaint looking row of shops, before they turned off into a small cul-de-sac, with a dozen or so detached houses.

"It's number twelve, the last one look," Juliette pointed at the end house, which bordered a field of high, swaying grass.

"Nice," Dave remarked, as he pulled up the handbrake and they both peered out of the window at the statuesque property, with the imposing bay windows and the double fronted garage.

Dave let out a low whistle, "It's a big house for one guy, are you sure he lives alone?"

"Shush," Juliette replied, as the front door swung open and Ben Rivers stood there, bathed in the dwindling evening light. Juliette fumbled with the seat belt, clumsily trying to extricate herself without spilling the trifle.

"Don't forget your bags," Dave said, with a bemused smile, "do you want a hand carrying them to the door?"

"Erm, no thanks," Juliette bent to grab everything, before waving Dave goodbye.

"Have a nice time," he said, resting his arm against the open window, "text me when you're ready to come home."

"I won't be too late," Juliette assured him, "thank you so much for the lift," she watched as he gave Ben a curt nod, before slowly pulling away.

"Hello," Ben greeted warmly, as he padded towards her, barefooted, "did your friend want to come in for a drink?"

"Oh no, he has to get back. He's my brother-in-law by the way."

Ben took the bags from her and led her into the house, "please, make yourself at home."

Juliette slipped off her shoes and gazed around at the minimalist décor. A few seconds later a scratching sound emanated from the opposite end of the long hallway. A furry head peeked around the door and then the most adorable dog was bounding towards her.

"Oh my gosh," laughed Juliette as the dog launched itself onto two hind paws, yelped with excitement and covered her with lashes of canine kisses.

"*This* is Heathcliff," Ben commented drily, "get down boy."

"Oh he's okay," Juliette protested, as his master pulled him away by the collar, "what type of dog is he?"

"A labradoodle, six years old and still thinks that he's a puppy."

"He is gorgeous," Juliette said, crouching down to pat him vigorously. Heathcliff cocked his head to the side in approval, as she rubbed his ears.

"He gets all the attention," Ben grumbled, but his face beamed with a happy grin. "Would you like a glass of champagne Madam?"

"Mmm, sounds lovely," Juliette took Ben's outstretched hand and rose to be caught in his arms.

"I've missed you," Ben kissed her mouth, "where have you and your friends been hiding?" Juliette's head swam with a dizzy desire, then she remembered Evelyn's Mam and a wave of sadness engulfed her.

She explained what had happened as they passed through a lovely cosy lounge into an ultra-modern kitchen diner.

"How terrible for Evelyn," Ben commented, "I'm glad you've told me. Would you like me to notify the course director and her lecturers?"

"That's lovely of you Ben, yes if you could, she may need essay extensions at least."

"She could defer the course for a while," he suggested, "I can imagine that university may be the last thing on her mind at the moment. Maybe she could come and see me after the funeral and we can discuss her options."

Juliette nodded, "I'll speak to her and let her know. Thank you, that's very kind." She beamed his way, *how lovely is this man*, she thought and how can he still be single?

"Right then," Ben plonked the bags of groceries on the table and switched on the CD player, "tell me what culinary feast you intend making me tonight."

Juliette whizzed around the kitchen, making the paella and warming the taco shells. Her head was a little fuzzy after drinking two large glasses of champagne, but she was having a fantastic time. Ben stayed in the room with her, chatting, passing her pots and pans and washing up the used utensils.

"I'm nearly done," she said, wiping at a damp forehead. As she gave the paella a last stir, Ben laid the table with plates and cutlery.

"Oh, I nearly forgot, there's tea lights and table confetti in my hand-bag, would you..."

"You think of everything," Ben replied, "I'm a lucky man."

She carried the pan of paella across the kitchen, placing it down in the middle of a lovely oak table.

"That. Smells delicious," Ben licked his lips with appreciation.

"I hope you're hungry," Juliette surmised, as she eyed the bubbling food. They clinked glasses, while Heathcliff curled around their legs, nose upturned at the delectable smell.

"So," Ben commented, between mouthfuls of food, "you're definitely a fantastic cook."

Juliette gulped down the chilly champagne, "thank you, I do love cooking, although I don't really have time to experiment much at the moment."

Ben nodded, "studying for an English degree isn't as easy as some think. It's a very time consuming subject. Are you finding it difficult?"

"No." Juliette shook her head fervently, worried he may think she was looking for sympathy, "I mean it *is* hard work, but I don't regret doing it. I love the subject, the university and have made some lovely friends. It's just the amount of reading really that can be challenging and the essays too, I'm just getting used to the referencing."

"By the third year, you'll be an expert," Ben assured her.

Juliette sloshed more champagne into her glass with a sigh.

"Are you okay?" Ben asked. "What's worrying you? Tell me."

"I'm worried about *you* to be honest Ben. I'm worried that your career could be in jeopardy because of me. Some of the students have noticed about us and I'm sure the staff know too."

Ben shrugged, "they probably do. Let them gossip. It's not like we're children Juliette, we're both consenting adults."

"I know," Juliette blushed, "I just don't want them accusing you of favouritism towards me."

"Is it the essay marking you're concerned about?"

"Yes," Juliette blurted out.

"It's sorted," Ben replied smoothly, covering her hand with his own, warm long fingers, "Brian Hodges is going to mark your essays. I've cleared it with Tarquin Haverstock."

Juliette's mouth hung open, "you've told the course director about us?"

"Of course, he's not an ogre, he's a great bloke."

"But...but" Juliette felt lost for words.

"I'm serious about you...about us," Ben looked at her darkly, "you're worth it."

Juliette felt heat infuse her cheeks, then she was up leaping towards him, balancing on his knee, as she smothered his face with kisses.

"You've finished your paella then?" Ben said with a slight chuckle, as they drew apart.

Juliette nodded and slid her fingers into his already tousled hair, "are you ready for raspberries?"

"Mmmm," came his reply, "with squirty cream?"

Thank heavens Molly had put two cans into the trolley, Juliette thought as she nodded dreamily. She almost floated over to the fridge;

a heady combination of passion and champagne made her steps feel literally buoyant.

"That's definitely an aphrodisiac," she said, pointing at the empty bottle.

"Do you want more?" Ben asked with a cheeky grin.

"Yes please. Ta-da," she set the trifle down in the middle of the table.

"That looks amazing," Ben said, gazing down at the mint sprigs, fruit and the generous sprinkling of white chocolate.

"It tastes even better," Juliette revealed, as she spooned him a generous portion, "I've made it a few times, it's the kids favourite dessert."

"It's delicious," Ben confirmed, "so, tell me all about your children."

"Well, Harry is ten, loves sports, music, computer games, the usual really, a typical boy. Molly is seven, very girly has inherited my wild hair, loves art, books, sleeping," Juliette laughed, "a lot of people say she is a mini me."

"And I bet they are absolutely lovely, just like their Mom."

Juliette blushed and was just about to ask about Ben's family, when her phone began ringing.

"I better get this," she rummaged in her handbag and fished out her mobile, "hello."

"Jules it's me," Marty's voice was distinct over the crackly signal.

Juliette's spirits deflated, "erm, hello. I'm kinda busy at the moment."

"Oh, did I interrupt you and your male friend?" His sarcastic tone could be heard clearly throughout the kitchen. Ben sat back, with a raised eyebrow and looked down at his empty bowl.

"What can I do for you?" Juliette said, with an embarrassed sigh.

"I want to take the children out next weekend, there's a family day at the park. I don't see why they should lose out just because you're being arsy."

Juliette felt her face flame with an angry heat and bit down on the expletive that threatened to erupt. "We can talk tomorrow okay?" She didn't wait for a reply, cut the call and placed it back in its case.

"That was my ex," a nervous Juliette began.

Ben held up his hands, "you don't need to explain."

"Oh but I want to, that's if you don't mind listening."

"Of course not," Ben gripped her hands, "tell me."

So Juliette told him the whole sorry tale, how they had met when they were teenagers, a snapshot of their relationship, his shady lifestyle which had resulted in his internment in prison. The detrimental effects it had on Harry and Molly. But most of all she wanted to assure Ben that she held no romantic feelings for him.

"He'll always be part of my life because of the kids, but I don't care about him romantically, haven't done for years. He let me down in so many ways, it's left me sort of scarred."

Ben leant forward to kiss the tip of her nose, "I think you are very brave, strong and gorgeous. I'm not going to hurt you; don't you realise I'm crazy about you."

Juliette's eyes widened, "really, but you...I just don't understand why you're not married by now. I feel the same way about you too, I can't stop thinking about you..."

Ben pulled her to her feet, "let's go listen to some music and dance."

They padded back into the lounge, it was dark now. Ben snapped on the lamps, which cast a seductive glow around the room. She stood waiting while he searched through his CD's.

Then a soft sound swooned around the room.

"Tell me what this is," Ben said as he took her in his arms.

Juliette cocked her head to one side, "oh my gosh, it's A Flock of Seagulls I think, but what is the song called?"

"Wishing," Ben said with a smile, "let's forget university and shady ex boyfriends, dance with me?"

Juliette of course was only too happy to oblige. She wound her arms around his neck as they spun around the room, at one point she stood on his feet and they waltzed around like a couple of tipsy teenagers.

"Ouch my toes," Ben said laughing.

"I'm sorry Sir," Juliette batted her eyelashes seductively then broke away from him to run into the kitchen and through the back door, out onto a beautiful patio. Heathcliff barked playfully beside her as she cooed over the pretty potted plants and the beautiful starry night sky.

Ben was behind her, panting breathlessly, "where are you going now woman?"

"I want to explore," Juliette threw her arms wide, "the world is huge and full of exciting possibilities."

"Let's start with my garden then," Ben said, catching her in a playful embrace, "did you know there is a little stream at the end. Village gossip says that fairies come out to play at night."

"Do they do your housework too?"

"Huh?" Ben looked puzzled.

Juliette laughed, "your house is immaculate!"

"That's because one, I live alone. Two, my kind neighbour Mavis is a brilliant cleaner and dog walker extraordinaire. Three, I'm hardly ever here."

"That's a shame," Juliette replied, "this is such a lovely house." She thought briefly of her tiny maisonette and a sadness washed over her.

Ben seemed to sense the change in her mood, "come with me," he said quietly.

They hopped over a line of steeping stones, to reach a gate that opened to the field.

"Watch your step," he warned, as she skirted around thorny weeds.

"How beautiful," Juliette gasped at the sight of the narrow, winding stream, the water looked luminous in the moonlight and it bubbled rhythmically over rocks, as it cascaded past them.

"Come in," Ben waded into the shallow stream, pulling her with him.

"Oh that feels divine," Juliette stretched her toes, curling them upwards to meet the gentle swell of the water, "and it is surprisingly warm."

"You look gorgeous; your hair is shining."

Juliette gazed up at him, then they were kissing passionately. She gripped his shirt, her hands slid underneath the fabric to touch warm, firm skin. His fingers ran down to the curve of her back, making her shiver with desire. Just then Heathcliff began barking, shackles raised as he foraged in the undergrowth, his nose following the scent of mice and hares.

"My dog the passion killer. Would you like to see the rest of the house?" His nose rubbed gently against her own.

"Yes," she replied huskily.

They headed back inside.

"This is my study," Ben showed her inside a small room that consisted of a table, computer and shelves of books. It smelt of lavender polish: fresh, sweet and clean. Juliette noticed a pile of marked essays resting on a trendy looking printer. There was a tall tower of paper sheets occupying the middle of the desk, she thought at first it may be Ben's own work but then she recognised Evelyn's name at the top of the page.

"Have you started reading it yet?" She asked with excitement.

"I have," Ben confirmed, "only the first four chapters, but it is extremely good. The writing flows beautifully. She is a talented lady."

"I hope a publisher thinks that too," Juliette ran her fingers over the cool, crisp pages, "it must be so fulfilling to write a book. Maybe one day she will become famous, like J K Rowling or Stephen King. She certainly deserves success; Evelyn is such a lovely lady."

"Maybe she will, I should get her autograph now. Come, I'll show you upstairs."

Ben settled Heathcliff on the rug with a tasty bone, before they climbed the stairs to the first floor.

"You've seen the bathroom," he indicated to the nearest door on the right.

Juliette nodded, "how many bedrooms does this house have?"

"Three. Which is great for when my niece and nephew come and stay."

He pushed open the first door, which led into an L shaped room, with a bed and a bucket of toys. The second room was the same, except for the bed spread, the first one had been a sunny yellow colour. This one was covered with roaring dinosaurs.

"And this is mine,"

Juliette followed him hesitantly into a large room, with bay windows covered in venetian blinds. It was painted in warm browns, with an imposing oak wardrobe and a king-size bed. Juliette glanced at the sheets, they were not silk, but they sure looked warm and comfortable. She perched on the edge, "this is lovely Ben."

"I'm glad you approve Miss Harris," he sat down beside her and cupped her face in his hands, "I've had such a great time tonight, when are we going to see each other again?"

He kissed her so tenderly that Juliette was left gasping, "soon."

The bed creaked gently as he pushed her back and Juliette felt cocooned inside the soft duvet.

Her whole body trembled as he parted her mouth with his own. She could hear her own moans mingled with his guttural groans, as they explored each other with their lips and their hands.

"Juliette," he whispered, as her head spun.

"Yes," she replied, her body ached for him. It had been so long since she had been held by a man. It felt divine. He felt divine.

Then from far away, she heard the sound of a phone ringing, a mobile maybe.

"Is that mine?" She asked groggily.

Ben released her and sat up, head cocked to one side, "It's yours. Do you want me to go get it?"

Juliette was very tempted to say no, come back to me, but thoughts of her children concerned her. She nodded and then rubbed at her temples, as he left the room. If it was Marty again, she might kill him.

She could hear him bounding back up the stairs, with Heathcliff yelping after him.

"A missed call," Ben said, as he passed her the phone.

"Oh it's my sister, I had better ring her back," she pressed redial and waited while they connected.

"Hi Jules," Marie's warm tone rang out.

"Is everything okay?"

"Molly's feeling sick and upset. She's crying and she wants you to come home. I can't do anything with her."

"Oh no," Juliette sprang to her feet, "tell Dave to come for me now and Maz, give her a kiss from me and tell her not to worry, I'll be back soon."

She cut the call and looked at Ben with regret, "I've got to go, my daughter's not well."

"Yes of course, then you must go." He looked disappointed.

"We could have another night out...maybe we could go watch a film and get a burger after?" Juliette fiddled with her hair, smoothing it down self-consciously.

"Great!" Ben's face cracked into a wide, beaming smile, "I'll let you decide then. Thank you for a lovely night, the food was delicious and so was the company."

"And it's been lovely meeting you too," Juliette crouched down to fuss a tail wagging Heathcliff.

They waited in the open doorway, arms encircled around each other. Ben pointed out each house, giving Juliette a brief run down on his neighbours.

"Number two is Martha, she lives alone with a harem of cats for company. Then at number six there's Bill and Josie, a retired couple, both worked for the police, terrible snobs but kind hearted. Next door is Samuel and Vanessa, city high fliers with money on their minds and then there's sweet Mavis, her husband has not long passed away. She keeps an eye out for Heathcliff and I help her out when I can."

"They sound lovely and it's so nice that you all look out for one another," she pointed at the neighbourhood watch sign, affixed to the flickering lamppost.

"It is a lovely area," Ben conceded, "I rented a flat in the city centre before this, it was close by for work, but an extortionate price and too noisy. I like my peace and quiet."

Juliette sighed, "I know what you mean. I'd love a garden and being part of a close knit community. Where I live there is no trust, every door is triple locked and it's cold and grey, but when I'm a teacher I'll be able to buy us something nice. A small house, nothing fancy with a colourful, wild garden, where I can sit in summer evenings, read and watch the world go by."

"I like your positive determination," Ben kissed the top of her head, "everyone should have a goal to aspire to."

"What's your goal Ben?" She asked, her face muffled against his chest.

"Funnily enough it's similar to Evelyn's. I'd love to have a book published, although mine would be boring academic research. I'd also like to travel more. I like visiting cities – Prague is next on the agenda."

A car's engine could be heard. Tyres swerved around the corner and they were dazzled by a set of headlights.

"I guess this is my lift," Juliette reluctantly released Ben, "it's been a wonderful evening."

"Thank you for cooking," Ben kissed her mouth softly and she felt desire stirring deep inside her, "see you at University?"

Juliette nodded and backed away, "bye."

She walked up the path towards the rumbling vehicle.

"Juliette!"

The sound of her name had her spinning around and just for a split second, she felt like running back to him.

"I'll wait to hear from you."

Chapter Seven

Evelyn sat alone in the lounge, staring at salmon coloured, flowery wallpaper and the flickering flames of the topaz fire. It was mid-afternoon, Sunday she thought. The days since Mam's death had fused into one, so without looking at the calendar, she wasn't exactly sure what day it was anymore. She knew it was the weekend, there had been children playing in the street all day, whooping and laughing as they raced up and down on bikes and scooters – no school for *them* today. She flicked on the television, *Songs of Praise* blared from the screen. Ah, so it *was* Sunday after all. She thought maybe she should eat something. Breakfast had consisted of a piece of fruit, washed down with sugary tea. She had skipped lunch, her stomach was in knots and she felt terribly sick. Evelyn felt stuck, trapped in a cycle of grief, that created a perpetual sense of sadness and tears, disbelief and shock. Images of Mam haunted her; her frail body in the hospital bed, the nurse pumping on her chest, the perplexed doctor declaring her dead at 3.30pm exactly, the cries of the other patients as they had lifted the sheet over her head. Had all this really happened? She thought with misery. She glanced across at Mam's chair, her glasses were still perched on the arm rest and there was one of her cardigans draped across the top. Evelyn shuffled over, picking up the clothing. It felt warm and soft, she lifted it to her nose, the smell of Lily of the Valley soap clung about it – Mam's favourite – her essence.

They had told her afterwards it had been her heart that had given up in the end, bought on by the complications of pneumonia. Evelyn knew deep down that Mam had wanted to die, but still she found it hard to accept that she was gone. Her laughter would never ring around the house again; her sweet smile would no longer brighten up the dullest day. For years she had warned Evelyn that her time was almost up. Evelyn hadn't taken much notice. Isn't that the way a lot of elderly folk complained? Now it had actually happened, Evelyn felt utterly heartbroken and lost without her lifelong companion. The sound of the letterbox flapping intruded on her thoughts. Another sympathy card maybe? Evelyn had a whole collection of them adorning the mantelpiece, the table, on top of the T.V. Beautiful poems of sadness and condolence, uplifting words to assuage the despair. In reality they made Evelyn cry even more, quiet sobs that racked her frame and left her gasping for air.

This morning when she had risen early to collect yesterday's milk, there had been the most beautiful posy placed on the doorstep. It was a thoughtful gift from the four young children who lived two doors down. Now they were resting in a crystal vase, Evelyn was drawn to the splashes of colour: reds and pinks and creams. Such pretty flowers, too vibrant for death she thought. A fresh tear glistened in her eye as she ruminated over people's kindness, the benevolence of the human spirit. Mam had lived in this neighbourhood all of her married life. She had been respected, admired, loved, oh she had been loved. A fresh wave of grief washed over her, sadness gripped her heart like a vice, the pain was bittersweet. Her eyes were streaming again, she reached for a tissue, wiped at her brow, her damp nose and wet eyes. Then she heard a different sound, a gentle tapping that emanated from the front door. The drapes had been pulled across the window days ago, no one could see into her grief stricken world. Dust motes hung in the air, tiny prisms of light that fell onto the furniture. Evelyn rose to stand in front of the mirror, a strange reflection stared back at her: red, puffy eyes, knotted flat hair, that hadn't seen a brush for days, pale cheeks and a pinched, blanched countenance. Her attire consisted of a stained dressing gown and threadbare slippers. How long had it been since she had put on a cycle of washing? She wondered. Visitors were not wanted at this difficult time she decided, maybe she should ignore it.

A memory flashed before her; a phone call from great aunt Gertrude, who had threatened to hop on the next train down with one of her famous Lancashire hotpots. At the time however, Evelyn had managed to persuade her distant relative that she was fine and coping. In truth she wasn't, but please let it not be her. The tapping came again, this time more insistent. Evelyn smoothed at her lank hair and pulled the belt of her dressing gown tight against her.

"Who is it?" She warbled, hovering in the hallway.

"Evelyn, it's me Jacob, I just want to make sure you're okay."

She breathed a sigh of relief. It was kind and chivalrous Jacob, Mam's friendly daycentre bus driver. Except he wasn't anymore, he never would be again. A fresh batch of tears welled, spilling down her cheeks, dropping onto the rug. Evelyn no longer felt them, her face felt numb. She stumbled towards the door. Jacob was good, Jacob was okay to let in. The locks were stiff underneath her clammy hands.

"Just a minute," she called, as she grappled with them.

"Hello," she said, facing a solemn looking Jacob. He removed his cap, tucking it underneath his arm.

"How *are* you?" He asked gently.

"You had better come in," Evelyn drew a deep, shaky breath.

They stood in the hallway, an anxious silence enveloping them. Jacob was shocked by her appearance, but tried not to show it.

"I bought you flowers and cake, shop bought of course," he smiled and held out the most beautiful spray of white roses.

"Thank you, they're beautiful," Evelyn sniffed and meandered through to the kitchen, "please excuse this," she motioned towards a sink full of dirty crockery, "I haven't been able to summon up the energy for housework."

"I completely understand…you've had quite a shock. It will take time to get over it."

Evelyn nodded, "I still can't believe that she's gone, it all happened so suddenly, what am I going to do without her?"

Jacob grasped her cold hands, "you'll carry on. That's what we do and I'll be here for you if you need any help with anything. Even if it's just a shoulder to cry on."

Evelyn's shoulders shook at his kind words, "she didn't get a telegram from the Queen."

"No, but she made it to ninety-seven. That's a grand old age. She was happy Evelyn, you made her happy. Sometimes though, there comes a time when people can't carry on anymore, they want to move on, to go to a better place."

"I hope wherever she is she's safe and with my dad, he'll look after her."

"There then," Jacob smiled gently, "I loved her too you know. Knocked me for six when I heard the news. Life can be cruel, but you just have to stay positive and cherish the good memories."

Evelyn's spirits lifted at Jacob's words. He was such a fine, kind man. Mam had been fond of him and Evelyn understood why.

"Would you like some tea?" She asked and for the first time in days, her lips lifted into a smile.

"Only if I can cut us a piece of this delicious chocolate cake," Jacob winked.

Evelyn nodded, "I'll fetch us some plates."

* * *

'Appointment with M', Will typed the words into the diary section of his phone and set a reminder for 8.30am. Although he really shouldn't have bothered. It was unlikely that he would forget his first ever visit to a midwife. The receptionist had been able to squeeze Hema into a cancellation, so they were going together tomorrow morning, bright and early.

"Feet up Will," Flora was hoovering, tugging a new contraption around that Max had bought her in the sales. Will lifted his legs and sprawled back on the sofa, squashing his paper and folders. If he closed his eyes for long enough, he could almost believe that none of this was happening. How on earth were they going to cope with a baby at nineteen? He was just a big kid himself. He couldn't even iron a shirt for goodness sake.

"Are you okay Will?" Flora was flicking the off switch and staring at him with concern.

Silence ensued, *should he confide in her?* The possibility of a major hysterical fallout however, stopped him.

"Yeah Mom I'm cool, just got a lot on with uni work."

"You should have a break, you've been working all weekend," she sat down beside him, "actually you look a little peaky, are you feeling unwell?"

Urm, yes! He wanted to shout, you are going to be a grandma.

"Would you like to come out with me and Dad?" Flora continued with a frown, "we're going for a meal tonight."

"Actually Mom, Jimmy's coming around, we'll order a Chinese and have a few beers if that's okay."

Flora patted his knee, "of course it is son, you enjoy yourself."

Normality resumed, Flora went off in search of her duster and Will was left chewing on his nails with worry. He had wanted to meet Hema, but she was resting after suffering a serious bout of morning sickness that had stretched into the afternoon. Will closed the door, pacing the room until she picked up his third call of the day.

"Are you okay?" He whispered.

"A little better yes."

"What have you told your parents?"

"They think I've got a sickness bug. I'm in quarantine," her tone quickened, "I've got to go, Dad's coming up the stairs."

Will gulped at the thought of Mr Kumar, "see you tomorrow?"

"Yes of course and Will try not to worry, everything will be okay."

Will cut the call with a heavy heart, everything really wasn't okay, but he was excelling at putting on a brave face for her. Inside he was terrified.

He endured another bad night's sleep. If tossing and turning were an Olympic sport, he would surely win a gold medal. He watched the sun's golden rays shining through the gaps in the blinds, as it rose to herald another day. Downstairs he padded, switched on the kettle and proceeded to make himself a strong coffee. He opened the fridge, but the thought of food churned his already delicate stomach. Ruby peered at him from her bed, confused at the sight of him so early in the morning. After a few hasty slurps, he pulled on a heavy duffle coat, slipped on his trainers and snapped on her lead.

"Let's go for a walk, eh girl?"

The streets were quiet, leaves crunched underneath his feet as he quickened his pace. He jogged through the entrance of the park, passing a lake that lapped gently. Birdsong greeted his ears. Ruby yelped with excitement at the ducks and geese gaggling near the shoreline. By the time he returned home he was sweating profusely, but feeling better. His head felt clearer and his nerves had settled into a strange calmness.

Max was sitting at the kitchen table, eating crunchy cornflakes, when Will appeared through the utility door.

"What on earth are you doing up?" Max exclaimed, following his words with an open mouthed gawp.

"Couldn't sleep," Will replied, crossing to the sink to pour himself a tumbler of ice cold water.

"I didn't think teenagers usually surfaced till lunchtime, on their days off."

Will bristled at the word 'teenager.' It seemed a juvenile term, considering everything that was going on in his life. "I'm nearly twenty Dad."

"Okay, it was a joke!" Max shrugged and opened his daily newspaper.

Will glanced at the clock, it wasn't even 6.45 am, but his dad was dressed smartly in a shirt and tie, ready for another stressful day at St. Mary's. Just then Flora waltzed into the room, a happy smile on her face.

"Oh hello Will, what a surprise to see you up so early."

Will rolled his eyes, "morning Mom, why are *you* so happy today?"

Flora's eyes flashed with excitement, "It's Monday, my favourite day of the week. Remember Will, I go to my flower arranging class, then it's lunch with Martha and finally helping at the elderly day care centre for the arts and craft afternoon."

Will nodded, "cool. I'm working lunchtime, so I er, won't be home till late afternoon." That at least was true. Mick the bar manager of the Students Union had text him yesterday, asking if he would help out with the dinner time rush.

"And I won't be back till after six love, it's parents evening at the end of the week, so I need to nag the staff into getting organised." Max popped his empty bowl into the dishwasher. "So Will, is Sophie doing voluntary this morning?"

"How should I know," Will said with a frown, "you're the one who works at St Mary's."

"Don't get lippy with me lad, I was just making conversation."

Will immediately felt guilty for snapping, "sorry. Why are you asking anyhow?"

"The nursery teacher has rung in sick," Max replied, as he closed his briefcase, "we could do with an extra pair of hands."

"I could text Soph if that helps. She should be in though, she was only saying the other day how much she is enjoying being in the nursery."

"It would be a big help if you could son, just as a gentle reminder," Max flung on his jacket, kissed Flora and strode to the door, with Ruby yapping at his heels in excitement. Flora waved cheerily until he had disappeared.

"Let's have some music shall we?" She fiddled with the CD player, until Cliff Richard's voice swooned around the kitchen. Will sighed, plugged in his ear phones and lost himself in the crazy, morning world of Radio One.

* * *

Sophie was still lazing in bed when Will's text pinged through.
'Just checking to see if you're going into St Mary's this morning?'
She read the message aloud to Ryan, who was wrapped tight in the duvet and still half asleep.

"Will's never messaged me about St Mary's before," she said aloud.

"Huh?" Ryan opened one eye, "who's Will?"

Sophie sighed, Ryan had the memory of a goldfish at times.

"My university friend, remember you got a signed ball for him?"

"Ah yes," anything to do with Chattlesbury FC had Ryan's interest piqued.

"His dad is the head teacher of St Mary's, where I'm doing voluntary?"

Ryan's head fell back on the pillows, "I know it."

Sophie doubted he did, but decided to drop the subject. She had other things on her mind, mainly her husband's suspicious behaviour. Just lately he had been acting very strange indeed. Disappearing late at night to take the dogs a 'midnight stroll', late back from footy practise, more nights out than usual. He seemed distracted and not his usual, charming self. It was beginning to worry Sophie, especially when they had received a series of telephone calls to the landline and no one had been on the other end. Or if they had, they were extremely quiet. Ryan had proclaimed that they were prank calls and nothing to worry about.

"We'll change the number," he had soothed. Sophie had to remind him that they had done that already four times.

"It's just fans," he had answered.

"Stalkers more like," Sophie had cut in scathingly.

Now there were other things bothering her, namely Ryan's lack of libido. Since their relationship had begun, Sophie had been fighting off Ryan's over amorous advances. But just lately, he had been distant, cooler towards her. Then there was his phone which was always glued to him and definitely never left unattended. All of these factors combined to make Sophie question his adherence to his marital vows. Heck, in plain words she thought he might be having an affair. She lifted the duvet slightly and glanced over his naked frame, looking for love bites or scratches, a sure tell-tale sign of infidelity, especially when one's wife hated love bites, considering them vulgar and immature. Thankfully there was none. Was she being paranoid? She wondered again. Sophie swung up out of the warm bed, determined to put the negative thoughts aside for the day. Maybe she could cook them a nice meal later and broach the subject with sensitivity and tact. She padded out onto the landing, calling the boys out of their slumber, then jogged downstairs to let the dogs out for their morning reprieve.

Straight from the school run, Sophie headed towards St Mary's. It was busy as usual, but thankfully there were plenty of parking spaces allocated for staff only. Max Bentley was out chatting to parents, when he saw Sophie he headed straight for her.

"Morning Mrs er?..."

"It's Mrs O'Neill, but please call me Sophie."

"Right. Okay, well just to let you know the nursery teacher has called in sick today."

"Oh dear," Sophie said with sympathy, "it must be all the bugs, working with the little ones."

"Yes staff absence is a real problem at the moment, but anyway, you will be having another teacher in with you this morning and then of course there are the teaching assistants."

"Okay, no problem," Sophie said cheerfully, "I'll help them get organised."

"How are you finding university Mrs O'Neill?"

Sophie paused to turn around, "oh I love it. The course is excellent, so interesting and I've made some lovely friends. Will is a great lad, you must be very proud."

Max Bentley looked surprised, but nodded, "I am. Thank you for your help here at St Mary's. Have a good day." He smiled and Sophie was struck by the likeness to Will. Then he was off, greeting another set of annoyed looking parents, with complaints on their minds.

Sophie walked down the warm corridor pausing to greet Gina, the learning support assistant. She was bent over, wiping smears of blood off a small child's knee.

"Hi Sophie, you've got me in the nursery with you today."

Sophie grinned, "that will be lovely." She liked Gina, with her warm personality and sunny smile.

Gina affixed a sticky plaster and chucked the boy underneath the chin.

"Off you go now and be careful!" They watched as the boy charged off, dragging his P.E bag and lunchbox on the floor.

"No running inside!" Marcia Bent appeared in the doorway of her office, a scowl on her face, "good morning ladies, as you aware, Cara is off again, so you will be having a junior teacher in with you today. Luckily, the children have a yoga session also, which will leave you free time to prepare resources for the afternoon and any other tasks you need to do."

"Thank you Mrs Bent, that's generous of you," Gina's smile didn't quite reach her eyes.

"Yes well, unfortunately when one staff member is absent, the rest of us have to muddle through," she clapped loudly, startling Sophie, "but I am sure that you are both quite capable." With an icy smile, she strode off down the corridor, straightening coat peg tags as she did.

"Sexual frustration" mouthed Gina. Sophie giggled and followed her towards the early year's section of the school.

The nursery was chaos, with children sprawled across the floor in various states of undress, as they struggled into their P.E clothing.

"Here you are, thank goodness," Mrs King whispered, as they trooped through the door, "the children have been acting like wild animals with Cara away."

Gina laughed, "they like their routine, that's all. It must be liberating for them, Cara can be strict at times."

Sophie stooped to help a tiny three-year-old tug off her shoes, "let's undo the laces first, shall we," she said patiently.

"Right class, I want everyone ready and lined up at the door in five minutes," a tall, lady with dark, wiry hair shouted, with her hands on her hips.

"We use this," Mrs King, the teaching assistant, cut in, "it seems to work." She produced a sand timer and turned it upside down. The children immediately scrabbled into their shorts and t-shirts, while keeping an eye on the flowing grains of sand. "And maybe we could have a little soothing music, keep them nice and calm." She flicked on the CD player and a gentle nursery rhyme wafted around the busy room.

The tall lady rolled her eyes, "I am so out of my depth with the little ones, I'm used to independent year six."

In no time at all the children were ready, apart from a few stragglers who thought it would be more fun to read a book. Sophie took them by the hand and joined the wobbly line skipping into the hall.

The yoga teacher was pulling out mats, she gave them a cheery smile, "leave them with me, I'll holler when it's all over," she chuckled, as she began arranging the children into a large circle.

"Thank Christ that's over. I'm Suzie by the way, key stage two teacher, SENCO and frustrated mother of three. Come on let's go grab a coffee."

Mrs King and Gina were already in the kitchen, watching the bubbling kettle.

"Make mine a gin," Suzie said drily, "I really don't know how Cara does this every day."

"No alcohol I'm afraid, but we do have cakes," Mrs King replied, as she placed a tin on the table.

Suzie sank down in a seat opposite Sophie, "so, you must be our new volunteer then?"

"I am and can I ask what SENCO is short for?"

"It's an acronym for special educational needs co-ordinator. Basically more pressure to add to the daily grind. You don't want to know, it would take too long to explain," Suzie waved the question away, "are you sure you want to go into teaching?"

"Erm I think so. I love being with the children."

"Sadly that's not what teaching seems to be about now-a-days. It's all paperwork, keeping up with new initiatives, stress and pressure, look at me, I used to be pretty before I went into teaching," she pulled out a cat compact mirror and inspected her features, "I look like death warmed up. This is what happens when you're under too much pressure," she pointed at a crop of lines etched beside her weary looking eyes, "maybe I should get botox."

Sophie gasped and shook her head, "don't do it. Botox is poison."

"But if it works, why not? The things we do to make ourselves look better eh?" She leant forward, picked up a cake and took a hearty bite, "Jesus," she cried, "where's the jam? This is bone dry."

"Jam?" Mrs King asked quizzically, "this isn't the Women's Institute you know dear – this is the produce of the PTA and you know how stingy they are. Plain fairy cakes will have to do us just fine."

Suzie wiped her mouth with a grimace, "well, I'm going to the staffroom for a bit. I've got tons of marking to do. Won't get my promotion sitting here eating and socialising will I? She winked Sophie's way, let out a hearty chortle then disappeared, her skirts swishing after her.

Sophie stared after her retreating figure, for once at a loss for words.

"Oh that's just our Suzie," Gina commented, with a wave of her hand, "a complete sociopath of course, but a brilliant teacher."

"Oh right," Sophie added a mental note to look up the meaning of that particular word when she got home.

"Watch what you tell her," Mrs King piped up from the book corner, "she has a nasty habit of repeating things and using them to her
advantage, friend or no friend. She's currently being groomed for management. Highly ambitious and ruthless. Makes Mr Bentley look like
a bloomin saint."

"Thanks for the warning," Sophie sat back, her mind was whirring
with thoughts of Ryan and what he was up to. This evening she was
going to confront him she decided, hopefully she was wrong about
him having an affair. Whatever his reaction was, it was time for them
both to face up to it; there was definitely something amiss in their
marriage.

* * *

The health centre was a short walk from Hema's house. Will had
arranged to meet her outside on the car park. He stood underneath a
towering oak tree, casting furtive glances around and glancing repeat-
edly at his watch. He was early and she was late; *again.*

"I'm so sorry," she explained, as she came round the bend, "Mom was
asking lots of questions this morning, it took me a while to get away."

"You're here now," Will mumbled, taking her hand.

"The sickness seems to have stopped though," she said cheerily, "I
managed to eat some toast this morning, without rushing off to the
loo."

"You look better," Will agreed, "are you ready?"

"I suppose so," Hema gulped nervously, "Will, you *are* okay about
me keeping the baby?"

"Of course, if you're sure that's what you want. Don't stress, you
need to stay calm."

"Okay and I am sure. It's the right thing."

Will smiled down at her, he was feeling much more positive today
about her pregnancy. He had confided in Jimmy last night, swore him
to secrecy, then told him everything. It was good to talk to someone
about it and offload his worries. His best mate had been shocked but

then strangely accepting of the whole situation. Apparently, Sadie had a scare a few months ago.

"It's not the end of the world," he had said philosophically to Will. Then they had talked about the practicalities: money, a place to live, that kind of thing. The biggest hurdle would be telling their parents, but Will was determined to stand up to them all, and to look after his girlfriend.

The door slid open and after announcing their arrival to a bored looking receptionist, they perched on cold plastic seats, waiting for their turn. The waiting area was full; people coughing, sneezing and muttering with impatience. Will's eyes were drawn to a young lady, balancing two young children on her knee. She looked weary and a little bit bedraggled. Will gulped down a nervous lump. He battled with his inner voice which urged him to up and run. Too late anyway, the neon sign was flashing Hema's name, directing them to room two. Hema knocked the door and they hung back in the corridor, nervous and awkward.

"Come in, come in," a cheery voice called. A pleasant looking midwife swung in her seat and surveyed them.

"Oh my, you two look as if you are both about to keel over, sit down." She pointed and waited for them to take a seat before continuing, "so, you think you might be pregnant?"

Hema nodded vigorously and grasped at Will's hand.

"Well the first thing we need to do is a test. Have you bought a sample with you?"

Hema produced a small vial filled with liquid from her bag. The nurse busied herself over the other end of the room, chattering about the weather and the weekends television. Will looked around the room at posters of pregnant women and foetuses at different stages. Hema's eyes followed his, widening at the pictures of the unborn child.

"I feel a bit faint," she whispered. Will looked with concern at her red cheeks and perspiring forehead.

"Excuse me," he said, "can she have a glass of water? She's feeling a bit hot."

"Of course," Jenny the midwife spun round, "it's so hot in this clinic, hang on while I open the window." Moments later, a cool breeze was wafting through the room, "here dear," she tipped bottled water into a plastic cup. Hema sipped at it thankfully.

"Are you okay lovey?"

"Yes I am now thank you."

Jenny's brow furrowed as she stared at the pregnancy test, "you *are* pregnant."

A silence stretched between the three of them. Will looked down at his feet as a sinking feeling began in the pit of his stomach. Now it had actually been confirmed by a medical professional it all seemed scarily real. What the hell were they going to do? He wondered. Last night's sensible pep talk was forgotten. In the cold light of day, the reality of the situation unfolded in front of him; he was nineteen years old and he was going to be a Daddy. Where was the sense in that?

Chapter Eight

Ann was sitting in the garden, enjoying the mild March weather. She lifted her face to meet the sun's rays, pondering on last night's family soiree. Her parents Betsy and Charlie had decided to throw a last minute surprise party for Ann's sister. It had been a good night; lots of mingling with distant relatives, scrumptious buffet food and way too much vodka. Her head was now pounding and her mouth felt dry and furry. It had felt good to have a weekend off from books and studying though, even if she was suffering the after effects. Jon was at the bottom of the garden, pegging out the washing. He looked very handsome today in a black suit and tie. Ann looked down at her own attire, a floaty black dress, sensible shoes and a warm, woollen cardigan. Today was Mam's funeral and they wanted to pay their respects and to support Evelyn. They had all been surprised that she had continued to attend university. Ben Rivers had suggested she take some time off, but Evelyn had been adamant that she was going ahead with her studies.

"I think it's time that we should be going," Ann shouted over the din of next door neighbour's lawnmower. Jon gave her a thumbs up sign, then headed back towards the house.

"Not really looking forward to this," he said, bending to tighten his shoe laces.

"No, nor me. But poor Evelyn needs her friends around her at the moment. She looked utterly heartbroken at university the other day."

"You've become fond of her haven't you," Jon said with a smile.

"I have," Ann replied, "I like them all; Will with his floppy hair and laid back persona, Juliette with her determination and positivity, Evelyn with her shy, gentleness. I even really like Sophie, she's disgustingly wealthy and ostentatious of course, but now I've got to know her she's funny and kind. They're a great crowd."

"I knew you'd love being at university, you've changed since you've been there." Jon said lightly.

Ann gazed his way, "I do feel different. Sort of calmer and more content if that makes sense."

"You make perfect sense to me," he kissed her softly on the lips.

"So, shall we get going?" Ann glanced at her watch. They were picking Juliette up on the way to the crematorium and time was ticking by.

"Thanks so much for the lift," Juliette gushed, as she strapped herself into the vehicle, "it would have taken me two buses to get there."

"No problem," Ann half turned in her seat, "you look stunning by the way."

Juliette smoothed down her black trouser suit, then fiddled with the cuffs of her matching jacket. Marie had straightened her hair last night and remarkably it had kept its shape, even through six hours of turbulent pillow tossing. She hadn't slept well, thoughts of Evelyn and Ben Rivers had kept her awake into the early hours. Yet again Marie had been lecturing her on the many negatives of embarking on a relationship with her 'teacher'. They had quarrelled for the first time in years, Juliette had told her to mind her own business, now she regretted speaking so sharply. Marie only had her best interests at heart, but she still managed to make Juliette feel like she was six years old again. As if on cue, a text pinged into her phone, an apology off her big sister. Juliette smiled and typed out a reply consisting of hugs, hearts and teddy bears. Life was too short to hold grudges against the people you loved. The death of Evelyn's Mam was tantamount to that. As the car whizzed up a hill and houses flashed past, Juliette's thoughts turned to Ben Rivers. They had been out on another date. A lovely evening which had consisted of a film, food, drinks, lots of chat and laughter. He had asked her if she wanted to stay the night. Her heart hammered as she recollected the heat in his eyes and his persuasive kisses. Juliette had reluctantly declined. Molly's stomach bug had lingered and now Harry had caught it too. Her children needed her and however much she wanted Dr Rivers, they would always come first.

"Looks like we're the first one's here," Ann commented, as Jon parked up in the almost empty carpark.

"Evelyn did say it was going to be a small, intimate service," Juliette replied, "but where is everyone?"

"Here comes Will and Sophie now," Jon was peering in the mirror as she swung her four by four into the space behind them.

"Hi everyone," Sophie air kissed Ann and Juliette's cheeks, "are we early?"

Will was lingering behind, staring down at his phone. He looked pale this morning and not his usual cheerful self.

Ann drew her husband to one side, "maybe you could talk to Will, somethings bugging him."

"What makes you think he'll confide in me?" Jon replied.

"You've got that kind of face; warm and welcoming. People open up to you." Ann winked up at him.

"Okay I'll try," Jon pushed her up a ramp and waited for the others to catch up.

"Oh, there's a few more cars coming now," commented Juliette, as they walked up the path towards the chapel. They waited outside, watching as more people arrived. Sophie slipped her arm through the crook of Juliette's.

"Is that Dr Rivers?" They both peered across at the car park, shielding their eyes from the glare of the midday sun.

"Oh my gosh," Juliette said with surprise, "it is and who is that with him?"

"It's Tarquin Haverstock," Sophie grinned and began waving manically. "How nice of them to come and show their support for Evelyn."

"Yes," Juliette replied, "how lovely." She watched as Ben strolled towards her. He looked extremely handsome and smart too; dark trousers, a white shirt and a snug fitting jumper.

"Hello there," Tarquin greeted, blowing on his hands to warm them. In comparison to Ben, Tarquin looked quite casual. He was wearing an untucked flowing shirt that was covered with black and white spots, large pointed collars and rolled up cuffs. Sophie thought he looked like a rock star with his blond spikes and his pierced eyebrow and ear.

"It's so lovely to see you," Sophie replied, addressing them both, but looking directly at Tarquin.

"Likewise," came the chirpy reply, "it's just a shame it's under such sad circumstances." They moved away to discuss Evelyn and how she was coping.

Juliette was left alone staring up at Ben, wishing she could kiss him.

"How are you?" His voice was warm and resonant. He moved a little closer, their fingers touched and Juliette felt a jolt of desire.

"I'm good," she cleared her throat and moved back a little, "are you going back to university after the wake? Only I need to get books from the library and I wondered if I could grab a lift with you."

"Sure, I'm dropping Tarquin back so hop in," he smiled, the loveliest smile that had Juliette's heart racing. They stared at each other for what seemed like an eternity, before Ann noted that Evelyn was on her way towards the chapel.

The car slowly snaked around the winding road, past the colourful flower beds and the emerald green lawns, before coming to a halt. An ashen looking Evelyn rose from the vehicle, followed by an older lady, who despite the morbid setting, looked jolly and friendly. Evelyn paused to speak to the vicar who clasped her hands gently and whispered something into her ear. There were now quite a few people congregating, talking in hushed tones. Evelyn spoke briefly to them, as she made her way towards Sophie, Ann and Juliette.

"Thank you so much for coming," she hugged Sophie tightly, then the others.

"I'm so sorry for your loss," Juliette said with sincerity
If there's anything we can do..." Ann trailed off, as Evelyn's eyes filled with tears at their kindness.

"It's just lovely of you all to come," Evelyn said, dabbing at her face with a hankie, "hello Will." She turned to embrace him, listening while he mumbled his condolences.

"Shall we go inside?" The vicar enquired gently. Evelyn nodded and followed him into the chapel. It was chilly, the walls were painted a neutral cream hue and there were long, arched windows that allowed prisms of the midday sun to shine through. Evelyn walked down the aisle, clutching a black patent handbag. Her gait was slow and heavy, but her back was straight and her head was held high. The strains of an organ swooned around the room; a subdued background noise, to distract from the realities of death.

The coffin was laid to one side, resting on a beautiful blue silk cloth. Evelyn stared at the dark oak veneer. She couldn't bear the thought of Mam being all alone in there, she touched the wood as the tears splashed down.

"Evelyn," Great Aunt Gertrude called, patting the seat next to her. Evelyn sank down and managed a watery smile, inside she was screaming, hold it together, hold it together.

"You're coping so well dear. Nora would be proud." The mention of Mam's name started the formation of fresh tears.

"I'm really not," Evelyn admitted.

"Come here lovey," Gertrude held open her arms and Evelyn allowed herself to be enveloped in the softest of hugs. She clung on as the vicar began speaking in loud, clear tones. He was telling the congregation all about Mam, describing her kind, sweet persona, her strength and determination. Her capacity for hard work, her resilience for coping when times were tough. The information had all come from Evelyn of course, with a little bit of assistance from Jacob. He had sat with her when the vicar had visited, supported her when she needed it most. She turned slightly in her seat to nod a thank you his way. Jacob was sitting with the day centre manager. Both of them looked sad and downcast, but when he saw Evelyn, his face lit up and the corners of his mouth stretched into a warm smile. The vicar had stopped talking, next they were singing 'All things bright and beautiful', Mam's favourite hymn. Then he was beckoning her up to the steps at the front. Evelyn stood nervously, looking around at the sea of familiar faces. The room was full with relatives, friends, neighbours, elderly folk from the daycentre. Even the milkman was here and the paperboy was lurking right at the back. People who had come to pay their respects, to say their final goodbyes. Evelyn no longer felt nervous. She was proud to speak out, to pay a tribute to her dear, beloved Mam. So she cleared her throat and the words came tumbling out.

"Mam had the most beautiful eyes, the warmest, dazzling smile, a kind, sweet demeanour and hands that toiled so hard to build a wonderful life. She was always unselfish, always forgiving, she had vibrancy and positivity and a perseverance until the very end. Mam was always there for her family and friends, she was a good listener and always gave excellent advice. She was fun and endearing, a bright, happy person that lit up the gloomiest of days. I'll miss her kindness and her unwavering support. But most of all I'll miss seeing her each day, our conversations, her laughter, even her stubbornness." A small titter spread around the room as people reminisced, "so this is a farewell until we meet again. I love you Mam, with all my heart. Sleep tight with Dad, I'll be thinking of you, when I look into the midnight sky, searching for the brightest star in the heavens, that will be you Mam. Rest in peace," the last words were high pitched and broken. Evelyn hung her head, feeling weary with emotion. Then the vicar and Great Aunt Gertrude were helping her back to her seat. There was a final reading and another hymn, before the service was over. Evelyn let out a shaky breath as they were led outside to the garden of rest, to look over the beautiful flowers.

* * *

The wake was held at Evelyn's house. Ann was in the kitchen help-ing Evelyn unwrap clingfilm from trays of food.

"Isn't it lovely of Dr Haverstock and Dr Rivers to come and pay their respects? They must be so busy," Evelyn sniffed.

"I'm sure they think you're worth it," Ann replied, "as do we all."

"That's so kind, thank you, I just need to powder my nose," Evelyn disappeared up the stairs, wiping at her moist eyes.

"Will she be okay?" Ann said with a frown.

"It takes time," Jon replied, "I'm sure she'll be fine." He pinched a breadstick and munched on it thoughtfully. "Looks like it's serious between Juliette and Dr Rivers."

Ann nodded, "yes, did you notice the way they were staring at each other?"

"Definitely love between those..." Jon broke off as Juliette backed into the kitchen.

"I need some more squash," she said, "the kids have drunk it all."

"Oh, yes," Ann pointed at the fridge, "It's in there I think." There was an awkward silence.

"Everything okay?" Juliette asked as she splashed water into the pitcher.

"Fine," Ann assured her, "we were just concerned about Evelyn and how she's coping."

"It must be difficult," Juliette replied, "but we can all help her at university and Sophie was going to invite her for tea one evening next week, for a bit of company."

"Great idea," Jon cut in, "er, I'm just going to have a chat with Will."

The lounge was packed full of people sitting and standing. There was soft classical music playing from the hi-fi system and the guests were talking in hushed tones. Will was embroiled in a conversation with Sophie about Chattlesbury Football Club. She flicked her hair as she explained about the long hours that Ryan had been training just recently.

"It looks like they're going up to the premiership," she beamed, "this new manager is working them hard."

"It would be awesome for the city if they were to go up. Imagine all the big clubs like Manchester United and Liverpool coming here."

Sophie nodded with excitement. Her mind swam with the thought of player's luncheons and night outs she could attend with famous A lister celebrity wives. That meant one important factor – shopping for new dresses, yay! Then her grin slipped somewhat, as she noticed Evelyn standing in the doorway, with her hands clasped.

"I'd just like to thank you very much for coming today and for your kind words, support and beautiful flowers and cards. There's a buffet in the kitchen, so please help yourself..." she trailed off as people moved forward to comfort her.

"Do you want food Will?" Sophie asked quietly.

"Huh?" Will looked up from his phone with a frown, "okay, thanks." Jon was looking his way with concern.

"You alright mate?"

Will nodded, "I suppose so."

Jon led him by the arm to the vacated sofa, "do you need someone to talk to? You're not yourself mate, are you having problems with Hema again?"

"Kind of," Will admitted, running a hand through his tousled hair, "she's pregnant Jon."

"What??!!" Jon was looking at him with shock and disbelief.

"The midwife thinks she might be four months, but we're going for a scan to confirm it."

"Bloody hell mate, I don't know what to say... are you happy?"

"I don't know," Will said with a sigh, "we're both only nineteen. How are we supposed to be looking after a baby? We should be enjoying ourselves, partying and travelling. Now we're both worried sick."

"So I take it you're going to keep the baby?"

Will nodded, "Hema's adamant. I have no idea how we are going to cope though. What do you think?"

"I think you'll be fine," Jon said slowly, "you'll have to be. But Will, what kind of support will you have? What do your parents think?"

"They have no idea," Will admitted with misery.

"Jesus," Jon said, "don't you think you should tell them?"

"Not really, they will hit the roof, and that's putting it mildly. Then there's Hema's parents, I don't even want to think of how they will react," Will shuddered with the thought of it.

"You've got to tell them mate, she won't be able to keep it a secret indefinitely. Won't she be showing soon?"

Will shrugged, "she's lost weight if anything. You're right though, we should tell them."

"I would," Jon urged, "get it out in the open. Or at least tell *your* parents, they're cool aren't they?"

"Mom is, not sure about Dad though," Will let out a shaky breath, "I don't know Jon, do you think we're doing the right thing?"

"It's your and Hema's decision at the end of the day mate, no one else can tell you what to do. Sounds like she's made her mind up though huh?"

Will nodded as he looked despondently down at the carpet. "This is life changing, so much responsibility."

"Well look, if it's any consolation, Ann and me, well we'd love children, but can't have our own for obvious reasons. Think of the positives; kids, they're great and I'm sure you'll have heaps of help once everyone's got used to the idea. Now come on, why don't I help you think of a way to tell your Mom without giving her a coronary."

He placed an arm around Will's slumped shoulders and heads bent together they talked.

Sophie was heaping food onto an already overflowing plate when Tarquin nudged her in the side, "save some sausage rolls for me," he said with a wink.

"There's plenty to go around," Sophie laughed, as she bit into a celery stick.

"Well would you look at this for a spread," Tarquin was impressed with the varied choice of food on the table.

"I helped," Sophie said proudly, "Although Evelyn made the cakes and I just iced them."

"They look scrumptious," he said, as he helped himself to two, "and how are you getting on with your studies Sophie? Has all the furore with the press died down now?"

"Oh yes, they've moved onto someone else now, thank heavens. As for my studies, I'm feeling more confident, thank you."

"Excellent," Tarquin poured himself a wine, "would you like a drink?"

Sophie held up her hand, "no, not for me. I'm driving, besides day-time drinking always makes me sleepy and bad tempered."

"Fair enough, then you're enjoying your course?"

Sophie nodded, "it's excellent, I'm loving the poetry module."

"That will be the fabulous lecturer no doubt," Tarquin looked across at Ben Rivers, who was talking to Juliette.

"All the lecturers have been good," Juliette enthused.

"Wait till you start year two, it gets even better. And Sophie, don't forget to make an appointment with your personal tutor, to discuss your progress. I'd like to tutor you myself, but I'm inundated with students at the moment."

Sophie was surprised by his words and felt a blush warm her cheeks. "Thank you Mr Haverstock, that's very kind of you."

"No need to thank me and please call me Tarquin, you know where my office is if you need any further help or advice." He moved away to join Ben's conversation and Sophie watched him with a feeling of bemusement. What a lovely man, she thought, he really was quirky, but so approachable and welcoming and so different to the men of the footballing world that she was used to. Her thoughts drifted to Ryan, her handsome, jack the lad husband. The pair of them couldn't be more different. There was no way that Ryan would drink wine for a start, to him that was a women's drink and only for sissy males, as he so eloquently phrased it, when on an ale drinking binge with Derek. As for their intellect, well Ryan wouldn't be able to name one classic novel, never mind read one. Their looks were so different too, Ryan was tall and muscular with perfect, chiselled good looks and sleek, shiny hair. Tarquin was small in stature, not much taller than herself, he looked a bit scruffy, but there was something wildly romantic about his untucked shirts, his messy blond spikes and his stubble covered dimples. Sophie found him surprisingly attractive and found herself checking his hand for a wedding band. Then she berated herself, I am a married woman, albeit not entirely happy, but lucky to have such a wonderful family none the less. Sophie moved away, putting distance between them. She noticed Juliette looking across at her with a puzzled expression.

"Are you okay Soph?"

"Yes, I'm fine," there was an unconvincing pause, "well to be honest Juliette I'm not really."

Juliette immediately steered her out of the kitchen, down the hall and through the back door into a beautiful, wild garden, just like the one she fantasised over owning. She waited while Sophie composed herself, drawing great gulps of air in.

"It's just personal stuff," she began, "nothing remotely interesting, you really don't want to hear this."

"Of course I do, what are friends for?" Juliette rubbed her arm soothingly, "come on, let it all out."

"Well, basically I think Ryan might be having an affair."

"An affair?" Juliette echoed, "what makes you think that?"

"Oh the usual; working longer hours than normal, being cagey about where he's been, strange phone calls to the house late at night where no one speaks." Juliette remained silent as Sophie continued her diatribe, "hiding his phone from me and the boys, then there's the personal side of our relationship. He seems to have gone off sex!" She whispered the last word, looking around to make sure there was no one else in the garden with them, "no cuddling, no foreplay, nothing!"

"Are you sure you're not being a teeny bit paranoid," Juliette advised, "maybe he's just overworked at the moment."

"There is that I suppose," Sophie conceded, "I don't know Jules, it's just not right between us. Our relationship feels strained, I'm really worried."

Juliette thought for a moment, she certainly was not fond of Ryan O'Neill – but an affair? It didn't make sense, Sophie was gorgeous. He was a fool indeed, if he *was* playing away.

"Maybe you should talk to him honey. It's not good to keep things bottled up, just voice your concerns in a calm and reasonable manner. I'm sure there will be some kind of explanation."

"I tried," Sophie said, her face taking on a sheen of misery, "just couldn't get the words out, then the boys were there and the moment passed. Call me crazy Jules, but I've just got this awful inkling that Ryan's been unfaithful to me."

"You're not crazy," Juliette soothed, "it must be difficult with all the attention he gets. Speak to him, that's all you need to do."

"Yeah, you're right. I'll see how things go between us. It could be nothing more than work pressure."

"Maybe you need a holiday," Juliette suggested, with a kind smile, "sun, sea and sand can work wonders you know."

"That's a fab idea! Thank you Jules, I'll make a detour via the travel agents on the way home."

"Everything okay out here?" Ann was peering around the door frame.

"Yeah great actually," Sophie offered Ann her packet of cigarettes, "want one?"

"I've stopped," Ann said with a smile, "not good for our adoption application."

"Good for you," Juliette piped up.

"We're going to be leaving shortly, are you coming back with us Juliette?" Ann asked.

Juliette blushed, "er, I'm getting a lift back to uni, but thanks anyway."

"No problem," Ann replied, "I'll go find Evelyn and let her know we're leaving. See you at uni in the week?"

"You sure will," Sophie said with a happy grin.

They said their goodbyes, then Juliette went in search of Dr Rivers.

* * *

Tarquin insisted that Juliette sit in the front passenger seat next to Ben.

"I'll squash in the back," he said, as he scrambled behind her.

The mid-afternoon traffic was quiet. Ben flicked on his CD player and Rick Astley swooned out of the speakers.

Tarquin warbled along, making Juliette laugh out loud.

"Jaysus Ben, have you no proper music?" Tarquin had stopped singing and was contorting his face into creases of displeasure.

"What's wrong with music from the eighties?" Ben said, glancing in the mirror with a grin.

"It's manufactured cheesy rubbish, that's what's wrong with it. Where are the real drums and the guitar riffs?"

"Have you got any Oasis?" Juliette asked diplomatically.

"Yes! Oasis! Wonderwall! Turn off this shite and I'll sing if I have to."

"Go on then," Ben said, snapping off his stereo, "I challenge you to do A cappella."

Juliette was shocked when Tarquin threw his arms wide and began singing loudly. Ben glanced at Juliette and rolled his eyes. She tapped along to the imaginary beat, trying not to chortle at Tarquin's high pitch shouting.

"Talk about pub singing," Ben commented with a laugh, then as Tarquin came to the chorus, he joined in too.

Tarquin emanated the sound of banging drums, as Ben reached across to encase Juliette's small hand in his own. She threw him an ear splitting smile, feeling ridiculously happy, "you guys are crazy."

"All the best folk are missy." Tarquin replied, "anyway, enough of my singing for one day. How do you think Evelyn really is?"

"She seems okay," Juliette replied, "it takes time to work through grief doesn't it? And then I don't think you ever really get over the death of a loved one. But she's a strong lady and me, Soph, Ann and Will, we are going to look out for her."

"Very commendable," Tarquin leant forward in his seat, "your friend Sophie. She's a fine woman."

Juliette turned around with surprise etched on her face, "oh yes, she's lovely."

"And she's married to Ryan O'Neill, the famous Chattlesbury FC striker? I've heard he's a philanderer and that's putting it politely."

"Oh, erm, I'm not really sure," Juliette paused, not wanting to gossip about her friend.

"Could never stand the game myself," Tarquin continued drily, "give me a book over a ball any day."

"Hear, hear," Ben echoed, "although I do remember thrashing you at a game of tennis once." Juliette looked across at Ben and smiled. He was so different from all the other men she had known. He made her happy, of that she was sure, but she felt confused about him all the same. What *was* their relationship? Was he now her boyfriend? Or were they still in the friend's stage and should she tell the kids about him?

Juliette bit her lip as she thought of Harry and Molly. They were staying over at Marty's the weekend, for the first time in years and she had been fretting about it for days. Molly was super excited, while Harry was rather more subdued.

"Do we have to?" He had complained, when she had explained that their Dad was taking them to the local fair then back to his flat for a "night of treats." Juliette's heart had constricted with worry. She had assured Harry that she was only a phone call away, she would be there in a heartbeat, if he needed her. After a bout of tear filled histrionics from Molly, he had grudgingly agreed to go. Now was not the time to tell them about Ben, she thought resolutely, too much upheaval would be no good for them. No, she decided, the best thing to do would be to keep things quiet between them, like they had agreed.

"What are you thinking about?" Ben cut into her reverie, as he swung his vehicle into the staff carpark.

"Just wondering what I'm going to do when the kids are away the weekend," Juliette played with her fingers and let out a sigh.

"Well here's me," Tarquin said, as Ben pulled up alongside a purple Volkswagen Beatle with Save the Whale stickers emblazoned across the back windscreen.

"What a cool car!" Juliette said with a surprised laugh, "I love the colour."

"It's a tip, but very reliable. Goodbye Juliette. Ben, I'll see you to-morrow."

Juliette turned to wave, then they were left alone in the car and the atmosphere turned electric.

"Come to my office," Ben said huskily, "I have something for you." Juliette sat quietly as he parked, then followed him out of the vehicle and up the winding path towards the humanities block. They squashed into the lift, with four other people. Ben pulled her towards the back, placing a possessive arm around her waist.

"You smell gorgeous," he whispered, as his lips caressed her hair.

Juliette shivered and looked up at him. In his smoky eyes, she saw her own mirrored desire. She barely noticed that the lift had stopped on the second floor and everyone had disembarked, leaving them alone. As the doors slid shut, they fell into each other's arms and warm kisses.

"Stay with me the weekend," Ben murmured, teasing apart her mouth.

"I want to," she admitted, "it's just Harry and Molly, I need to be there for them."

"I understand," Ben said, his breath hot against her ear, "but think about it okay, I want to be with you properly Juliette."

"Okay," Juliette's arms wound around his neck, then they were kissing passionately and she could feel the cool metal of the handrail riding against her thighs. Urgently he lifted her up, leaving a trail of nips and kisses down her throat and to her uncovered collarbone. Then his hand was cupping her breast and she was lightheaded with desire.

"Well I never," the uttered words were tinged with shock.

Juliette lifted heavy lids to stare at a group of gawping women. She sprang away from Ben, as she recognised the lady's voice belonged to Carol the gossip. A groan emitted from her lips and this time it was fuelled with dismay.

"Excuse us ladies," Ben said smoothly, taking Juliette's hand and striding past them.

"Ben stop!" Juliette said after he had practically dragged her up the corridor and to his office door, "what are we going to do, now everyone will know!"

"Let them know, let them gossip," Ben said, as he fumbled with the door key, "Don't worry about them, they're not important." He snapped on the light and Juliette followed him inside.

"But I do worry Ben, I worry about you, your job here, your reputation. That woman can be mean, she can make life difficult for both of us."

"Don't worry about her, she's not important."

"You're important Ben," Juliette stopped, blushing furiously, do not get carried away and admit how much you like him, her inner voice screamed.

"So you care about me then?" He teased, "careful Juliette, it's written all over your face."

"You're incorrigible," Juliette laughed, pushing him away, "now, where's my surprise?"

"Oh that old thing, hang on," he opened the desk drawer with a tiny, silver key, then passed her a square white box. "This is for you; I hope you like it."

Juliette looked at him quizzically and slowly opened the box. She gasped when she saw the contents. Inside, on a bed of cream satin, lay the most exquisite silver bangle.

"Oh wow," Juliette lifted it out with shaking fingers. She raised it to the light and admired the numerous charms that hung off it, "this is so pretty. Ben, thank you, so much. You really shouldn't have."

"Do you like it?" He asked as he unclipped the catch and slipped it onto her wrist.

"I love it, it's beautiful."

"As are you," Ben said, his eyes dark and stormy with emotion, "it was my mother's."

Juliette gasped, "I can't accept this, it's too much Ben, what about your sister? Does she not want it?"

"My sister has enough," Ben insisted, "I've been waiting for some-one special to give this to and now I've found her. My mom would be proud."

"Oh," Juliette's voice broke with emotion and her eyes filled with tears, "I will cherish it forever."

As the sun set and the evening was lit up by silvery moonlight, Ben took Juliette in his arms and she clung on, never wanting to let him go again.

Chapter Nine

Sophie was striding through the busy city streets with a happy, beaming smile on her face. In her arms she clutched a pile of glossy, exotic looking brochures and in her handbag was the print out confirmation of the holiday she had just booked. The thought of ten nights at the Crystal Palace, five-star hotel in Lanzarote for the end of June lifted her spirits. She didn't even care as the drizzle began and her immaculately straight hair began to fluff. Mam's funeral had been draining and since she had left Evelyn's house, Sophie had been pondering on death and worrying over her friend's grief stricken state of mind. Sophie's frazzled feet had almost taken her to the travel agents of their own accord. Once in there, she had been ushered into a seat by a grinning camp man called Byron, who had fired up his PC, then proceeded to talk her into an all-inclusive holiday package, that promised fun, relaxation and excitement all rolled into one. Now here she was, heading towards the grey stone walls of the multi storey, daydreaming about sun, sand and the rolling waves of the Atlantic Ocean.

It was almost the end of the first year of university and the football season was drawing to a close. Sophie was looking forward to jetting off on a plane, she wanted to feel hot sunshine caressing her skin, soft sand seeping between her toes and cool water lapping her naked thighs. It was going to be ten nights of pure, undulated bliss; fine food and cocktails, set amidst a wild, rugged landscape. She wrinkled her nose at the sight in front of her; a graffiti strewn fountain surrounded by rubbish and birds that cawed and shrieked as they flew overhead. Yes, it was definitely time for a holiday. The rep had assured her that the hotel was top quality, with fabulous amenities and right in the centre of the resort. He had managed to book her a family room, with what promised to be a fantastic sea view. There was also a water park attached to the hotel, which was guaranteed to make the boys and Ryan euphoric.

"We're all going on a summer holiday," she sang, as she flicked on her windscreen wipers and pulled out onto the busy main road.

Sophie imagined Ryan's face when she told him the good news. He would be excited of course, he loved his holidays and it was just what he needed after a gruelling football season. They would be able to spend time as a family, with no clingy Derek to worry about. Her neurotic mother would have to cope alone and there would be no Chattlesbury Football Club pestering on the telephone. It was going to be just perfect she thought, no footie, no fans, just her, Ryan and a pair of exuberant twin boys, cast adrift in a family orientated idyll. Although no doubt Ryan would be purchasing a beach ball to practise his right foot flick and his headers, but Sophie could cope with that, if it meant they were to be all together. A honking van suddenly swerved across the lane in front of her, the man in the driver's seat shook his fist and mouthed something unintelligible. Sophie slammed on the brakes, gripped the steering wheel and wished herself on a plane, flying above the line of miserable looking commuters, away to a slice of paradise.

When she arrived home thirty minutes later, she was surprised to see Amber's car parked up on the driveway. She had not heard from Amber in weeks and she wondered why she had turned up without texting her first. Ryan was home too by the looks of it. Sophie felt a flicker of annoyance – could they never be alone? Unopened mail was sticking out of the box and Ryan's football boots were flung upside down across the doormat. Sophie kicked them to one side in irritation and slotted her key into the lock. The door swung open but no dogs or children rushed to greet her. No of course not, they boys had gone to a friends for tea and were not due back for another couple of hours and Heidi had probably taken the dogs out for their afternoon stroll. The house was quiet, too quiet. Sophie slipped off her shoes and padded down the hallway.

"Hello," she called, poking her head around the lounge architrave. There was no reply, the room was empty and pristine looking, this morning's debris had been tidied away. Lavender furniture polish clung in the air, sickly and sweet and balancing on the coffee table was a fresh posy of tulips, that Heidi must have brought in with her. Then she heard it, the sound of laughter. She cocked her head to one side and listened closer. Yes, it was definitely laughter, a man and a woman's coming from the direction of the conservatory. Sophie tip-toed through the kitchen, surprised to see Amber's long leather boots spread over the floor. Her designer rain mac had been deposited on the back of a stool. Girlish giggles wafted through to Sophie.

"Oh it's so big," she heard Amber clearly gush.

"Feel it," came Ryan's husky reply.

Sophie froze, *what the hell was going on?* She felt a coldness settle over her and a sense of foreboding.

"I shouldn't really," she heard Amber titter, "but you're a hard man to refuse."

Right that's it, Sophie gritted her teeth, clenched her fists and marched through into the conservatory. She gasped at the scene in front of her. Ryan was stood there shirtless, flexing his left bicep and jiggling his chest muscles, while a practically salivating Amber was running a hand across his bulging muscles.

"Wh-what the hell is going on?" Stuttered Sophie.

"Oh hello babes," a nonplussed looking Amber tossed her long tresses, "Ryan was just showing me which exercises are best for the arm muscles."

"Like hell he was," snarled Sophie, "what's really going on here?"

"Calm down babes," Ryan said chirpily, "it's just a bit of fun."

"It looks more than that to me," screeched Sophie, "you two make me sick," she turned on Amber, "every time you're here you're fawning all over him. You're a married woman for god's sake!"

Amber opened and closed her mouth a few times, her face growing pinker by the second.

"I really don't think you should talk to me like that Soph. It's just a bit of harmless fun, you know how me and Ryan are together."

"Why don't you feel your own husband's muscles and leave mine alone? Why are you always here Amber? Are you two having an affair?" Sophie's eyes narrowed into angry slits.

"Don't be soft darling," Ryan soothed, but his stance was fidgety and nervous.

"I'm your best friend," whined Amber, "how can you accuse me of something so revolting."

"Are you my best friend though?" Sophie thought of protective Juliette, of sweet, kind Evelyn, honest but loyal Ann, youthful, brave Will and was overcome by the realisation that they were her true friends, Amber was like her mother; selfish and superficial.

"Something's going on," Sophie stared hard at Ryan, "just lately you've been acting incredibly shifty. You're never here, always working late or out with Del," she spat his name in fury, all the pent up angst and frustration welled out of her.

"Someone mention me?" As if on cue, Derek appeared outside the open door of the conservatory. He was pulling a wheelbarrow full of garden refuse and looked grubby and windswept. Sophie could have laughed, there was something quite comical about Derek's gormless face, gawping at his employers, but the seriousness of the situation pressed upon her. This was her marriage, her life and she was livid. If there had been an ornament nearby she would have hurled it at Ryan's perfectly gelled head, instead she placed her hands on her hips and ranted, "you never make any effort with me or the children. When's the last time you took us all out as a family?"

"Now hang on a bit," Derek jumped to Ryan's defence, "he's been working hard Mrs O. It ain't right you screaming at him like a banshee."

One death glare from Sophie had Derek fall silent.

"Aren't me and the kids enough for you anymore?"

The lack of reply fuelled Sophie's wrath, "who is she then? Some strumpet from Chattlesbury FC? Another player's wife? If it's one of my friends I'll throttle her and you."

Ryan wiped a sheen of perspiration from his brow. He looked queasy and rather frightened.

"I don't have to listen to this...this shite," he snapped, "come on Del, let's go for a spin."

"You stay right where you are!" Sophie screeched at her gardener, "if *he* wants to leave, then *he* can go alone."

Derek hopped from foot to foot, torn between allegiance to Ryan and wanting to keep his job.

"Tell her babes," Ryan pleaded with Amber, "tell her she's being ridiculous."

Amber observed him for a moment, "it's not me Soph honestly. I wouldn't do that to ya, even if I do admit that Ryan is pretty hot, there's no way I would shit on my friends. I do have some morals."

Sophie observed her stricken face and wringing hands. The usual façade of cool superiority that surrounded Amber had vanished. "I believe you," Sophie said with a nod.

Ryan sighed with relief, "there you go then, hysterics over."

"I said I believed Amber, not you." Sophie sniffed, willing her eyes to stop watering, "I don't trust you Ryan and you know I'm right not to."

Ryan rolled his eyes, "darling you've got this all wrong, me and the opposite sex have always got on. I can't help it if I attract the women."

Derek nodded with agreement, "they throw themselves at him Mrs O. It ain't his fault."

Ryan threw Del a look of warning, *don't give too much away*, it said.

"You can help it," Sophie snapped, "you don't have to encourage it. You could remind them that you're married. But you don't want to do that, you love the attention don't ya Ryan?"

"Right enough of this stupid chat, I'm off to the club, there's an open day for families. They need me for publicity."

"What about your own family?" Sophie said sadly.

Ryan opened his arms and moved towards her but she halted him with a shake of her head and a blocking hand.

"Just go," she said wearily.

Ryan flung on his discarded shirt and legged it outside. Seconds later they heard the thrum of a vehicle starting and the screech of tyres as he departed.

"I'll just leave this here," Derek tiptoed away, muttering something about hormonal women.

"Are you alright babes?" Amber asked warily, "you can't seriously think I'd be shagging your bloke?"

Sophie's lower lip trembled, then she was bursting into tears, "sorry," she wailed, "I don't know what's wrong with me."

"Come 'ere," Amber pulled her into a rough embrace, "it's me who should be apologising. Maybe I was a bit forward with Ryan. I don't mean anything by it though, I'm just a bored, desperate housewife."

Sophie sniffed, "are things no better between you and Martin either?"

"Not really, that's married life eh?"

"Is it? Sophie said with misery, "I'm beginning to wonder."

Amber rubbed her arm, "look at us pair, like a sad couple of old married hens. Maybe *we* need a night out. A good girly chat, fine wine, no husbands, no kids."

"I want to go out as a family in honesty Amber. You know I've booked a holiday for the four of us."

"What a great idea," gushed Amber, "just what you need to get you and Ryan back on track."

"Not if he's been cheating," Sophie said firmly.

Amber shook her head and looked at her with pursued lips.

"What?" Sophie exclaimed, "surely you can't think it's acceptable for him to be unfaithful?"

"Look honey," Amber began, "no, it's not okay to cheat, but people do make mistakes, that's what makes us human and you never know what really goes on in a marriage."

"Are you saying this is my fault?" Sophie was shocked at the implications of her friend's words.

"Of course not!" Amber snorted, "why would anyone want to cheat on you? All I'm saying is that it doesn't mean your marriage has to end if he has."

Sophie let out a shaky breath, "if Ryan O'Neill has played away, then that's it, marriage over."

Amber's eyes turned wide like saucers, "you don't know for sure he even has. Let's not jump to conclusions. Come on, try not to worry. Why don't you tell me all about this holiday you've booked? I'm well jealous."

They slumped down on the soft conservatory seats and Sophie grudgingly told her about the spur of the moment madness that had gripped her.

* * *

An hour later, the boys were home and Amber had left. Derek had sloped off early, citing he was off out for his wedding anniversary. Sophie had snapped at him, angry that he had cheated on his wife with her own mother. There had been no messages from Ryan, she was beginning to regret the way she had screeched at him. Had she acted like a shrew or a 'banshee' as Derek had so eloquently termed her? She lay on the bed, rubbing at her throbbing temple, wishing she could rewind the afternoon and approach the subject of Ryan's fidelity differently.

"You okay Mrs O'Neill," Heidi stood in the doorway, feather duster in hand, surveying her sympathetically.

"Just a headache," said Sophie wearily, "you can get off home Heidi, I'll be down to watch the boys in a minute."

"You want me get some pills?"

Sophie smiled at her housekeepers broken English and the concerned look on her face.

"No I'm fine thank you," Sophie swung with determination up off the blissfully soft, fresh smelling sheets and smoothed her untidy hair.

Heidi nodded, then disappeared down the landing, humming softly.

Sophie pulled back the window netting and shielded her eyes. The sun was dipping, a blazing orb in a blood red sky. She gasped at the wondrous sight and watched with longing as a plane crossed over, leaving a trail of white smoke billowing behind. Looking at the heavens, her thoughts turned to Evelyn, she wondered how she was faring and searched in her pockets for her phone. Evelyn answered on the third ring, a soft warble, that tugged at Sophie's heartstrings.

"Are you okay Evelyn?" She asked.

"Yes I'm fine dear," Evelyn sounded tired, "it's been a long day, but I think it went okay."

"It was a beautiful service," Sophie replied, her eyes glistened with tears for Evelyn's and her own emotional pain.

"Are you okay dear?" It was typical of Evelyn to be so altruistic. Sophie's chest constricted with affection for her friend. There was no way she could burden her with her worries and woes, with everything she was enduring at the moment.

"I'm good thank you Evelyn," she assured her, "I just wanted to make sure that you are okay and if I can do anything to help. You know I'm here for you and please do come for tea next week. I don't like to think of you alone."

Evelyn sighed, "well I do have to get used to it, but yes, yes, I would love to come."

They organised the day and time, then Sophie rang off, satisfied that Evelyn sounded okay. No sooner had she cut the call, her phone was buzzing again. It was flashing 'Mom', Sophie groaned, leaving it to go to her message inbox, she would pick it up later, when she was in a better frame of mind. No such luck! A minute elapsed before the phone was buzzing yet again. Sophie snatched it up, worried something may have happened to Yvonne.

"Hello Mom,"

"Sophie," her mother's husky tones crackled over the line, "I've just had poor Ryan here and he was very upset. Why are you accusing him of having an affair? What a preposterous idea, as if."

Sophie blew out her irritation, "I can't believe he's gone crying to you."

"Well he needs to speak to someone darling," there was a pause, "now stop this foolishness, call him, put your sexiest negligee on and make it up to him."

"Is that your answer for everything – sex!" Sophie was annoyed, it was typical of her mom to take *his* side.

"It works for most men," Yvonne cackled, "he'll soon forget all the hurtful things you've said when he sees you all dressed up."

"Can I remind you Mom, I haven't done anything wrong."

"Apart from being horrid to him and embarrassing him in front of Amber," Yvonne reminded her, "It will be all over the village next you know honey. Ryan's not having an affair. I'm afraid you're just being silly and jealous."

"I am not," Sophie seethed, "I do have my reasons."

"Really," sniffed Yvonne, "and who's put these ideas in your head? You know you haven't been the same since you started university."

"What do you mean?"

"I mean all this learning has gone to your head and the people you're mixing with well, how can I say this, aren't our class."

"What?!" Sophie clutched the phone, "don't be such a snob Mom, this isn't the fifties, no one cares about class anymore."

"They're not our type then," Yvonne persisted, "a lot of these students don't live in the real world. All they care about is complaining, demonstrating about things, waving placards, dying their hair and shouting about world peace. Now it's rubbing off on you, you used to be fun, but it's all study, study, study, books, books, books. What about your husband and kids? What about me? I hardly see you anymore."

"That's because I'm studying for an English degree," Sophie replied huffily, "It's hard work, I have to set time aside for it. As for my university friends, they are all lovely and very clever. What's wrong with intellect? It's refreshing to talk about something other than Chattlesbury FC and make up."

"At what expense darling? Maybe your family should come before university shenanigans. All this learning is no good for your mind. You're fragile Sophie, you always have been. I hate to say this to you darling, but I'm afraid you've changed and not for the better."

Sophie had the urge to scream, *yes for the better,* "are you accusing me of being a bad wife and mother, because I'm a student? Have you forgotten which century we are living in."

Yvonne sensed she may have overstepped the mark, "I'm not saying that, I just…"

"Good," Sophie snapped, feeling anger bubbling somewhere deep inside her, "because you're not exactly the perfect mother, are you?"

Sophie closed her eyes and recollected her childhood; watching Yvonne spiral into alcoholism, after the disappearance of her husband, Sophie's Dad, Anthony. She shuddered as she remembered the long line of different men that came and went throughout her formative, teenage years. Even now, Yvonne was still unsettled, drifting along aimlessly, still looking for Mr Perfect. How bloody dare she lecture me, thought Sophie.

There was no reply from the other end and Sophie wondered if her mom had cut the call, but then she heard light breathing. Maybe she had gone too far with those cutting words. Sophie knew how it felt to be down. When the rest of the world thought you had everything, but instead you were stuck in a cycle of loneliness and emptiness. Hankering for more to complete oneself, but not sure what exactly that entailed and how to go about obtaining it. Sophie rubbed at her throbbing temple, "sorry Mom."

"It's okay," Yvonne's tone was brisk and high pitched, "I shouldn't have interfered. I'm worried about you Sophie."

"Oh, everything will be okay with me and Ryan. You're probably right, I'm being paranoid. Maybe university *has* changed me and not for the better." Sophie stared at the shelves of books dotted around her bedroom. Her expensive ornaments had been packed away, replaced by bits of paper. Maybe it was time to get them back out, in the hope of recapturing a feeling, a sense of contentment from the past. Maybe it was herself who needed to make more of an effort with Ryan and the boys. Was she a good enough wife and Mother? She pondered on this, as she stared misty eyed at the family portrait hanging on the wall. There, that is what is important, her conscience nagged. Sophie said her goodbyes to her Mom, then went down to the kitchen, where the boys were blowing bubbles and the dogs were yapping playfully. Sophie smiled at their gaiety, their innocence, their simplistic outlook on life.

"Come here boys," she called. They ran into her arms and she embraced them tightly.

"What's wrong with your voice Mom?" Josh asked.

"Nothing honey, Mommy just got a bit emotional. I love you both very much."

"Yuck," replied Jake.

"Eurgh," Josh pulled a sicky face.

"Now play in the garden," Sophie said, with a ruffle of their hair, "you're making the floor wet and slippy."

They raced outside, whooping and laughing.

Sophie stared at her reflection in the kitchen mirror, have I changed?

She decided to text Ryan, four simple words: sorry, please come home.

Then she made herself a cup of herbal tea and perched on a breakfast stool, ruminating over what she should do and pondering on ways to make amends.

* * *

Juliette had insisted that Molly and Harry each take a cuddly toy with them to Marty's flat.

"To remind you of home and that I'm thinking of you," she said, as she squashed Dino the one eyed dinosaur and Sparkles the pink, fluffy unicorn into their overnight bags. Harry had rolled his eyes with the superior nonchalance that only a ten-year-old boy can muster. Molly however, the eternal enthusiast, had decided to pack another two cuddly toys *and* her favourite doll: disco Barbie.

"In case Daddy has no toys or Disney DVDs," she had revealed, with wide eyed consternation. Juliette had turned away, so her daughter had missed the grimace that crossed her features. It had been years since her children had spent the night at their Dads. Prior to his internment in prison, Marty had lived with his mother, the ghastly Brenda and she had no inclination to have Harry and Molls at her house, even if they were her own grandchildren. Apparently, Marty's 'Ma and Pa' would be popping in over the weekend, along with others of his shady family. Juliette had therefore been worrying herself sick about the 'sleepover' and had even been looking for excuses to cancel her children's little excursion. She was almost hoping for a last minute stomach bug to swipe throughout the flat, so she could keep them in their beds, warm and safe.

Too late, here he was now, pounding on the front door like some demented madman, demanding to be let in. Harry slouched off to open it, in his usual, can't-be-bothered with-my-Dad gait. Juliette busied herself with wiping chocolate smears from an otherwise pristine Molly. She smelt sweet; banana shampoo and baby oil, Juliette kissed the top of her head and tickled the sides of her.

"Mommmmyyyyy, stop," Molly shouted, succumbing completely to the tickle monster, aka Juliette.

"Never!" Crowed Juliette, as she chased a panting Molly around the kitchen. Her daughter squealed with delight and curled herself into a tight ball on the linoleum floor. Juliette bent to ruffle her hair, nip at her rosy cheeks and blow onto her uncovered tummy.

"Marty's here," Harry surveyed the scene before him and managed to gravitate his eyeballs into the biggest roll ever.

"It's Dad to you," a gruff voice followed him into the kitchen.

"Oh hi," Juliette wiped a sheen of sweat from her brow and forced her lips into a smile.

"Dadddyyyyy," tickle monster was forgotten, Molly sprang to her feet and pounced into Marty's open arms.

"Hi there," he laughed, "how's my favourite girl?"

"I'm not a girl, I'm a princess," came the serious, wide eyed reply, "one day my prince will come," she sang, as Marty hoisted her onto his hip.

"Have you been watching Snow White again?" He asked.

"It's Cinderella silly," Molly replied, wriggling free to execute a perfect pirouette.

Juliette wondered if she should limit Molly's TV time. Her obsession with Disney films was bordering on the obsessional and it was beginning to infringe on her wardrobe too. Princess gowns were now a must have when gift shopping. Molly beamed with delight with each dressing up outfit she received, and the more jewel encrusted, frill bearing, satin swishing the better. There was the positive that she had an abundance of outfits to choose from for the school's World Book Day though, Juliette conceded.

"Hey Jules," Marty nodded her way, giving her the once over, as he did most of the female population, "how are you?"

"Fine," she replied stiffly. She would have liked to have snubbed him completely, but Harry was staring at her with the oddest expression. A mixture of worry, fear, is this okay? His troubled eyes enquired. Juliette gave herself a proverbial shake, lighten up buttercup, she told herself.

"Have a fabulous time tonight you guys," she gushed, giving Harry and Molly a big thumbs up, "did you pack your toothbrushes?" Their blank faces revealed the answer to be in the negative. Molly pulled on Harry's sleeve, challenging him to a race to the bathroom. As soon as they were out of ear shot, Juliette turned to face Marty.

"Please look after them," she pleaded, her stomach churning.

"Of course I will," came Marty's snappy reply, "everything's organised, so don't fret. They're going to have a grand old time."

Juliette nodded gratefully, "well, I'll leave my phone on, just in case you need to contact me urgently."

Marty waved away her words, "look Jules, I'm sorry about the other day, hassling you on the phone. You're right, it's none of my business who you see, or what you do with your life, so I er, apologise."

Juliette stared his way, surprised at his sheepish look.

"But you are welcome to come this evening," he continued, with his usual cocky swagger, "if you're that worried..."

Juliette shook her head firmly, "you know I can't do that. I don't want to lead you on Marty. You'll always be part of my life because of the children, but you and me... well, we're over. Our relationship is going to be purely platonic from now on. I hope you understand that."

"I do," Marty replied grudgingly, "I'm trying really hard to sort myself out Jules, this time I mean it."

Juliette smiled, "I believe you," her chest felt a little lighter as she listened to his words and surveyed his freshly shaven face and clean attire. He even smelt nice she acknowledged, with relief. The hard, rough exterior had abated somewhat and his attitude seemed to be improving.

"This job is suiting you then?" She enquired.

"It's fine," he replied with a broad smile, "the people are cool and the pays not bad."

"I'm glad," Juliette replied with sincerity, "it's good to see you on the up and maybe in the future, for Harry and Molls, maybe we could be friends?"

Marty nodded, "I'd like that."

Harry and Molly came charging back into the kitchen, like mini whirlwinds.

"We're ready," Molly shouted, arms spread high, "can we go Daddy?"

"Cuddles first," Juliette knelt down and was almost knocked back by the force of enthusiastic kissing and squeezing.

"Have a great night," Juliette ruffled their hair, "be good for your Dad."

"We will," sang Molly, before she raced off down the hallway.

"Will you be okay Mom?" Harry was looking up at her, his eyes wide and twinkling.

"I'll be absolutely fine." She nodded enthusiastically, "I've got chocolate, marshmallows and a night of watching whatever I want on the t.v. You have fun Harry, love you." She squeezed his shoulders reassuringly and smiled, as he dashed off to catch up with his younger sister.

Marty picked up the bags, "see you Jules," his smile was melancholy, "thanks for being so nice, about everything... you're a top bird. I'm sorry I've been such a shit to you. I really messed things up, huh?"

Juliette threw him a rueful smile, "let's start again... from now," she suggested. Although she did not feel ready to embrace him, she felt that they had reached a turning point. The thought of them becoming friends was now, not so ridiculous after all.

He walked a few steps then turned to say, "I'm never going back in there Jules. This time it's for real. I'm going to devote my time to being an awesome Dad."

"Good luck Marty," Juliette replied simply, as he disappeared down the concrete stairs and into the chilly night air, with her beloved children bounding after him.

* * *

Half an hour later she was wrapped in her fluffy onesie, hair tied up, face scrubbed clean of make-up, popcorn tipped into a bowl and her love ballad CD playing softly in the background. Juliette padded through to the lounge, splashing wine into a plastic tumbler. She sank onto the soft sofa, reaching across to check her phone for messages. There was no catastrophe so far, no pleading text from Marty to come and get Harry and Molls. Juliette felt herself relax. Her mind wandered to Ben Rivers, he had messaged her this morning. A simple hello, how are you? It made her feel ridiculously happy to see his name flashing in her inbox. Apparently, this evening, Ben was going for a last minute family birthday meal at his sister's house. He had sent her a picture of the gift he had purchased; an exquisite scarf decorated with pretty flowers and butterflies. She was touched that he had thought to ask her opinion. Of course she had replied that she loved it. The L word, carefully she typed it, daydreaming of his gorgeous face, his expressive hands, his husky, sexy voice. Impulsively she text him, 'hello, I miss you,' sending it before she had chance to regret it. But then she did regret it. How needy does that sound? She fretted with a wince. He's probably cringing into his dessert right now.

Suddenly, there was a bang at the door. Juliette jumped in fright, sloshing wine down herself. Hoping it was not the party loving neighbours, religious groups or salesmen, she tip-toed down the hall, to peer through the peep hole.

It was her sister Marie, grinning and waving madly, "let me in Jules."

Juliette flung back the lock, a bemused expression on her face, "hello," she began, "to what do I owe this honour?"

"Hiya kiddo," Marie breezed past, bringing with her the aroma of food, "I've been to pick up the Chinese. Just thought I'd check up on you, while I'm in the vicinity. Has the toe rag left with my niece and nephew?" she peered into the empty lounge.

"Yes, he's gone and Maz, he was trying really hard to be nice. He apologised and made this emotional speech about how he's changed and I don't know, I sort of believe him this time, he was kinda sweet and sincere, different."

Marie opened her mouth and stared at her for a few moments, "Really? I hope he does mean it Jules, I really do."

"Sit down," Juliette instructed, "would you like a drink?"

"Go on then," Marie sat back, kicked off her shoes and wriggled her toes with relief, "I've been on my feet all day. We had two funeral collections, flowers everywhere."

Juliette clicked her tongue in sympathy, "so, what brings you out on an evening and where is Dave?"

"Oh he's watching the footy, I've left him to it. Anyway, do I need an excuse to come see my kid sister?" Marie feigned a look of offence.

"Of course not," Juliette swirled milk on top of a soggy teabag, "it's very lovely to see you," She passed her sister the daisy painted mug and smiled at her vibrant, newly dyed, purple hair, "your hair looks pretty, it suits you."

"Well out of the two of us, you were blessed with the most beautiful red curls, I had to make do with mousy brown straggles that need pepping up from time to time," she winked.

Juliette laughed, "you are gorgeous!"

"I've got some news."

"Let me guess," Juliette pondered for a minute, "Mom's gone and won the lottery, Dad's quit his dire job and Dave's taking you somewhere exotic and exciting for your birthday?"

"Oh, erm, actually," Marie looked as if she was going to burst with happiness, "I'm pregnant!"

"What?!" Juliette shrieked.

Marie looked up at her with moist, glistening eyes, "only a couple of months. It's very early days, but it looks like the IVF has worked this time."

Juliette bent forward to hug her sister gently, "that is the most wonderful news. I'm so happy for you!"

Marie placed a trembling finger against her lips, "no one else knows though Jules, apart from Dave of course, so it's between me and you okay?"

Juliette nodded in agreement, "of course, I understand."

"We're telling the parents tomorrow," she continued, "I'm blessed, finally."

Juliette swallowed down a lump of emotion. Maz had been trying for a baby for years and had remained stoically cheerful as each disappointing month had passed. Juliette knew how much it meant to her and Dave too.

"You are going to be wonderful parents. Mom and Dad are going to be thrilled and think how excited Harry and Molls will be to have a baby cousin to cuddle and fuss over."

Marie held up her hand, "It's still so early though Jules, I'm scared to get too excited. I'm afraid something's going to go wrong."

Juliette had never seen her confident, opinionated sister look so vulnerable, "try to look on the positive," she squeezed her fingers, "get plenty of rest and relaxation. Please let me help, with anything: shopping, housework, damn, I'll even do your laundry and ironing."

"You have enough to do yourself," Marie replied smoothly, confidence restored again, "Dave's on my case twenty four seven. He won't let me lift, hoover, he's been terrific. But I really could do with a helper in my flower shop, if you know of anyone who is creative and green fingered."

"I can ask around," Juliette replied, "see if any of my student friends need a part time job working for a demanding but lovely boss. Drink your tea and tell me everything; due date, name choices, colour of the nursery?" They laughed together companionably, then settled back for a girly chat.

* * *

"Your Chinese will be stone cold," Juliette remarked some time later.

Marie fiddled with the bulging white plastic bag where prawn crackers protruded at an odd angle, "oh it will soon warm up in the microwave. Anyway, tell me how it's going between you and Mr Lecturer."

Juliette's eyes twinkled at the mention of Dr Rivers, "really well," she gushed, "he is so lovely Maz."

"Is he?" Marie's eyebrows were raised in a sceptical look, "I'd like to meet him, before I decide on that."

"Only if you promise *not* to interrogate him," Juliette replied with a sigh.

"I might have a few questions for him," Marie acknowledged, "you know, shoe size, favourite pop artist, what his intentions *really* are."

"I can answer those," Juliette blustered, feeling both defensive and protective, "his feet are big, like his hands. He loves eighties music. As for his intentions, I do hope they are on the corruptive side," Juliette laughed, "he makes me happy, I love being with him."

Marie stared straight into her eyes, "are you *in love* with him? And don't lie Jules, I know you and I know you've never been like this over a guy before."

Juliette flushed, ducked her head to stare at the rug, "I don't know. We're still getting to know each other. It's far too soon to get all mushy and serious. Er, do you want more tea?"

Marie ignored her pained look of let's change the subject, "only I don't think you've ever really been in love Jules."

"I have!" Juliette cried, as an image of her eight-year-old self flashed before her eyes, "Jamie Stott, the prince in the school adaptation of Snow White, remember, I adored him."

"Now I know where Molly gets her love of all things Disney," Marie chortled, "weren't you a dwarf in that and didn't Jamie Stott marry Susan Spencer, the school bully?"

"I played Sneezy," confirmed Juliette, "and yes he married her. They both work in the police force now, can you imagine it? Susan Spencer and Jamie Stott, Chattlesbury's very own detective duo, catching criminals all day."

"Speaking of criminals. Did you love Marty?"

"I honestly thought I did at the time, but retrospectively, I think I got it confused with infatuation. He was always the school heart throb wasn't he? A little bit rebellious, a little bit dangerous. Now I know we were so unsuited, way too different."

"And you were always way too good for him, that's a fact," Marie sniffed, "but hey, you made Harry and Molls, something to be proud of."

"Exactly!" Juliette sipped thoughtfully at her wine, "maybe you're right Maz, what is love anyway?"

Marie burst into song; a Howard Jones classic track: 'What is love?'

"I'm being serious," Juliette rolled her eyes, "quit with the singing, you'll make it rain."

"Well I can try to define it for you Jules, but really it's all about personal preference."

"Go on then," Juliette urged.

"Love isn't hearts and flowers. It's not big, fancy words. It's not even romantic gestures. It's believing in a person unconditionally. It's making someone laugh through the tears and the pain. It's holding someone's hand when they need a friend. Supporting them and helping them, looking out for their best interests. It's just bloody being there," Marie paused, "and don't even get me started on dashing good looks."

"People can't help how they look," Juliette thought of Ben's gorgeous face and his lean physique, "attraction is important too."

"I know that," Maz huffed, "okay, but just because someone looks nice on the outside, it doesn't necessarily make them a nice person. Looks can be superficial and deceiving. Love is fancying someone, even when they have a spotty, period face."

Juliette laughed, "that's me! Always get a shiner once a month on my chin."

"I've got a confession Jules," Marie set down her mug, "I almost had an affair."

"What?" Juliette spluttered, "but you and Dave, you're rock solid, what happened?"

"It doesn't matter now, I was young, foolish and flattered by the attention of some cad. I had my head up my own arse, couldn't see what was really important. Basically, I lost myself for a while. But I didn't, have an affair I mean."

"No, you didn't," Juliette interjected firmly.

"Life can be so bloody hard sometimes. Everyone's just muddling through, trying their best to make it a happy one. You just have to keep fighting."

"Wow! Marie," Juliette gasped, "have you ever thought of being a motivational speaker, or even a marriage guidance counsellor?"

Marie swiped at her with a cushion, "get away with you, I'm happy in my flower shop. But you Jules, you're going to be somebody, I just know it. It's in your genes, that fight, that spirit and you've always been different. A special kind of."

Before Juliette could reply there came another bang on the door.

"It's just the neighbours," Juliette exclaimed, frustrated to be interrupted in her sister / sister bonding session.

"Better answer it," Marie got to her feet, "I really need to get going anyway."

"Just wait here," Juliette rushed down the hallway, a fixed, go away expression on her face. In her haste, she forgot to look through the spyhole, flung the door open and stumbled over the door ledge into the arms of none other than Ben Rivers.

"Woah," he laughed, "pleased to see me?"

"Ben!" A smile lit up her face, her fingers slid up firm chest muscles.

"You missed me, I came," he took her hands, kissed her mouth.

"All this way for me? But, but your sister's birthday."

"Irrelevant, she's happy with her family and her wine. Whereas you," he took her in his arms, "need something more."

There was a cough from behind. Juliette turned to see her sister advancing on them with a no nonsense expression on her face.

"Hello there, it's good to meet you at last," Marie took Ben's hand and shook it firmly.

"Erm, Ben this is my sister Marie, Marie, Ben," Juliette winced a little at the cool gleam in her older sibling's eyes.

"The pleasure is all mine," Ben said smoothly, extracting his hand.

Juliette threw her sister a look of warning.

"I'll be on my way," Marie leaned in to give Juliette a quick hug, "enjoy your evening," she gave Ben a curt nod as she passed him.

They watched until she had disappeared down the stairwell. Then Juliette gazed at Ben, as he slowly closed the door.

* * *

There was a brooding passion in Ben's eyes as he lifted her chin and kissed the soft tip of her nose.

"So you're all alone then?"

"Yes," she mumbled, her voice sounded husky and breathless, even to her own ears. She cleared her throat and stepped away from him.

"Would you like a drink? Something alcoholic maybe? I've got brandy left over from Christmas, there's wine in the fridge, or an alcopop if you prefer."

"Wine would be great, thank you."

Juliette led the way into the kitchen, "I apologise for my attire, I wasn't expecting visitors and I do like to be comfy," she pulled at the fluffy fabric of her onesie, threw him an embarrassed grin.

"You look extremely cute," he teased, reaching around to pull at the round tail that rested above her buttocks, "and strangely erotic."

Juliette skipped playfully away from him, heading for the fridge, "is Prosecco okay?"

"Perfect."

"So, how was your sister's meal? Did she like the present?"

"It was edible I suppose," Ben revealed, "burnt sausage casserole followed with sunken cake. Her partner cooked. Although what he lacks in culinary skills, he makes up for in other departments, or so I've heard. And she loved the present."

"Good, here," she thrust the glass of bubbly at him, acutely aware that her hands were trembling slightly.

"She wants to meet you."

Juliette smiled, "how do *you* feel about that?"

"Extremely proud that I am able to show off my gorgeous and extremely lovely girlfriend at last."

Juliette's smile slipped, she moved abruptly towards the sink, running herself a large glass of water.

"What's wrong?" Ben watched her with a puzzled expression, "are you ashamed to be known as my girlfriend?"

"Oh no!" Juliette cried, aghast at the thought that she may have upset him, "it's just that we're hardly teenagers."

"How shall I address you then? My lover maybe? No, not that either."

Juliette blushed, "friends?"

"We are more than that and you know it," he grasped her hands, "why do you keep pushing me away?" When there was no reply he continued, "I know you want me Juliette."

Juliette stared into his warm, brown eyes, felt her stomach flip with desire, "I do," she answered truthfully, "I guess I just don't want to get hurt."

"I'm not going to hurt you," he replied softly, "have you not realised by now? I'm crazy about you."

Juliette's eyes grew wide like saucers, "I'm sorry, I care about you too…a lot, and I'm not frigid, it's just that it's been so long…" she trailed off, wishing the floor would swallow her.

"We can take it slowly," Ben soothed, "I'm a patient man."

"That's just it, I don't want to wait anymore," Juliette fiddled with her fingers, her cheeks flaming with colour.

"How about we listen to music, relax," his lips had curled into the loveliest smile, "what is this playing? It has to be the cheesiest song I have ever heard."

Juliette cocked her head to one side and laughed as the sound of birds tweeting could be heard, "oh it's Minnie Riperton – loving you, not exactly the coolness of Oasis, but it has a sweet ambience to it, don't you think?"

"Yes, if you're five. Oh, but Miss Harris, are you trying to seduce me?"

Juliette snorted with mirth, "oh yes, clad head to toe in my sexy rabbit suit? I'm positively sizzling."

Ben pulled her into his arms, "are you naked underneath this wickedly erotic playsuit?"

He tugged at the zip, slowly sliding it down to her stomach which Juliette sucked in self-consciously. The parted fabric revealed a sheen of soft skin, the tantalising curve of a cleavage.

"You really have no idea how attractive you are? Hmmm?" Ben slid his hands inside. They were cool, made her jump slightly and almost seemed to be emitting sparks as they hovered mercilessly.

Juliette shivered, her eyes like liquid pools of longing, as she instinctively turned her body towards him. Ben dipped his head, brushing her lips with his own, so warm compared to his firm, cool hands. Her knees turned wobbly and she gasped with desire.

"Come with me," she whispered, mind made up.

"Are you sure?"

"I'm sure," she took his hand, pondered briefly on the state of her bedroom, hoping that she had remembered to tidy it. Thank goodness she had washed the sheets and vacuumed underneath the bed yesterday. They hurried through the flat, both stumbling over furniture in their haste.

The sheets were heavenly; soft, lovely and smelt fresh of hibiscus conditioner. Juliette sank down on top of them, pulling him with her.

They became a tangle of limbs, head spinning kisses and sweet murmurs. Juliette closed her eyes and succumbed to the delicious feelings that he invoked in her: warmth, desire and love. Yes love, she recognised it now, in the flip of her stomach, the tremble of her fingers as she opened his shirt, the constant thoughts of him that spun her head, the longing and the passion. This was much more than pure fondness; this went way deeper. She wondered if she should tell him, three short words that could change their relationship forever. It floated on her tongue, those words that her body screamed should be vocalised, but then she was overcome with pleasure, his searching hands and lingering kisses distracted her and she allowed herself to be carried away on waves of pleasure, an ocean deep with love.

Chapter Ten

"I can't drink anymore," Hema was frowning at the cup full of water, clutched in her hands.

"You're supposed to drink a pint, aren't you?" Will reminded her gently.

"My bladder is full," Hema replied, "how much longer are we going to wait?"

The maternity block of Ambleside Hospital was busy, staff hurried past them, indistinct blurs in blue uniforms, some clutching papers, others wheeling patients, linen and drugs. A man with a mop swiped at the floor next to them. Will wrinkled his nose at the strong smell of disinfectant, and ladies perfume. There had to be at least twenty women waiting besides them, some sat alone, some were accompanied by nervous looking men and other grinning females; potential grandma's maybe or excited aunties? One woman was sprawled across two chairs, continuously rubbing her protruding stomach, while her young off spring darted around the room, pretending to be zombies or some other monstrosity.

The screen above them flashed number eighteen. Great, Will thought, looking down at their number twenty ticket.

"Not much longer," he assured her, flashing her a smile and a wink, in an attempt to lighten the atmosphere, but inside, Will's stomach was churning with nerves. Last night he had almost told Flora about the pregnancy, they had been alone at the dinner table, Max was working late again. Something stopped him, fear over how she would react; would she disapprove and disown him? He doubted it, his mom was one of the sweetest, kindest person you could wish to meet. Yet still he put off telling her. Maybe this evening, with a scan picture to confirm the reality, maybe he could confide in her. Hopefully his dad would be out, yes pretty certain he would be, Mondays were his swim night, even better; no Max Bentley lurking around the house.

"I think we're the youngest here," Hema whispered. Worry lines were etched across her forehead. Will was tempted to smooth them away, kiss the fear and trepidation off her pretty face. He glanced at the couples dotted around him; women in dungarees and maternity smocks, clutching the hands of middle aged, greying men.

"We're definitely the coolest," he replied with a wink. Hema smoothed her flowery tunic and fiddled with the bangles on her wrist.

"Everything will be okay, won't it Will?" she looked at him, with wide, honey golden eyes, "I mean just because we're younger, it doesn't mean things can't go wrong?"

"Don't stress, you need to stay calm. Everything is going to be cool, don't worry."

"I wish I could believe that," she said tersely, "I didn't know for months Will, I drank wine at Christmas, ate soft cheese, I can't help but worry."

"You weren't to know, let's just wait and see what the professionals have to say," he reached across to take her hand, squeezed it lightly. Number nineteen flashed on the screen, but there was no rush for the sonographer's room. A few minutes passed before their number appeared, red and stark against the cool whitewash of the hospital décor.

They both jumped to their feet. Hema lifted her bag onto her shoulder and let out a shaky breath.

"Come on," Will said, with a gentle smile. They picked their way across the floor, avoiding feet and handbags. The door was firmly closed, Will rapped at it. It swung open and a lady with a welcoming smile ushered them inside. She was young, looked barely in her twenties, but her demeanour was calm and professional.

"Hello Miss Kumar," she rifled through a pile of notes and proffered her hand for Hema to shake.

"I'm Will," he said, after she had gazed at him expectantly, "Hema's partner."

"Hello both, I'm Sandra and I'll be performing your scan today. If you have any questions, please don't hesitate to ask."

They stood awkwardly for a few moments, looking around the dimly lit room. It was small, with a half raised bed and a corner full of medical looking equipment.

"Okay Hema, I need you to get up on the bed and pull your bottom clothing down a little okay?"

Hema climbed onto the bed, wriggling herself into a comfortable position.

"Are you okay Hema?" Sandra asked briskly.

"Yes," Hema replied, lifting her tunic to reveal a bare stomach and midriff.

Will swallowed, there was definitely some kind of bump going on there. It was small and raised, but definitely different to the normally flat, taut skin. They waited nervously, Will clasped her hand as Sandra squirted a strange blob of clear looking gel over her stomach.

"Oh, that's cold," Hema breathed in sharply.

"Sorry," Sandra said, as she swivelled in her chair and fiddled with some knobs, "You're doing really well. I'm just going to place a transducer now over your stomach and we'll be able to have a look at your baby."

Hema smiled at Will who gulped and grinned back with excitement. He leant forward in the chair and together they peered at the monitor to the side of them. There was nothing except a black, fuzzy screen. A few minutes passed, whereby the sonographer pressed down over Hema's stomach, then they heard it. A loud whooshing sound.

"Ah, here we are, that's the heartbeat by the way."

"Will!" Hema gasped with happiness, a huge smile wiped the frown lines off her forehead.

Will shifted in his seat, his mouth wide open with shock, "oh my god," he breathed, as a blurry image appeared on the screen.

"There is the heartbeat," the sonographer pointed at a flipping image, "strong and healthy."

"That's our baby Will," Hema's eyes were streaming, tears spilling over, as she gazed in awe at the screen. Will kissed her forehead, her nose, her lips, "our baby," he confirmed, his voice a tremulous echo.

* * *

The Student Union bar opened at midday. Sophie was already there ten minutes before, pacing outside and glancing at her watch. She had been into the city centre this morning for a dose of retail therapy. Now her arms were aching, from carrying bags overflowing with designer clothes, make up and lingerie. Her weekend had flown by and had consisted of a kid's party at the local play den and then a family meal with her mother and on / off boyfriend Roger. Sophie had drunk too much wine and was now suffering the consequences. Her sunglasses shielded red, tired eyes. She frequently sipped at a bottle of Evian, determined to assuage the sick feeling that churned her stomach. But at least her and Ryan had managed to patch things up and were on friendly terms again. Was she happy she wondered – maybe?

"Hey girlfriend," a soft voice wafted towards her.

Sophie turned to smile at Juliette as she walked buoyantly towards her, "hi honey."

They hugged briefly.

"What's all this? Has Christmas come early?" Juliette asked, as she stared down at Sophie's purchases.

"Oh, I just needed some new things," Sophie said sheepishly, acutely aware of Juliette's lack of finances.

"Ok," Juliette replied, "but where are the books?"

"I'm tired of buying books," Sophie said with defiance, "they're really cluttering up my house."

"Are you okay Sophie?" Juliette asked with concern, as she noted her friend's pale countenance.

Sophie inspected a perfectly manicured hand, "in fact I'm having second thoughts about the whole university thing. It's all getting a bit boring."

"Boring? I thought you were loving being a student?" Juliette was puzzled by Sophie's sudden change of heart.

"Yes, well, my family has to come first and my grades so far have been dire. I kind of feel I'm wasting my time here Jules. Maybe I'm just not the sort to be a successful student. Maybe I should stick with shopping and footballer's wife's luncheons."

Juliette's eyes narrowed, "I know you don't believe that. Are you still having problems at home?"

Sophie sighed with resignation, "My mom thinks that it's all down to me coming to uni. I've changed apparently."

"Maybe it's a change for the better?" Juliette suggested gently, "have you considered that it might be a teeny bit of jealousy, that you're making something of your life, change is good! Don't give up, not yet honey. You've had a couple of low marked essays – so what? This is only the first year, we're all learning, getting used to essay writing, referencing. It's hard, but I'm sure you can do it. You just need to concentrate, forget this," Juliette pointed at the bags, "it's all superficial rubbish, use your brains Sophie, follow your dreams."

Tears sprang to Sophie's eyes, "but what about Ryan, the boys, my mom and friends."

"They really should be supporting you and if they aren't then stand up to them. Show them you can do this."

"Is it worth it though?" Sophie swept a hand around her surroundings.

"Absolutely," Juliette placed a comforting arm around her shoulders, "what you are doing should be applauded. You're working hard to improve your prospects. There's so much more in this world than being a wife and mother. You can do this Soph, *I* believe in you."

"You are such a lovely person Juliette, a true friend, thank you and you're right, I'm going to carry on and I'm determined to succeed."

"That's the spirit, now come on, the bars open, let's go get a drink and wait for Ann to explain why we're all meeting here."

* * *

"I'm your new personal tutor," Wilomena Smythe was explaining to a happy Ann, "your original lecturer is unfortunately away from work, so lucky you has me for the next foreseeable future."

"Oh that's fine," Ann was feeling extremely laid back this particular day. Any other day she may have argued, demanded to know why her original personal tutor was no longer available. "Stress and depression," Melanie whispered from behind her, answering her unspoken query.

"So, your grades so far have been excellent. How are you finding the course?" Wilomena was tapping her desk with a posh looking pen and looking expectantly at Ann.

"I'm enjoying it," Ann confirmed, "so far the lectures have been informative and interesting. Although it can be a challenge to read all the allocated texts. Also, the seminars never seem long enough."

"Ah yes," Wilomena replied, nodding enthusiastically, "I do love a good discussion. I'm afraid we do work under a very limited time frame but Ann, maybe you could highlight your concerns on your student satisfaction sheet."

"I already have," Ann replied, holding up a completed form.

"Excellent, leave that with me," she ceremoniously filed the papers on top of a towering in try. "Now have you any concerns or issues you would like to discuss with me?"

"Apart from the extortionate price of tea in the canteen? No, everything is fine."

Wilomena threw back her head and laughed heartily, "this is why I insist on bringing a flask. I agree, the price is way too high and not even PG Tips. The catering staff insist that students want to drink Darjeeling or English Breakfast. Maybe we should instigate a review of the food and beverages facilities here at Chattlesbury. What do you think Melanie?"

Melanie nodded, "the bacon isn't crispy enough either and the hot chocolate is just watered down slush, urgh," she shuddered at the thought of the offending hot drink.

"Well then Ann," Wilomena changed the subject, "I recommend that after the primary texts, you endeavour to familiarise yourself with critical pieces and maybe discuss these briefly in your essays. That will help you gain even higher marks. Also, I know this may seem awfully premature, but you really do need to be considering a plan for your dissertation. I've seen many students fail because they were unprepared, now is the time to be exploring what authors and themes you may wish to discuss. The first year is in many ways the least stressful year of an English degree. Although I'm sure that some may disagree with me. But it does give you more time to think ahead. So overall Ann, you are doing exceptionally well. Jolly well done, keep up the good work and do come and pop in if you require advice." She scraped back her chair and took Ann's hand, pumping it vigorously.

"Thank you Ms Smythe," Ann glowed from the unexpected praise.

"Oh do call me Wilomena, I shall see you in European Mythology. Goodbye Ann, goodbye Melanie." The lecturer pulled her cardigan tighter around her midriff, then picked up a dainty watering can and proceeded to tip liquid into the numerous spider plants that were dotted around her office.

"I like her," Ann said, as Melanie wheeled her down the corridor.

"I do too, she's a nice person with a good heart. Her partner is a complete loser though. A philanderer, a snob, an educated rogue."

"Really?" Ann declared, shaking her head, "why does she tolerate it? Such a clever lady."

Melanie sniffed, "loves him I suppose. Have you had the pleasure of meeting Dr Patrick Smug Sullivan? He's a creative writing lecturer mainly, and also specialises in American Literature. Long haired hippy, thinks he's irresistible to women everywhere. Carries condoms in his back pocket just in case he gets lucky with any of the younger students."

"What?" Ann was shocked, "that's disgusting."

"Exactly," Melanie agreed, tucking a tendril of hair behind her ear, "a total leech, grossly unfaithful to Wilomena. He tried it on with me once, nearly lost his nuts because of it."

Ann shook her head, "I would not tolerate that, but her personal life is her own I suppose."

"Yes it is, it must be awful for her though, but apparently he is very suave and charming, has her wrapped around his tiny digit, she keeps forgiving him, so who is the biggest fool – him or her?"

Ann looked back up the corridor, "well, let's not gossip. I'm here to complete an English degree. I'm not in the business of judging others."

"If only more of the university staff were like you Ann, but anyway, why are we all meeting in the bar on a lunchtime?"

"I have some news, I thought it would be nice to share a bottle of wine when I tell everyone."

"Oh this sounds intriguing, can't wait." Melanie jabbed the button to call the lift and chatted animatedly about the local gig her and Tasha were attending at the weekend.

* * *

For the first time in her life Evelyn was running late. This morning she had sat in her dressing gown, stirring her porridge with a 'I really don't want to go anywhere' feeling. It was raining again, which only added to her lethargy; grey clouds were covering the sky and thunder rumbled ominously in the distance. The clock on the mantelpiece ticked slowly by, as she missed one bus then the other. At eleven o'clock she shook off her maudlin thoughts of Mam, stared critically in the mirror and gave herself a good talking to; pull yourself together she berated her pale, frizzy haired reflection. She was feeling a little bit hyper after consuming two pots of tea, all by herself, as she sorted out outstanding post and pondered what day she should do the food shop. Since Mam's death, her stomach had been tied into a tight knot of anxiety, her weight had plummeted by ten pounds and her thoughts were occupied by death and mortality. She worried about her own health; the niggling bad back, her worsening eyesight. For the first time she wished that she had siblings to confide in. Who will look after me? She fretted, but then she spied a charity bag in amongst the takeaway menus. It was collecting for cancer research and it made her think of all the many people that were fighting numerous horrible diseases around the world. Maybe it was the indomitable British spirit inside her, or maybe it was her beloved Mam's last words but Evelyn knew she had no choice but to carry on. To push aside the crippling grief and face each day with positivity. So, by late morning she was showered, dressed and ready to leave the house, with a firm smile fixed on a façade to hide the numbing pain.

On the way to the bus stop she paused to speak to persistent neighbours asking after her welfare. Evelyn was torn between feeling touched by people's kindness and fed up with having to repeat the same mantra: I'm fine, life goes on. Truthfully she was not fine; her heart had been beating rather erratically the other day and her state of mind was fragile. Visions of Mam lying in the hospital bed haunted her. She was sure that had she been admitted to hospital sooner, they may have been able to save her. Guilt and grief consumed her and therefore each night she found it hard to settle; sleep ultimately eluded her. During the bus journey into the city centre, she rested her head against the cool, dusty glass, yawning as she watched motor vehicles streaming past. She had been to the solicitors a few days ago to sort out all the finances. Mam had left everything she owned to Evelyn, apart from a small donation to the local Dogs Trust. The house was paid for and there was a substantial amount in her personal savings account. Thankfully, money was one factor she could tick off her worry list.

Since the funeral, Great Aunt Gertrude had been staying with her, but this morning she had left for Lancashire, satisfied that Evelyn could cope alone. Gertrude was a great conversationalist; chatty, loud and opinionated. She had distracted Evelyn with debates on politics, British history and entertainment of the 1960s, which she had heralded as being a great era. Since her departure, the house had been eerily quiet, every creak seemed amplified. Dust had settled over the furniture and the garden was overgrown. She felt like Miss Haversham from Great Expectations, secluded and forgotten, rambling alone in a large four bedroom, turn of the century detached, watching the world go by from yellow netted windows, while spiders weaved silvery webs in the cornice and magpies nested on the derelict chimney stacks. Yet today she had ventured out. A phone call from Sophie had spurred her out of her sad reminiscence and out into the bustling world. Watching the busy commuters whizzing past, reminded Evelyn that life really did go on.

The bus rumbled to the city centre stop and Evelyn joined the line to disembark. As she was skirting past a man who was sneezing profusely, she heard her name being called and looked up the flight of steps which led to the upper deck. Will was bounding down towards her, closely followed by Hema. Their faces were glowing with happiness and Evelyn felt her heart lighten at the sight of them.

"Hello there," she greeted warmly, shifting her books onto her other hip.

"Hi Evelyn, here let me," Will took the books from her arms, before she could protest, "every time I see you, you're weighed down with books."

"I've been working on the poetry essay," she confided, "almost finished. Hema, how are you dear?"

Hema reached across to hug Evelyn gently, "I'm good thank you. I'm so sorry to hear about your Mam, I hope that you are okay?"

"Oh I will be," Evelyn replied, reaching out to take Will's hand as he helped her from the bus, "but thank you for your concern."

"So, we're meeting Ann and the others in the bar. Sherry for you Evelyn?"

"Not on a lunchtime," Evelyn replied with a laugh, "I would be asleep for the rest of the day."

They walked up the busy path, following the signs for the university.

"Will you come for a drink?" Will asked Hema gently.

"My lecture starts in urm," she glanced at her watch, "ten minutes, but you go and enjoy yourself and text me when you get home later."

"Be careful," Will kissed her softly, "have a good afternoon."

"See you handsome."

"Later beautiful."

They turned in opposite directions, Will caught up with Evelyn who had wandered off to give them some privacy. They chatted about the poetry essay, while making their way towards the Student Union bar, down a flight of stairs they trooped, past the reprographics shop where printers churned noisily.

"We should get one of those," Will pointed at a mannequin in the window, that was wearing a Chattlesbury University logo with the words 'learning enables us to be free,' emblazoned across the chest.

"Oh yes and also a mug too, as a keepsake."

"After you," Will pulled the door open and waited politely for Evelyn to step inside. Music thrummed from the bar, a loud disco beat that shook the pictures dotted on the walls. Sophie and Juliette were already seated, sharing a bag of peanuts as they chatted to the bar manager Wayne.

"Here he is, my best barman. I was just telling these lovely ladies how natural you are at this job." He slapped Will's back heartily, "you'll have to try a cocktail, Will can make a fantastic 'sex on the beach'."

Juliette's nose wrinkled, "I'm not really one for spirits, what's it in anyway?"

"Vodka mainly," Will replied with a smile, "with a measure of schnapps and cranberry and orange juice to water it down."

"See," Wayne said smugly, crossing his arms, "told you he was good."

"I love cocktails, we will definitely have to share a pitcher on our next night out," Sophie said with enthusiasm, "Evelyn come sit here," she patted the vacant space on the sofa, then enveloped her in a tight embrace.

"Good to see you Evelyn," Juliette leant across to pat her hand.

"Well hello," Ann called to them from across the room. They turned towards her and Melanie as they paused at the bar, "is sweet, white wine okay with everyone? We'll only have one, as I know some of you are driving."

The whole table chorused their approval.

"This room looks so different in the daylight." Evelyn commented, looking around at the bare tables and the deserted dance floor.

"Oh yes, the staff / student Christmas party," Juliette reminisced with a dreamy, far away look on her face, "that was the night Ben and I first got together."

"How are things going between you dear?" Evelyn asked with interest.

"Really well thank you Evelyn," Juliette replied shyly.

"She means fantastic," Sophie interjected, "and at last it's out in the open."

"What's out in the open?" Melanie asked, as she plonked down a tray of wine and glasses.

"Jules and Doctor Rivers are officially an item," Sophie answered for her.

"Wow, that's excellent! About time too," Melanie nudged Ann, "another reason to celebrate."

Ann passed the wine around, then held her glass high, "to Juliette and Ben."

Juliette blushed, "but what was *your* news Ann?"

"Oh just a little letter I received this morning, confirming that Jon and I have passed the initial checks to adopt a child," she held a piece of paper high and began waving it manically, her face beaming with happiness. Will, Evelyn, Sophie and Juliette surged forward to embrace her. Cries of 'great news' and 'fantastic' ricocheted around the room.

"To Ann, Jon and their future child," Sophie held her glass high, urging the others to follow her lead. There was a clinking sound as glasses tapped against each other.

"How about a bit of pop music to help you celebrate?" Wayne fiddled with the CD player then turned the volume up, as Katy Perry's 'Firework' reverberated from the speakers.

Sophie was on her feet, swaying her hips in time to the upbeat tempo, "come on Will, dance with me," she pulled him onto the empty dancefloor, spinning him around and sashaying against him merrily. Wayne urged them on with claps of encouragement and wolf whistles.

The others settled back in their seats and listened with interest, as Ann explained all about the adoption checks that her and Jon had undertaken and what would happen next in their quest to adopt a child.

A few songs later and the student union bar was beginning to fill up. Alone behind the bar, Wayne was rushed off his feet serving punters. He beckoned Will over, "fancy another last minute shift?" Will was happy to oblige, he needed the money desperately at the moment; every penny counted. He bounded behind the bar, reaching for the chrome cocktail glass, then began expertly shaking spirits together, tipping blue liquid into frosted glasses and grinning charmingly at the groups of ladies hanging over the beer trays.

"Look at Will, he's in his element," Sophie smiled fondly, "such a lovely lad."

Juliette nodded in agreement, "what's his dad like? Ann was saying they don't get on."

"Very career orientated by the sounds of it. Quite serious and reserved, but I suppose you have to be when you're a head teacher. It must be such a stressful job."

"Yes," replied Juliette, "a lot of responsibility. Oh no!" She gazed towards the door, grimacing as Carol the gossip and her group of friends flounced in.

"Urgh," Sophie pulled a face.

Melanie had noticed the group appearing too, she broke off her conversation with Ann to converse with the others.

"Someone needs to smash apart that coven of witches. Wanna hear some gossip about Carol? I've heard on a weekend she likes to dress up as a..."

"I really don't want to know," cut in Ann.

"No," Evelyn patted her arm, "don't stoop to their level dear."

Melanie let out an irritated sigh and twirled her ponytail, "you lot are way too nice, let's just say that her fiancé, wouldn't be too happy if he knew what she got up to on a girl's night out and there she sits in judgement of others because she is way too hypocritical to acknowledge her own vices."

"Forget about her," Ann tutted, "who's been to see their personal tutor?"

"I have an appointment in about half an hour," Juliette replied, "with Brian Hodges."

"Me too dear, but with Dr Rivers, shall we walk over together?" Evelyn was already on her feet, collecting up her belongings.

"I think I'll go to the library, do some work on the poetry essay," Sophie cut in, "Ann, would you like to accompany me?"

"Great idea," answered Ann, "maybe they have some books on successful adoption."

Just as they were about to leave, two beaming student representatives paused at their table.

"Hello ladies, can I tell you about a demonstration rally that some of the students have organised tomorrow in the city centre?"

"What's it about?" Ann asked, her interest piqued.

"Tuition fees, we believe they should be abolished, or at least cut drastically. School leavers are foregoing their right to a university education because of all the debt they will accumulate. We're trying to make people aware, through a peaceful protest of course, of the financial obstacles that now put off many people coming to uni. We would appreciate it if you could show your support at the rally and join your student friends in a march throughout the centre." She handed out leaflets, smiling brightly, "hope to see you there tomorrow."

"This is awesome," Sophie cried enthusiastically, "my first ever demonstration. Please say you'll all be able to come."

"I'll be there," Ann confirmed, "what about Evelyn and Juliette?"

"If I can get a babysitter, sure, why not?" Juliette nodded.

Evelyn was looking dubious, "I really don't know whether this is a good idea, aren't I a little old to be demonstrating?"

"Of course not!" Ann replied impatiently, "age is irrespective. We all need to do our bit to

stand up against this capitalist government and their unfair legislation. It's time to kick

against the establishment. Let's make placards ready for tomorrow and stand with our

student brothers and sisters, united!" She balled her hand into a fist and shook it heavenward.

Just behind her Melanie was chuckling, "Ann, do you even pay tuition fees?"

"That's not the point," Ann declared with a sniff, "I'm supporting my peers. This world has

become so accepting. Whatever happened to free speech and revolution? It's time to rebel

ladies."

"Like they did in the 1970s?" Melanie replied, "shall we wear flares and paint flowers on our

clothes."

"Anyone care for a spliff?" Juliette said with a laugh.

Evelyn was clutching her throat in consternation, "I think that's illegal Juliette."

"I know," Juliette hugged her gently, "I'm only joking. Come on let's leave Ann and Soph to organise the placards. You and I have important meetings with our personal tutors."

* * *

"Well it's warming up," Juliette declared, as they crossed the courtyard, "look at the beautiful flowers." She pointed to a vibrant collection of daffodils.

"I love this time of year," Evelyn declared, "when nature is shaking off the icy hold of winter and the world is starting to bloom again."

"How poetic," Juliette said with a smile, "you can tell that you are a writer."

Evelyn blushed, "I've always been the same. A daydreamer Mam used to call me."

"How are you coping Evelyn?" Juliette asked quietly.

"To be honest dear, I still can't believe that she's gone. The house is so quiet without her." She shook her head sadly.

"Well just to reiterate, you know we are all here for you; me, Soph, Ann and Will. If you ever need anything; help, advice, a shoulder to cry on, please don't be afraid to let us know."

"That is so very kind of you dear, thank you."

"Everyone needs support," continued Juliette, as she slipped her arm through Evelyn's, "you're not alone."

"Hi there ladies," the friendly security guard was standing in front of the sliding doors. Juliette flashed him her ID card, but he waved them through without looking. She was feeling excited that she was going to Ben's office. Her weekend had been fantastic, she had not been able to stop grinning, as she relived the evening they had spent together; the passion, love, fun they had shared. Then the next morning, before the kids were due to arrive back, she had cooked them crispy bacon sandwiches with oodles of tomato ketchup, washed down with sweet, warming tea. He had kissed her lovingly on the doorstep, then reluctantly they had parted. Juliette had spent all of Sunday day-dreaming about him and longing to see him again. After much con-templation soaking in a bubbly bath, she had decided that she was going to tell Harry and Molly all about him and finally admit that he was her boyfriend. That description made her smile, for they were far from teenagers, but it was too soon to describe him as her partner, so boyfriend it was and she couldn't be happier.

The lift whizzed them upwards and Juliette chatted happily to Eve-lyn about her children, explaining how well they were both doing at school and how they were growing into the most loveable, kind, thoughtful pair. Why on earth was she worried about introducing Ben into their lives? She ruminated, they would love him for sure and he in turn would be enchanted by their impeccable manners, and lovely dispositions. Overall, Juliette thought, life was pretty bloody good at the moment. She wished she could wave a magic wand and alleviate some of Sophie's problems and ease Evelyn's grief.

"Is this our floor dear?" Evelyn asked, peering at the flashing num-ber sign, "I've forgotten my spectacles."

"It is," Juliette steered her down the corridor, pausing to direct a Spanish student towards the languages block, "here's their office," she whispered with excitement. The air was still and quiet around them. Juliette noted the door to Ben's and Brian's shared office was ajar. She raised her hand to knock then paused as she heard the sound of a heated conversation, emanating from within.

"Her name is Juliette," she heard Ben say angrily.

"She's your *student*," Brian replied tersely, "your whole career is in jeopardy here."

"Why? Because one student has complained?" Ben sounded angrier then she had ever heard him. Juliette's heart sank with forebearing but still she listened, placing her finger to her lips to silence Evelyn who was trying to speak.

"It wasn't just one, there was a whole group of them. They're accusing you of favouritism Ben, they're threatening to go to the Dean. You are doing so well, didn't Tarquin suggest you are in line for a promotion. And what about Helena, surely you know she's in love with you. She's going to be heartbroken Ben."

"I don't care," Juliette heard the sound of Ben's fist thumping down on the table and jumped in fright.

"Do you love her?" Brian asked slowly.

There was silence, total utter silence. Juliette felt her heart tearing apart, as tears welled in her eyes.

"Okay, maybe that was too personal. Is she worth it then?"

Again silence, cold unnerving quiet. Juliette glanced at Evelyn, taking in her friends horrified face. She shook her head as the tears spilled over, *say something you bastard.* There was no reply, then Juliette decided that she had heard enough, she ran blindly down the corridor, pushing past other students, away from heartache, away from pain and away from her almost boyfriend: Ben Rivers.

Chapter Eleven

Will was refilling the alcopops section behind the bar, when Evelyn burst back into the room looking for Sophie and Ann.

"They left not long after you," he informed her, "is everything okay?" Evelyn looked anxious and was wringing her hands. Will wondered if she was upset about her mam and prepared himself for an emotional outburst. But instead, Evelyn shook her head and replied, "I'm fine Will, but somethings happened with Juliette, she's very upset and I can't find her anywhere."

"Try the library," he replied. He watched her rush out of the bar and shook his head with bemusement.

"Women eh?" Wayne commented drily, "like a different species, don't ya think?"

"Sometimes," Will ran a hand through his hair and checked his phone. Hema had sent him a picture of a nursery room, complete with baby accessories and a new-born curled underneath a broderie anglaise blanket. Even Will had to admit the infant was cute, with fair, curled hair, wide blue eyes and a cheeky smile. He was still buzzing with excitement from seeing the baby scan. He had a picture stored in his back pocket. When Wayne had his back turned, Will surreptitiously pulled it out to gaze at it with wonder. The midwife had pointed out the baby's arms and legs, on the screen it looked like it was waving at him. The whole procedure had been extremely emotional and the good news was that the baby was perfectly healthy and due around the end of August. So they were going to be parents, they had both decided then, that they couldn't keep it a secret any longer. It was time to be open, time to grow up and face up to the reality. Now all they had to do was tell their parents.

The rest of his shift dragged by. The bar fell quiet again as students petered off to their afternoon lectures. As a distraction, Will worked on his poetry essay, re-editing an already completed piece of work, checking for spelling and punctuation errors. Wayne let him finish half an hour early, after Will had helped him drag a new stock of beer barrels into place. He was sweating profusely by the time he had finished, but their afternoon tips had been good. Wayne pressed a twenty into his hand and jokingly told him to spend it on hair gel. He bounded across the city centre, rushing for his bus. He wanted to get home before his dad. He planned on testing the waters with Flora first, he guessed her reaction to be one of shock then supportive acceptance. With his Dad however, he had no idea of the reaction. It was dependant on two main factors; his present mood and how things were progressing at St Mary's.

When he arrived home he was dismayed to see his father's car parked up on the driveway. Will slunk in the house, threw his coat off and hovered in the hallway. Ruby came bounding towards him, ears up, tail wagging.

"Hello girl," he stooped to pet her. He could hear his mom chattering away on the telephone. Will strode through to the kitchen where his Dad was seated, nose in his laptop.

"Evening," Max Bentley said, his eyes fixed firmly on the screen.

Will mumbled a greeting, then crossed to pour himself a drink. His stomach was in knots and his breathing was faster than normal.

"You're back early," Will turned to peer at Max.

"Thanks for the welcome," Max responded with a frown, "for a change, everything is calm and seems to be running smoothly at St Mary's, so I thought I'd sneak off early, being the boss and all that."

"That's wonderful to hear love," Flora had appeared in the kitchen, a vision of domestic bliss, in a flowery dress, with a pink apron tied around her midriff.

"Hi Mom," Will nodded her way, "what's for tea?"

"Oh you and your stomach William," Flora chuckled good naturedly, "as a matter of fact I've made a stew, with homemade crispy dumplings."

"Awesome," Will smiled brightly, inside he was longing for a takeaway kebab and chips.

"So," Will pressed, "will you be in all night?"

Max looked up in surprise, "as a matter of fact, I'm going to the local pub quiz with Uncle Evan, would you like to accompany us?"

Will sighed inwardly, "sorry, no can do. Essays to finish, books to read."

"That's what I like to hear, my son, sensible and focused at last."

Will felt a sweat break out on his forehead, "so, er Mom, what are you up to this fine evening?"

"Well," she began happily, "I was going to go with your Dad, but Brenda's coming over and we're doing a spot of flower arranging for our class next week." Flora frowned, "also, next door neighbours are having a garden party with fireworks of all things. The poor dog will be terrified, so I really do need to say with her."

"Sounds cool, urm what time will Brenda be over?"

"Not till after eight. Will are you okay? You look awfully pale."

"Just tired Mom." Will yawned theatrically to highlight his point.

"Go and rest," she insisted, "You don't want to be ill. Good job my stew has lots of garlic in it." Flora ushered him out of the kitchen into the living room, "sit down and watch some mind numbing television, rest your brain." Will did as he was bade, before the adverts were rolling on the screen he was asleep, head cocked to one side, dreaming of wheeling Hema down the aisle of a maternity suite, while she screamed in pain.

Will woke hours later, feeling groggy and light headed. He stumbled to his feet and into the kitchen where his Mom and a small lady with icy blue hair sat laughing, surrounded by dried flowers and ribbon.

"Hello sleepy," Flora beamed, "your stew is in the pot, I couldn't bear to wake you, you looked so comfortable."

"What time is it?" Will spluttered, as he lurched towards his phone.

"Eight thirty love, don't worry I've wrapped the dumplings in foil so they didn't spoil."

"Well where's Dad?"

"At the quiz. Will, don't you remember him telling you? This is Brenda by the way."

Will mumbled her way, as he tried frantically to switch on his mobile.

"Brenda helps me with Sunday school, with the little ones dear. She plays the flute, and very accomplished at it she is too. I think your phone needs charging."

Will shook his dead phone, in an attempt to will it to life.

"You youngsters with your phones," Brenda piped up, "my son is exactly the same, can't live without it."

All three of them jumped as a firework erupted right outside the window.

"Mary mother of god and all the angels, has bonfire night come early?" Brenda was trying to peer through the swaying venetian blinds.

"It's just the neighbours dear, they did warn me earlier they were having fireworks," Flora patted her hand and frowned at Ruby, who was cowering underneath the table, tail wedged firmly between a pair of shaking legs.

"I really need to charge this," Will was searching through a drawer full of nick-naks. He pulled out a chewed pen, battered headphones, before his hand grasped a black plug.

Flora watched him as he unplugged the radio, cutting the sounds of Cliff Richard abruptly.

"Would you like some hot chocolate Will?" She asked kindly, perplexed by the anxiety which emanated from him. Will was usually so laid back, so carefree, but just lately he had been acting strange: tense, quiet and not his usual effervescent self.

Before Will had chance to answer, there was a heavy thudding on the front door. The bell rang two, three times, before Flora could rise to her feet.

"Whoever is that at this time of night?" Flora pulled her cardigan tighter around her as another explosion ricocheted the night air. She disappeared down the hallway as Will stabbed at the on button of his mobile. Then he heard shouting and the hairs on his arms flew upright. Seconds later Mr and Mrs Kumar burst into the kitchen, faces contorted with rage.

"So here he is, hiding behind his own Mother," Mr Kumar shouted loudly, pointing a gnarled finger at Will. Will took a step backwards, almost tripping over Brenda who had risen and was peering at the uninvited guests over her spectacles. Flora was staring at Will, a frightened look on her face.

"Will, what on earth is going on?" She asked, clutching her cross pendant in consternation.

Mr Kumar spun round to face her, "your son is what is going on. I'm here to give him a good hiding."

"I say," sniffed Brenda, "there's no need to be so aggressive."

"Leave my mom alone," Will found his voice, pulling Flora behind him.

"You swine, I should beat you black and blue for what you have done to my daughter."

"I don't think so Mr Kumar," Flora pushed Will aside, "just because their relationship has ended, it does not give you the right to come shouting at and threatening my son. Hema is young and beautiful and I'm sure given time she will get over it…"

"You really have no idea do you!" Mr Kumar sneered, "ask your son what's really been going on."

Flora stared at Will with puzzlement, "Will?" She queried hesitantly. Will gulped with fear, "where's Hema?"

"None of your damn business," roared Mr Kumar, "if I have my way, you won't be seeing her *ever again.*"

"The mother is as deluded as the son," Mrs Kumar cried, "how could my precious daughter have got mixed up with someone so… so shabby in morals. The whole family are delinquents."

A steely coldness had settled in Flora's eyes, as she turned towards the older woman.

"And how dare you, come into my house and abuse my son. Get out the pair of you, before I call the police." She picked up the cordless phone and held it like a weapon.

There was silence for a moment as they stared at each other.

"Get out!" Flora repeated.

"You," Mr Kumar jabbed a finger at Will's chest, "haven't heard the last of this. Maybe you should fill her in," he nodded his head towards Flora.

"My daughter is going to India," shrieked Mrs Kumar, "you're not part of her life anymore," and with a sweep of her sari, she stormed out of the house.

"You can't do that," Will said slowly, "you can't banish her, she's done nothing wrong. Blame me."

"Oh, I blame you alright. You disgust me. I'm warning you to stay away from my daughter," his eyes were cold and flinty, "if you know what's good for you." With a growl he followed his wife, banging the door with such force that the windows rattled.

Flora noticed that not only was Brenda staring at them with an open mouth, but the neighbours were hanging over the fence, festivities forgotten in the stampede to witness the altercation. As she rushed over to close the windows, Judith, their nosy neighbour and church organist called, "everything okay in there?"

"Erm yes, everything is just fine." Flora banged the windows shut, then pulled the blinds down. "Brenda I think we should continue this another time, I need to speak to Will."

Will passed Brenda her coat and helped his mom usher her out of the house.

"See you in church Sunday?" Brenda asked hopefully.

"Yes of course, I'll be there."

Once the door was firmly shut, Will let out a shaky breath, "you were amazing Mom."

He turned to go back into the kitchen, desperate to text Hema.

"Not so fast," Flora snapped, "I think you owe me an explanation. Your phone can wait."

She filed into the living room and perched on the sofa. Will tagged behind, feeling overcome by a myriad of emotions: fear, guilt, trepidation.

"So the thing is Mom, erm..." he broke off as heat flooded his face.

"So?? Tell me Will, I'm not as naïve as I look and promise I won't be shocked."

"Well, okay, Hema and I have been seeing each other again."

"Is that it?" Flora's tone was imperious. "I had my suspicions Will, but really such an over-reaction from Mr and Mrs Kumar. I won't be going in *their* shop again."

Will picked at a loose cushion thread, "there's something else, I...she's, well..."

"Oh for heaven's sake, spit it out son," when there was no reply she rose to her feet, "I'm going to carry on with my flower arranging. Really Will I'm annoyed, poor Brenda has been sent off home and we were having such a lovely time, I..."

"The thing is Mom, she's pregnant."

Flora was puzzled, "who?"

"Hema of course," he watched her face pale, "I'm going to be a Daddy, you're going to be a Nan."

"What?" Flora spluttered, "is this a joke Will?"

"I'm deadly serious for a change. We've had it confirmed, the baby's due in August."

The clock on the mantelpiece ticked rhythmically, as Flora digested the news. She closed her eyes for a full two minutes, Will guessed, before making the cross sign against her breastbone.

"Oh my dear son, whatever will your father say?"

* * *

Marie's flower shop was stationed on Hilton High Street. It was a quaint affair, tucked between a butchers and a shoe shop and opposite a beautiful park. 'Marie's Memories' had been fully operational now for seven years and was growing from strength to strength. Word of its beautiful flower arrangements and charming staff had spread and now as well as numerous local orders, customers were flocking from other neighbouring towns. The shop was painted a romantic rose pink, with splashes of green writing. Buckets of pretty flowers covered the pavement leading to the shop and trailing hanging baskets decorated the window. On this particular day, Marie was crouched in the window, concocting a new design which she had entitled simply, spring weddings. There were bouquets of roses, freesias and trailing lobelia, interspersed next to crystal goblets and lucky horseshoes, and in the middle hung a short lace cream dress, perfect for the modern, spring wedding. Marie was almost finished, she was taking a break and watching the world go by, so when Juliette came rushing down the street, she already knew from her facial expression that there was something wrong.

The bell tinkled above the door, (as it does in all romantic flower shops) Juliette scurried inside and sank down onto the nearest stool.

"Dear sister, how lovely to see you," Marie pierced the pins back onto the cushion and admired her window display, "finished at last. What do you think?"

"What? Oh yes, lovely," Juliette looked down at her fingernails, which had been mercilessly chewed on the journey over here.

"Jasmine, make a brew will you?" She called to the young sales assistant, who was wrapping sprays of lilies into cellophane. "she's going off to uni in September, Cardiff of all places. I really do need to start advertising for a new assistant. Did you ask around Jules?"

There was no reply, Juliette was immersed in her own thoughts.

"I'm also thinking of dying my hair yellow and running naked around the park for comic relief," Marie waited for her sister to acknowledge the absurd statement, but there was silence.

"Jules," she shouted, "earth to Juliette."

Juliette's glazed expression lifted, as she stared at her sister with dismay, "you were right," she whispered, "I never should have got involved with him."

Marie sighed as she climbed out of the window, "what's happened?"

Juliette exhaled shakily, before explaining what had transpired.

"You really shouldn't be listening in on other people's conversations," Marie berated her.

"I thought that you would be on my side," Juliette cried.

Jasmine brought their tea over and then retreated back behind the counter, where she watched them with wary eyes.

"Of course I'm on your side! But maybe after you left, maybe he declared his undying love for you," Marie swallowed and forced an encouraging smile.

"I doubt that," Juliette shook her head vehemently, "he had the opportunity and I waited for him to say something Maz, I willed him to stand up for us, but nothing. He said nothing and the language lecturer I told you about, the gorgeous, brilliant, classy one, she loves him too and he knows it."

"Why don't you confront him then?" Suggested Marie gently, "go back to uni and give him a piece of your mind if it makes you feel better. Give him the chance to defend himself."

"Like he defended me?" Juliette snorted, "I think not! No, I've made my mind up, it's over between us. It never would have worked anyway, we're too different, from two completely different worlds."

"What are you going to tell him then?"

"I'll think of something," Juliette confirmed, mind racing, "I'm sure he'll soon get over me and move onto a different student." There was a tinge of bitterness to her last words.

"But you liked him so much," Marie regarded her as she sipped at her tea, "are you sure you're not acting rashly?"

"I'm sure," there was a hint of defiance in Juliette's eyes. "I'll be fine."

Marie rose to her feet, "I hate to see you like this Jules, I know you're not fine, but if your mind is made up…and maybe it is better to end it now, before you get too involved."

Juliette sniffed, inside she felt her heart was breaking, already too involved, she admitted inwardly.

"I'm going to get my children, they need me." Juliette picked up her belongings and made for the door, "time to concentrate on Harry and Molly and my career."

"I'm always here for you Jules, remember that…" Marie watched in dismay as her younger sister walked away, out into the breezy day, where the tears cascaded unseen.

* * *

"Mom are you okay?" Will was pacing the living room, while Flora sat silently, gazing into the distance, "Mom!"

Flora jumped to her feet, "I'm making tea."

"Then what?" Will demanded.

"Then we talk…we sort this mess out…we decide on the best course of action, to…"

"It's already been decided, we're keeping the baby."

"Of course you are," Flora said, eyes wide, "but it's not going to be easy love. Come on," they trooped into the kitchen and waited for the kettle to boil.

"Now," Flora began, once they were seated at the table, "first, how on earth are you going to cope financially Will? Babies are expensive, how are you going to support them both?"

"I have savings," Will explained, "probably enough to put down a deposit on a flat."

Flora stared hard at him, "how are you going to live day to day? Food, bills, baby equipment, clothes."

"I'll have to get a job won't I," Will said with impatience.

"You already have a job," Flora replied.

"I mean a proper job," Will glanced at his mom nervously, "I think that I should leave uni."

"But Will," Flora was aghast, "you're doing so well, the first year is almost over. What is Hema planning on doing?"

"Deferring her course? I don't know, we haven't discussed it in depth."

"Well maybe you need to have a heart to heart." Flora sipped at her tea thoughtfully, "don't make any decisions about uni, not yet. Let's just let the dust settle, let things calm down."

"Then what?"

"Then we tell your father."

Chapter Twelve

Sophie woke up to a bright, warm spring morning. She flung back the duvet, practically skipped to the shower, and dressed while humming happily.

"I'm going to my first ever demonstration rally today," she chirped to Ryan, who was lying spread like a star fish underneath the warm duvet.

"Jesus," his head peeked out of the fabric, "I hope you know what you're getting yourself into."

"It's just a peaceful revolt against tuition fees, capitalism, erm you know that kind of thing."

Sophie dragged her straighteners through her golden hair and looked expectantly at her husband, "I'll be back to make tea, don't worry."

As if on cue, Ryan's stomach rumbled loudly, "avoid the press then." He turned over with a humph, signalling the conversation was over. A few moments later, his phone was vibrating across the bedside table. Ryan shot upright and grabbed it, pulling it underneath the duvet. Sophie watched him in the mirror as he fumbled frantically.

"Anyone exciting?" She asked, her voice sounded shrill in the quiet still of the bedroom.

"Just a mate. Hey" his tousled hair peeked round towards her, "why don't we have a takeaway tonight darling, save you cooking."

"Okay," Sophie pouted happily at her reflection.

"You look beautiful," Ryan said smoothly, "my gorgeous girl."

"Always and forever?"

"You bet," his head fell back on the plump pillows. Sophie blew him a kiss, then tiptoed from the room.

Downstairs was chaotic, the dogs were barking like crazy and chasing around after an exuberant Josh and Jake, as they whirled around the garden. Their school had an inset day, but that had not stopped them from rising early.

Sophie watched them from the window, "where on earth do they get the energy?" She mused to her housekeeper, as Heidi struggled across the kitchen, holding a basket full of ironing.

"They non-stop," agreed Heidi, dumping the crumpled clothes on the work station.

"Thank you for looking after them this morning," Sophie smiled warmly, "I should be back for lunchtime." The harassed looking housekeeper waved her away, as she plugged in the iron.

"Be good boys," Sophie called, laughing as they raced to embrace her. Then they were off, running to the tree house, with the dogs chasing merrily after them.

Sophie reversed her four by four carefully past Ryan's gleaming sports car then joined a line of traffic heading into the city centre. She loved this time of year; when the days were growing lighter and the weather was warming up. She wound down the window and inhaled the bracing countryside air. A flick of a switch and music filled the car; an up tempo pop beat that had Sophie crooning along exuberantly. Then her phone was ringing, Sophie turned down the radio and reached forward to answer the call. She sighed as her mother's husky tones emanated from the loud speaker.

"Hello darling."

"Mother, what a pleasant surprise, what can I do for you?"

"I just rang to see how you are darling."

"I'm fine," Sophie responded cheerfully, "just on my way to uni."

"And how are things between you and Ryan?"

"Good," Sophie glanced in the mirror, annoyed to notice the man in the car behind flashing his lights. This is a thirty zone she mouthed, hoping he could see her face in the steamed up mirror. Seconds later he was whizzing past and powering directly in front of her.

"Tosser," Sophie screeched, as road rage over powered her and her car swerved dangerously close to a ditch.

"Pardon?" Yvonne Fletcher cut in.

"Not you Mom, just some boy racer, that's all. Everything is fine with me and Ryan by the way. You must have caught me on an emotional day. I think I may have over reacted. Sorry to have worried you."

"Well okay, as long as you're alright."

"How are you Mom?"

"Oh me? I'm okay, it seems to be everybody else with the problems. Roger still hasn't got the hint that our relationship is over. I sat him down last night and tried to explain, but he seems to think it's just a rocky patch and that we'll be fine. Now his daughter is coming to stay with us over the summer, he's planning all sorts of days out and I really don't think I can bear it."

Sophie grimaced at the mention of her mother's current boyfriend. She really did not like Roger, with his gelled back hair and his lecherous innuendos, his booming voice and over bearing persona. Yet she did feel pity that this was another of her mother's failed relationships, another notch on the bedpost, as Ryan so eloquently phrased it. Sophie was just about to advise that her mom needed to be more forceful and maybe with the help of Ryan they could physically kick him out, when Yvonne changed the subject.

"So how is Derek? Has he mentioned me?"

Sophie gritted her teeth, "no, my gardener hasn't mentioned you and I really do suggest that you forget about Derek. He's a married man."

"But is he happy?" Yvonne sniffed, "We're so well suited you know darling. He's a Virgo and just perfectly compatible for my star sign."

"Stuff and nonsense," was Sophie's verdict, on the subject of astrology.

"His aura is wonderful, so calm and relaxed. Did you know darling his life number is six, the same as mine. Maybe we are destined to be together…" Yvonne trailed off, her thoughts overcome with the romanticism of it all.

"And maybe you need to concentrate on your current relationship. Here's an idea, why don't you be alone for a while Mom?" Sophie suggested.

"Alone?" Yvonne shrieked, aghast with the thought of it.

"Yes on your own for a change," Sophie continued, warming to her theme, "it's all about independence Mom, girl power and all that. You don't need a man, I'm sure you could cope."

"Alone?" Yvonne replied, her voice a tremulous whisper, "of course I need a man darling. Who would do the decorating, carry the heavy shopping bags, open doors and whisk me out to swanky restaurants? Just because you are at university with all those awful feminists, please don't try to enforce their mantra on me. I'm an old fashioned lady at heart, I need love and romance in my life. I need a prince."

Sophie stifled back a laugh, she is serious she thought with a shake of her head, my mother is officially deranged and stuck in a 1950s housewife sitcom.

"Look Mom, I'm coming into the city, I need to concentrate, can I call you later?"

"I suppose so, but I may not be here. I'm having a full body exfoliate and it takes hours apparently."

"Okay, have a nice day, I'll speak to you soon." Sophie cut the call and steered her car around the huge city centre roundabout. She followed the signs for the university with a happy smile on her face. How could she have considered dropping out? Where would she be now if she was not at uni? Most probably with her mother in a beautician's chair, followed by a wine fuelled lunch with Amber. No, Sophie decided, stick with uni, complete the course then see what opportunities the world had to offer. If Evelyn could carry on, with all that she had been through lately, then Sophie was sure that she herself could succeed.

Feeling positive and optimistic, Sophie swung into the multi storey car park, pulled the handbrake up and rubbed the lipstick off her teeth. She was surprised to see Ann a few spaces away, clutching a placard and chatting to Melanie. They greeted each other warmly.

"Oh wow, have you made these Ann?" Sophie pointed at a banner daubed with red paint, 'say no to tuition fees!' it read.

"She was up half the night," Jon said, with a weary shake of his head, as he pulled an armful of leaflets from the back seat of his car. "I think these are to be distributed to the public." He passed them to Sophie, then bent to kiss Ann.

"Behave yourself," he warned her.

Ann smiled cheekily, "who me? Of course, see you later handsome."

"Bye beautiful."

They watched as Jon reversed away from them and down the exit ramp.

"Shall we go meet the others?" Melanie suggested. They made their way out onto the bustling street, swerving around the lines of pedestrians.

"It's busy," Melanie commented.

"Good," Ann replied, "the more people we make aware of these issues, the better."

"I wonder if the lecturers will be here today?" Sophie mused, her thoughts on Tarquin Haverstock.

"Doubt it," Melanie replied, "too busy plotting their next amazing lecture, or marking tons of essays. They'll be plenty of student ambassadors there though. It should be fun, come on." They crossed the main street, turned a corner and then approached a loud crowd of people milling about.

Evelyn, Will and Juliette were already there, hanging on the outskirts of the protestors.

"Blimey," gasped Melanie, "there's megamouth McLaren," she pointed at a young lady who was standing on a chair, shouting into a megaphone. Sophie gawped at the crowd of people before her.

"I didn't think there would be this many," she said, "there must be hundreds here."

"I guess this is something our fellow students feel passionately about," Ann replied.

"Hi everyone," Sophie hugged Evelyn and Ann, "is Hema not here?" She addressed Will, who was looking handsome and relaxed.

"She couldn't make it," he replied smoothly, hands in pockets, as he looked around him with interest, "I've seen quite a few of the English students though."

"Is this a good idea?" Evelyn asked, clutching her throat, "I'm afraid I'm a little bit agoraphobic."

"We can stay at the back," Juliette replied quickly, "you'll be fine."

"Yes," piped up Ann, "get in the spirit Evelyn, let your revolutionary side appear."

"Listen up everyone," megamouth McLaren was yelling into an up-turned megaphone and waving her arms in the air to attract attention, "I would like to thank you all for coming here today. We really do appreciate your support. The plan is to march through the city centre, distributing flyers and making people aware of what we are demonstrating against. Then we meet back here, where there will be a few special guests speaking about what it means to be a student in today's capitalist economy." There were rousing cries and waving of banners. The excitement in the air was palpable, which was further heightened when music boomed out of towering speakers, Marc Bolan's 'children of the revolution' had the crowd swaying and stamping feet, adrenalin flying. "Let's go!" The crowd surged forward and Sophie felt herself being pushed from behind.

"This is so exciting," Sophie dug in her bag and lifted her phone high, so she could capture video footage, with the sole intention of uploading it onto her Facebook wall and sharing it with her social media friends as soon as possible, how cool would that be and she wondered how many likes that particular post would accumulate.

As they moved slowly forward, the student ambassadors at the front began chanting, "what do we want?" and the crowd replied, "to end tuition fees." The next lines were shouted even louder, "when do we want it?" "Now!" Banners were rocked exuberantly and people clapped and raised their fists. Evelyn was looking at Juliette and wondering whether she should broach the subject of Ben Rivers. The poor girl looked as if she had not slept for a week. There were dark circles underneath her pretty eyes and her complexion was pale.

"Juliette, are you okay?" Evelyn touched her arm, pulling her back a little from the others.

"Yes I'm fine," Juliette replied, looking straight forward.

"What we overhead," Evelyn continued, "I'm sure Dr Rivers didn't mean…"

"It's over between us," Juliette interjected, "and I'd rather not talk about it Evelyn."

"Oh okay," Evelyn felt stung by her friend's brusque manner, Juliette was usually so warm and talkative, "but did he explain?"

"I haven't er, spoken to him yet," Juliette felt a shiver of unease run down her spine. Ben had texted her three times last night, asking her out on another date. This time he wanted to take her to the theatre. Juliette had ignored them all, she smarted with anger each time she replayed that horrible overheard conversation, between him and Brian Hodges. She felt betrayed and badly let down. But her mind was resolute on the matter, their fledgling relationship was over, even though her heart felt like it was breaking in two. Boy it hurt, the thought of never kissing him again. This was going to be hard, she conceded, but she had to be strong, their worlds were so different and she couldn't bear the thought that he may find his career in jeopardy because of her. Next to her, Evelyn had changed tack and was chatting about the poetry module. Juliette pushed thoughts of Ben Rivers to the back of her mind and concentrated on discussing poetic form and stanza.

They marched past shops and stalls, where shoppers paused to gawp their way and listen to their unified chanting, "end tuition fees now!" Across the main road they filed, causing chaos for the busy morning traffic. Horns were tooted and some commuters rose from their vehicles to see what all the commotion was about. Juliette breathed in the smell of baking potatoes, sizzling sausages and warm sugar laden donughts, as they trooped down the main street. Then Megamouth McLaren bought the crowd to a sudden halt. She had stopped to talk to members of the public and along with a dozen or so student union representatives, was distributing flyers.

"I guess this is our chance to mingle," Ann said, as she passed a leaflet to an elderly couple pulling a huge shopping trolley. They took it without stopping, mumbling something about catching their bus.

"Here," Ann passed a handful to Juliette, Evelyn, Sophie and Will.

Juliette attempted to press the leaflets into passer-by's hands but noticed that most of them seemed to be avoiding her, looking down at the ground, refusing to meet her eye and scurrying past. Some were blatantly rude, a group of teenagers stared at her as if she had two heads and a line of men in business suits tutted with disapproval.

"You need to get a job!" One man called as he strode past with a shiny briefcase.

Some kind people stopped to listen to Ann ranting on about the extortionate cost of going to university, but many others were openly hostile.

Juliette noticed a group of middle aged looking men laughing at them. It was a large group of twenty or so, they were stood outside a Chattlesbury Football Club merchandise shop. Some were clutching glass bottles of alcohol and stumbling about.

"Look at those guys," she whispered to Ann, "drunk this early in the morning."

"Football hooligans by the looks of it, ignore them."

No such luck, the group decided to come over and stand directly to the side of them.

"Hey Swampy," a bearded man called, "aren't there any trees for you to hug around here?"

Juliette swallowed nervously and looked down at Ann, "I think we should make a move."

"No way!" Ann cried, "I'm staying put."

"Bloody students," a different man yelled, "leeching off hard working folks wages, nothing better to do than stand around demonstrating."

"Get in the real world love," there were snorts of laughter and back slapping galore.

Ann had heard enough, she could feel the anger bubbling inside of her, "get lost you bozos," she yelled back.

"Ann!" Juliette reprimanded her, "shush."

"I will not shush," Ann replied tersely, "this is a peaceful protest, it's not going to be spoilt by a group of brainless hooligans."

"Who you calling a hooligan?" The bearded man strode towards them, egged on by his mates.

"Well I'm looking at you," Ann challenged, her eyes cold and flinty.

He towered over her, his mouth drawn into a mean line, "look lady, just because you're in a wheelchair, don't think I'm gonna let you get away with saying that."

"Well what *are* you going to do then? We have every right to demonstrate, I suggest you move on and leave us to it."

"Can you believe this broad?" bearded man turned to face his cronies, "maybe you need to get a life love, instead of worrying about this shite. Here," he thrust an alcopop at her.

Ann batted it away and it slipped from his hands, shattering on the floor.

"Uh-oh," the group of men sang.

"That's enough," Juliette said, heart racing, "leave us alone, please."

"Oh you're a pretty one ain't ya," he lifted a curl and fingered it slowly.

"Leave her alone," Will was beside her, with a frightened looking Evelyn and Sophie, grasping his arms to hold him back.

"Hark at this here kid," there was a bout of raucous laughter as bearded man sauntered to stand right in front of Will, "you going to make me boy?"

Will stared stonily back, into a pair of watery blue eyes. His fists were clenched tightly by his sides, as he watched the other man smirk, as his gaze travelled the length of him.

"Are you old enough to even be at university?" He chucked nastily, "there's a bit of baby fluff on your chin, better shave it off," he reached out to grasp Will's face. Instinctively Will stepped back and the other man stumbled forward, falling onto his knees. There was an audible gasp that emanated from the man's friends.

"Oh, you've done it now kid," one warned.

Will watched defiantly, as the bearded man struggled to his feet.

"I suppose you think you're funny, don't ya," the man rasped, "let's see if you can beat me at a fist fight then."

Before Will could reply, he felt a right hook collide with the tip of his mouth. Will dodged away from him, but the man was still advancing.

"Come on you pansy," the man snarled.

"Leave him alone!" Ann cried, attempting to wheel herself between them. Will's face was hot and he could taste blood; bitter and metallic on his tongue, but there was no way he was backing down. On the contrary, he felt a surge of anger rise inside him. Will indulged the rage, let it wash over him. For the second time in his life, he felt control slipping away. The first time he had lost it was with a nasty playground bully: Andy Mallett. They had both been fourteen and had quarrelled because Will had refused to let him copy his history essay. Blows had been exchanged and a visit to the headmaster's office had ensued. But ever since then Andy Mallett had left him well alone, even viewing him with a renewed respect. Now-a-days he greeted him like an old friend instead of a teenage foe. Thus Will realised the importance of asserting yourself and standing up to bullies. This bloke towered over

Will and definitely had the upper hand, where physical strength was concerned. He was broad and bulky, with huge fists and a fat, folded neck. But Will was lithe, quick and agile and not about to back down to a bully of the worst kind; one who abused women and a disabled one at that.

Young, reckless Will saw red and surged forward to rugby tackle the man to the ground. There they rolled on the floor, kicking and punching. Will raised his arms to shield his face, while around him the other men cheered their bloodthirst and the women screamed. Sophie and Juliette fell beside Will, trying to help him. Juliette grabbed a fistful of the hooligans jacket and tried to pull him away, but he shrugged her off roughly and she tumbled backwards, rolling towards the gutter, where she heard the sickening thud of her head, as it bumped against the kerb.

"Juliette!" She heard Evelyn call her name. Her sight swam for a few seconds and bile rose in her mouth as the back of her head throbbed with pain.

Seconds later a siren wailed and a group of policemen rushed forward, their batons raised.

The fight had spread and now there were about a dozen people involved in the fracas. Bottles were hurled against shop windows, where they shattered on impact. Sophie bit down on Will's assailants hand, adrenalin flowing. The man shouted a tirade of profanities and released his grip. He spun towards her, fists raised, ready to strike.

"The coppers," someone shouted in warning. Two policemen grabbed bearded man and bundled him into the back of a vehicle.

"Oh my god it's the riot van," gasped Sophie, "it's okay Will, the police are here now." She turned to thank a figure in blue, but he grabbed her by the arm.

"You better come with me missus," she felt strong hands push her into the van and looked around in shock.

"I haven't done anything," she called to a police officer, who was grappling with Will.

"You too son."

Will fell breathlessly on the seat next to Sophie.

"Are you o-okay Will?" Sophie stuttered. Her eyes scanned his face, his lip was bleeding and there was a purple bruise forming above his eye.

"Oh no, you're hurt," Sophie rummaged in her bag, pulled out a tissue and mopped gently at Will's mouth.

"Mrs O'Neill, Mrs O'Neill," someone outside the van was screeching her name.

"It's a reporter," Will mumbled, "duck behind me."

Too late, Sophie gaped as camera's flashed, blinding her with their vibrant light.

"Are you hurt Mrs O'Neill? How did it start? Did you throw the first punch Mrs O'Neill?" A barrage of questions filled the air, like rapid machine gun fire. Sophie was almost relieved when a screeching woman plonked down in front of her, shielding her from the camera's and further interrogation. The doors were shut firmly, then they sped away, horns blaring, across the city, heading towards the police station and the cells.

"Oh my god Will, what have we done!"

* * *

"Four hours later we were all released with a caution," Sophie was explaining to a concerned Evelyn the next morning, "public affray, can you believe it?" She gripped the phone to her ear and appraised her reflection, pale and lacklustre, after a grand total of two hours sleep. Evelyn drew her breath in sharply, "how is Will dear? His face looked terrible."

"I think he's okay," Sophie replied, "his Mom came to pick him up, said she was taking him to accident and emergency to be checked over. How was everyone else Evelyn?"

"Oh Ann was fine dear, angry as usual. I can't help wondering that none of this would have happened, if she had controlled her temper. Juliette had a nasty bump to her head, we took her to the first aid station at the uni, just to be checked over. She had quite a lump, but I've spoken to her this morning and she assured me she is okay."

"Poor Juliette," Sophie paused as she heard the front door rattle open, "I'll ring her later and Evelyn, you haven't forgotten that you're coming for tea tonight?"

"Are you sure dear? I don't want to be a nuisance."

"Not a nuisance at all, you are very welcome. The boys are looking forward to meeting you, so see you later."

Sophie rang off, then walked through the hallway, where Ryan stood, engrossed in the newspaper.

"Hi honey," she began, "I was just going to make a sausage sandwich, would you..."

"I don't believe this," Ryan cut in, rasping heavily, "you're page two in the local rag."

"Only page two?" Sophie joked, "well what does it say?" She leant towards him, trying to peer over his shoulder.

"Look," Ryan spluttered, holding the newspaper aloft. His face had turned an unbecoming reddish hue, "oh.my.god. They've mentioned the club and there's a full frontal shot of *you*. This is a complete disaster."

"Oh calm down Ryan," Sophie shook her head with annoyance, "it can't be that bad." She pulled the paper from him, then swallowed as she skimmed the page. "Local footballer's wife in mass street brawl," she read aloud, "Sophie O'Neill, wife of Chattlesbury Football Club's key striker, Ryan O'Neill, was arrested yesterday following a student rally which turned violent." Sophie gasped.

"You said you weren't arrested," Ryan accused, as he grasped the stair banister for support.

"I wasn't," Sophie replied with conviction, "the press are exaggerating as usual," she turned her attention back to the black and white print.

"Mrs O'Neill was seen by one bystander shouting profanities and attacking a man before police intercepted and took her into custody. A police spokesman declined to comment on Mrs O'Neill's activities, but did confirm that the matter had been dealt with and the Dean of the University had been notified. One witness described the students as behaving like a 'pack of wild animals.' A student ambassador told reporters that it was a peaceful demonstration against the spiralling costs of tuition fees and condemned the 'reprehensible actions of a small minority of students.' Chattlesbury University thanked the police for their swift action in diffusing the incident and stated that they strongly oppose all acts of violence, deeming them to be repugnant and inexcusable. An internal investigation is to be undertaken by the Student Union and measures are to be taken to ensure it does not happen again."

Sophie flung the newspaper away with disgust and stormed back into the kitchen, "I can't read any more of this tripe."

"This is terrible," Ryan wailed, placing his head in his hands, "I warned you not to get involved. I'm embarrassed of you Sophie, you're not some, some teenager and who the hell is this geezer?" He stabbed his finger at a picture of her comforting a dazed looking Will.

Sophie glared at her husband, "he's my friend Ryan and *we* were the innocent party, if you remember me explaining. Will was just defending himself and others. How often have you been in the tabloids with Mickey; boozing, gambling, wild night outs, general bad behaviour?"

"That's different honey. We're men just being men. You're supposed to be a lady."

"Sexist as well as stupid," Sophie muttered, as she slammed the fridge door and stared down at the oozing leg of lamb. "I'm starting tea. Evelyn will be here in a few hours and she's had a real tough time of it just lately, so try your best to be nice."

"Oh great, more student vigilantes and in my own house too. Why couldn't you have invited Amber?"

Sophie spun around, "and watch you two fawn over each other?! No thank you. Evelyn is a sweet, gentle lady. Stop being so ridiculous. Now, why don't you take the boys to the park, so I can get on with the cooking."

"I'm tired," Ryan snapped, "I think I'll just go for a lie down." He backed away, avoiding her steely gaze. Then his phone was ringing and all thoughts of his wife left his mind, as Chattlesbury Football Club's number flashed on the screen.

With a heavy sigh, Sophie began prepping for the evening meal, determined to make it enjoyable for her lovely, endearing friend Evelyn.

Chapter Thirteen

"I think we should tell him Will," Flora was hovering in the doorway, whispering to her spread eagled son. Will removed his bulky headphones and pulled himself upwards on the squeaky bed. He presumed that the 'him' referred to his father and shook his head in disbelief at her words.

"Are you crazy Mom?" He replied slowly, "he's still in a mood over the demonstration thing."

"Well now Will, is it any wonder? You were almost arrested and your picture *is* all over the local newspaper. You know how much he worries about us and his job. A good reputation is crucial to him, surely you can appreciate that." Flora paused to exhale shakily, "it was all over St Mary's you know, the staff, parents, all gossiping about your misdemeanour."

Will's mouth drew into a thin line, "I've explained what happened Mom, it wasn't my fault."

Flora scurried across to embrace him, "I know darling and you were terribly brave."

Will pointed to his bruised face; his swollen lip and his purple eye, "this is what bravery gets you," he responded with rueful acknowledgement. "I'm just thankful that nothing was broken."

"How is Hema?" Flora asked carefully.

"Mr Kumar's not speaking to her apparently and her mother's watching her like a hawk. Her brothers have threatened to kill me, but apart from that, she's fine."

"Oh Will," Flora sighed, "it can't be good for her or the baby, all this stress."

Will jumped up, "don't you think I know that? I've been racking my brains, trying to think of a solution."

Flora perched on the edge of the bed, "I've been thinking too Will and I have a suggestion to put to you."

Will turned to peer quizzically at his mom.

Flora swallowed, "move Hema in here with us."

"That would not work," Will's reply was swift and adamant, "we need our own place."

"How are you going to afford it Will," Flora implored, "it makes perfect sense, we have two unused bedrooms, one with an en-suite. This house is big, more than big enough for another person and a-a baby."

"It wouldn't work," Will sighed, "look Mom it's nice of you to offer, but what about Dad? How would he feel about Hema moving in with us? I doubt he would agree to it. He doesn't even know about the baby yet, for God's sake. He's going to go ballistic."

"Will, please don't blaspheme," Flora chastised him, "it's not as bad as it seems. Truly it isn't. I want to help you and Hema and as the baby's future Gran, I really can't see you destitute and out on the street. You would *all* be very welcome here. In fact I quite like the idea of having a baby in the house."

Will gawped at his mom, softening as he searched her face. He saw only kindness, love and sincerity, "but what about Dad? He might hate the idea and Hema – what will she say?"

"Leave your father to me," Flora said with determination, "talk to Hema," she urged, "let her know that she would be welcome here."

Will paused to think. The idea of living here temporarily was not entirely crazy, but the thought of his dad's reaction sent a shiver down his spine. Then there were her family to consider. What a mess! Will placed his head in his hands, blinking with frustration.

"Don't worry son," Flora soothed, "it will all work out. Let's deal with this," she clutched his hand firmly, "together."

* * *

Across the city Sophie was fussing over last minute preparations, namely the seating plan for this evening's grand dinner. She had decided to place Evelyn to the side of her, with the boys and Ryan opposite. She was in a fluster because her mother had decided to invite herself last minute, despite Sophie's protestations.

"Surely you have enough food to go around," Yvonne had whined, "I'm all alone here Sophie and I never get to see you anymore."

So without further argument Sophie had acquiesced and was now setting an extra place at the dining table. Fortunately it was a long table, which stretched the length of the room, seating up to twelve people. It was decorated with potted spring flowers, to add a dash of colour and in the centre stood a majestic candelabra, which Sophie only used for special occasions. The table cloth was pure white, soft and freshly ironed, the cutlery gleamed and the napkins were twirled elegantly. It all looked very sophisticated. Sophie had instructed Ryan to fetch champagne from the local wine store, who in turn had sent Derek, she wanted to spoil Evelyn, she wanted everything to be perfect.

Dwindling sunlight streamed through the French windows, adding a cosy ambience to the room. Sophie lit the candles and ushered the inquisitive dogs out of the way. Ryan stuck his head around the door and tutted loudly, "bit posh ain't it?" He then went onto complain about the table centre piece, stating that Sophie's candelabra resembled an artefact from the Victorian era. Sophie pushed him out of the way with a bounce of her hip and flounced into the kitchen, where the succulent smell of roasting meat bought a rumble to her stomach. Yvonne arrived early for a change, plonking herself down and grumbling about 'ghastly Roger and his sciatica.' Sophie was just about to warn her mother not to drink too much when the doorbell rang. Evelyn looked lovely in a grey cotton dress and pretty chiffon scarf. She had been to the hairdressers for a wash and style. It curled softly around her neck and had been tucked behind her ears to show off a pair of cluster pearl earrings. Sophie fussed over her, pulling out her seat and pouring the champagne into sparkling crystal goblets. The boys were behaving like angels; sitting still and chatting animatedly to Evelyn, even Ryan had forgotten his earlier truculence, he was charming their guest with impeccable manners and listening attentively as she described her home.

"It's far too big for me," she began shyly, "since Mam passed away, I'm afraid I've neglected it, the whole house needs a lick of paint and the gardens could do with a bulldozer."

Ryan laughed, "a property can never be *too* big."

"Ain't that the truth," Yvonne readily agreed as she slurped back her drink like it was pop.

Sophie jabbed him underneath the table, frowned at her mother, before turning to Evelyn with a concerned smile, "We have a gardener, I'm sure he could help, free of charge of course."

"That's very kind of you dear but I can manage."

Yvonne's eyes had lit up at the mention of Derek, "Oh Evelyn he's a terribly good gardener. Extremely conscientious and has the most perfect hands. He's promised to trim my bushes, so overgrown they are and I'm all alone too."

Ryan burst into laughter, "what about Roger?"

Yvonne lifted her nose, "incapacitated poor darling," her tone was haughty, "and Derek is so professional and gifted with all things green. Is he here tonight sweetheart?"

Sophie glared across the table, "yes, he's working mother and after that he's off home to his *wife*."

"Oh, I thought maybe he could join us for dinner," Yvonne suggested with over eagerness.

"Hey that's a great idea, I'll go find him," Ryan winced as another stiletto tip dug into his shin.

"Mother, would you like to help me serve the food?" Sophie said through gritted teeth.

Once they were in the kitchen she spun towards her, "he's not staying for dinner and that's final."

Yvonne backed away, palms up, "calm down darling, if it's the food you're worried about, I'd be happy to share mine."

"It's not the food," she said in a low whisper, "he's an employee, a married employee. Didn't you always warn me not to get too friendly with the staff?"

"Well yes, but Derek is like family darling. He told me that Ryan is like the brother he's never had. I think their relationship is sweet. But as for your housekeeper, I have my reservations. She told Derek she was going to see a male stripper the other day. A woman her age, fawning over half naked men. Isn't she married?"

"What Heidi does in her spare time is up to her," Sophie said, slamming the oven door, "maybe you should stop fawning over married men!"

Yvonne pouted, "It's just a bit of fun darling. Right now, with the burden of Roger's ill health, I need some excitement in my life."

"Just remember we have a guest," Sophie said with bad temper, "I want this to be a good night for Evelyn, she's been through a lot. Please be nice and behave."

"I'm always nice," Yvonne tossed her hair, picked up the vegetables, then strutted back through to the dining room.

Sophie was extremely pleased with the meal that she dished up. The lamb was mouth wateringly tender, the potatoes were crisp and golden, the veg was steamed to perfection and the gravy was dark, rich and full of flavour. It was a veritable feast, the finale was the most delicious shop bought summer berries gateaux with thick, whipped cream.

"Absolutely bostin," Ryan declared, as he sat back and patted his belly, "good job I'm at the gym tomorrow."

"That was delicious Sophie," Evelyn crossed her cutlery and wiped daintily at her mouth, "thank you very much."

"You are very welcome Evelyn, I'm so glad you enjoyed it and a little surprised it was such a success."

Ryan belched into his napkin, "she usually burns everything."

By now Ryan's lower legs were covered in bruises.

"More champagne?" Yvonne asked spiritedly, as she filled up Evelyn's glass.

Evelyn turned to listen to Josh and Jake, as they suddenly began describing their formidable teacher.

"She has white hair and false teeth and the biggest nose you could ever imagine. She has a basement in her house, where she locks up naughty children. She eats pigs hearts for breakfast, with sprouts."

Evelyn laughed loudly at the randomness of the conversation and the wide eyed sincerity of a nine year old's vivid imagination.

"Can we be excused pur-lease," Jake turned huge, pleading eyes to his mother, who waved them away with a happy smile. They bid good night to the adults, before charging up the stairs.

Sophie began clearing away the dishes, while Yvonne quizzed Evelyn about university.

"How do you find it darling?" Yvonne drawled, "being surrounded by young ones?"

"Mom!" Sophie protested, "there are a lot of mature students on the English course."

Evelyn chuckled, "anyone over the age of twenty one is classed as a mature student, it seems, but truthfully age is no barrier to learning."

"University is awesome, I've met some great people," Sophie reached out with her free arm to pat Evelyn's shoulder.

"And I've made some lovely friends," Evelyn agreed.

"Of course it's okay if you have a long term career in mind," Ryan piped up, "My Sophie wants to be a teacher. What do you want to do Evelyn?"

All eyes turned to Evelyn who stared blankly back, "well I'm not at uni because of a career goal. I haven't worked for years, I was Mam's sole carer you see and will be picking up my old age pension soon. An English degree is something I have always wanted to study. It's more for personal satisfaction than any long term monetary incentive and also, I just love reading and it will help with my erm writing."

"Evelyn wants to be a writer," Sophie said with a proud smile.

"A writer?" Yvonne echoed, "how wonderful. What kind of genre do you write? I adore erotica, can't beat a bit of smut."

"It's a romance mainly, with a sprinkling of mystery and adventure too."

"Has Dr Rivers read it yet?" Sophie asked, as she scraped a plate of scraps for the dogs.

"He hasn't finished it yet dear. He must be awfully busy with his lectures and his marking. I'm in no rush though."

"And busy with Juliette too," Sophie chuckled.

"Oh erm, I'm not too sure about that."

"Why? What's happened?" Sophie asked.

"I think they just had a fall out dear," Evelyn replied quickly.

"I *knew* something was up with Juliette. She's been in a weird mood for days. I hope he hasn't hurt her."

"What's this?" Yvonne eyes lit up at the prospect of gossip, "your friend is having a love affair with a lecturer?"

Sophie scoffed, "hardly an affair. They were both single."

"How exciting," Yvonne replied, a faraway look in her eyes, "maybe I should go to university. I need to meet new people."

"It's disgusting," Ryan burst out, "a teacher and a student, pure filth as far as I'm concerned, aren't there rules against those kind of shenanigans?"

Sophie rolled her eyes, "don't be ridiculous Ryan. Juliette isn't some vulnerable, love struck teenager. They are both mature, fully consenting adults."

"Still not right," he grumbled, "she's there to study and don't you get ideas about any fancy lecturers."

Sophie blushed as an image of Tarquin Haverstock accosted her thoughts, "well I think it's romantic."

Just then the sound of the doorbell chimed throughout the house.

"Who the devil is that?" Ryan sprang up and twitched at the curtains.

Sophie wondered why he was acting so nervously, "I'll go get it then, shall I?" She banged the plates down and trooped through the hallway. Whoever it was had given up using the doorbell and was now thumping rapidly on the door. A shadow was outlined through the frosted glass and Sophie realised that they were standing right against the frame, she could see their breath fanning out in wisps.

"Who is it?" She called, feeling a shiver of trepidation. There was no reply, just the sound of heavy breathing. Sophie called the dogs to her, one of which began growling. She slipped the chain over the lock and opened the door a crack. At first she was unable to see anything, except for the blinding ray of the sensor light, then suddenly a face appeared in front of her, eyes wide and frightening. Sophie squealed and jumped back, clutching her throat with shock. "Ryan," she called.

Her husband careered down the hallway, "what's up?" he demanded, "who is it?"

"I don't know," Sophie whispered, "don't open it."

The banging began again, this time accompanied by shouts, "I know you're in there Derek, answer this door or god help me, I'll bash it down."

"It's Del's wife," mouthed Ryan.

"Let her in," Sophie decided.

Ryan stood there motionless, "I don't think that's a good idea."

Sophie tutted, barged him out of the way and flung the door open. A wild eyed woman with bushy, dark hair greeted her.

"Hello," Sophie began, "I don't think we've met, I'm Sophie, Sophie O'Neill."

"I know who you are," the woman retorted, "where the hell is my husband?"

"Oh Derek's working…in the garden of course. Would you like to come in?"

"Too right I would," the woman stepped inside, bringing with her a trail of muddy footprints, "in there is he?" Without waiting for a response, Derek's wife stormed through into the dining room. Evelyn and Yvonne abruptly stopped their conversation to stare at the peculiar looking woman with the rain mac and riding boots.

"So which one of ya is it?" The woman voice had taken on a husky growl and she looked absolutely livid.

"Mrs erm," Sophie was mortified to realise that she did not know her own gardener's surname.

"Steeple, it's Mrs Steeple with three 'e's"

"Would you like to discuss this with your husband somewhere more private, I'm entertaining you see."

"Like someone's been entertaining my husband?" Mrs Steeple's face contorted into an angry scowl, "now which one of ya has been cavorting with him?"

Sophie noticed her mother's blanched countenance and trembling hands.

"Is it you?" Mrs Steeple pointed to Evelyn.

"Of course it's not," Sophie answered for her friend and stepped towards her protectively.

"Whose are these then?" Derek's wife dug in her pocket and threw what looked like a scrap of fabric down onto the table.

Evelyn looked down with shock at her dessert bowl, where a pair of red, satin knickers had landed.

"Because they certainly ain't mine," Mrs Steeple's face and neck was scarlet.

Behind her she could hear Ryan tittering, "go and get Derek," she turned on her husband, giving him one of her death stares.

For once Sophie's mother was sitting mutely. Sophie felt anger bubbling up inside her and longed to yell at her irresponsible mother.

Instead she breathed shakily, "I think there has been some kind of misunderstanding Mrs Steeple," she began politely, "would you like to sit down and maybe have a drink."

Sophie felt like grabbing the bottle and downing a mouthful herself.

"No, I would not like to sit down and don't try to placate me, I know Derek's playing around with someone." Her lower lip wobbled and Sophie felt a pang of sympathy for her.

"He's never at home, always here or down the pub. No time for me, mysterious phone calls late at night, then today I find these in his bed drawer."

Sophie did not know how to respond, but she certainly knew how Mrs Steeple felt. Hadn't she been feeling exactly the same way and worrying herself sick over Ryan's strange behaviour of late. Sophie felt a surge of antipathy rise against Derek and Ryan and every other male with a wandering eye.

"What's occurring here then?" Derek's gruff tone resounded from the doorway.

"I'll kill ya," Mrs Steeple spat in fury, "I know you're having an affair, don't try to deny it."

Sophie noticed his eyes flicker to Yvonne and prayed that Mrs Steeple hadn't seen the silent interaction.

"This ain't the time or the place for histrionics," Derek said casually, "I'm at work."

"You disgust me," Mrs Steeple screeched, hands raised like talons, she surged towards him. Derek dodged behind Ryan who looked as if he was enjoying the whole spectacle.

"No Mrs Steeple," Sophie held her back, "is he really worth this re-action, this upset?" The lady went limp in her arms and began sobbing loudly.

"You disgust me," Sophie shouted at her gardener, "you're fired!"

"You can't fire Del," Ryan spluttered.

"Watch me," Sophie replied with conviction, "get out!" Derek trudged out of the room, head bowed, mumbling sullenly.

Soon after Yvonne left, citing a headache as an excuse. Sophie waved her away, feeling furious. Ryan, longing to escape the distraught Mrs Steeple, offered sheepishly to take Evelyn home.

"I'm so sorry Evelyn," Sophie apologised as she hugged her friend at the door, "this doesn't usually happen at tea time."

Evelyn hugged her back, "I've had a lovely time dear. The food was delicious and poor Mrs Steeple, it certainly isn't your fault that she turned up the way that she did. I do hope that she will be okay."

"I hope so too," Sophie replied, "see you at university."

Once they had left, Sophie helped her reluctant guest into the kitchen.

"Whatever am I going to do?" Mrs Steeple said with a loud sniff.

"Everything will be okay," Sophie soothed, "here," she passed her a tissue, "I'll put the kettle on and we'll have a good chat. See if I can help you sort this mess out."

* * *

The following week heralded much excitement amongst the English students. The presentations for European Literature were due and the majority of the class were in the library preparing and running through last minute rehearsals. Ann was stationed in a study booth listening to Sophie run through her speech.

"Does it sound okay?" Sophie asked, she felt rather queasy, her stomach was in knots and she had been unable to face breakfast this morning.

Ann gave her a big thumbs up sign, "it sounds excellent."

"I am so nervous," Sophie said shakily, "I'm worried that I'll let you down Ann. You're so confident and articulate and you've been stuck with me."

"Nonsense," Ann declared, "don't make disparaging remarks about yourself. I'm sure you will be fine, but if you're struggling, I'll help."

Sophie smiled gratefully and looked through the glass to where Juliette, Will and Evelyn were seated, laughing and conversing, "I suppose we should join the others huh?"

"Yes, why not," Ann wheeled herself forward, while Sophie held the door open.

The topic around the table had moved from presentations, to discussing the disastrous demonstration rally. Melanie was sitting on the table, swinging her legs and chewing an over ripe banana.

"Apparently after the police left, the crowd pretty much dispersed. Leon Broome, the Student Union president was fuming, he had a twenty minute speech prepared and had managed to get one of the local councillors to speak on our behalf as well."

"I kinda' feel bad now," Will mumbled.

"It wasn't your fault dear," Evelyn smiled his way, "you were extremely brave."

There was a chorus of approval around the table.

"Uh-oh look out, here comes Megamouth McLaren."

The student union rep was heading straight for them.

"You'll be happy to hear that the Dean has decided not to take any further action," she began loudly, "of course he wasn't happy to hear that *some* of his students were brawling."

"They were defending themselves against an unprovoked attack," Melanie responded calmly.

"Yes," Ann interjected, "the press concocted a completely false account of the situation. It seems that wild exaggeration sell newspapers these days."

Megamouth McLaren sniffed with disapproval, "yes well, we haven't yet planned another rally but maybe next time you could give it a miss." With that she flounced off.

"I certainly will *not* be attending another student demonstration," Evelyn admitted.

"Neither will I," Juliette and Sophie said in unison.

"Oh I don't know," Ann suggested with a smirk, "I enjoyed the feeling of student camaraderie and rebelling against authority. It's just a pity that a small minority of yobs spoilt it for us."

The library's archaic clock began chiming and people flooded towards the exit.

"Looks like it's time for our first lecture of the day."

As they were collecting their belongings, Sophie nudged Juliette, "I think someone is looking for you."

Juliette looked up to see Ben Rivers leaning against the reception desk.

"Can I speak to you Miss Harris," he called, "in private."

"Oh," Juliette's stomach flipped, "I'm just off to my lecture."

"This won't take long."

He strode across and pressing his hand into the small of her back, directed her towards a vacant study booth.

"I heard that you bumped your head," he began, as he banged the door shut, "are you okay?"

"Yes, yes I'm fine. It was nothing."

"I hardly call a street fight nothing. Why didn't you tell me?"

Juliette stared up into brooding dark eyes.

"In fact, why haven't you been returning my messages?"

"I've been really b-busy," she stammered, a flush spread to her cheeks and guilt racked her.

"Too busy for your boyfriend hmm?" He stepped towards her, his hand gripping her own possessively.

A memory of an overheard conversation flashed in her mind and she felt a surge of anger, "I wanted to talk to you about that Ben."

"About what? Us?"

"There is no us," Juliette whispered.

Ben stared at her until she tore her eyes away, to stare down at the speckled floor.

"We're not right for each other Ben. We come from two totally different worlds," the wretched words slipped from her lips, while inside her heart was breaking. Do not cry, she told herself, as she bit down on her bottom lip and waited for his response.

"So that's it? I'm dumped?" His voice was cold, devoid of emotion.

"We can still be friends," Juliette pleaded.

With an incredulous look he turned away, "not fair Juliette, I don't know what's going on with you, but you know where I am when you come to your senses." He pushed the door open then was gone, striding away from her.

Juliette hung her head, overcome with misery, but her friends were still waiting outside and she needed to be strong.

"Are you okay dear?" Evelyn asked tentatively. No one was speaking, they were all watching her and the atmosphere was tense. Juliette shook herself, swallowed down the heartache.

"Come on you guys, let's go smash these presentations."

* * *

The class was full when they arrived, but they managed to squeeze on a table at the back. Right next to Carol the gossip and her cronies. Juliette groaned, took her seat and shuffled some papers to look busy.

"Are you all ready for the presentations?" Carol called.

"Oh yes," Ann replied with a sickly sweet smile, "let's hope you are too."

"What class have we got this afternoon?" Carol continued, with a nasty chuckle, "oh yes, Introduction to Poetry, with the hunky Dr Rivers."

Juliette jumped up and faced her foe, "you can stop with the nasty remarks because it's over between us. No doubt that will please you, so just shut up with your incessant bitchiness."

For once Carol was shocked into silence. Then Wilomena Smythe appeared at the front of the class and all attention turned to her.

"Right class," she clapped her hands three times, "I'm looking forward to watching your group presentations, so without further ado, let's get started!"

Chapter Fourteen

Wilomena decided to go round the class from back to front, so therefore Will's group were the first ones to present. Evelyn and Juliette followed him to the front, where the lecturer was fiddling with a microphone on a stand. She tapped it three times, before it rumbled to life.

"There you go," she said with a smile, "all ready for you."

Will opened his mouth to speak but Wilomena changed her mind and interrupted him.

"Hang on there young man, let's just add to the ambience," she dimmed the lights, then slunk to the back of the class, with her notebook and pen in hand.

Evelyn was petrified, her heart was racing and her hands were clammy, she wiped them on her skirt and stood focussing on Sophie's head as Will began the presentation. The minutes ticked by as he gave a brief overview of Norse Mythology. Then it was her turn to discuss the Valkyries, Odin and Valhalla and the bravery of Brynhild. The words flowed easily enough and with the help of the microphone could be heard over the sound of her knees knocking together. She breathed a sigh of relief when her turn was over and she could pass the responsibility on. Juliette was great; confident and clear, she interspersed her discussion with vibrant slides and pictures depicting scenes of Norse Mythology. The whole class were silent and listening with interest, apart from one occasion where a phone rang out, the shamed student was subsequently sent out of class by an annoyed Wilomena.

"Fantastic," Wilomena gushed, when Juliette had finished, "class, can we show our appreciation?" There ensued a round of applause and murmurs of approval. Evelyn hurried back to her seat and wished Sophie and Ann good luck, as they made their way to the front.

Ann and Sophie's presentation was on Celtic mythology and in particular the obsessive and disruptive traits of Celtic romance. Ann gave a brilliantly descriptive and lively overview of the Celtic history, then Sophie described the famous love affairs of Tristan and Isolde and Lancelot and Guinevere. Sophie struggled at first with her speech, she stumbled over her words and lost her place a few times, but with Ann's gentle assistance she managed to finish with confidence. Ann was talking about further reading for the students if they were interested, when Wilomena motioned to her watch.

"Sorry to halt you," she explained, as Ann wheeled past her, "we are working within a limited time frame, to ensure that all presentations can be fitted in, but Ann you were wonderful." Ann thanked her happily, then re-joined the others to watch the remainder of the presentations.

"That was excellent!" Ann commented, as they made their way down to the canteen for food and beverages.

"It certainly wasn't as bad as I imagined it would be," Evelyn replied, as she searched for a vacant table. The canteen was packed full, but they managed to find room on the squashy sofa's next to the exit. Juliette plonked her folder down, then made her way to the toilets. As she rounded the corner, she spotted Ben with his back to her. Juliette gulped and was just considering going to apologise to him, when she saw who he was talking to. Helena Mulberry looked sickeningly beautiful today, her hair was piled high in a sophisticated twirl and she was wearing the prettiest cotton dress, that showed off shapely legs and slim ankles. She was chatting to Ben who had his head bent towards her. Neither of them were aware of her watching. Juliette was over whelmed by a horrid feeling of jealousy, Brian Hodges' words rang in her ears, Helena Mulberry loves him too and how can I compete with her. She looked down at her faded jeans and old, comfortable cardigan and cursed her outdated wardrobe.

Quickly she ducked into the ladies, dug in her rucksack for make-up and comb then proceeded to cover her full lips in a pink rose hue. She widened her eyes with mascara, then smudged her cheeks in a plum glow. As she was loosening her hair and combing it out, the door opened and in floated Helena Mulberry. Juliette watched in the mirror, as she washed her dainty hands and smoothed her perfect, feminine clothing.

"Oh hello," Helena said, as she caught her eye in the mirror, "you're Juliette yes?"

"That's right," Juliette replied crisply.

"I heard all about the demonstration rally, I hope you weren't too badly hurt."

Juliette marvelled at the university gossip circuit and wondered if Helena had heard about her and Ben's relationship. Ex relationship, she reminded herself miserably.

"I'm fine thank you," Juliette replied, looking down at the stainless steel taps.

"Oh right, well have a good day," Helena nodded her way with curt politeness, before clacking out of the toilet.

Juliette breathed shakily, she loves him, she loves him and now that we are over she will hook her claws into him. Juliette rushed out of the toilet, but Ben was gone. Brian Hodges had accosted Helena Mulberry in the corridor, they turned to stare her way and he whispered something, before coolly nodding in her direction. Juliette held her head high and walked briskly past.

Back at the canteen, she joined Sophie in the jacket potato queue.

"Are you okay Jules, you look as if you've seen a ghost."

"I'm not feeling too well," Juliette replied, "I think I might go home after lunch."

"And miss Introduction to Poetry?" Sophie's eyes were wide and incredulous, "Jules, what's going on, what's happened, you and Ben were so happy."

"It's over," Juliette said through gritted teeth, "I really don't want to talk about it, I'm fine honestly. Apart from a splitting headache."

"Here," Sophie dug in her bag, "I always carry an emergency supply of paracetamol."

Juliette reluctantly took the tablets and washed them down with some bottled water.

"Now you can stay," Sophie said firmly, "I won't mention him again, unless you *want* to talk about it. You know I'm here for you right?"

"I know, sorry, I don't mean to be such a grouch bag, come on let's indulge ourselves with a pudding too."

* * *

Will was helping Evelyn dissect a poem, in preparation for their afternoon lecture, when he received a text from his mother.

'**I'm telling your father,**' it simply read.

A cold sweat broke out on Will's forehead, quickly he typed his reply, '**wait till I get home.**'

Flora had been pushing him all week to announce the news that Max was about to become a granddad. She had only gone and bought wool to start knitting a blanket and a book of traditional baby names. Now Hema was on his case too.

'**Have you told him yet?**' she had messaged him earlier.

'**I need to wait for the right time,**' he had responded.

Now she wanted to meet him, in about two minutes time. Will excused himself and made his way towards the courtyard. He jogged down the path, past clusters of students chattering and eating their lunch. It was sunny and bright, without a cloud in the sky and the temperature was steadily rising. Hema was sitting on a bench, surprisingly early. She looked so pretty, Will felt his heart constrict with love for her. Now she had passed the first trimester she had a certain glow about her, the sickness had abated and her appetite had returned. Her hair was thick and luxurious and her complexion was radiant.

"Are you enjoying that?" Will asked, watching with amusement as she chomped on a chocolate covered donught.

"I had a sudden craving for sugar," Hema replied with a smile.

Will took her in his arms, covering her mouth with kisses, she tasted sweet; sugary lips that responded with eagerness.

"How are things at home?" Will asked.

"Not good, Dad still refuses to speak to me and Mom just keeps shaking her head and tutting. They are finding it hard to accept Will, I'm surprised that Dad and my uncles haven't stormed down to your father's school."

"I *am* going to tell him, I was just waiting for the right time. He's always so stressed out just lately."

"I'm still shocked by your mom's proposal, it's very kind of her Will, to offer me a home."

"And not entirely crazy," Will said gently, "how would you feel about coming to live with us?"

"What about your father? He was against us from the start, I can hardly see him agreeing to me moving in."

"Well we can't live with your family can we," Will replied briskly, "let's see how Dad responds to the news first."

"*When* are you going to tell him though hmm?" She stoked his chin, "I'm starting to show and it won't be long until baby arrives. We need to buy things Will: a pram, cot, clothes even little things like nappies cost an awful lot."

"I'll tell him," Will vowed, "soon and don't worry about getting things for the baby, I have money stashed away."

"That was for a car," Hema protested, "you were so excited to get your own wheels."

"You are more important," Will reached across to place a hand against her protruding stomach, "and this one is going to have the best."

Hema laughed, leaned her head against her shoulder, "I'm happy Will, now I've got used to the idea. We're having a child and I couldn't be happier."

"You make me happy," Will hugged her tight, "I feel I can take on the world with you by my side." They sat in comfortable silence, listening to the sound of distant, rumbling traffic and birds chirruping in the trees overhead and Will felt contentment and deep love for the woman in his arms.

* * *

Juliette followed the others into the classroom, it was warm, the windows had been propped open slightly, allowing a gentle breeze to rock the blinds and lift papers.

"Shall we sit towards the back today?" She suggested with nervous unease.

Ann looked her way with sympathy, "of course Juliette, you pick the table."

Juliette sank into a chair with her back to the front of the class and sipped at her water. The room soon filled up, there was much chattering and laughing, the students were excited for the impending end of year one. She heard a voice greet Ben Rivers and immediately stiffened. Melanie the notetaker was looking her way, a frown creasing lines on her youthful forehead.

"Okay class, all eyes on me please, we have a lot to get through today," Ben's voice commanded silence. Juliette waited for him to start but there was no further noise. She realised that all the others around the table were looking her way and reluctantly turned around to face him. Brooding dark eyes flashed at her, making her head spin and her stomach somersault. Then he began speaking and with a sigh of relief she picked up her chewed pen and began making notes. The lecture was excellent; interesting and lively. Juliette listened as Ben read out a beautiful poem about unrequited love by W B Yeats. His eyes bore into her as he read the last line, 'for he gave all his heart and lost.' Then he snapped off the projector and mumbled to the class to take a coffee break.

"Phew!" Sophie announced brightly, "that was some reading huh?"

"Very heartfelt," Melanie replied, as her eyes flashed in anger towards Juliette, "it must be horrid to have your heart broken by a player."

Juliette opened her mouth to retaliate, but how could she explain what she had overheard.

Evelyn jumped to her defence, "well really a love affair is between two people and not really anyone else's business, we shouldn't judge."

Melanie's face softened, she leant towards Juliette, "why don't you speak to him, the poor guy is in bits," she whispered.

"I – I can't," Juliette scraped back her chair and fled from the room.

"Whatever has happened?" Ann asked, "is their relationship over?"

"It looks like it," Evelyn said with a sigh, "but I'm sure that Juliette has her reasons."

"You could cut the atmosphere with a knife," Sophie muttered, "maybe I should go after her."

"I think she needs to be left alone dear," Evelyn advised, "let's try and keep this low key, for Juliette's sake."

"Everybody knows anyway," Melanie declared, "Ben's not coping well with it, that's obvious, it's starting to infringe on his professional life too."

"Seems to me that it's their business," Will piped up, "maybe everyone should worry about their own lives."

There were nods around the table, then the topic of conversation changed to something more mundane, as Juliette made her way back into the classroom.

"Did anyone see EastEnders last night? What a cliff-hanger," Sophie began reliving the whole episode. While the others listened attentively, pretending not to be interested in the Ben and Juliette saga.

"Sorry," Melanie said quietly, as Juliette took her seat, "it's none of my business."

Juliette nodded, "okay," her eyes were drawn to the front of the class, where Ben had reappeared, clutching a cup of coffee. He looked as handsome as ever, his face was lined with stubble that added to his attractiveness. He was wearing a smart navy suit, a crisp white shirt that accentuated his dark eyes. But his face looked strained and his mouth was down turned. Juliette's heartstrings were tugged, concern for him overrode her own wounded pride. She considered going to speak to him, to apologise for her earlier abrupt behaviour, but then she noticed Carol watching her and the feeling passed, leave it alone, her conscience wailed, you've done enough damage for one day.

"So," she said, when there was a lull in the conversation, "my sister is looking for a part time assistant in her flower shop, no experience required, just a willingness to learn, creativity and a good eye for colour. Anyone interested?"

Will's eyes lit up, "I know someone who would be ideal. My Mom's been going to a flower arranging class for years, she's pretty talented and very enthusiastic."

"That's brilliant Will, ask her to send her CV to Marie's Memories, here, I'll jot down the address." She passed him a scrap of paper then froze as she noticed Ben heading their way.

"Evelyn," he began with a smile that had Juliette's stomach flipping madly, "I just wanted to congratulate you on your novel. What I've read so far is excellent, you are a talented lady."

"Oh thank you," Evelyn replied, as her fingers fluttered to her mouth.

"I would recommend that you send it off to as many literary agents and publishers as possible. Work through the Writers' and Artists'

Yearbook. I have a recent copy in my office if you would like to borrow it."

"Do you really think it's good enough to be published?" Evelyn asked, eyes wide with delight.

"I do," Ben confirmed, "it needs editing of course; grammar, punctuation and a thorough spell check, but yes the actual story line is brilliant, original and interesting. The characters are humorous and the style of writing is lively and engaging. I definitely think it has potential."

Evelyn clapped her hands with delight, "Dr Rivers, I must thank you for taking the time to read my manuscript, I thought you may find it boring, what with it being predominantly a woman's book."

"Oh no," he said with a laugh, "us men like romance too, we just won't admit to it." He stared at Juliette for a moment before turning away, "right then, let's proceed with the seminar."

* * *

Once the painful discussion of love poetry had finished, Dr Rivers went around the class handing out student satisfaction surveys.

"Could you please fill them in before you leave," he called over the excited chatter.

Juliette picked up her biro and stared down at the first question, on a scale of one to ten how would you rate the module overall. She quickly completed the paper, ticking mostly nine and tens. This wasn't due to bias, she truthfully believed the module to be stimulating and enjoyable and led by a well informed, articulate lecturer, who always endeavoured to make the classes interesting. The fact that he was also absolutely gorgeous would also help him achieve a good response, Juliette conceded with rueful envy, as she noticed a few young female students swooning over him.

"I'm off," announced Will cheerfully, stuffing his pens into his rucksack.

"Would you like a lift Will?" Ann asked, "Jon and I are going to the shopping centre, that's not far from yours is it?"

"Yeah, cool," Will replied, "give the bus a miss this evening."

He helped Ann towards the door, with the others trailing behind.

Juliette hurried past Ben, who had been accosted by students asking last minute questions on the final poetry essay.

They managed to squeeze into the lift together and hung on, as it whooshed them down to the ground floor.

"Jules and Evelyn can hop in with me," Sophie decided, "see you later guys."

"Well done again on the presentation Sophie," Ann called, as Will wheeled her down the exit ramp.

Jon was already there waiting, hazard lights flashing at double yellow lines.

"All the disabled spaces were taken," he complained, helping Ann into the passenger seat. A driver behind was papping with impatience, "yeah, yeah," Jon hopped back in and pulled away sharply. The traffic was busy, as lines of rush hour traffic built up on the main city roads.

"How are you mate?" Jon asked, peering into the mirror at Will, as he relaxed in the back.

Will grinned, "all good."

Ann was messing with the radio, flicking from station to station, in the hope of finding some music that reflected her positive, upbeat mood.

"The presentations went really well," she told Jon, "ah this will do," Ann settled for Queen playing 'Bohemian Rhapsody'. Jon immediately began warbling along, tapping the steering wheel in time with the fast tempo.

"So the adoptions really going through for you?" Will asked, "you're going to be parents?"

"Hopefully mate, we have everything crossed. It's just a waiting game, takes an age for everything to go through."

There was a slight pause, "what about you, is everything sorted now?"

Ann stared at her husband, a puzzled look on her face, "why are you asking Will that?"

"Ah, urm," Jon winced as he remembered that Will had confided in him, "sorry have I put my foot in it again?"

"Will?" Ann turned around to face Will who was shaking his head.

"It's alright Jon. It's going to come out eventually," Will raked a hand through his hair, "Hema's pregnant."

"Oh lord," Ann was taken aback, "and you're both happy about it?"

"Not at first," Will conceded, "it's taken a bit of getting used to, but we had the baby scan and it was just amazing."

There was a slight pause, as Ann digested the news, "so when is baby due?"

"End of August."

Ann smiled, "well I'm happy for you Will, congratulations."

"Thanks, but can you just keep it between us at the moment, there's a few people we still have to tell."

"Yes of course," Ann replied, "looks like it's not just us that's celebrating," she reached for Jon's hand, they linked fingers and grinned with happiness, while Will pondered on the best way to break the news to his father.

Flora was in the kitchen as usual, when Will arrived back home and let himself in. He could hear her banging about and singing along to Cliff Richard's 'mistletoe and wine.'

"Isn't it a bit early for Christmas songs?" He enquired with a grin.

"Oh Will, I'm just playing his greatest hits CD, you know the one your dad bought me for my birthday."

"I know it," Will replied, he had heard this song so often, he had memorised the words, "where is the old miser anyway?"

Flora tutted, "he's still working of course. Have you spoken to Hema?"

Will nodded and helped himself to a couple of purple grapes that were hanging from the fruit bowl, "she was touched by your offer

Mom and not entirely against it, we would rather have our own place though."

"You could eventually," Flora insisted, with a happy smile, "this would be a short term fix, until you've finished uni and got a job. I think it's an excellent idea."

Will took his dear Mom in his arms and hugged her gently, "you're the best Mom in the world, have I ever told you?"

"Oh get away with you," Flora batted him lightly, "you'll have me crying next."

"So, who is coming for tea?" He motioned towards the extra plates set out.

"Uncle Evan and his new lady friend," Flora replied with excitement, "I've made a chicken chasseur, completely from scratch and a trifle, won't that be lovely son?"

Will winced, "sounds great Mom, I'm going for a shower." He bounded up the stairs, with the dog chasing after him. As he was pulling off his clothes, he noticed a text from Hema flashing.

'**You have to tell your dad tonight.**'

'**Is everything okay Hema?**'

'**No, my dad wants to hold a meeting with your parents.**'

Oh cripes, Will felt a surge of indignation, we're not children, he wanted to yell.

'**Don't worry, I'll sort it.**'

Will threw the phone down and hopped across the landing into the shower. As he was towelling himself dry, he heard the doorbell ring and Flora welcoming uncle Evan.

"This is Grace," Evan boomed, as he introduced his lady friend, "now, where's the boy?"

Will froze on the stairs, annoyed by the patronising reference.

"Here he is," Flora replied patiently, "and he's hardly a boy Evan, he's nearly twenty."

"He's still at school isn't he?"

"University dear, it's a lot different."

"Hello Will," uncle Evan shook his hand firmly then slapped his back, "just got up?"

"You joker," Will said with a tight smile, "I've had a busy day."

"Reading books?" Evan replied with disbelief, "at your age son I was in the army, completing my training, crawling through fields of mud and learning how to shoot a gun."

"That was a long time ago," Flora said with a sigh, "thank goodness national service is no longer compulsory. Now come on through and make yourself at home." While Flora fussed over Grace, Will was left to entertain his bombastic uncle. Luckily for Will, Max arrived home just as Evan was wittering on about the good old army days.

"Will, Evan how lovely to see you both," Max said with a smirk, as he threw his coat over the balustrade.

Will breathed a sigh of relief and escaped into the kitchen to pour himself a lager.

He turned to look at uncle Evans new lady 'friend.' Grace was slender, tiny in height and stature, with flowing black hair and pencilled on eyebrows. She was wearing the oddest colour tights, a kind of dusky pink, which were teemed with a grey woollen skirt. She seemed nice enough though, she was smiling and chatting to Flora, as if they were a pair of old, reunited friends. Flora was asking how long they had known each other and Will was surprised when she replied they had met six months ago. The old bugger had kept that quiet, he thought with amusement. Evan was a widower, ten years ago Will's lovely aunt Rose had passed away. He still remembered the smell of her perfume now; sweet and fresh, she had been very similar to Flora; kind and happy, without a bad word to say about anyone. Will was glad Evan had found someone else though. It must be hard being alone, day in, day out.

When everyone had been given a drink, Flora ushered them through to the dining room to take their seats. She then proceeded to fill the table with a variety of dishes. Will stared at the burnt casserole and gave it a good stir before anyone else had noticed. He felt a pang of sympathy for his mom, she tried so hard, but cooking was definitely not one of her talents, but maybe something else could be.

"Hey Mom," he said as she passed round the extra crispy potatoes, "how do you fancy a job?"

"A job?" She echoed, "doing what?"

"Working in a flower shop, it's Jules from uni – her sister owns it."

Flora clutched her throat, "but Will, I haven't worked for twenty years, don't you need experience?"

"Nope," Will replied, with a shake of his head, "they are going to train the successful candidate up. You should go for it Mom, you certainly have the talent."

He pointed at the frames of dried flowers on the wall.

"Those posies are so pretty," agreed Grace, "it must be lovely to be a florist, such an artistic, interesting career."

"What do you think love?" Flora looked across at her husband, who was spearing a piece of broccoli.

"I thought you were happy at home," Max grumbled, "we don't want two stress heads in the household."

"I hardly think a part time position in a flower shop is going to stress Mom out," scoffed Will, "it will do her good to get out the house and have a bit of independence."

"I don't think I have much chance of getting it son, but I'll think about it," Flora said, there was a twinkle in her eye, as she contemplated making up bouquets *and* getting paid for it.

"You should have more self-confidence Mom," Will replied with a cheeky grin, "I think you have a good chance of getting it, so make sure you apply."

"So anyway," Uncle Evan cut in, changing the subject, "how is university going?"

"It's going okay," Will answered, "year one is almost over and I have to say I've enjoyed it."

"I suppose it's all late night raves, followed by afternoon lectures," Evan guffawed at his own wit.

"Nothing like that," Will said smoothly, "everyone works blooming hard, English is a difficult subject."

"And the second year is going to be even harder," Max peered over the frame of his glasses, "that's when the grades really matter."

As if sensing the atmosphere between father and son, Evan changed the subject again, "How's life in the primary sector dear boy? Still enjoying being a head teacher?"

"I wouldn't say I'm enjoying it," Max swallowed a mouthful of tough chicken, "the stress of course is phenomenal. Only last week, a head teacher friend of mine keeled over with a heart attack, teachers are dropping like flies with depression and anxiety, even the teaching assistants have been taking time off."

"I'm a teaching assistant," Grace cut in, "have been for fifteen years. The job role has changed so much since when I first started, before we were washing paint pots and giving out the milk. Now we are having to take classes and contribute towards the planning. It's mad."

"Well of course that's down to the government, they have been eroding the teaching profession as a graduate career for years now. Supply teachers are expensive, don't know the children and are a drain on resources, that's why teaching assistants are being utilised more for cover."

"I hope that you pay your teaching assistants then Mr Bentley, our head teacher doesn't even give us a thank you."

"Oh, urm, my staff do know that they are appreciated of course, extra potatoes anyone?"

The rest of the meal passed by, Flora was up and down refilling people's glasses, then bringing out the largest trifle Will had ever seen.

"Mmm," he said as Flora spooned a huge wad of oozing cream and sponge into his bowl.

"So Will, are you dating?" Evan questioned, "I would have thought a good looking boy like you would have them lined up, but when I asked my sister she said you were in between girlfriends."

"Oh Evan, that's Will's personal business, don't grill him," Flora replied for him.

"He doesn't have time for girlfriends," Max Bentley announced, "needs to sort out a career first."

"I can do what I want," Will said through clenched teeth.

"Max, can you get my glasses from upstairs? I have a headache start-ing," Flora frowned at her husband. Max scraped back the chair and plodded up the stairs. There was an awkward silence around the table.

Uncle Evan reached across to slap Will's back, "plenty of time for careers eh? You enjoy yourself."

Grace began chattering about her dreams of going to university, "I would love to do a film studies degree, cinematography fascinates me, purely for fun though of course. I'm thinking of enrolling when I retire."

"That sounds exciting dear," Flora replied, her face tilted at an angle.

Suddenly the door burst open, Max entered with a puzzled look on his face. In his hands, he clutched a paperback book.

"Why have you got a book of baby names in your bedside drawer Flora?"

Chapter Fifteen

Juliette was sitting on a park bench, enjoying the dwindling sunlight, when a rubber ball rolled at her feet. Seconds later a young boy raced towards it, and snatched it up with a playful look, then he was off, back to his friends on the grassy hill area, just adjacent to the round-a-bout. Juliette watched them as they threw the ball high to each other and whooped with laughter. She smiled and searched the crowds of children for Harry and Molly. The mild temperature and balmy evening had bought families to the park, dogs trotted on long leads and chased through the bushes after squirrels and other small rodents. She watched as a young couple strolled hand in hand, looking amorous as they gazed into each other's eyes. Juliette moved along to the end of the bench to make room for them. There was Harry, she could see him hanging upside down on a climbing frame, while Molly whizzed down a slide nearby. She waved at them with a happy heart, glad that she had given in to their pleads and bought them out into the fresh air.

Juliette looked down at the poetry anthology in her bag, she should really be studying, but essays were the last thing on her mind. Thoughts of Ben Rivers occupied her mind and she felt overwhelmed with guilt, but she was too proud to contact him, too embarrassed to admit that she had listened in to a private conversation and worked herself into a stupor over it. That she had acted rashly and their relationship was now over and she felt completely and utterly bereft. Yet deep down she knew she had done the right thing, Ben's career was in jeopardy because of her and for what? Just a feeling of fondness, why had he not declared his love for her? when she was damn sure that she loved him and would willingly proclaim it from the roof tops if he asked her to. No this was inevitable, it would never have worked between them; her living in a council flat with two children by another man, him in his middle class detached house and his bachelor lifestyle. So yes, Juliette knew it was the right thing to do; finish the relationship now before he had a complete grip on her heart, walk away with her head held high and a 'it was fun while it lasted' attitude. So why did she feel so miserable, why did she feel so heartbroken and lost?

"Are you okay sis?" Juliette spun around to face Marie.

"What are you doing here?" Juliette exclaimed, wiping at a sudden tear that had sneaked out of the corner of her eye.

"I went to your flat and guessed you might be here. You're just like Mom, can't abide being indoors when the sun is shining."

"Well I have to make the most of it, we don't get that much sun in this country," with that Juliette burst into tears.

"Hey, hey," Marie's arms wound around her, comforting and warm, "come on now, don't upset yourself."

Juliette nodded and searched blindly in her bag for a crumpled tissue, "I told him Maz, I told him it's over."

Marie sighed and sunk down on the bench next to her, "I think you've done the right thing, Dave does too. I know it hurts like crazy at the moment Jules, but you need to be strong. That guy shouldn't be letting other people run you down you know."

Juliette nodded, "you were right, about him, I don't know what I was thinking getting involved with an academic. My last serious boyfriend is an ex criminal, talk about polar opposites."

Marie chuckled, "you were blinded by lust and who can blame you, that guy was hot, I have to admit it."

"He was, he is," a memory of Ben covering her naked body with kisses flashed through her mind and she felt heat flood into her face.

"Looks aren't everything Jules, haven't I told you that? It's what's inside that matters, the way you behave and treat others around you. Sense of humour is highly over looked in relationships I believe."

"Like you and Dave?" Juliette chuckled.

"Exactly. Woo-hoo, I've made you laugh, mission accomplished."

Juliette leant her head on her sister's shoulder, "I'm so lucky I have you. Thank you for always being here for me."

Marie gave her a quick squeeze, "it's okay and you're going to be fine Jules, really you are."

"I am," Juliette said with determination, "the eternal optimist, that's me."

"That's why we all love you so much," they sat in silence for a moment, each lost in their own thoughts.

"How are *you* feeling? Are you enjoying being pregnant?" Juliette stared down at her sister's stomach, which looked the same as it usually did.

"I feel good," Marie replied, with the hugest grin, "no sickness so far. Sometimes I forget there's a baby in there, oh apart from I keep having a craving for Chinese rice, chips and gravy."

Juliette laughed, "it was hobnobs with Harry and liquorice all sorts with Molls."

"Dave is so happy Jules, he won't let me do a thing, I feel like I'm being wrapped in cotton wool."

Juliette smiled, then fell silent, happy for her sister but sad that she herself was alone. As if reading her thoughts, Marie gently pushed a tendril of Juliette's hair behind her ear.

"You'll find someone sis, there's plenty more fish in the sea."

"Oh yeah?" Juliette stared doubtfully off into the distance, "all the nice guys are either married or gay."

"Nonsense, what is it Molls is always singing, one day my prince will come? That applies to you too."

"I thought I'd met him," Juliette confessed, "I knew it was too perfect."

"Perfection is boring and highly overrated in my experience, no, what you need is a down to earth bloke like Dave, someone funny and kind, someone who'll take care of you."

"I won't be holding my breath waiting Maz and in the meantime, I'm concentrating on forging out a fabulous career and looking after what's important in my life." She pointed straight ahead, "those two."

* * *

Max Bentley was laughing lightly as he pointed at the book in his hands, "so, what's this Flora? Have you something to tell me?"

There was a deathly silence in the room. Flora glanced at Will who was gawping at his father.

"Well?" Max continued, as he flipped casually through the paperback, "why on earth would you have a book of babies names?"

"I…I," Flora was stammering and turning pink, "it just caught my eye that's all."

Max shook his head, "you and your antique fairs, haven't we got enough rubbish about the place?"

"It's not Mom's," Will said quietly, fists clenched underneath the table.

"Well it's certainly not mine," Max chortled, "but at least it's traditional names. You would never believe some of the children's names now-a-days: Sky, Blue, Summer, whatever happened to good old Elizabeth or Mary. I wonder if Max is in here…" he flipped through the book, "ah yes, here it is. Well would you believe it means greatest."

"I say, is Evan in there?" Will's uncle was unaware of the terrified vibes emitting from his sister.

"Yes it's Gaelic, meaning young warrior and Flora means flower."

"Oh how lovely," Grace clapped her hands, "and very fitting considering you would like to be a florist. This must be an omen Flora. I already know my name means Gods favour, but what does Will mean?"

"It's a shortened version of William of course," Flora cut in, "and it means strong willed."

"That is definitely fitting of my son," Max said with a laugh.

"Anyway," Flora jumped to her feet, "why don't Will and I clear away, then we could have a game of charades."

"Mom stop," Will said quietly as he screwed a napkin into a ball.

"Or maybe we could all go down to the Fox and Goose."

"Mom!" Will shouted. Everyone turned to stare at Will shocked.

"Don't shout at your mother," Max snapped, "have a bit more respect."

"It's okay dear," gabbled Flora, as she began collecting dishes.

"It's not okay Mom, it's time to be honest," Will stared defiantly at his father.

"What the devil are you on about?" Evan said as he scraped the remains of his trifle, before Flora could swipe it away.

"Will?" Max looked at him with questioning eyes.

"Hema's, well Hema is," Flora went to stand behind Will, placing a comforting hand on his shoulder, "pregnant." There, the words were out and Will felt as if a huge weight had been lifted from his shoulders.

"Pregnant?" Max scratched his head, "that didn't take her long. You've had a lucky escape there son."

"Who is Hema?" Evan looked at Flora with a blank expression.

Max answered for her, "Wills ex-girlfriend," then realisation dawned, "it's not...no it can't be."

Slowly Will nodded, watching as Max's pallor turned pale. There was complete silence, apart from the rhythmic ticking of the antique clock. A few moments later it chimed as it turned seven o'clock, but still the silence continued.

"Dad?" Will ventured.

Max Bentley shook his head, "you broke up Will, months ago, this can't be right, it must be someone else's."

"We got back together just before Christmas," Will spoke clearly, "Hema didn't want anyone to know."

"So you lied?" Max roared, fist thumping the table, "you blatantly lied, to me and your mother?"

Will jumped to his feet, "you're not exactly easy to confide in, are you Dad."

"This isn't my fault," Max blustered, "don't you dare turn this around on me and you Flora, you knew Hema was pregnant and you didn't think to *tell* me, your husband?"

"I…I" Flora was wringing her hands and close to tears.

"Don't yell at Mom, it's not her fault. If you weren't such a crap husband and father, maybe we could have spoken to you."

"I don't believe this," Max turned away from them.

"Soooo," said Evan slowly, "Will's ex-girlfriend is having a baby and it's his?"

"You're not helping Evan," Flora said shakily, "it's alright son," she patted Will's back.

"No it's not alright," Max spun back towards them, his face contorted in anger, "how is a nineteen year old, who can't even make himself a sandwich, going to look after a baby hmmm? Any suggestions, because at the moment, I'm finding it hard to look on the bright side."

"I'm sure Will and Hema will cope, with our help of course," Flora said.

"What about her parents, what do they have to say about all this?" Max fumed.

"They weren't happy love, Mr Kumar threatened Will, I almost rang the police."

"What??" Max shouted, "you mean her parents were here in this house and nobody told me. This gets worse. How long *have* you known Flora and how far gone is Hema?"

"She's five months," Will replied calmly, "and we're keeping the baby, irrespective of our age."

"Haven't you heard of contraception?" Max cried, flinging his hands up.

"Of course," Will retaliated, "it was an accident."

"We have to deal with this love, it doesn't matter how long I've known, it's done now, let's just stay calm and talk it through," Flora stared at her husband with pleading eyes.

"What about your career Will, uni?" Max leant on the table for support, "have you considered adoption?"

"That's it," Will had heard enough, he stormed past his father, shook off his crying mother, flung open the front door and left the house, heading outside, away from his parents, away from everything.

"Will, Will, come back please," Flora wailed, as Grace attempted to comfort her.

"So does this mean I'm going to be a great uncle then," Evan boomed, as everyone turned to look his way with disbelief.

* * *

Will dug in his pocket for his phone and shivered. He had left the house without a jacket and the evening air was cool on his skin, making it pucker into goose bumps. A couple walking their dog stared his way, as he increased his speed and broke into a jog.

'**Can you meet me?**' he text Hema, '**I'm at Jimmy's**'.

He turned down Franklin Avenue, up Main Street, heading towards his friend's house.

Jimmy answered the door looking dishevelled and half asleep.

"Will!" He exclaimed, staring his way, "you alright mate?"

"Not really, can I come in?"

Jimmy held the door open wide, "you look bad mate. Have you told him?"

"How did you guess?"

"I can tell by the look of ya," Jimmy shooed him inside, "Sadie' upstairs, we'll go in the kitchen."

Will waited while his friend broke the top off two lagers, "get down ya."

They supped on the bitter alcohol, "so what happened?"

Will relayed the incident, adding a few expletives as he described his Dad's reaction.

Jimmy whistled, "at least it's out in the open eh?"

"I suppose so," conceded Will, "It's so frustrating though, he treats me like one of his primary school pupils; always lecturing me on the way to behave, do this, don't do that, I'm sick to death of it."

"What about your mom mate, what was her reaction?"

"She's cool," Will said with a nod, "wants Hema to move in with us."

"Would that work though Will; you and Hema living with your dad?"

"Nah," Will replied, "of course it wouldn't. I'll just have to think of something else."

"Put yourself down on the council list, if you're lucky you might get a flat around here."

"Why does Will need a council flat?" Sadie was leaning against the door frame, wearing a shirt of Jimmy's, which just covered the top of her thighs.

"Oh it's nothing sweets," Jimmy threw her a warning look.

"It's alright mate, may as well tell her, she's going to find out in another four months anyway." Will pushed a hand through his tousled hair, "Hema's pregnant, she's due in the summer and we're keeping the baby."

Sadie's mouth opened and closed a few times before she found her ʾice, "OMG, you're going to have a baby? But you're so young."

ʾe're both almost twenty," Will replied through gritted teeth. Al-
Will thought highly of Jimmy, who he had been friends with
ʾry school, his feelings of fondness did not stretch towards
Sadie was a loud mouth, a gossip and completely ditzy.
ʾrised when they had hooked up, but who was he to
ʾh problems of his own, without getting involved
ʾs.

ʾ her out of the room, "I need to talk to Will
ʾd warm the bed eh?"

Sadie pouted but did as he directed, "maybe I'll drop Hema a text, make sure she's okay," she called as she plodded back up the stairs.

"Can I crash here tonight?" Will asked, spinning towards his friend, "I can't face my dad at the moment."

"Course you can," Jimmy replied, "a bit of breathing space will do you both good. Do me a favour though mate, text your mom, I don't want her banging on my door at two o'clock in the morning, when you haven't showed up."

Will nodded his agreement and fired off a quick message to Flora, telling her not to worry and that he would be back tomorrow.

Then the doorbell was chiming and Jimmy had disappeared to answer it, leaving Will to fret over the fallout at home. He hoped his poor Mom was okay.

"Will," Hema rushed towards him, arms outstretched. Will buried his face in the arch of her neck, she was warm, smelt sweet and fresh. Boy, was he glad to see her.

"You told him then?" She asked fearfully, her eyes were wide and her bottom lip trembled.

Will kissed her quickly, "it's done," he confirmed.

"Was it bad?" She asked, twining her fingers around his.

"Yep, what I expected, he hit the roof, raged about a bit, but at least he knows. You shouldn't have to hide away, I refuse to feel ashamed. This little one," he caressed her stomach gently, "needs us both to be strong, so from now on we do what's best for us okay? No interference off anybody."

Hema nodded quickly, gazing up at him with glistening eyes.

"Stay here tonight, stay with me and don't go back to them."

"Will I can't," Hema implored, "they'll come looking for me."

"I want to be with you," Will replied, his voice husky and emotional, "they can't keep us apart any longer."

"Shush," Hema placed a comforting finger to his lips, "we *will* be together, but first we need to make plans, we need time to figure out where we go from here. We're going to be okay Will, everything's going to be fine. Please don't get upset."

Will swallowed, "I'm okay, as long as you're by my side I'm good, no great. Did I tell you my mom's been scouring baby name books?"
"Oh that's sweet, at least baby has one grandparent that's excited."
"They're biblical names: Esther, Martha, good old Mary."
Hema winced, "maybe we could do a bit of research ourselves?"
"That's an idea," Will replied, his tone lightening, "hey Jimmy."
Jimmy poked his head around the door.
"Can we use your laptop?"
"Yeah course, it's over there," he pointed out a red Hewlett Packard wedged against a pile of books.
"Come on," Will said taking Hema's dainty hand, "let's go and make some decisions for ourselves."

* * *

The following day at university, there was much excitement between the English students. A notice had been pinned to the information board and also uploaded onto the Hive computer system, detailing an end of year trip to the Bronte Parsonage Museum.
Evelyn and Ann were in the library working on the remaining poetry essay.
"It sounds so exciting Ann, a trip to Haworth to see where some of the greatest writer sisters in the world lived."
"I've been already," Ann replied a little grouchily, "a beautiful place, but it wasn't very wheelchair friendly, from what I can remember."
"Oh," Evelyn's face fell, "so you're not coming?"
"No," Ann said with a shake of her head.
"But Ann that's not fair, surely if we complain, they may be able to organise a trip more suitable."

"Complain Evelyn? why I think I'm rubbing off on you at last." Ann grinned, "no, it's fine honestly. On that particular day, we have a meeting about the adoption, so I really don't mind."

"How exciting dear," Evelyn searched the table for her pen, which had rolled underneath her vast folder.

"How exciting for *you* Evelyn," Ann replied, "you've written a novel which has been endorsed by a respected academic, you must send it off, listen to Dr Rivers."

"I will, I mean I'm going to," Evelyn smiled, a sad bittersweet smile, "it's just I've been so busy with the house and organising Mam's affairs, I truthfully haven't had the time."

"How are you coping?" Ann asked in her usual, no nonsense manner.

"I'm getting there slowly. I still can't believe she's gone dear, I miss her so much."

"You're doing remarkably well Evelyn, you've hardly missed any lectures. Your Mam would be very proud of you."

"It's what she would have wanted; continuing with life."

"And you're succeeding Evelyn. The first year is almost over and look how well we've all done."

"You especially Ann. You will make a wonderful lecturer."

Ann smiled, "oh we all have our dreams. Some take longer to reach, but I'm sure we'll all get there. Now, let's crack on with this last essay and then we can relax and enjoy a well deserved summer break."

Chapter Sixteen

Sophie was carefully applying eyeliner and humming along to her pop party cd. On her dressing table was a plethora of make-up; expensive foundation and sparkling eyeshadow, three different shades of lipstick, which she would combine to create a killer pout. Her hair had been professionally styled and cascaded in soft waves around her shoulders and to top it all off, she had been into the city to purchase body shimmer from the huge department store. Now she just had to decide what to wear. The curtain rail was full of hanging, sparkling dresses, pick me, pick me they called. There was the blue one with the revealing split, which was gorgeous but the red jewelled short number was also exquisite. Then there was a long silver maxi number with a glittering bodice and a slinky black number with ruffles in all the right places. Decisions, decisions, Sophie gazed in the mirror, sucked in her cheeks and applied a sweep of soft plum blush.

Ryan staggered out of the en-suite, looking flushed from his power shower. He collapsed on the bed, stark naked and closed his eyes.

"You can't sleep now," Sophie screeched, "help me decide what to wear."

Her husband opened one eye and glanced at the row of dresses.

"Red one," he said with a predictable wink.

"I think the silver one. I've got some lovely glittery sandals which will go perfectly."

"Why don't you show off your legs," he replied with a yawn, "you've got a lovely set of pins."

Sophie smiled at his compliment, "I wore the red one at the last Football party. How about the black? It's very classy."

"Will you wear stockings with it?" he enquired, interest piqued.

"I might do," Sophie teased, "if you're lucky."

"Go for the black then,"

Sophie nodded happily and picked up the first of the lipsticks.

"Erm Soph," Ryan began softly, "I was wondering if you would agree in reinstating Del."

Sophie frowned at the mention of their sacked gardener.

"I don't know Ryan, have you forgot what happened with his wife the other week? The poor woman was distraught. He's become way too familiar with my mother and his work has been slacking."

"Isn't that their business," Ryan wheedled, "they are grown adults. Who are we to judge?"

"When it's bought to my door, it *is* my business. Poor Evelyn must have been traumatised witnessing that altercation."

Ryan laughed, "you gotta admit, it was funny. Your mom's face was priceless, especially when she threw her knickers on the table for everyone to see."

"Yes well, hopefully Mom has come to her senses. As for Derek's job, I'll think about it."

"Great," a twinkle appeared in Ryan's eyes, "Hasn't your mom given Roger Sciatica the boot yet?"

"I have no idea," Sophie answered humourlessly, "I haven't spoken to her since it all kicked off."

"She's babysitting tonight though right?"

Sophie sighed, "she insisted. Please don't mention Derek, we don't want to encourage her with this crazy infatuation. I just wish she would spend some time on her own."

Ryan shrugged, "some women need a man to look out for them."

"I suppose so," Sophie agreed, "anyway, have I told you about the class trip to Haworth?"

"Where the blooming eck is Haworth?"

"Up North somewhere, I think. Oh Ryan it sounds so exciting, we're going to the Bronte Parsonage Museum – Emily, Charlotte, Ann?"

Ryan stifled another yawn, "who's Emily Bronte, is she dead?"

"Yes, she's dead," Sophie tutted, "she was the most fantastic writer. Jules leant me Wuthering Heights, I couldn't put it down, so dark and passionate. Then there's Jane Eyre, which was written by her sister, I've got that on my to be read pile."

"I hope there's not going to be any trouble in Haworth. You're not demonstrating again are you?" Ryan pulled himself up into a sitting position.

"Of course not! It's an educational visit."

Suddenly the dogs burst into wild barking. Ryan was up peering out of the window.

"It's just your mom," he said with relief.

"Who were you expecting? You had better get dressed then, or she'll be developing a crush on *you* next."

Will hurried into his dressing gown and went downstairs to let Yvonne in. A few minutes later, there was footsteps on the stairs, "coo-eee, can I come up?"

"Yes Mom," Sophie called, as she blotted her lips on a piece of tissue.

"Oh darling what beautiful dresses," Yvonne gushed, as she stepped into the room.

"Thanks Mom, I'm wearing the black. How are you?"

Yvonne air kissed her daughter's cheeks, "I'm okay darling. I have the most wonderful news."

Sophie paused in her beauty ministrations to gaze at Yvonne.

"Roger has left."

"Oh Mom, well maybe it's for the best. He wasn't making you happy after all."

"It certainly is for the best," Yvonne replied, "it wasn't working between us and the feelings had completely gone, we were more like nursemaid and patient."

"Well then, now is your chance to be an independent woman," Sophie said with fervour, "maybe you could enrol at night college, spend time with girlfriends. Haven't you always wanted to be a yoga teacher? Follow your dreams Mom, it's never too late."

Yvonne laughed, a girlish high pitched giggle, "me at night college? I don't think I could bear it darling, homework at my age? No silly, I'm not alone. Derek's moved in and everything is just perfect."

Sophie gaped at her mother, "have you gone completely mad?" She squeaked.

Yvonne clutched her throat theatrically, "do you always have to be so negative Sophie? Of course I haven't gone mad. In fact, I feel completely sane and certain about this one. Derek and I have spent a lot of time together talking and erm, well let's just say the spark is definitely there between us."

Sophie grimaced at the sexual innuendo, "he's married Mom, what about his poor wife!"

"He's not happy with her, hasn't been for a long time," Yvonne sniffed, "I know you don't approve Sophie, but Derek and I, we have a connection. He makes me feel young again."

"Probably because he's half your age," Sophie pointed out.

"He makes me happy," Yvonne insisted, wiping at her eyes with a lace handkerchief, "can't you just be pleased for me?"

Sophie sighed with resignation, "I suppose so."

Yvonne grinned, "hoo-ray! I'm not a child darling, you don't need to worry about me."

"Oh but I do," Sophie replied, "just be happy Mom and... and try not to hurt others in the process okay?"

"Yes daughter," Yvonne wrapped her arms around Sophie's shoulders, "you look beautiful by the way. Go on and enjoy your night – have a ball."

* * *

The end of season football dinner was held in the most prestigious banqueting suite that Chattlesbury Football Club owned. It was a magnificent room with a crystal chandelier, sumptuous carpets and a posh polished dance floor. Running the whole length of the room were glass sliding doors, which directly led to the stadium balconies, from which the entire football pitch could be seen. Sophie was out there, surveying the thousands of tiered seats, the huge floodlights, the gigantic screens and the emerald green, grassy carpet before her. It was an impressive sight and a shiver ran down her spine as she thought of her Ryan playing football here in front of thousands of spectators. He was still at the free bar, socialising with his footballer pals, she could see Mickey lining up the shots, while yelling down her husband's ear. The doors slid open and a group of young women clattered onto the terrace. Sophie smiled politely at them, not recognising the faces. They were new girlfriends, accompanying new players, brought in to shake up Chattlesbury Football Club. To try to help get them up into the premiership. Sophie listened for a while to their small talk, before she wandered back inside, searching for their table.

After a quick peer at the seating plan, she made her way to table number two, which was directly in front of the stage. There were a few people already dotted around the large, oval table, drinking and talking. Sophie slid into her seat and smiled brightly at a red headed, buxom lady to the left of her, before helping herself to a large glass of champagne. She was relieved to see Ryan wandering across the dance floor in her direction and waved to grab his attention.

"Honey," he drawled, planting a kiss on top of her head, "this is Coach Malone's wife."

Sophie suddenly remembered that dear coach Jones, who had devoted half of his life to Chattlesbury FC, had been replaced.

"Hello there," Mrs Malone said in a plummy, posh accent, "call me Muriel, please."

Sophie took her proffered hand and shook it gently, "Sophie...Sophie O'Neill."

"Oh gosh yes of course, you're the main man, the one with golden feet," she nodded up at

Ryan, "I've heard all about you."

Ryan threw her one of his most charming smiles, "all good I hope."

Muriel nodded, but Sophie noticed a glint in her eye, "and you're his lovely wife, a model I hear?"

Sophie almost spat the champagne from her mouth, "I think you have me confused with someone else. I've never done any modelling."

"But you could have honey," Ryan gushed, colouring slightly, "remember the time that agent approached you at a match and gave you his card?"

"Yes, he was a scout for a topless modelling agency and remember I told him where to stuff his card," Sophie replied sweetly.

"Good for you," Muriel interjected, "so what *do* you do Sophie? please don't tell me you shop all day and visit beauty salons."

"I have been guilty of that in the past," Sophie conceded with a laugh, "I'm a student studying English."

"What, here at Chattlesbury university?"

"That's the one," Sophie grinned.

"A fabulous university!" Muriel gushed, "my daughter is in her second year, studying sociology."

Sophie was shocked she had a daughter old enough to be at university, Muriel's face was like porcelain; smooth and devoid of lines and wrinkles.

"This is my first year." Sophie said with a nod, "it *is* a wonderful university. I've met some amazing people there."

Ryan nudged her, "nearly as interesting as the footballing world – eh?"

Sophie remained silent, but Muriel piped up with a scathing, "really?" Sophie decided she liked Muriel.

* * *

Half an hour later everyone was seated and the first course was served; caviar with toasted crackerbread and a red onion dressing. Sophie stared down in dismay at the food on her extremely posh plate, pushing it around with her fork.

"This is seafood, right?" Sophie whispered to Muriel.

"I presume so," Muriel replied, "revolting by the looks of it. Shall we have champagne and crackerbread instead?"

Sophie giggled and held out her glass.

"So," Muriel began as she chomped on the cardboard like bread, "what are the lecturers like on the English course? The sociology ones are a quirky bunch from what my Gwennie has told me."

"Absolutely brilliant," Sophie replied, "extremely knowledgeable, clever, make the lectures interesting. I really can't fault them and they were so good when I had the trouble with the press."

"Ah yes, the press can be an intrusive lot, but glad the university could help."

"The course leader was fantastic," Sophie gushed dreamily, "so supportive."

"Really," Muriel glanced her way with interest, "what's his name? I might know him."

"Tarquin Haverstock, he's a bit of a hippy but a lovely, lovely man. Small, blonde hair, piercing eyes, dazzling smile..." Sophie trailed off.

Muriel stared at her for a moment, "I know him, he's a relative of a close friend."

"Really?" Sophie was curious and excited, both at the same time.

"Yes, Mr Haverstock is quite the romantic hero. A proper gentleman," she pointed around the table, "not like these lot here."

"Oh, I really don't know him that well," Sophie felt a sudden pang of guilt and looked towards her husband, who was talking animatedly to coach Malone.

"He had his heart broken you know," divulged Muriel, "spectacularly."

"What happened?" Sophie was all ears.

"His fiancée, she died. Leukaemia, terrible it was. Never been in a relationship since and that was almost a decade ago."

"How awful," Sophie declared, "the poor man."

"Yes," Muriel crossed her cutlery together, to signify to the hovering waiter that she was finished, "he's been through some tough times. Anyway, enough maudlin gossip, we need to get rid of this awful caviar aftertaste - care to dance?" Sophie looked up at Muriel who was already on her feet, shimmying around. She allowed herself to be dragged onto the dance floor, where they began bopping to the up tempo beat. The dance floor was empty, Sophie smiled self-consciously, smoothing her dress down, but Muriel seemed oblivious to the other people in the room, she was flinging herself around energetically, making Sophie laugh in the process. Then she noticed Ryan bent over one of the women on their table; a striking brunette with an impressive cleavage, her smile faltered as she watched them flirting with each other. Muriel it seems had noticed too.

"Take no notice of her, a desperate, lonely woman who loves any male attention."

Sophie sniffed with disapproval, "it looks like Ryan is encouraging her."

Muriel tutted with sympathy, but declined to comment. Sophie had the uncomfortable feeling that the new coach's wife knew more about her husband than Sophie would have liked. There was an aura of disapproval emanating from her, each time she looked Ryan's way.

"We'd better sit down," Sophie decided suddenly, "looks like the main course is on its way."

Duck a la orange with a rosti potato tower and spring vegetables was served next. Sophie ate the whole thing and washed it down with copious amounts of champagne. The portions however were tiny and she was still hungry by the end of it.

"I detest this nouveau cuisine," Muriel complained, "give me old fashioned pub grub any day. Can't beat a man size pie and mash." Sophie laughed, remembering all the times she had starved herself on one faddy diet after another.

The group of women opposite had left half of their meals, one of them; a painfully thin, well known model, had only ate her vegetables and orange sauce. Sophie watched them as they trooped out to the terrace for their fifth cigarette.

"Those poor, deluded women," Muriel whispered, "they think being stick thin will get them a rich husband?"

"I used to be like that," confessed Sophie, "always worrying over my figure, but since I've started uni, I've realised there are more important things in life."

"Thank Christ you came to your senses," Muriel belched behind her fist, "I come from a long line of chefs, was encouraged to indulge and enjoy food, hence my appearance."

"You have a lovely figure," protested Sophie, "you're curvy and womanly."

"Ain't that the truth," Coach Malone was patting his wife's hand, looking at her with tender pride.

"What do you think Ryan?" Sophie piped up, feeling a sudden surge of anger for her vain husband, "women shouldn't have to constantly worry about their weight – agree?"

Ryan took a swig of beer and viewed Sophie with an air of arrogance, "there's nothing wrong with looking after yourself honey."

"Yes, but true love is based more on just good looks and a toned physique, don't you think?"

"Oh get off your soapbox, you're not at university now."

Sophie gasped at her husband's words and his bitter tone, furious that he had publicly humiliated her. Muriel glanced sideways at her with sympathy, "more champagne?" She refilled Sophie's glass without waiting for a reply.

"I think I need the bathroom," she said as she scraped back her chair.

Sophie weaved across the dancefloor and into the luxurious ladie's powder room. She locked herself in a cubicle and fumbled in her bag for a tissue. Tears were stinging the back of her eyelids and she berated the way she had spoken at the table. It was Ryan's night not hers. It was his turn to shine and here she was, her head full of university and Tarquin Haverstock. Too much champagne had loosened her inhibitions and bought out her angry side. Her head was starting to throb and as she scrutinised her reflection in her compact mirror she noticed her cheeks were bright red.

The sound of the door squeaking open intruded her thoughts and she heard a chorus of high pitched girlish laughter.

"Wow, this party is just awesome," one breathless girl announced.

"I know right and the footballers are so totally gorgeous," another replied.

Sophie smiled to herself and was just about to open the door when she heard her husband's name mentioned.

"Ryan O'Neill is looking extremely handsome tonight girls, don't you agree?"

There was a chorus of approval.

"I feel for his poor wife though."

"Why what's happened?"

There was a pause, "well I shouldn't really say, but he's completely unfaithful to her isn't he?"

"No way!" There was a shocked silence.

Sophie's heart began thudding and the blood whooshed through her ears.

"I mean she's totally gorgeous, why would he cheat with club groupies?"

"I heard she's a bit of a battle-axe, totally up herself and did you hear the way she was bragging about being at university. Why would you want to study with all that money?"

"Maybe she doesn't satisfy him?" There was a gaggle of cruel laughter.

Sophie flung open the cubicle door, "and maybe you should check there's nobody listening before you gossip about other people's marriages," She stared with anger at the small group of women. The nearest to her opened her mouth and stared at Sophie with shock, while another mumbled an apology.

"Oh, don't let me stop you," Sophie said with a sweep of her hand, "I'd love to hear where you get your information from."

"It's just rumours that's all," the blonde with a face that looked as if it was in pain simpered.

"That's crap and you know it," Sophie blew out her anger, "how many?"

There was complete silence. Sophie turned on the taps, splashed cool water on her face, oblivious to the make-up which began running down her cheeks in rivulets.

"How many groupies has my husband shagged?" She spoke slow and calm, while inside her stomach churned.

"Just the two I think," the one nearest to her mumbled.

Sophie almost chuckled at their indifference, "oh that's okay then, here's me worrying it was double figures." The sarcasm dripped from her, "just go." When they made no move Sophie bellowed, "GO!"

Then she was alone, shaking with fury and a strangely triumphant sense that she had been right all along. She had not been paranoid, he *had* been screwing around after all. Suddenly bile rose into her throat and she stumbled forward to bend over the lavatory and regurgitate the entire contents of her lavish meal. Once she had finished retching, she felt better; in control and calmer. Quickly Sophie swilled her hands, then with her head held high walked purposefully from the toilet. On the way she paused at a vacant table to pick up a deserted pint of beer, then carried on, weaving across a now packed dancefloor. Ryan was sitting where she had left him, signing autographs for some dizzy looking blonde, his smile saccharin sweet as he conversed with his adoring public. Sophie felt a surge of bitter anger rise and she almost stumbled. From the corner of her eye she noticed Muriel gazing her way, apprehension dawning in her eyes, as she realised what Sophie was about to do. Sophie didn't think, didn't give herself chance to consider whether her actions were the wisest. The glass tipped in her hand as she stood behind him. Whoosh! Brown liquid covered Ryan's head and shoulders, spattering the pristine white tablecloth. The lady he was with shrieked and jumped away as foam landed on her micro mini dress.

"What the…" Ryan gasped, the shock of the cold liquid leaving him breathless. He spun around to face his wife, his eyes widening in shock as he registered the anger, the coldness in Sophie's steely gaze.

* * *

The bouncers asked them politely to leave.

A hundred or so pairs of eyes watched them both being escorted from the lavish room, down the stairs and out through the wide reception doors.

"Calm down," one warned, "or we'll call the coppers."

"Call a taxi and go home," the other advised.

Ryan was immediately on the phone to Derek, jabbering into the ear piece.

"Yes Derek I need you to come now…I know it's early, just come." Ryan cut the call, flipped his phone shut and stared hard at Sophie.

"What the hell are you playing at? I was only talking to her Soph, you really need to get a hold on your jealousy."

"Oh yeah, just talking were ya?"

"Look at the state of me, I've never been so embarrassed in my life."

"Now you know how I feel," Sophie yelled, feeling completely out of control.

"What? You need to go to the Doctors babe," Ryan was genuinely puzzled by his wife's behaviour, "and maybe give up the booze. How dare you throw a drink over me, in front of everyone too. What's coach Malone going to think?"

"I couldn't give a monkey's what anyone thinks," Sophie sobbed, the tears flowing freely, "how about considering my feelings. Did you think about me while you were having grubby affairs?"

Ryan stopped pacing, swallowed nervously, "don't know what you're on about. You're drunk!"

"Not drunk enough," Sophie spat out, "I know Ryan, I know all about your dalliances with... with groupies."

"Babe you've got this all wrong," Ryan held out two placating hands and made a move towards her.

"Keep away from me," Sophie said with quiet determination, "it's true isn't it? You've cheated on me and more than once."

"It's just vindictive gossip," Ryan said wildly, "jealousy, that's all this is. People trying to stir it up, trying to cause trouble between us."

"Look at me Ryan, look at me and tell me the truth."

A silence stretched between them, Sophie watched a muscle twitching in Ryan's jaw. His eyes were wide with fright and his lips drawn into a tight line, as if he was afraid to speak.

Sophie knew it was true then, he had never been a good liar, even with all his practise.

"I want you out the house. Tonight," she walked away, clacking down the drive, not sure where she was going but desperate to get away, for time alone to think.

"Sophie," Ryan called her, "it was nothing babe, it meant nothing, it's you I love."

Sophie spun towards him, digging in her pocket, her fingers wrapped round her lipstick, she hurled it at him, "you disgust me. Our.Marriage.Is.Over."

With those words she turned away, wiping at the tears cascading down her cheeks. Sophie forced her legs to move forwards, walking until she reached a lamppost which she leant against for support. The light above her flickered and she watched as cars on the main road whizzed past.

"You alright there love," it was the burly bouncer, standing hesitantly nearby, "come inside, I'll make you a cuppa and we can ring you a taxi." Sophie allowed herself to be led gently back inside, Ryan had disappeared, but the party was still raging on, muffled music floated down from the upper levels. Sophie accepted the tissue that was thrust at her, while her benefactor made a quick call, she placed her head in her hands, numb with shock; what the hell was she going to do now?

Chapter Seventeen

Will was woken to the sounds of the radio; chattering voices and cheesy adverts pulled him from a fitful slumber. He sat up feeling groggy and lightheaded from lack of sleep. The cold leather sofa had offered little comfort throughout the night. He had almost fallen off a few times and woken up with one arm and leg dangling precariously. The evening had stretched interminably slow, he spent much of it watching eerie shadows creeping along the walls and ceilings and listening to the sounds of creaking, emanating from the bedrooms above. It seemed each hour that passed the room grew darker, a full moon peeped from behind silver clouds that slowly drifted by. At one point, Will could have sworn he had seen a fox, peering in at him through the French windows, then it had vanished and Will wondered if it had been a trick of his over tired imagination. By five O'clock Will was wide awake, fretting over Hema and replaying his father's reaction. As a distraction, Will decided to explore Mrs Forsyth's opulent bookcase. Much of it consisted of romances, but right at the bottom, wedged into a corner he found a hardback copy of 'Ash' by James Herbert. He snapped on the lamp and settled back to lose himself in a tale of horror that had him gripped. He hardly noticed the sounds of his friend Jimmy rising and padding softly down the stairs.

"Good book?" Jimmy was standing in the doorway, a cup of steaming coffee in his hands.

"What time is it?" Will asked, as he folded an edge of the page over.

"Just gone six," Jimmy replied with a casual shrug, "Dad and me are off out to work in a bit."

Will swung himself into a sitting position, "and I should get going. Thanks for letting me crash mate."

Jimmy patted him on the back, "no problem, I hope you can sort everything out."

"That's what I'm about to do," Will said with determination, "can I borrow this book?"

Jimmy looked down, "yeah, it's one of my Dad's, don't think he ever finished it."

"It's good," Will grinned, "give me a break from reading the classics."

"So text me yeah," Jimmy said, as he passed Will his coat, "if you need any help, advice or just a game of pool."

"Will do," Will was already bounding out of the door, full of youthful energy, "cheers mate."

The streets were quiet, with only a few early morning dog walkers out. It was still dark, the lamp lights buzzed as he jogged underneath them, all around him curtains remained closed as people slept on, warm in their beds. Will glanced down at his phone. He had two missed calls from his mom and a cute message from Hema, telling him that she loved him. Will slowed his pace as he neared his house, he noticed that the whole of the house was bathed in light, which streamed through gaps in the curtains. Once he was halfway up the path, the dog was barking as she sensed his imminent arrival. Flora was already there, door wide open a look of pure relief on her face.

"Oh Will," she began, embracing him tightly, "I've been so worried."

Will noticed her tired countenance and felt a surge of guilt. "I'm fine Mom, I just needed some space."

"Will, your Dad and I, we've been talking, most of the night actually. I think he's come round to the idea."

"He's going to have to," Will said curtly as he extricated himself from her grip, "where is he?"

"I'm here," Max stood in the hallway, tall and imposing, "come through Will, we need to talk."

"Haven't you got to get off to St Mary's?" Will mumbled as he trooped into the kitchen.

"Not for an hour at least," Max sank down in a chair.

"I'll make us a pot of tea," Flora busied around the sink as Will sat opposite his father.

"I can't say I'm happy about your predicament," Max began slowly. Will cursed and rose to his feet.

"Sit down," Max instructed, "please." He waited while Will reluctantly complied.

"Your Mom and I have been talking, we're both exhausted but that's not important."

"I had to get away," Will replied, folding his arms in a sullen gesture.

"It's okay," Max held up a hand, "we understand. It must have been extremely difficult carrying this burden. I'm sorry you couldn't come and talk to me Will."

Will stared in shock at his father but remained silent.

Max swallowed, "I know I'm not always the easiest person to be around, but I am your father Will and I'm," he nodded to Flora, "we're here to help you."

Will nodded with uncertainty, "so what now."

"Now we deal with it. You're going to be a Dad, it's time to step up Will."

"I've already thought about leaving uni, getting a job. Jimmy said he could get me work."

"As a plumber?" Max asked, "is that really what you want to do?"

"There's not much alternative, is there? I have to support Hema, financially as well as emotionally."

"When did you get so grown up huh?" Max said with a rueful smile, "you already have a job Will."

"A job in a student bar? That's hardly going to support us is it? No, I need something full time, some way of bringing in a regular income to pay for everything we'll need."

"We can help," Max said firmly, "let us help you."

"How?" Will sniffed nervously.

"Don't leave uni," Max said firmly, "come and live with us. We can help support you financially until you have finished your studies."

"You mean it?" Will said shakily, "but what about Hema? Are you really happy having her live here with us, because if you're not then I'm gone too."

Flora winced at Will's stubborn defiance and glanced at Max, trying to gauge his reaction. His face remained impassive, calm and controlled.

"I'm getting used to the idea," Max conceded, "and I'm willing to give it a go, if you are."

"Hema is very welcome here," Flora said with a soft smile, "your dad and I, we can't believe we're going to be grandparents in our forties. That's kind of young, don't you think?"

"How do you think I feel, I'm only nineteen," Will replied with a grin, "you'll be great Mom." He looked at his Dad, opened his mouth to say something, but then changed his mind, feeling strangely self-conscious, with his father sitting there, watching him.

Will scraped back his chair, "I'll speak to Hema."

Max rose to his feet and held out a steady hand to his son. After a slight deliberation, Will shook it firmly, "here's to future sleepless nights," Max said with a smile, "and working together as a family."

* * *

Sophie pressed snooze on the alarm clock for the fifth time this morning. It was no good, she had to get up in just one more minute. But the duvet was so warm and the bed was so soft and comfortable. Getting up meant showers and chores and having to put on clothes, combing hair and brushing teeth, all things that expounded energy, of which Sophie was in short supply. She flung her arm out to the left and felt the corner of a chilly pillow. Where was he, she wondered sleepily, where was her husband? Her head was throbbing and the inside of her mouth felt dry and sore. There was a glass of water on the bedside table, one which she did not remember pouring. She was thankful of it now anyway. Quickly she swallowed a large mouthful, then cursed as a stream trickled onto her naked skin. It made her jump, it made her skin pucker, it made her eyes snap fully open, then the memories came, tumbling into her confused, sleepy mind. Reminding her of last night.

Of course she was alone. Last night's revelations had made sure of that. Sophie swung her legs out and staggered to her feet. There was a sickness in her stomach, a dull aching that worsened with each flashback. Dodgy caviar, dancing, toilet gossip, anger, reaction and the pint of beer in her hand, she remembered so clearly tipping it over her darling husbands head. The satisfaction she had derived from humiliating him. Vengeance had been on her mind and she had indulged the urge, Ryan had been embarrassed, in front of his friends and work colleagues. Then he had been terrified when he found out why, why she had acted so aggressively, so irrationally. Gullible Sophie had at last found out; her husband was an unfaithful toad.

The journey home alone in the taxi had been full of hysterics. It was like reality had actually sunken in. This was not a game, this was not a television show. This was her life, this was her children's life. And, oh God the children; Josh and Jake, how could she tell them what their father had done. How could she explain how he had lied and cheated, not just on her but them too. He had let them down too. Ryan had smashed a huge whole in their precious family and it was completely broken. Broken by lies and lust and selfishness. Sophie had wailed and ranted, stamped her feet, hurled back her head and screamed in pain. It was like Ryan had physically punched her, knocked the life out of her. All of this outpouring had transpired in the back of a black taxi, emotions had taken hold and for a while, Sophie had acted like a wild woman. Then when the driver had pulled over and threatened to kick her out, then her sanity had returned and she had quietened down, with just the tears flowing and the occasional hiccup permeating the enclosed space.

So she had arrived home, a terrible state, hair sticking up, make up smeared. Her mom thought she had been attacked and had vowed to call the police. Then Sophie had taken her into the kitchen, closed the doors and told her everything that had happened. At first Yvonne had been in denial, proclaiming it to be a complete prank, a wind up, nothing but evil gossip. After a lot of heated persuasion she had finally accepted it; her son-in-law *was* an unfaithful toad. Yvonne had opened a bottle of wine, closed it and made coffee instead. Never one for a crisis, she had sat there simpering that she couldn't believe it, that they could work through it, that it didn't mean they had to divorce. Angry Sophie had ranted at her mother, proclaiming her to be just as bad as Ryan. Then she had unceremoniously kicked her out, checked on her sleeping boys and flopped down exhausted onto the bed.

Now she was in the bathroom, wiping at mascara streaks, smoothing down frizzy hair, attempting to present a picture of normality. She knocked gently on the twins' room, peeping her head around the door. They were still sleeping, golden haired cherubs, curled in their warm beds, oblivious to the chaos and upset that had transpired. Sophie went to gently shake them from their slumber, watching them with love as they stirred and stretched, shaking off the vestiges of sleep.

"Time to get up boys," she said cheerily, "I'll go make you some breakfast."

Josh was bouncing on his bed before she had left the room, full of energy and zest for the coming day.

Downstairs looked a mess, was a mess. Sophie's clothes were strewn across the floor, she vaguely remembered flinging them off in a fit of rage. A shiny stiletto was upside down in the dog's bed, a stocking hung from the lampshade. How the hell had that got there? She wondered. A fit of passion but not in a good way maybe? There was a sudden noise from the hallway, a key turning in the lock. Quickly Sophie snatched up her discarded attire, throwing them in the laundry basket. She breathed a sigh of relief, as Heidi peeked her head around the door.

"Hello Mrs O'Neill," she said cheerfully, "you want me to do breakfast?"

"Yes please," Sophie was relieved to see her housekeeper. Then Josh and Jake were skidding into the kitchen demanding to know what food was on offer.

Heidi chased them around playfully with a tea towel, "I do you omelette," she told them gasping for breath. They took pity on their elderly housekeeper and settled down on high stools to watch the morning t.v.

Sophie ran herself a large glass of water and gulped it down.

"What about Mr O'Neill?" Heidi asked as she whisked the eggs, "does he want omelette too, or maybe a bacon sandwich?"

Sophie glanced towards the boys, who were engrossed in a noisy cartoon, she drew the housekeeper to one side.

"Mr O'Neill's not here, but I don't want to worry the boys, so please don't say anything."

Heidi's eyebrows raised slightly, but she nodded quickly, "I finish breakfast and then I start on the ironing," she pointed behind the ajar door, where a basket of crumpled clothes overflowed in the corner.

"Thank you," Sophie replied, "I'll drop the boys at school and then I'm off to St Mary's."

Sophie wandered back up the stairs in a daze. She considered ringing St Mary's and cancelling today's voluntary, but then decided that it would be more beneficial to keep her mind occupied and be busy. Her thoughts turned to Ryan and she wondered where he had slept last night. As if on cue, her phone vibrated in her hand. It was a text message from her husband, full of apologies and pleas for her to talk to him. Sophie gritted her teeth, wiped the messages from her screen and searched in her accounts setting, looking for ways to block his number. Then her inbox was flashing again, this time it was her mother.

Sophie decided not to even read the message. Her mother was so predictable, she would be championing Ryan of course, even though he had behaved appallingly. Sophie thought of his infidelity and shuddered. This was bad, this was final. Why had she not been enough for him? He knew how much she loved only him.

Sophie found herself in floods of tears. She hurried into her bedroom, closed the door and flung herself on the bed, where she released a tumultuous outpouring of emotion. After a few minutes of sobbing into her pillow she felt better, relieved somehow. She turned onto her back and lay observing her rings. Decisively she pulled them off and her finger immediately felt bare, with a tier of white ring lines looking stark against her spray tan enhanced hands. Carefully she wrapped her wedding, engagement and eternity rings into tissue and placed them into her jewellery box. Then she was up on her feet and trooping with determination to turn on the shower. She would carry on she vowed, she would show everyone she could cope alone. Who needed a lying, cheating rat of a husband anyway? Even if it was the legendary Ryan O'Neill.

At the school gates Amber was waiting. Sophie spotted her friend in the melee of parents, children and teachers; dressed in designer gear, perfect hair and make-up, sunglasses fixed firmly in place, even though the day was dreary and full of dark thunderclouds. Amber wasted no time in getting straight to the point.

"I've heard all about it darling," she gushed, "it must have been awful for you."

"The boys," Sophie whispered, pointing at an oblivious Josh and Jake, "I can't talk now anyway, I'll see you... soon."

Amber surged forward to embrace her tightly, "you were right Sophie. Your intuition was spot on. Call me okay, I'm on your side."

"Thanks," Sophie backed away, feeling tears burning the back of her eyelids, "I'm just carrying on as normal."

"If you need to talk, anytime..." Amber trailed off with a sympathetic glance.

Sophie nodded, turned away and rushed back to the safety of her car. Then she was reversing backwards and driving away, watching the figure of her friend become smaller in her mirror.

For half an hour she drove around, wasting time, listening to the beep of the incoming messages and the incessant chatter of the radio. At one point she pulled over to take deep breaths and stave off the increasing feeling of panic she felt surging inside her. When she finally arrived at St Mary's she was late, the primary school was quiet, with all the children in registration. Sophie took a deep breath, told herself she could do this, life had to go on. Then she fixed her mouth into a wobbly smile and strode across the car park. As she opened the doors with her fob, the heat hit her and she wondered why the radiators were boiling hot at the beginning of May. The corridors were full of coats and lunchboxes, she passed through them quickly, head down, scurrying towards the sanctuary of the nursery. Mrs Bent the deputy was hovering outside, peering through the gap in the window, she jumped as Sophie approached her.

"Oh hello Mrs… erm, Mrs?"

"O'Neill," Sophie replied with a wince.

"I was just preparing my paperwork," the deputy divulged stiffly, "the nursery teacher is being observed this morning. Are you helping today?"

"I certainly am," Sophie replied with a bright smile, "I'll just erm… go on in then." She skirted past the deputy, pushing at the door. Inside the nursery was quiet and calm, the children were busy at activity tables and playing on the carpet with various toys. When they saw Sophie there was a loud chorus of 'hello's' and manic waving. Sophie tiptoed through to the kitchen, trying not to cause attention, but already there was a small circle of children pulling at her skirt and pleading for her to play with them. Cara lead them gently away, giving Sophie chance to peg up her coat and squash her bag into a vacant locker.

Mrs Bent had found a seat right in the middle of the room and was watching the children carefully. She was jotting notes down and frowning slightly as she focused on Cara and her literacy lesson with the older children. Sophie paused for a moment, undecided where to go, when there was a cry from the water table and a huge swell of foamy water sloshed onto the floor. She hurried over with a mop, utilising her most placating voice to diffuse the argument which had begun over a plastic crocodile. Soon enough it was cleared up and the children were playing again like angels. Sophie wandered over to the role play area and allowed herself to be prodded and poked by a three year old nurse who declared that she was having a baby. She stifled down a laugh, feeling happy that she had come today. The children were taking her mind off personal issues and she felt much happier. Cara had moved to the interactive whiteboard and motioned her over to help with behaviour management. A particularly energetic boy was rolling on the floor, looking everywhere but at the nursery teacher. Sophie squatted down next to him, encouraging him to look at the moving letters on the screen.

"That's an a," he said proudly, looking up at her for approval.

"Well done," Sophie affixed a smiley face to his jumper. His attention was snared and she relaxed back for a few moments. A young girl with red pigtails plonked herself on Sophie's lap, clapping each time Cara asked a question. Sophie sneaked a look at Marcia Bent, whose face was blank, devoid of emotion. In comparison, Cara was exuding enthusiasm and happiness and Sophie inwardly acknowledged what a wonderful teacher she was.

Then the bell was ringing and the hours observation was thankfully over.

"I shall give you feedback at lunchtime," Mrs Bent said snootily, as she picked up her papers and left.

"Thank goodness that's over," Cara said with a sigh, "and thank you for your help Sophie, you were amazing."

The children settled down for fruit and milk time, allowing Sophie chance to make a drink for the nursery staff.

"Have you thought of applying for a teaching assistant position?" Cara asked, her head cocked to one side, "you're a great support Sophie and it would give you experience before you apply for teacher training."

"What a wonderful idea," Mrs King the nursery assistant echoed, "there's a part time job going for September, do you think you might apply?"

"I…I'm not sure," Sophie replied hesitantly, "I have university to think of as well."

"It's only sixteen hours per week, mornings I think," Cara informed her, "maybe you could fit it around your studies. I would be happy to give you a reference, if you want to that is."

"I'll think about it," Sophie said with a grateful smile, "thank you for thinking of me."

"It's a pleasure," Cara replied, "now, I think we should take the children outside for some fresh air, it's such a lovely day and we have mass in…" she glanced at her wrist watch, "twenty minutes."

"The nursery go too?" Sophie asked, a little shocked, "aren't they a bit young?"

"It can be a trial," Cara conceded, "but they have to get used to going, it's all about being part of a catholic school."

Sophie helped the children into their coats, for a quick whizz around the play areas bikes and scooters, before ushering them into the toilets to try to go, even if they didn't feel like going. Then they were off, following a long line of classes weaving across the car park and onto the path leading to the adjacent church. Sophie gasped when she entered the church, it was beautiful with its high, stained glass windows, the polished oak row of seats and the numerous candles dotted around. The priest was at the front of the aisle, welcoming the staff and children into the church. As Sophie neared he took her hands in his own warm ones and gave her the most beatific smile.

"Welcome my dear," he said in a quiet tone, "may God be with you."

Sophie followed Cara to the right of the altar, where they squashed onto two long benches. They instructed the children to remove their coats and waited while the rest of the school trooped in. Then it was quiet and the mass began. As the priest began a reading, Sophie's thoughts wandered to Ryan. She found herself reminiscing over their own wedding, the vows they had taken and she felt an incredible sadness wash over her. Right at this moment she didn't know what she was going to do about her unfaithful husband, but she knew for certain that things would never be the same between them again. The trust had been irrevocably broken and she felt alone and frightened, scared for her children and the prospect of an uncertain future.

Chapter Eighteen

"Mommy, what a pretty bangle, can I wear it, can I wear it?" Molly was sitting at Juliette's dressing table, playing with the hanging charms and turning it over in her small hands.

Juliette was refitting the freshly cleaned duvet cover, but when she heard the words she dropped the sheet and hurried over to take the bracelet off Molly.

"Sorry sweetie, I need to put this back in its box," Juliette carefully wrapped it in tissue, closed the box then placed it high out of the way of prying fingers. Next week it was going back to its rightful owner: Ben Rivers. There was no way she could keep his family heirloom, not now that their fledgling relationship had ended. Molly was delving in her jewellery box again, the pretty bracelet forgotten. She pulled out a string of pearls, wrapped them around her neck and preened in the mirror. Juliette smiled at her daughter, "I have a ring to go with those, would you like to try it on?"

"Yes!" Squealed Molly, "I'm going to put my fairy dress on and watch Harry Potter with Nanny."

"Again!" Juliette hooked her hands into claws, "tickle monster's coming to get you."

"No, not tickle monster!" Molly jumped off the stool and ran around the other side of the bed, giggling profusely. Juliette picked her up, plonked her on the cushiony bed and tickled her neck, under her armpits and the sides of her stomach. They were both laughing loudly and Harry stuck his head around the door to see what the commotion was. When he saw them both rolling about with glee, he rolled his eyes and went back to his toy soldiers.

"Stop Mommy!" Molly kicked her legs in the air and wriggled away from her.

"Okay, okay," Juliette replied breathlessly, "tickle monster's gone back to sleep."

Molly skipped out of the bedroom, in search of her DVD, leaving Juliette alone to ponder on what she could wear this evening.

The weekend had rolled round again and Juliette was off out, for a meal with her sister Marie, her brother-in-law Dave and a friend of theirs. Clive something or other, Juliette couldn't remember his last name. It wasn't a date, Marie had insisted, just a friendly get together at a local curry restaurant and then a short pub crawl through the city centre. Initially Juliette had said no when she had first been invited. No way! Was this some kind of blind date? She had screeched on the phone to her sister. But Marie had been adamant there was no ulterior motive, no romantic match making, just friends having a drink and a night of fun and conversation.

"He's just lost his Mom," Marie had informed her emphatically, "he just needs a night out and you could do with one too. You've been moping around all week."

Juliette knew it was true, she *had* been moping. Ben Rivers constantly occupied her thoughts and she felt pretty miserable, so maybe tonight would be good for her. Maybe it would take her mind off him. The first year of university was drawing to a close, with only a few lectures left. The summer stretched before her, promising warmth, sunshine, relaxation and the horrible realisation that she wouldn't see him for three whole months. Fortunately, Marie and Dave had invited Juliette and the kids to their caravan for two weeks in August, this would keep her occupied, but still the thought of not seeing him over the summer made her feel physically sick and already she was yearning for year two to begin.

Juliette sighed and slid open the doors to her wardrobe. She couldn't decide what to wear, her fingers paused over her jeans, but then skipped on to her dresses and skirts at the back. It was warm this evening and although she wasn't bothered about impressing Clive, she still thought she should make an effort. It had been ages since she had been into the city for a night out. So finally after much deliberation, she decided on a short, floaty, periwinkle blue dress and matching sandals. A flower in her hair and a slick of lip gloss completed her attire. Juliette went into the lounge and sat down next to Molly.

"You smell nice Mommy," Molly said as she cuddled close to her, "where are you going?"

"Just out for a meal with Aunty Maz, I won't be late."

"Is Aunty Maz going to have her baby soon?" Molly asked, eyes wide with excitement at the prospect of having a baby cousin.

Juliette chuckled, "not yet sweetie, the baby's not coming until the winter."

"Why does it take soooo long," Molly was bouncing up and down.

"Because," Juliette replied, hugging her tight, "it takes time for the baby to grow. It stays in her tummy safe and warm, until it's ready to come out. But Aunty Maz is going to have a picture taken soon, It's called a scan."

"We can see the baby in her belly?"

Hmm, mmm," Juliette replied with a smile.

"Wow!!" Molly was enthralled, but only temporarily. Soon she was engrossed with the action on the television screen. Juliette wriggled out from underneath her and went to check on Harry, who was in his bedroom surrounded by soldier figurines.

"You okay buster?" she crouched down beside him, ruffling his hair with affection.

"Yep," came his succinct reply.

"How's school going?" She asked tentatively.

"Good," he looked up at her with a broad grin, "I've been picked for the football team. Dad said he'll take me for a practise over the park."

"Oh Harry that's wonderful," Juliette grinned, feeling pride swelling inside of her, "we'll have to take you shopping, get you kitted out," she paused as she thought of Marty, "and I'm so glad you're getting on with your dad."

Harry looked at her with suspicious eyes, "you're not getting back together again are you?"

"No," Sophie said with conviction, "but we're trying to be friends. Is that okay with you?"

Harry shrugged, "yeah, that's cool."

Juliette kissed the top of his head, laughing at the subsequent look of disgust on his face.

"Mom, pur-lease, I'm not five!"

"Okay, sorry," she held up her hands and backed out of his room, softly closing the door behind her. Then there was knocking on the front door. Her mother stood there, small, rosy cheeked, eyes twinkling as she surveyed her youngest daughter.

"Hello Mom," Juliette had the breath knocked out of her as Violet embraced her tightly.

"You look pretty," Violet said with a wink, "I've heard this Clive is a bit of a catch."

"What?" Juliette said aghast, "No! It's just a friendly drink. I'm not interested in him romantically!"

Violet bustled into the kitchen, plonking down her bag, "still hankering after that lecturer?"

"How did you..."

"Marie told me of course," her mom interjected, "you don't need a man like that love."

"Like what?" Juliette asked, in a small voice.

"From what I've heard he sounds a snob."

"No, he really isn't. He's lovely..." Juliette trailed off flushing.

"That lovely he can't even defend you huh? Not much of a gentleman by all accounts." Violet grasped her by the arms, "forget about him. Has he contacted you?"

"No," Juliette replied miserably, "but I did end the relationship, he said he would wait to hear from me."

"Rubbish," Violet tutted, "why isn't he beating down your door if he thinks that much of you?"

Juliette hung her head and Violet looked at her with sympathy.

"I'm sorry I don't mean to be blunt, but you can do better sweetheart. It's time you enjoyed yourself. Have fun, be a flirt. The world is your oyster you know." She chucked her under the chin and smiled, "now go and enjoy yourself and don't worry about the time, I'll have a kip on the sofa if I get tired."

"Thanks Mom," Juliette moved the blinds to look outside, "is Marie here?"

"She's waiting outside," confirmed Violet, "go on with you now. Me and the kids are going to have a lovely night so don't you worry about us," she ushered Juliette towards the front door, "don't forget your bag and remember if you can't be good, be careful."

Juliette laughed at her mom's lascivious wink, hugged the kids, then hurried out the flat and down the flight of concrete stairs.

Marie was waiting, revving the engine and chattering away to Dave in the passenger seat. As Juliette neared the car, she noticed a figure in the back seat which shifted slightly as she opened the back door and squeezed in.

"Hello kiddo," Marie turned around to flash Juliette a sparkling smile. Juliette reached forward to hug her sister and then her brother in law. "This is Clive, otherwise known as Rambo for his love of all things Sylvester Stallone."

"Oh hello," Juliette smiled his way, and was a little disconcerted when he surged forward to embrace her.

"Hello Juliette, I've heard a lot about you, very pleased to make your acquaintance," Clive had a thick Midland accent and a shock of ginger hair, "and it's nice to meet a fellow ginger."

"It's nice to, erm, meet you too."

"Right, buckle up, we're off!" Marie pushed down on the accelerator and the car shot forward. Juliette relaxed back and observed Clive surreptitiously. He had wide lips, a large nose and dimples that seemed out of sorts in his chiselled jawline. He was chatting animatedly to Dave about cars and every so often he broke into a chuckle. Although he wasn't what Juliette would class as conventionally handsome, there was something appealing about his merry face and his twinkling eyes.

"Fancy a sherbet lemon?" He thrust a bag of yellow sweets towards her.

"No…thank you," Juliette replied politely, *what am I doing here?* she thought to herself, *I could be at home in my onesie.*

As if sensing the awkwardness, Marie caught her eye in the mirror, "how are the kids?"

"They're fine, being spoilt by Nan at this very moment."

"That's good. So I hope you two are hungry," she looked towards both her and Clive, "it's a new restaurant we're going to. An eat as much as you can buffet!"

"Sounds bostin!" Clive replied, while Juliette fixed a smile onto her face.

There was a silent pause, then Dave and Marie started talking amongst themselves about the cost of baby apparatus. Apparently the pram she wanted was too expensive in Dave's opinion. Juliette listened distractedly, eyes turned to look out of the window at the houses flying by.

There was a slight cough in her ear and Juliette noticed that Clive seemed to be edging closer to her.

"So," he began, placing his arm casually at the back of her, "Marie tells me you work in the social club, Rowfers?"

"That's the one," Juliette replied, moving away slightly, "only part time, I've been there years."

"And you're at school as well?"

"University," Juliette corrected him, "yes, I'm in my first year of an English degree."

"That must be hard work," he commented, as he popped another sweet in his mouth.

"It has been hard work, but very enjoyable," Juliette smiled, her thoughts on Ben Rivers. She wondered what he was doing this evening, whether he was out with another student.

"Never bothered with school myself. Books give me a headache."

Juliette laughed politely, "maybe you've read the wrong ones."

"Oh yeah," he drawled with a cheeky wink, "maybe you could advise me on which one's I *should* read. What is it all you women rave about – Fifty Shades of Gray?"

"I prefer the classics," Juliette replied stiffly.

"Oh I loved Fifty Shades," gushed Marie, "couldn't put it down."

"If you like erotic fiction Maz, there's lots of other books you could explore."

"Erotic fiction?" Dave cut in, as he turned around, "don't you mean porn?"

Juliette blushed as the men chuckled, "I really wouldn't know, I haven't read that genre."

"Yes, that's what they all say," Dave teased, "I bet you've got a secret stash Jules."

"Mom loves Mills and Boon," Marie said with a chuckle, "some of their books are really racy you know Jules."

"I can imagine," Juliette replied with a smirk, "apparently some of the English lecturers secretly read them too."

"They must be a barrel of laughs right?" Dave said, "just chatting about books and academia all night."

Juliette jumped on the defensive, "some might be, I wouldn't say they're all like that."

"Okay, okay," Dave held up his hands in surrender, "let's change the subject."

"Yes, forget about books for the night Jules, let your hair down," Marie swung the car around a corner and into the multi storey car park, "I hate these places, how tight are the bends and why are the pillars so close to the parking spaces." Subsequently Dave got out and waved her into a pair of white lines. Then they set off, passing darkened shop windows, until they arrived at the brightly painted restaurant.

The Spice of Bengal was busy, most of the tables were occupied with couples and large groups chattering and laughing. The air was thick with the heady aroma of spicy food. It was all very jovial and Juliette felt herself relaxing as a harassed looking waiter motioned them across to a cute window table. There were candles and pink napkins which were swirled elegantly into crystal wine goblets. Juliette was surprised at how pretty it looked. Clive pulled out a chair for her and Juliette shrugged out of her cardigan, before sinking next to her sister.

"This is romantic," Marie said with a wide grin, "don't you think Jules?"

"Very cosy," Juliette said with a cough.

Dave motioned to the hovering waiter, ordered two bottles of wine and a plate of poppadum's. Then they settled back into an easy conversation.

"You will never guess where we're going for our anniversary," Marie said, with a squeal of excitement.

"Paris?" Juliette ventured, knowing how long her sister had hankered over going there.

"Even better – Prague!"

"Prague?" Juliette echoed. She bit her lip as a memory of Ben Rivers telling her he wanted to go there, flashed through her mind.

"Yes Prague," Marie replied with a shake of her head, "for two nights."

"Well…that's wonderful," Juliette trailed off, distracted, "what will you do with your shop?"

"I have staff. They can cope without me for a weekend, and oh Jules, I received an application from your friend's mom for the part time position. She sounds perfect and is coming in to see me next week."

"That's great," Juliette said with a smile, "I hope she's successful."

Marie stared at her for a moment, "shall we go to the ladies?"

Juliette followed her across the busy restaurant and into the toilet.

"Are you okay?" Marie asked gently, "you seem a little distracted, aren't you enjoying yourself."

"I am," protested Juliette, "sorry."

"You're thinking about him aren't you Jules? It takes time to get over a break up, I do understand you know."

"It hardly even started," Juliette replied sadly, "I'll be okay, sorry I haven't been much company, I'll make more of an effort, I promise."

Marie rubbed her arm and surveyed her sympathetically, "enjoy yourself okay, this is just a friendly meal with people who care about you and Clive, poor bloke could do with a bit of fun at the moment, be nice to him please."

"As long as he doesn't get the wrong impression Maz, I'm really not interested in anything romantic."

Marie winked, "you have to admit Clive is kinda cute huh?"

"I suppose so," Juliette replied grudgingly.

"Come on," Marie said with a laugh, "let's go eat."

The food was delicious. The all you can eat buffet was bursting with a variety of dishes to choose from. Dave and Clive went up for seconds, while Juliette and Marie finished with an extremely sweet Indian ice cream.

"That was lovely," Juliette said as she wiped at her mouth.

Clive nodded in agreement, scooping up thick sauce onto his nan bread. Marie and Dave were deep in conversation about their upcoming holiday, making plans for sightseeing. Juliette gazed at Clive and wondered if she should broach the subject of his mother. Then Clive began talking about her, telling Juliette of all the wonderful Indian dishes she used to make from scratch.

"I'm so sorry for your loss," Juliette said, when there was a pause in the conversation.

"Thanks, we knew it was coming. It's still hard though, my sister's not coping well at all and Dad's just in denial. I guess that's what grief does to you, people cope with it in different ways."

Juliette nodded, decided to change the subject.

"What do you do for a living Clive?" She asked.

His eyes lit up, "got my own fish and chip shop. Worked there since I was seventeen, then when the owner retired I sorted a bank loan, bought it and been managing it ever since."

"It must be great to own a business," Juliette said enthusiastically.

"I'd love a restaurant by the sea one day, that's my goal."

Juliette smiled across at him, he was a nice bloke she thought, there was an easy going vibe emanating from him and he had kind eyes. She realised that she liked him and was enjoying his company. She told him about her dreams of becoming a primary school teacher and he declared she would make a brilliant teacher.

"You don't know me," Juliette laughed, after he had finished complimenting her.

"You have that sense of authority about you," he whispered, "I love a woman who can take charge."

Juliette blushed and looked down at her empty bowl, "it's years off yet, but I'm determined to get there."

"I believe you," he said, leaning across to tuck an errant strand of hair behind her ear.

Juliette jerked backwards and he immediately apologised. Then there was an awkward silence.

"Right then you guys," Marie said, clearing her throat and looking quizzically from Clive to Juliette, "shall we go and have a few drinks?"

Once the bill was paid, they left the restaurant and crossed the busy main road to walk towards the canal area of the city. It was where all the best bars and pubs were, so Dave proclaimed. Juliette was surprised to see a high volume of people milling about, there were police patrolling the area too. It was a hive of activity and they soon found themselves being ushered inside a trendy looking wine bar.

"Buy one get one free on the shots," a young girl in a black velvet jumpsuit enticed.

"I can see why," Marie drawled, as they looked around the quiet bar. They knocked back the drinks then set off again. As they were walking up a winding hill, Juliette noticed a sign outside a small, tucked away pub advertising eighties disco and karaoke.

"Let's go in here," she said with excitement, pulling at Marie's arm.

The bouncer tipped his cap at them as they entered and Juliette grinned as she looked around the busy pub. There were waitresses hurrying around carrying trays of food and a line of elderly men perched on stools at the bar.

"Oh look, there's a table, quick," Marie hurried across, flinging her bag and coat down. Juliette sauntered after her, leaving the men to order the drinks.

"I LOVE eighties music," Juliette shouted in her sister's ear as she bopped away to Wham's 'Freedom'.

"We should put a request in," Marie delved in her bag, extricating a pen and slip of paper. Then she was off, weaving across the tiny dance floor, jabbering into the DJ's ear.

Juliette relaxed back and spent a few moments people watching. There was a mixture of young and old, groups of singles and couples enjoying the friendly ambience. She was glad she had made the effort to come out tonight. She needed this, a night away from study and thoughts of a dream relationship. This is reality, she thought looking around, this is my life.

"Stop daydreaming Jules," Dave was back from the bar with a tray of drinks, he set them down and smiled her way with fondness, "Clive and I were just discussing karaoke, to sing or not to sing."

Juliette smiled at Clive, "I think you should, definitely."

"Only if you do too," Clive said with a wink.

"We should," Marie was back, shouting with excitement, "let's do karaoke!"

"No, no karaoke," Juliette was aware that her words were slurring, she knew she had drank far too much. Her head felt fuzzy and suddenly everything seemed hilarious, even Clive's dire jokes. It felt good to loosen her inhibitions and it felt good to have some male attention.

"Oh come on Jules, it'll be fun and it can't be any worse than *that*," she pointed at the stage where a buxom lady was staggering around and warbling 'I will survive' completely out of tune.

"Okay," Juliette agreed, with a snigger, "but only if the lads go first."

"You're on!" shouted Clive as he jumped to his feet. He conferred with Dave for a few minutes, before disappearing.

Juliette leaned closer to her sister and together they pored over the song sheets.

"How about a Queen track?" Marie enquired, "radio ga-ga? I love that."

"Are you joking," Juliette cried, "that's way too hard. We need something simple, fun and girly."

"I know," Marie gushed, "leave it with me," she scribbled down her choice, then shimmied her way up to the sweating D.J.

Juliette noticed her phone beeping and an image of Harry appeared on the screen.

'We love you Mommy' it read and underneath was the most exquisite photograph of her two children, sitting astride their Nan's knee. Juliette felt overwhelmed with love, like her heart was literally melting, she typed out the reply adding five lines of kisses.

"Have you got children Clive?" She asked with a bright smile.

"Unfortunately not. Not yet anyway," he threw his arms wide, "but I'd love a whole football team, when I meet the right girl anyhow."

"I'm sure you will," she replied with a laugh, liking his enthusiasm.

They were interrupted by the D.J calling their names. Clive and Dave bounced up to the stage, took up the microphones and belted out 'Prince Charming' by Adam Ant. It was accompanied by all the dance moves and Juliette and Marie were bent over with laughter. When they finished they was a tumultuous round of applause, cries of 'more' and liberal foot stomping.

"It'll be us next," Marie warned, as she drained her fruit juice.

"How can you do this sober?" Juliette asked, amazed.

"I don't need alcohol to have a good time, although it does help and after this little one is born, I'm sure I'll make up for it," Marie rubbed her stomach tenderly.

Juliette leant forward to embrace her sister, "I'm so happy for you Maz."

"Get away with you," Marie replied, "now don't get all emotional on me Jules."

Clive and Dave were back, breathless and euphoric, "your turn," they teased, pointing fingers. Their names were being called, Juliette rolled her eyes, "tell me again, why I let you talk me into this," she mouthed.

"Come on spoil sport," Marie grabbed her hand and pulled her across the pub.

The steps to the stage were slippy and Juliette wobbled precariously as she climbed them. The pub had grown quiet, all eyes looking their way. Juliette felt sick and nervous, maybe this wasn't such a good idea, she thought, as she faced the packed pub.

"Right girls, take it away!" The exuberant D.J shoved microphones into their hands and motioned for them to look at the screen. As the background tune started, Juliette's spirits sank even further. What a song choice! She glared at Marie, who was looking at her with an innocent smirk upon her face. Then she was being nudged and she reluctantly opened her mouth and began singing. Madonna's 'Like A Virgin' seemed to drag on and on. Juliette felt herself blushing furiously as the pub rang out with wolf whistles. One man near the front even suggested that they do a raunchy dance to go with the lyrics.

"Go on darling," he leered, "show us your hip movements."

Dave and Clive were laughing uproariously, provoking Marie's dance moves to become even wilder. And she was stone cold sober for goodness sake and pregnant! Juliette willed the song to speed along and was relieved when the final verse popped up on the screen. Just as she was opening her mouth to screech a high note she noticed a familiar face at the bar, looking her way. Was that? No it couldn't be! Oh my Lord it was Brian Hodges. Juliette immediately snapped her mouth shut, leaving Marie to warble alone. Her eyes scanned the back of the room, wondering who he was with. There she was, her arch love rival, Helena Mulberry sitting at a table chatting to the European Literature lecturer and another man she didn't recognise. Juliette gulped with fear, surely he wasn't here? He couldn't be. Then she saw him; Ben, leaning against a stone pillar, looking gorgeous and brooding and staring her way with an amused look upon his lovely face. Juliette felt mortified with embarrassment. Without thinking she thrust the microphone back at the D.J and jumped from the stage. On the way down, she landed awkwardly on her left ankle and let out a cry, as pain shot up her leg. Could this get any worse? She fretted, as Clive surged forward to help her to her feet.

"Are you okay?" He asked, his face a picture of concern.

"Yes, yes, I'm fine," Juliette wriggled away from his touch and noticed Ben's smile had turned to a frown.

"What the heavens are you doing Jules?" Marie questioned, "you left me all alone up there."

"Over there," Juliette tried to motion surreptitiously with her head in Ben's direction.

"Oh no!" Marie's line of vision focussed on him for a few moments, "just ignore him."

Marie helped her back to their table, where Juliette took a large glug of wine.

"Do you want to leave?" Marie whispered.

"No," Juliette shook her head adamantly, a flicker of desire stoked inside her, as she caught his eye again. Then it was quickly doused as Helena Mulberry wound her arms around him.

"I need another drink," she announced, inwardly seething, how quickly he had moved on, "same again?"

Juliette flounced off towards the bar, mentally reminding herself that their relationship was over, so therefore he could hug whoever he pleased. Still, it hurt and she was surprised by the strong pangs of jealousy that were invoked inside of her.

At the bar, Juliette waited patiently behind a rowdy hen party. She waved her twenty pound note in the hope of catching anyone's eye.

"Hello Juliette," the sound of her name sent shivers down her spine, as she spun towards him, almost falling against his torso. That delicious, firm torso that she had stroked with passion.

"Oh hello," now was a good time to feign nonchalance, she thought.

"It's great here, isn't it?" Ben smiled her way, "I see you're with your sister?"

"Oh, urm yes and my brother-in-law and friend," she emphasised the last word.

"I'm with the university lot," Ben explained, "it's our end of year work drinks. A tradition if you can call it that."

"Oh that's great," Juliette smiled up at him, loosing herself in his warm, brown eyes.

"Would you like to order?" Ben lifted his hand and immediately a young bar girl was looking his way expectantly.

"A bottle of dry white please," Juliette replied, "thank you."

There was an awkward silence, then Ben cleared his throat.

"What's happened Juliette, what's changed between us?" He looked sad and Juliette felt a rush of guilt and sympathy. When she didn't answer he leaned closer, took her hand in his larger one. The pressure of his warm fingers was like an aphrodisiac and she felt her head spinning.

"I'm sorry," she mumbled, tearing her hand away, "I can't do this." Then she was lurching away from him, stumbling to the toilets, desperate to get away before she blurted all her hurt and anger out. Not now, not tonight. Tonight she should be doing happy, tonight she could pretend she no longer cared for him, but not when he was so close, not when he was touching her with so much tenderness she could almost cry.

Thankfully the ladies was empty. Juliette sank down on a bench, staring at her reflection in the neon lit mirror. She smoothed down her wild curls and reapplied a sheen of lip gloss. What could she say to him she wondered, he did deserve an explanation, of that she was certain, the poor man must be completely bewildered by her change in attitude. Right, that's it, she thought, I'm going to tell him. I'm going to admit to listening in on a private conversation and let him know what he's done wrong. Juliette wished that she could turn back time to that day, wish that she had stayed in the bar with the others, wished she had not overhead Brian Hodges bad mouthing her, for once she welcomed ignorance over knowledge. Above all, she wished that she could erase the silence from Ben, that cold, lengthy silence where she waited and waited for him to declare his feelings for her, defend her, to say something, to say anything. This was hopeless. Juliette closed her eyes briefly then with a heavy heart she made her way back into the rowdy pub. Pushed through the crowds and edged towards the large table of lecturers. He wasn't there, for a moment she stared at Helena Mulberry, watched her laughing with Brian Hodges.

"Where is he?" She mumbled, glancing at the empty seat next to her.

"He's gone," Brian Hodges stood up, "he's left Juliette and maybe it's for the best."

"Best for who?" She hissed, angry at this little, opinionated man.

Brian shrugged, "you finished the relationship Juliette, this is your doing."

"Brian…" Helena Mulberry touched his arm, "maybe you should stay out of this."

"I heard you," Juliette said firmly, "I heard everything you said, the poison you put into his head. I *am* worth it, I am worth fighting for."

"Are you okay Jules?" Marie was by her side, glaring at Brian Hodges.

"Yes, I'm fine," Juliette replied with conviction.

She smirked down at a gawping Brian Hodges and an embarrassed looking Helena Mulberry.

"You know for all your fancy qualifications, for all your so called intelligence, you're really not nice people. *You're* not worth it." Juliette tossed back her head and flounced away, heart hammering, while beside her Marie patted her back and looked her way with admiration.

"Well done Jules, well done darling."

Chapter Nineteen

The final weeks of university rolled by; end of term essays were handed in, books were returned and the final lectures were attended by a tired class of students, looking forward to the long summer break. Max and Flora had officially invited Hema to live with them temporarily. Her parents knew and had surprisingly been accepting of the situation. Will had held her hand as she broke the news to them that she was moving out to be with him and the baby would be living with the Bentley's for the next foreseeable future. Her father had glared but nodded his assent and Mrs Kumar had shuffled off into the kitchen and pointedly ignored them both. There had been tears from Hema, she had been sad for a day or two but then the excitement of moving in with Will had taken over and they were both excited for their future together as a family.

The warm spring month of May had coaxed Evelyn out of her house and she was able to work in the garden and feel the sunlight on her face. At times she still felt overwhelmed with grief for her dear, departed Mam, but it was getting easier and she was looking forward to the summer with hope. Hope for good health and hope for success. Evelyn had tentatively began sending extracts of her novel off to publishers. She had taken Ben's advice and was working through the Writer's and Artist's Yearbook. His gentle encouragement had boosted her confidence and she finally believed that she had a talent worth sharing.

Ann was relieved that the end of year was almost upon them. For weeks she had toiled on the remaining essays, she was tired and looking forward to lazy days spent with Jon; her rock, her best friend and her soulmate. The adoption process seemed to be taking forever, they had been assigned a social worker; a lovely lady called Rose who spent time with them, advising, chatting, making them think long and hard about the arduous adoption process. Jon and Ann were determined, they were fully committed to offering a home to a child in need. And Ann's dreams of becoming a lecturer had intensified, she loved being at university, she loved the setting, the people, the chance to impart knowledge and in turn continuously learn. Life was good and Ann was happy, happier than she had been in a long time.

Sophie just managed to hand her last essay in, with an hour to the deadline remaining. She raced across town and into the registry and with a huge sigh of relief handed in her poetry assignment. She was doing okay, but no, truthfully she was struggling. Ryan had moved out leaving her with a huge mansion of a house, two children and a menagerie of animals. Some days she forgot to rise, sometimes she felt so down and brow beaten that she curled up into a ball and allowed Heidi to take over the care of the children and the organisation of the house. Tears ran often, but with the help of her friends, Sophie managed to soldier on. Continually telling herself that she could do this, she could cope, she could be strong like Juliette.

Ah, Juliette. The eternal optimist, the self-sufficient girl from the bad neighbourhood that has big dreams, a burning ambition to better herself and her beloved children's lives. The bracelet went back to Dr Rivers and with it her dreams of a romantic, happy after. Now Juliette is focussing on her studies. Already she has begun reading texts from some of the year two modules that interest her. She is looking forward to the second year and taking one more step towards her dream of becoming a primary school teacher. But first there is the class trip to Haworth and the Bronte Parsonage Museum, which they all agree will be the perfect way to conclude an exciting and inspiring first year.

Chapter Twenty

"It's here, look," Evelyn pointed with excitement, through the early morning mist, at the large approaching vehicle. The coach pulled up outside the entrance to the universities main reception and with a loud hiss the doors opened inwards.

"Okay everybody, transportation has arrived," Wilomena Smythe shouted above the noisy chatter, "please board the vehicle." She stood to one side, clutching a board and pen, dressed rather out of season in a tartan dress and thick tights.

"Ladies first," said a cheerful Will, as he held out a chivalrous hand and helped Juliette, then Sophie and Evelyn up the high steps. The driver winked their way and bade them a good morning as they passed.

"Is it?" Sophie grumbled, "I'm usually fast asleep this early on a Sunday morning."

Evelyn glanced at her watch, "it's eight o'clock dear, I never sleep past seven, even on weekends."

"Oh ignore me," Sophie replied with a watery smile, "I'm just being a grouch, sorry."

"It's fine dear," Evelyn patted her hand, "you don't need to apologise."

Juliette swung her rucksack into the overhead bag holdall and squashed next to Sophie, "are you alright?" she asked, noting with concern her friends pale countenance.

"Not really," Sophie replied quietly, "but I think I will be."

Juliette noticed her friends normally immaculate bitten down nails, "how are you coping?"

Sophie sighed and blew into a tissue, "I'm worried about the boys, they miss him like crazy."

Juliette knew without asking who the 'him' referred to: Ryan O'Neill, Sophie's cheating snake of a husband.

"Stay strong," Juliette advised, "it's hard, but you're doing well."

"Thanks Jules, you're a good friend," Sophie smiled her way, "anyway, let's enjoy ourselves today, no more negativity. Haworth here we come eh?"

"Absolutely," Juliette settled back, ripped open her boiled sweets and then passed them across to Evelyn and Will.

Soon they were following the blue and white signs for the M6 North. Trees and pylons flew by as they sped up the motorway. Then they were passing acres of lush green farmland where sheep and cows grazed lazily and wind turbines spun in the morning breeze. Juliette tried not to stare as Ben Rivers rose to his feet at the front of the coach and stretched above him. He was wearing a tight fitting white shirt which rose to reveal wisps of dark hair. A flashback formed in her mind, his bare torso pressed against hers as he trailed a line of kisses across her face and neck. Juliette swallowed and averted her eyes to look out of the window at the flock of birds that were swooping overhead.

"What happened between you guys?" Sophie whispered.

"It just didn't work out," Juliette replied cagily.

"Looks like we're both single then," Sophie slunk lower in her seat, "wake me up when we get there."

The miles passed by quickly in the stream of quiet traffic. Then they were pulling into services and Wilomena Smythe was announcing that they would be having a half hour comfort break.

"Soph," Juliette gently shook her friend awake, to join the line of other students disembarking from the coach.

"How are you Mrs O'Neill?" Tarquin Haverstock smiled broadly as he helped her off the thrumming vehicle.

Sophie winced at the sound of her married name, "please call me Sophie," she replied, "and I'm fine thank you, how are you?"

"I'm grand as ever," Tarquin replied, with a cheeky wink, "how have you found your first year at Chattlesbury university?"

"Oh, it's been great," Sophie replied with enthusiasm, "I had a bit of a bumpy start, but I think my grades are finally looking up and my writing skills and critical thinking have vastly improved."

Tarquin smiled, his eyes twinkled with merriment, "I'm glad to hear it missy. I'll look forward to seeing you in year two then?"

"Absolutely," Sophie replied with conviction. She watched as he wandered off to join the other lecturers.

"So," she said, turning towards Will, "how is the father to be?"

"Pretty cool actually," Will grinned, "so you've heard the good news then?"

"We have," interjected Evelyn, "congratulations Will. How is Hema?"

Will nodded, "she's doing okay, now the sickness has passed. Now she's living with us, Mom is spoiling her rotten."

"My sister Marie was impressed with your Mom Will. Flora, is that her name? She thinks she has a real talent for floristry."

"Yeah, she's always been creative," Will replied with a proud smile, "she was over the moon to be offered the job. Can you thank your sister for me?"

"No need to thank her," Juliette insisted, "Marie is just chuffed to find someone who loves flowers as much as she does. I think they'll get on brilliantly."

Their made their way through the foyer of the services and lined up to purchase drinks and pasties before seating at a formica covered table.

"It's strange without Ann here," Juliette commented, "I hope the adoption meeting goes well for her."

"She's arranging a meet up dear," Evelyn replied, "sometime over the summer. I'm sure that she will tell us all about it."

"I'm going to miss you guys," Sophie said with a sniff, "but it will be nice to have a break, how long do we have off – three whole months?"

"Yes," Juliette confirmed, as she looked wistfully across to Ben Rivers, "a long time huh?"

They chatted amongst themselves about their plans for the summer.

"What are you going to do about your holiday Soph?" Juliette asked, as she stirred her sugary tea.

"I don't know," Sophie replied with a frown, "it's all paid for and too late to cancel now. I was thinking of going alone with the boys."

"It's been years since I went on holiday," Evelyn said, "you know I have never been abroad. When I was younger it was always caravans by the sea in Dorset or Cornwall."

"Really?" Sophie replied, looking her way with wide, incredulous eyes, "well Evelyn, why don't you come with me this year."

"On holiday dear? But surely you have family or other friends you could take?"

Sophie snorted, "my friends are all on their third or fourth holiday of the year and wouldn't deign to go to Lanzarote. No," she emitted a tight laugh, "they compete to go to the furthest, most exotic destinations possible: Australia, The Maldives, South Africa on safari with rich American business men. As for my mother, who is now incidentally shacked up with my much younger gardener, they from what I last heard are going on an all-inclusive package trip to Goa. It's all very tantric between them at the moment."

There was an awkward silence.

"So it seems I'm all alone," Sophie continued, "please come Evelyn. It will be fun. The break will do us both good. You've been through so much and what with my crumbling marriage, I could really do with a good friend to spend some time with."

"I don't know dear…" Evelyn was tempted, but not entirely convinced.

"I think it's a great idea," Juliette encouraged.

"Sounds cool to me," Will said chirpily, "go and enjoy yourself Evelyn."

Sophie gripped Evelyn's arm, "it won't cost you a penny, it's all paid for. Obviously you'll need a bit of spending money, but I can help out if money is short."

"I'll pay my way dear, I insist."

"Is that a yes?" Sophie squealed.

"Why not," Evelyn said brightly, "it sounds lovely and just what the doctor would order for us both I think."

"Fantastic," Sophie cried, throwing her arms around her, "let me tell you all about it."

The remainder of the journey passed quickly. Soon they were leaving the motorway and making their way towards the village of Haworth. The grey steel structures were replaced by the most beautiful green fields, bordered by crumbling stone walls. They passed quaint olde worlde cottages and an aptly named 'Wuthering Heights' pub, before the coach wound its way up tight bendy roads. Up they climbed, following the signs for the car park.

"Okay ladies and gentlemen," Wilomena Smythe began, "it's almost ten thirty, the sun is shining and we've arrived at our destination. Have a fabulous day, explore the museum, the church and the lovely shops. Please be back here at three o'clock for our journey home."

Juliette rose to her feet and stretched, "how pretty it looks," she commented, as she peered out of the window, "where to first?"

"The museum?" Evelyn replied.

The Bronte Parsonage was just a short walk from the car park.

"It's a lot smaller then I imagined," Evelyn remarked, as they trudged up the path towards the house.

"I was envisioning a sprawling country estate," Juliette agreed, "it is in a beautiful setting though."

"Wait up guys," a breathless Sophie was digging in her handbag for her camera, "group selfie time!"

Will, Evelyn and Juliette huddled close next to her as she snapped away. Then she was taking pictures of the pretty garden, and the archaic stone residence. Many of the students had headed straight to the shops and church, but the lecturers were queuing up to enter.

Juliette stood behind Ben Rivers, breathing in the scent of musky aftershave. He was so close, she could almost touch him. Instead she curled her hands into tight fists and turned to look at the rooms which were on either side of them. They packed into the dining room, staring at the books, the table and the fireplace. They were all busy taking pictures but when Juliette looked up, she noticed Ben staring her way. He motioned her over.

"Come with me," he whispered. Juliette shivered and followed him out of the room and up a creaking staircase to the first floor.

On the way, Juliette paused to admire an antique Grandfather clock and a portrait of the Bronte sisters.

"This is lovely," she said, as they stopped outside Charlotte's bedroom. Juliette's heart was racing, her stomach flipping as she looked sideways at his handsome profile.

"I thought you would like it. It's a real gem."

"They were all so very talented," Juliette gushed, as she admired the beautiful dress behind the pane of glass.

"They were," he inclined his head, "I know why Juliette, your sister told me."

"Oh," Juliette was shocked, "I don't know what to say."

"I'm sorry," Ben faltered, "it was a silly conversation which got over heated. I'm sorry you overheard it."

"No," Juliette shook her head firmly, "it's okay, really."

"It's not okay though," Ben insisted, "I don't care what anyone else thinks Juliette, I care about you."

But not enough, wailed her inner thoughts.

"I care about you too Ben, but this, us, it's not right. It wouldn't work." She felt her heart constrict with anguish, but all she could think about was his compromised career, his livelihood, she couldn't be part of destroying it.

"Are you sure?" He raked a hand through his already tousled hair.

"Yes," Juliette said in a small voice.

Ben nodded, looked at her with sad eyes, then took a step back, "friends?"

"Friends." Juliette smiled, "always." They touched hands briefly, gazing at one another, then Sophie was bounding up the stairs and interrupting them.

"Jules, you should see the kitchen, it's got one of those cooking ranges that I've always wanted...oh, I'm sorry, I didn't realise you were talking," she turned to leave, but Juliette called her back.

"It's okay Soph, we've finished," and as Ben walked back down the stairs she whispered to herself, "it's over."

The remainder of the day was taken up with sightseeing around the church and grounds, then they walked down a steep hill, marvelling at the old cobbled streets and the quaint shops. Both Juliette and Sophie made purchases for their children, while Evelyn treated herself to a beautiful chiffon scarf that was a bargain with fifty percent off. After asking advice, Will bought Hema a pretty handbag, which was decorated with multi coloured sequins.

"That will be lovely for university," Juliette commented, as he paid for it. "Oh, I forgot about the pregnancy, what will Hema do about her studies Will?"

"She's deferring her course for a year. She's determined to go back to it though, still wants to be a social worker."

"Fantastic!" Juliette replied, "I've heard there is a great crèche at the main campus if you're stuck for a babysitter."

"Mom's already making plans," Will said with a grin, "she's offered to help out."

"I think it's lovely," cooed Sophie, "you *will* bring the baby in to see us won't you Will? I can't wait to have a cuddle."

"Course I will," he replied with a laugh, "this baby is going to have so much fuss."

They strolled back up the hill. Even though it was a Sunday, Haworth was busy. The warm sunshine had bought people out. Will swerved around a line of mothers with pushchairs, who were chattering and laughing loudly. He stared down at the young children strapped into their buggies, a few were sleeping peacefully but there was one who was bright red and squealing. He watched a little nervously as the young Mom hunted around for a comforter, then soothed the baby gently. He still couldn't quite believe that he was going to be a Dad, the thought scared him still, but there was also a feeling of excitement and now the shock had worn off and the parents had been told, Will was happy. In a few months' time he would be meeting his son or daughter. Both him and Hema had decided that they wanted the sex of the baby to remain a surprise, so they had been purchasing white newborn clothes and Flora had started knitting the most exquisite cream blanket.

"Where to for dinner?" Evelyn asked expectantly, as her stomach rumbled loudly.

"How about there?" Sophie pointed to a pub with a board outside, which advertised two for one on meals.

As they were nearing the door, a jolly looking man intercepted them.

"Come and dine in my café," he implored with a broad smile and twinkling eyes, "friendly staff, delicious food and a warm, laid back ambience. You can stay as long as you like, there's no rushing in Haworth."

He was right, the café was lovely. They sat at a pretty, gingham covered table, sipping tea from china cups, as they waited for their hot meals to arrive.

"What a beautiful day," sighed Evelyn. The window next to their table was ajar and they could hear bird song over the chatter and the distant sound of piped music.

"I'm glad I came," Sophie said with a nod, "I'll be honest, I nearly cancelled."

"It will do you good to socialise," Juliette replied, patting her arm, "don't lock yourself away, you haven't done anything wrong."

"We're all here for you Sophie, Ann is too," Evelyn said with a kind smile. Sophie smiled her thanks. Then a few seconds later, her phone was beeping.

"I've received a text from her," Sophie replied, holding her phone aloft, "she says the meeting went well and she hopes that we're having a great time."

"Tell her it's been great," Evelyn replied, "so this is it, our first year is over."

"I don't know about you guys, but I've loved the first year of university." Juliette said, "Aren't we all clever, passing our essays and attending the lectures."

"Yeah," replied Will, "I had my doubts at first, but Chattlesbury uni is growing on me."

"It's been hard work," confirmed Evelyn, "but yes, I have enjoyed it, what about you Sophie dear?"

There was a pause, then Sophie spread her arms wide, "it's been blooming fantastic. I've met some lovely people." A tear formed in her eye, "You guys really are great friends, I'm blessed to have met you."

"Let's have a toast, with proper English tea, who needs champagne!" Juliette held her dainty china cup in the air, waiting while the others raised theirs.

"Here's to Chattlesbury university. Here's to learning and aspirations and finally, here's to friendship and dreams."

Chapter Twenty-One

It was a hot, muggy, August night. Will was in a deep, contented sleep, his chest rising rhythmically up and down.

"Will, Will," she whispered in his ear, gently shaking his shoulder.

"What?" Will's eyes flickered open as he turned towards her, "do you want to cuddle?"

"No! It's too hot."

"Okay," Will heaved away from her, kicking the sheet from his sticky legs.

The sound of his name came again, "I can't sleep."

Will sighed, "it's the middle of the night. Try, please Hema."

There was silence. Will thankfully relaxed back into the pillow, feeling sleep pulling him under once again.

"I've been having pains." The words said so casually had him sitting bolt upright.

"Where?" He rasped, peering at the clock.

"Where do you think Will – my neck?" She spluttered with laughter. "Your stomach?"

"Yes and my back too."

"How long for?"

"Oh the past couple of hours."

"What?" Will swung himself up out of the bed, "are you sure it's not those pretend pains?"

"You mean Braxton Hicks?" Hema replied, with an air of superiority. "Don't think so, they feel kinda intense. Ouch," she flinched as another wave of pain washed over her.

"Okay, we both need to just stay calm," Will wafted his hands up and down, "shall I ring the hospital?"

"I think so," Hema replied as she rolled into a sitting position.

"Where are you going?" Will asked, "shouldn't you be resting?"

"No Will," she said with a smile, "movement is good for the baby. Remember what they told us at the ante natal classes?"

Will thought briefly of the fortnightly classes they had recently attended, the breathing techniques they had learnt, the videos they had watched of women giving birth, the yoga and the lectures on breast feeding.

"I'll get the phone," he rasped, trying to stay calm, "you just stay here and concentrate on your er… breathing."

Will jogged down the stairs, searching frantically for the handset. Where the devil was it? He thought, as he picked up a pile of magazines and scanned the room. Into the kitchen he rushed, looking around at the pristine work tops. Ruby looked at him sleepily, one eye open as she struggled out of her bed to welcome him.

"Hello girl," he ruffled her furry coat, "where's your mom put the phone eh?"

Then he saw it, in the fruit bowl, nestled amongst the over ripe bananas. With shaking hands he rustled through the midwifes paperwork, until he found the number of the maternity suite.

As he was speaking to a nurse, the door opened and Flora wandered in yawning and pulling her floral dressing gown tight around her midriff. Her hair was set in rollers and there was a beauty mask covering her face. Will had the sudden urge to laugh, but managed to contain himself, as he was instructed to bring Hema up to the hospital.

"What now?" He enquired, "shouldn't we wait till the morning?"

"I recommend you bring her in Mr Bentley, babies don't clock watch you know, they come when they are ready." Suitably chastised, Will thanked her, then cut the call.

"Is everything okay Will?" Flora asked tentatively.

"Hema's having pains," he explained, "they want to admit her."

"Oh goodness," Flora cried, "but the babies not due for another two weeks."

"I know," Will replied, "it might be a false alarm, but better to get her checked over."

"Have you got the bag ready?"

"Yes," Will motioned towards the hall, where a sports bag was crammed full of baby paraphernalia, "I'll call a taxi."

"I'll drive you," Flora insisted, "just let me get dressed."

Suddenly there was a cry from upstairs. Will took the steps two at a time as he bounded up.

"Hema," he said breathlessly as he burst into the bathroom.

She was bent over, clutching her stomach and staring down at the pool of water at her feet.

"Have you had an accident?" He slipped on the wet floor.

"No I haven't had an accident," she replied with a grimace, "my waters have broken!"

"Oh Jesus, right don't panic, Mom, Mom we need to go NOW."

Flora was on the landing, hopping into her trousers and blouse, "okay, okay, I'm ready."

"What's going on," Max Bentley lurked behind her, scratching his head. When he saw the water and heard the groans of pain from Hema he gulped, "do you need me to come too?"

"No dear," Flora turned towards him, "go back to bed, I'll call you."

Max looking relieved, shuffled back into the bedroom.

"Are you okay?" Will asked softly, as he helped Hema down the stairs.

"It hurts Will," she grasped onto the banister.

"Breathe, breathe," he urged, "come on Mom, let's go."

Flora sped across the city, running red lights and swerving around roundabouts.

"Mom slow down," Will cried from the back, he had never seen Flora driving so recklessly, she was usually so slow and sensible.

"There's no one about," Flora replied, but thankfully she did let up on the accelerator.

"Owwwwww, make it stop!" Hema shouted.

Will patted her perspiring forehead with a handkerchief he had found on the back seat.

"Nearly there," he soothed.

"I need to push," Hema wailed.

"No! don't push, not yet," Will replied.

Hema grasped his hand, cutting through his skin with her long nails, "I WANT TO PUSH."

"Okay, okay," Will squatted down beside her open legs, "Mom are you there yet!!"

"Just here," Flora sighed, "I just need to find a parking space."

"Just leave it anywhere," Will shouted with panic, "Bloody hell, is that the head?"

Flora screeched on the brakes, and spun round to look, "Mary mother of God, yes, that's the head Will. Hema, push, push darling come on you can do it."

There was an almighty screeching wail, that seemed to go on forever and that resounded in the night air. Then a perfectly formed baby slipped into Will's hand. For a moment there was complete silence, Will stared in wonder at the blinking newborn and the baby stared right back up at him.

"Oh, oh..." Flora crossed her breastbone then burst into tears.

"Will, is the baby okay?" an exhausted Hema struggled upwards.

"It's a girl Hema, it's a girl," Will kissed the baby's head, cradling her in his shaking arms, "look, she's beautiful, just like her Mom."

As Flora jumped out of the car and sprinted up towards the hospital foyer, Will and Hema gazed down at their beautiful daughter who grasped their fingers tightly, opened her tiny rosebud mouth and then cried and cried and cried.

An hour later, Hema was settled in a bed on the maternity suite.

"You did well," a midwife patted her hand, "that certainly was a speedy birth."

"Is she okay?" A concerned Will asked, as his eyes flitted over a sleepy Hema.

"Yes she's fine, no need to worry, she just needs rest."

"And the baby...is she okay?"

"Very healthy," the midwife smiled down at the sleeping newborn beside them, "six pounds ten is a good weight."

Flora was leaning over the cot with tears glistening in her eyes, "she's the most beautiful baby I've ever seen."

"Are you okay Nan?" Will went and hugged her tight, "thank you for getting us here."

Flora wiped at her eyes, "I'll go and ring your dad, he's probably been out of his mind with worry."

"Okay," Will watched her leave the room with a smile.

The baby was stirring and began to cry softly. Gently Will lifted her up and bought her round to Hema.

"Is she hungry do you think?" He asked, as he stretched out on the bed against Hema.

"Probably, if she's anything like her daddy," Hema took the baby, pulling open her gown so she could latch on.

"You were amazing," Will said, gently kissing Hema on the head, "I thought births took like hours and hours."

"I guess I was just lucky," Hema gazed down proudly, "isn't she beautiful Will."

"Perfect," he agreed, feeling as if his heart would swell with love and the sudden urge to protect them both.

"Are you happy Will?" Hema asked, her lips rising to meet his.

"I've never felt so happy," Will said, full of emotion, "thank you Hema, thank you for giving me a beautiful daughter."

They were both quiet as they gazed down with love at the suckling baby.

"What shall we call her?" Will whispered.

Hema looked across at the fluttering blinds and the golden day that was dawning in front of them.

"How about Esme?" she replied thoughtfully.

"Esme, I like that," Will replied, "no, I love it. What does it mean Hema?"

"It means loved Will, it means loved..."

To be continued...

About the Author

From a young age Julia Sutton has loved creative writing. She has written poetry, children's stories and most recently women's contemporary fiction. 'Dreams' is the first novel in a planned series of books and has taken just under a year to complete. Julia spent her evenings and weekends working on her novel, scribbling in notebooks and tapping away on her computer. She was overjoyed to finish it, and ecstatic to be offered a publishing contract with Creativia. She received the contract on her 44th birthday and celebrated with a bottle of bubbly.

By day, Julia works in a primary school, surrounded by lovely staff and children. When she is not chasing around the playground, she is walking her dog, listening to music, spending time with her family and writing. Writing stories is her passion and she finds great fulfilment in expressing herself through the written word. She finds inspiration occurs during everyday activities; relaxing on a Sunday morning, strolling through the park on a warm, sunny day, overhearing titbits of a conversation while waiting in a busy shop. Her house is full of notes, the scattered ideas that appear at the most impromptu moments and must be recorded before they are forgotten.

One of Julia's favourite hobbies is reading, she loves immersing herself in fictional worlds and enjoys reading a wide range of literature. In 2005 she achieved a lifelong ambition of completing an English degree at the University of Wolverhampton, where she was able to indulge her passion for books and also meet a group of lovely people, some of which have become lifelong friends. It was this time at university, which Julia utilised as inspiration for her novel 'Dreams.' The idea of a group of strangers meeting at university took hold and she thought it would make an interesting storyline to explore their lives, dreams and aspirations.

Her plans for the future are to complete the second book of the 'Dreams' series. At the moment she is researching and planning out ideas for the storyline. She has also started writing a series of children's books which she would like to finish.

Julia was raised in Wolverhampton, England and happily still lives there with her husband and two children. She loves travelling abroad, but is always glad to be back home with her friends and family.

Julia enjoys connecting with others on social media and has a Facebook author page: https://www.facebook.com/julia.sutton.author

You can also find her on Twitter:
https://www.twitter.com/juliasu48342015

Printed in Great Britain
by Amazon

10863112R00166